Tara Moss has made the transition from international top model to international crime-writing success as the author of the bestselling novels *Fetish* and *Split*. Tara has enjoyed writing stories since the age of ten. She earned a Diploma from the Australian College of Journalism in 1997, and in 1998 won the Scarlet Stiletto Young Writer's Award for her story, *Psycho Magnet*. Her novels have been nominated for both the Davitt and the Ned Kelly Awards, and are available in six countries in four languages. Her in-depth writing research has seen her tour the FBI Academy at Quantico, and spend time in squad cars, courtrooms, morgues and criminology conferences around the world. Tara has also taken polygraph tests, shot guns with the LAPD, flown with the RAAF Roulettes and much more. She immigrated to Australia in 1996, and is a proud Australian/Canadian dual citizen. She resides in Melbourne with her husband, Mark. *Covet* is her third crime novel.

**Visit Tara Moss at her website:**
**www.taramoss.com.au**

D1260582

# *Covet*

# TARA MOSS

HarperCollins*Publishers*

* 'Australia's No. 1 Crime Writer'
  Source: ACNielsen BookScan sales figures January 2003 to June 2004

**HarperCollins***Publishers*

First published in Australia in 2004
by HarperCollins*Publishers* Pty Limited
ABN 36 009 913 517
A member of HarperCollins*Publishers* (Australia) Pty Limited Group
www.harpercollins.com.au

Copyright © Tara Moss 2004

**HarperCollins***Publishers*
25 Ryde Road, Pymble, Sydney, NSW 2073, Australia
31 View Road, Glenfield, Auckland 10, New Zealand
77–85 Fulham Palace Road, London W6 8JB, United Kingdom
2 Bloor Street East, 20th floor, Toronto, Ontario M4W 1A8, Canada
10 East 53rd Street, New York NY 10022, USA

National Library of Australia Cataloguing-in-Publication data:

Moss, Tara.
  Covet.
  ISBN 0 7322 7672 1.
  1. Serial murderers – Fiction.
  I. Title.
A823.3

Cover design by Darian Causby, Highway 51 Design Works
Cover photograph: Steve Lowe
Cover images of city skyline and sand dunes: Australian Picture Library
Inside cover author photograph: Gavin O'Neill
Printed and bound in Australia by Griffin Press on 70gsm Bulky News

5 4 3 2 1        04 05 06 07

*For Mark*

*covet vb* **1.** to desire inordinately, or without due regard to the rights of others; desire wrongfully. **2.** to wish for, especially eagerly. **3.** to have an inordinate or wrongful desire.

# Covet

# PROLOGUE

The kettle screamed.

Brother and sister looked up, but only one moved to silence it. Ben Harpin remained sprawled in his favourite armchair, feet up on the coffee table. He did not budge an inch while his sister rose from her place on the couch to attend to the making of tea.

'White thanks. No sugar,' he said as she walked away. 'I'm trying to cut back.'

'No sugar,' Suzie assured him as she disappeared into the kitchen.

*He likes ice cream. I'll serve it with ice cream*, Suzie thought as she poured hot water into the teapot and pulled on an oven mitt. The pie would be ready by now. She opened the oven door and hot, sweet-smelling air billowed out, blowing her dark fringe back and stinging her eyes for a moment. She bent over, squinting, and coaxed the deli-bought apple pie out with one hand. It had been warmed for ten minutes to give it that fresh-baked feel, and now it looked simply delicious. Suzie

1

poked at it gingerly and licked the sticky remains off a fingertip. *Mmm, sweet.*

Ben's kitchen was set up for a real homemaker, and so was the rest of his suburban house. It had every Mixmaster, six-slice toaster, slicer-dicer, super blender, cappuccino machine and fancy knife set any aspiring supermum would want. And as far as size was concerned, the living room alone dwarfed Suzie's tiny bachelor pad in Malabar. But even with all these things she privately coveted, Suzie couldn't quite feel envious of her brother. Ben's estranged wife, Lisa, had walked out after barely two years of marriage, and now Ben lived in this big family house on his own, the proverbial white picket fence surrounding nothing. The Mixmaster was collecting dust in a cupboard along with sets of Royal Doulton china and various unopened wedding gifts, and the freezer was brimming with frozen meat pies and TV dinners. What a waste.

'That smells good,' Ben shouted from the living room.

Suzie snapped herself out of her ruminations and focused on what she had to do.

'It's coming. Hold your horses.'

She slipped off the oven mitt and grabbed a cake knife from a drawer. She cut a big piece of the pie, almost a quarter of the whole thing, and placed it on a plate. Then she fished around for the handful of pills in the pocket of her slacks, safely sealed in a Ziploc bag. *There you are.* The capsules were blood red, yet benign in appearance, *almost like jelly beans*, she thought. She held the bag up, mesmerised by the little capsules inside. She had to urge herself to hurry. If she really was going to do this, there was no time to dilly-dally.

She pulled on a pair of dishwashing gloves to protect her hands and slid one of the sharp, expensive knives from the block on the bench. Now she really was committed. If her brother walked in she would have trouble explaining what she was doing. She just needed another minute or two. Carefully, Suzie prised six of the capsules open with the tip of the knife, and one by one poured their glistening crystal content onto a strip of baking paper on the cutting board.

She eyed the substance with amazement. It was derived from the dried wings and body cases of the beetle *Catharis vesicatoria*, found in Italy, southern Russia and Spain.

*Spanish fly.*

It was highly illegal, but the man she had confiscated it from had sworn it was the real thing, in pure crystal form, straight from the black market in Asia. She hoped he was telling the truth.

A bit clumsily, she cut a few holes in the top of the slice of apple pie, the crust crumbling a little as it broke, and then, with as steady a hand as she could muster, she shook the tiny colourless crystals into the openings she had made, using the baking paper as a funnel and the knife to make the pockets in the pie a little larger to accommodate the new ingredient.

When she was done, Suzie was not entirely happy with the result. She was no domestic goddess, but even by her standards this looked wrong. The crystals had not really dissolved. Perhaps he would think it was some kind of sugar? No, it just didn't look right.

*The ice cream.*

Vanilla ice cream fixed everything. Two big dollops covered all sins and the dish was ready to serve. She took a deep breath.

'Coming ...' she called, and walked back into the living room carrying a tray with the pot of tea, two cups and saucers and Ben's slice of apple pie.

He removed his feet from the coffee table. 'Wow. This looks delicious. Since when did you come over all domestic?'

She set the tray down and smiled at him. 'I have my moments. I'll just get the milk for your tea.'

'Aren't you having any pie?'

'Oh yeah, I am. Not enough hands. Go ahead and start.'

She walked off to the kitchen again and washed her hands before cutting herself a slice from the remaining, untouched portion of pie. In a moment she was back with her plate and a small jug of skim milk.

'The milk is skim and the ice cream is low fat,' she told him.

'Thanks. Dr Mike says the sweets will kill me. And the beer.'

She nodded and poured some milk in his tea. He was already halfway through the pie, eagerly shovelling it into his mouth, ice cream melting across the plate.

Ben had put on a lot of weight in the past few months. At first, after Lisa left, he had dropped a few kilos. Now he had an unattractive paunch and didn't appear to be getting any exercise. Ben wasn't as disciplined as Suzie. Suzie liked to keep herself strong. It didn't surprise her that the doctor had said something to him.

'So how's work?'

'What work? The building trade ain't what it used to be,' he said with a full mouth.

She watched his lips as he spoke. There was ice cream gathering in the corners. 'No big jobs coming up then?'

'No. Things are slow.'

She took a sip of her tea. 'Why don't you take the opportunity to get away for a while? I could mind the house for you.'

'What for? The plants are already dead.'

She smiled.

'Nah, I should really start looking for work again.' He didn't sound too convinced of his own motivation.

She noticed that Ben had almost finished his apple pie, and she hadn't touched hers at all. Her slice should be safe, but somehow she didn't like the look of it. She found she had no appetite. Would he notice?

'So you don't have anything exciting coming up?'

'Not really. No.'

Now he was scraping up bits of crumbled piecrust with his fork and eating those.

She took another sip of tea. 'When do you think you'll get around to selling this place?' she asked. 'It's a beautiful house. You should get good money for it. You almost own it outright, don't you?'

'What is this, twenty questions?'

She laughed. 'Come on, are you selling it or what? Do you have a real estate agent yet?'

'No.'

'Will Lisa get much of the money, do you think?'

'Look Suz, we're separated, not divorced.' A touch of anger. 'I'm not going to just suddenly sell the house.'

'Suddenly? It's been almost a year! She's shacked up with that guy, Ben,' Suzie pushed, aware that it wouldn't take much to send him over the edge. 'Surely the courts wouldn't want you to support her. You don't have any children. You wouldn't owe her anything.'

He pushed his plate away, frowning, his face flushed.

'Calm down, Ben. I'm just saying she shouldn't be entitled to anything after what she's done.'

'It's none of your damn business, sis. It's between Lisa and me. She's ... she's ...'

He got up and stormed off into the kitchen.

*Oh no ...*

'I didn't mean to upset you,' she offered, following right behind him and trying not to panic. She had not considered that he would even be able to get to the kitchen once he consumed her preparation. She wasn't sure if everything was cleaned up properly. At least he had finished his pie before he got up. But would he find anything strange in the kitchen? Would it matter now?

'It's just that you have to face facts, Ben,' she continued as calmly as she could, looking around for telltale signs of what she had done.

He didn't answer her, but stopped by the fridge and opened it. She stood in front of the countertop with her arms crossed, hoping he wouldn't look past her at the cutting board. Over her shoulder she could see that although she had tossed the empty red capsules in the bin, the baking paper was still on the bench, sprinkled with the remnants of the cantharidin crystals. Not that he could possibly guess what they were.

But she needn't have worried, as Ben seemed preoccupied with getting himself a beer. Suzie saw that the fridge was empty except for a slab of Victoria Bitter and a package of Chinese takeaway that looked past its use-by date. Ben grabbed a VB, ripped the top off and took a swig. He shook his head and slammed the fridge door, bottles rattling as it shut.

Since Lisa had left him for Heinrich, their German accountant, Ben hadn't got off his arse to do anything about a divorce, or the house, or much else, really. It certainly didn't sound like he had a real estate agent or lawyer putting the wheels in motion. He had been avoiding the issue all this time, just as Suzie thought. Anyway, it hardly mattered now. The conversation only reinforced what she already knew. It was too late for him. The decision was made and Suzie was here to get her plan under way. Unlike her brother, she was not prone to procrastination. It would all be over soon.

*Get him away from the kitchen . . .*

Beer in hand, Ben walked over and stood beside her at the counter. Suzie's heart went up into her throat at his proximity to her carelessness. *You idiot!* He would have no way of knowing what it was, but what if he touched some crystals with his bare hands? Would it do anything on contact? What if they struggled and she accidentally touched some of it herself? She couldn't risk that. She had to move them both away from it. *Fast.*

'You don't know what it's like being married,' he said with a bitter, humourless laugh, leaning back on the counter. 'Hell, you don't even know what it's like having a boyfriend! You never got over your bloody teenage sweetheart and it's been two decades, so don't talk to me about my marriage.'

Her eyes narrowed to slits.

She hoped the cantharidin would hurry up and work. *Soon.* It had been perhaps fifteen minutes, maybe twenty. How long would this take?

'Look Ben, I'm not the one with the failed marriage, drinking all day and living on the dole. Don't try to make this about me,' she said, and started to walk away, hoping to lead him back into the living room.

He grabbed her by the elbow.

A thousand violent reflexes flickered through her mind. Moves she had learned and mastered, and would use on instinct. But Suzie held fast.

'Who the fuck do you think you are? Like you're so great! Some ugly goddamn spinster working with psychos all day. You can't even get a boyfriend. What makes you so high and mighty?'

She spat on him.

Ben raised his hand to strike her. He probably would have hit her if she were a bloke. Instead, after a moment, he deflated and wiped the spittle from his cheek. 'I'm sorry, Suz. I didn't mean that. You know I'd never hurt you. It's just that . . . Fuck, why don't you ever see anyone? Mum and Dad used to wonder all the time. Your damn job doesn't help. It makes people hard. Just don't go criticising my marriage. If you were married you'd know it isn't easy.'

*Maybe I didn't use enough? What if that slippery bastard Barton lied and it's something else? If that stuff is just some crystal meth or E in a bloody capsule, I'll nail his arse . . .*

Then Suzie heard a strange sound that started in the depths of her brother's belly and grumbled loud until it came out in a terrible burp.

'Uh . . .' Ben covered his mouth and stumbled back.

Suzie took a step away. 'Are you okay?'

'I feel a bit . . .'

Another rumble, this one louder.

'Maybe you drank too fast?' She took another step.

The colour had drained from Ben's face, and Suzie could hear his stomach rumble again. This time he moaned in agony and held himself around the waist. Before long he was doubled over, clutching the kitchen counter.

'I . . .'

A spray of vomit burst from his mouth, covering the countertop in splatters of pie and blood.

'Oh my God!' Suzie covered her mouth, backing towards the living room. It was disgusting.

Another spray, this one more solid.

'Ben?'

Her brother fell to the kitchen floor and convulsed, holding his guts. He lay on his side, blood trickling out of his nose onto the linoleum. In moments he threw up again, coating the floor in a fleshy, red substance and remnants of pie. Blood was everywhere, filling the room in a swamp of repulsive sick.

'I'll call triple O! Just hang on!' Suzie ran into the living room and picked up the phone. 'Hello? Hello, this is an emergency! My brother is sick! We need an ambulance right away!'

The dial tone rang steadily in her ear.

Suzie calmly put the phone down and made her way to her brother's favourite armchair. Breathing slowly in and out, she put her feet up on the coffee table and tried to relax. She pushed the dark fringe back from her face. Her eyes wandered to the empty plate on the coffee table where Ben's apple pie had been. She blocked from her mind the horrific sounds of sickness coming from the kitchen. She imagined that she could not hear her brother's cries for help, that she could not detect the ever-growing stench of blood and poison filling the house.

Suzie thought about her future. She thought about love.

Looking at her watch and finding it was already 4.32 in the afternoon, she picked up the television remote control and flicked to Channel Ten. Brooke and Ridge were playing out a scene in *The Bold And The Beautiful*, holding each other passionately as Brooke's eyes misted over. Suzie turned the volume up high, drowning out the unpleasant sounds in the next room.

There was nothing anyone could do for him now, and she knew it. His time was over, but hers had just begun.

# CHAPTER 1

*Damn.*

Makedde Vanderwall braced herself against a relentless wind, her curses blown away by its force.

*Dammit!*

Wind whipped across the open expanse of cemetery to the crest of the hill, blowing her blonde mane forward across her face, tangling it with each gust so it caught in the corners of her mouth. Bent forward by the gale, she flipped up the collar on her black trench coat in retaliation, but it did little to ease her gooseflesh or tame her thick, wind-mangled hair.

The Canadian West Coast had endured a long winter and spring had not yet dared to raise its head. The hard earth at Makedde's feet would be dying for sunlight and warmth, but there was none to be found here. Not today.

In her right hand she clutched a card and a small spray of pale yellow baby roses, gripped tight so they wouldn't blow away. They were gifts for a friend. She had braved the weather to pay her respects to Catherine Gerber, and although she felt a gnawing loneliness at that moment, she was not alone. Her father, Les, and his girlfriend, Ann Morgan, sat in a minivan a few metres away, waiting for her patiently and giving her space to do what she had to. But she didn't have long. In a few minutes they would need to drive her to the airport, where she would board a long flight to Australia.

*Dammit, Catherine. This is no birthday party, is it?*

She forced a smile, but it faded with the next gust of wind.

The hilltop memorial held a small wall of marble plaques marking the final resting places of cremated loved ones. On her many visits, Makedde, or Mak as her friends called her, had developed a morbid habit of perusing the names and dates on the plaques, and adding up the varying years of life. Henry Lee Thompson 1898–1984. Eighty-six years old. Josephine Patrick 1932–2001. Sixty-nine. Her friend's marker was on the bottom row, right-hand side, and she was one of the younger ones in this block of memorials. She had been only nineteen when she was murdered, practically a child. In fact, south of the nearby Canadian–American border, Catherine would have been legal to drink as of today, her twenty-first birthday. This day should have been a coming of age for her. *It should have been a big party*, Mak thought.

She reached down and pulled some dry, blackened roses from the metal holder by Catherine's plaque and let them blow out of her hand in a gust of wind. She watched them for a moment as they took flight and disappeared in the valley of gravestones below. She recognised the white ribbon holding them together. It was her previous bouquet.

*Am I the only one who visits her?*

She couldn't help but feel a flash of anger directed at Catherine's neglectful foster parents.

*Don't waste your thoughts on them. You have much bigger fish to fry.*

Mak placed her flowers in the holder and felt some minuscule and short-lived sense of satisfaction. At least Catherine had fresh flowers now, bright and cheerful, as she would have liked them. The yellow petals seemed to be the only colour for miles: the sky, the cemetery, the wall of plaques — it all seemed so grey and depressing.

*Don't cry, dammit. Don't.*

She had one more thing she needed to do. Makedde knelt on the hard stone tiles in front of the memorial, the numbing cold seeping through the knees of her jeans. She bowed her head for a moment to get up her courage, and with a deep breath she ripped open Catherine's card.

HAPPY 21ˢᵗ BIRTHDAY!

*I miss you, Cat. Your friend always, M.*

Mak pushed her hand flat against the marble square and closed her eyes for a moment. Then she slid the opened birthday card into one of the ridges around Catherine's plaque so it stuck in place. The wind would take it soon, but it was the best she could do. She crumpled the envelope into a ball and put it in her pocket.

*I've gotta go now.*

Mak stood up and brushed off the knees of her jeans. It was time for her to fly across the globe to Sydney, Australia — a beautiful destination for most people, but this would be no holiday. Makedde was the prosecution's key witness in the trial of the sadistic Ed Brown, the man who had abducted nine young women and murdered them senselessly; slaughtered and defiled them, and in the process had captured the public's imagination as the epitome of evil, his acts making gruesome news headlines across the world. He had savagely ended Catherine's life, and Makedde herself had been terrifyingly close to being his next victim. She had promised her dead friend justice for the wrongs that had been done to her, and although she could never truly make things right, taking the witness stand to help convict Ed Brown was one thing she *could* do. After a long and troubled eighteen months, the time had finally come for her to testify in court.

*We'll lock him away forever, Cat. I promise. And he won't be able to hurt anyone else ever again.*

What lay ahead would be no easier if she dwelled on her loss. It was too much to bear thinking about.

'I love you, Catherine,' she whispered. 'I'll get him for you. Wish me luck.'

She turned away from the bank of memorials and walked towards her father's minivan, prompting Les and Ann to look up from their conversation in the front seat. Her father offered a solemn nod through the foggy windscreen and Ann started the engine.

Mak got in. 'Alright, let's go.'

They pulled away in silence as she stared out the window, disturbed by the way a string of letters carved into cold marble could slowly take over the once vivid memories of her late best friend. Time blurred memories of the dead, even when the pain of their leaving remained fresh. Her mother and Catherine were slowly fading, like a dream upon waking, fragmenting and growing indefinite. She could no longer keep hold of them as they slipped away into the shadows.

★ ★ ★

Makedde's carry-on bag was at her feet, her boarding pass in hand. She had her warm turtleneck pulled up to her chin and the trench coat wrapped tightly around her. She could still feel the chill of the icy wind that buffeted Catherine's memorial. She was vaguely aware that some of the passers-by in the airport terminal were looking at her. Her father and Ann were also looking, their faces etched with concern rather than curiosity.

'Don't worry, I'll be fine,' she said, wondering if any of them would really buy her false confidence, herself included.

Standing tall in her heeled boots, Mak's gaze was level with her father's deep blue eyes. Les Vanderwall was still handsome in his early sixties, even though the past two years seemed to have aged him ten. At present he suffered from an uncharacteristic pallor thanks to a serious peptic ulcer that had recently taken a turn for the worse, unsurprisingly perhaps, considering his daughter's involvement in the upcoming murder trial. It had been an unfortunate two years for both of them. None of it was her fault, of course, but Mak felt somehow responsible. Losing Jane would have been more than enough. But then there was all *this*.

That worried look. *Dammit, Dad, don't look at me like that.*

'You will do fine, Mak. In fact, you'll do better than fine. You are one of the strongest young women I know.'

It was Ann Morgan who spoke. The clinical psychologist wore a brave smile and her admirable armour of calm was contagious. She was petite and rounded, with short, stylish auburn hair and warm brown eyes — a deceptively gentle exterior housing a sharp intellect and strong spirit. One of her hands rested comfortingly on Les's arm as he stood tense and silent. The relationship between Les and Ann had blossomed in the past several months. He had regained most of the weight he'd dropped after Mak's mother, Jane, lost her battle with cancer. The occasional smile had even returned to his face, despite the considerable challenges of late.

*Thank God he is no longer alone in that big house, his wife dead, his world empty. Thank God Ann has brought some life back to his private world . . .*

'Thanks,' Makedde replied. *You're pretty strong yourself*, she thought.

'Just think of the weight your testimony adds to the prosecution's case. He'll be locked away forever.'

With every ounce of her being, Mak hoped that was true.

'And then you can get on with your life, Mak. You'll have that PhD under your belt and all this behind you in no time.' Ann stepped forward to squeeze Mak's hand gently. Mak gave her a quick, heartfelt hug in return.

'That would be nice,' Mak replied. Her thesis was not on track. Her life was nowhere near on track either. With any luck this trip truly would put that regrettable chapter of her life to rest, and she could finally move on.

*Oh Dad.* She turned to embrace her father. His face was so pale.

The retired detective inspector was stoic as usual, one of that old school of strong, silent men. His pallor worried her, as did his tense look. He had to take it easy. Mak hated it when his brow was furrowed like that. She couldn't help but notice it was always herself who caused it. Theresa, her younger sister, never once made that brow furrow. And it sure wasn't Theresa who had given him that damned ulcer ... Theresa with the benign hubby and the happy bouncing baby girl. Theresa who had never done anything wrong, or risky, in her whole life. Sometimes Mak wondered if they were even related.

*It's okay, Dad. Just a little longer and this nightmare will be over.*

Her father had wanted desperately to go to Sydney with her, had fought every step of the way to come along, but Dr Olenski would not allow him to travel. If he had followed all of Dr Olenski's advice a year ago, he might have been practically cured on a course of antibiotics already. But no. This was Les Vanderwall, formerly Vancouver Island's most formidable detective inspector, and he didn't take orders from anyone. Stress had aggravated his condition until he was now touch-and-go for surgery in the next few weeks.

'I should get going,' Makedde announced, and glanced anxiously at the sign behind her.

VICTORIA INTERNATIONAL AIRPORT. DEPARTURES THIS WAY.

The 'International' part of the airport's name was really a bit misleading. Rather than a huge, bustling airport full of international jetsetters bound for all corners of the world, the airport was international only because it had some departures to Seattle, a mere forty-minute flight away. Looking at that sign, Mak felt it was almost impossibly hard to leave the tranquil safe-haven of Vancouver Island, the home of her youth. She would be flying straight into the centre of a media circus. She would have to relive her ordeal in court. She would have to testify while *he* sat there in the dock, only metres away. He would be right there in the same room as her.

ED BROWN THIS WAY.

If only Andy had aimed that bullet a little more to the left, it would have been over already. But of course such thoughts were pointless and frustrating, and led her straight into another area it was best not to dwell on — the whole muddled situation with Detective Andy Flynn.

*Just get on the plane, Mak.*

'I should really get to the gate lounge.' This time she meant it. 'I'll see you in a week or so. Dad, *please* take it easy and do everything the doctor says, okay?' Les nodded bleakly. At his side, Ann, too, gave Mak a nod, as if to say that she would personally see to it that he got better. 'This will be over in no time.'

'Have a safe trip.'

'I will. I'll be fine.' She gave the two of them one more hearty embrace. 'Say bye to Theresa for me,' she said. Her sister had not come to the airport, which was par for the course. 'I hope Connor's birthday is a blast.'

Ann's son, Connor, had a big eighteenth coming up. It was good that Ann would be there to help organise it. The relationship was still fragile, since Ann and Connor's father had split a couple of years before. Mak wondered what Connor thought about her dad, now that he was on the scene. Was it awkward?

Ann nodded. 'We'll see you soon.'

Finally Mak broke away, making exaggerated kisses and doing an impersonation of the Queen's wave, her hand held like a twisting spoon. 'Ta ta!' she said, doing her best to ease the tension. 'I love you.' She rounded the corner to walk through security.

'You'll be fine. It'll be a stroll in the park,' she mumbled to herself, staring at the ground as she walked.

'What was that, ma'am?'

It was a bulbous-nosed airport security guard, looking at her with bright eyes that wandered momentarily down her body and back up again. He probably hadn't even realised he'd done it, or that she'd seen him do it.

'Oh nothing,' she said politely. 'Just muttering to myself.'

Mak chucked her carry-on bag onto the conveyor and watched it disappear into the X-ray machine. She tried to walk past the guard and through the electronic scanner.

'Hey, how tall are you?' Now the guard was standing on tiptoe, far too close for comfort, clearly pleased with himself for being the fifty-thousandth person to ask about her unusual height. She noticed with distaste that he smelled of pickles and poor hygiene.

'Six feet and a little,' she said. 'And you must be what? Five-seven?'

He nodded. 'You guessed it, honey. And I *lurve* big women.' He swayed towards her a fraction. Ah, yes, canned pickles. Charming.

'You know, the National Center for Statistics say that the height of the average man is five feet nine inches.' She looked him over. 'Hmmm, below average ...' She left him with that thought and strode through the metal detector, taking her carry-on as it rolled out the other side of the X-ray machine, and headed to her gate without further interruption.

# CHAPTER 2

'I wanna be loved by you,' Marilyn Monroe crooned. 'You and nobody else but you ...'

Suzie Harpin hummed along as she vacuumed the house, cutting a swathe of spotlessness through each of the rooms. She ran the vacuum head over the carpet again and again, detouring around the hefty garbage bags full of clothing and junk she had rounded up and arranged against the walls, like hay bales awaiting collection.

'I wanna be loved by you, *alo-o-o-ne.* Boop boop beedooo ...'

Suzie had the stereo up loud, delighted to have found a CD she liked amongst Ben's boring Led Zeppelin, AC/DC and Skyhooks albums. That type of music was not to her taste. There was nothing romantic about 'Living in the Seventies' or 'Long Way to the Top (If You Want to Rock 'n' Roll)'.

She noticed the sky growing dark outside the large living room windows, and she flicked off the vacuum cleaner. Giving a cursory look along the street, Suzie closed the curtains and checked the time. It was already early Monday evening in this sleepy western Sydney suburb and there was still so much she wanted to do before she headed home to get ready for work. She wasn't used to keeping these hours and the lack of sleep had really hit her, but she was tough and she soldiered on. Her newfound domesticity excited her, and she threw herself into the role as fervently as she did any new project.

She had begun her chores by taking down all of Ben's photos: the wedding photos that he still had around for some reason that Suzie could not comprehend, the goofy happy snaps with fishing mates, the old photo with his surfboard. They had gone into the first garbage bag. There was a lot more to be thrown out, but she'd made a start.

Soon she would have to tackle the *clean-up*. The clean-up was going to be so much worse than she'd thought.

'I wanna be kissed by you . . .'

Not one to waste time even when she was tested by physical exhaustion, Suzie started the machine again and worked away, pushing the droning vacuum cleaner along the carpet of the hallway. She made it right up to the bathroom door before she finally turned it off.

She frowned.

Plugging her nose with two fingers, she stepped into the bathroom and stopped short at the small pool of blood hardening around the carcass of her brother. She was not sure what to do with the body in the long term, but that was okay. There was no great rush. She had several days to get everything ready, and she didn't have to worry about anyone snooping around in the meantime. But the rising stench would not do. She would have to get him in the bathtub before he made more of a mess, then bag him and move him somewhere more convenient.

*Oh, what a stench . . .*

It was with great interest and a sense of serendipity that Suzie had come across Spanish fly and learned of its powers. Spanish fly had, she knew, a somewhat inflated reputation for enhancing sexual prowess. It was believed by some to inflame and arouse, but only by way of a bit of poisoning. Cantharidin was in fact a blistering agent, and like all poisons, the deadliness was in the dosage. Suzie had been careful to administer a sufficiently large amount of the pure form of the poison to terminate her brother, but the result was so much messier and less efficient than she had anticipated. Everything the pie had come in contact with — his lips, tongue, throat, stomach and entire digestive tract — had been ripped to shreds. But who knew it would take so long? Almost five hours had passed before Ben died. Suzie was not pleased.

While she was still watching her favourite soap opera, Ben had managed to somehow get himself up off the kitchen floor and stumble down the hallway to the bathroom to relieve himself when the poison's grisly destructiveness had progressed all the way to his urinary tract. Imagine the shock and horror she felt in seeing him stagger past, losing his balance a few times in the process, leaving a bloody handprint on the wall and a mess of sick down the perfect carpet.

Terribly inefficient.

But never mind.

Now he was dead and she could get on with it. Suzie grabbed a mop and bucket from the kitchen and began the long and unpleasant task of making the bathroom presentable.

# CHAPTER 3

Which nineteenth-century French painter started pointillism?

*Georges Seurat.*

'Excuse me ...'

Bolivia and which other country are the only two landlocked nations in South America?

*Umm ... Paraguay.*

What was the name of the cyclone that devastated Darwin on Christmas morning, 1974?

'Excuse me, Miss Vanderwall?'

Makedde looked up to find a deeply tanned Qantas airline steward addressing her. She fumbled around to take off her headset, tearing herself away from Coldplay's moody tunes and letting the onboard trivia game penalise her for not choosing one of the multiple-choice answers.

'Um, hello.'

'Miss Vanderwall?' The pretty steward had her blonde hair pulled back in a tight bun, and she wore some of the darkest lip liner Mak had seen in some time. It was hard to take her eyes off the heavily drawn burgundy line as it moved with each syllable.

'Yes? That's me,' Mak replied.

'We'll be preparing to land soon,' the lip line said. The attendant squatted in the aisle beside Makedde's seat and continued in a conspiratorial whisper. 'We wanted to let you know that there will be some people to meet you at the gate in Sydney.'

'People?'

'It seems that the media may have been tipped off about your arrival. Some Qantas ground staff have been organised to escort you through a more convenient exit.'

'Really? Why thank you. That's very kind.' *The media?* 'Oh,' Mak added, remembering that the police had organised an airport pick-up, 'I have some people waiting for me —'

'That's okay, Miss Vanderwall. They have been informed also. It's all organised.' The steward nodded and smiled politely, as if to say, I know *everything.* 'Hey, are you feeling okay?'

Mak felt a little ill. 'I'm fine,' she lied.

The steward patted her arm in a familiar way, and leaned closer, cocking her head to one side, the lips held tight, eyes wide. She was bubbling over with unspoken questions, waiting for any sign that she could go ahead and start probing. She hovered for a few moments and when Mak failed to confide any deliciously gruesome details she said, 'Well ... good luck. I hope you enjoy your stay,' and stood to leave.

*Enjoy your stay?*

Mak couldn't help but feel queasy imagining that she had spent almost thirteen hours on this plane without even considering the possibility that everyone around her might know who she was, what had happened to her and why she was there.

Creepy.

'Um, can you help me with something?' Mak asked, just as the steward turned to walk away.

'Sure, what can I get you?'

'Do you know the name of the cyclone that devastated Darwin in 1974?'

'Sorry?' The drawn lips formed a confused pout.

'Never mind. It's not important.' Mak hated being posed a question and not knowing the answer, no matter how irrelevant. 'Thanks for letting me know about the, uh ... welcome party.'

The steward smiled sweetly and disappeared up the aisle.

Makedde yawned and stretched her sore muscles, her mind frantically running over the possibilities of what might be in store. There had been plenty of headlines back when the killings were still taking place and Sydney was in the grip of its fear and fascination with the Stiletto Murders, but she had hoped the trial would not attract the same amount of interest. Perhaps her hopes were in vain, if the steward's news was anything to go by. That wasn't a comforting thought. She couldn't stand the idea of seeing poor Catherine's beautiful face in the papers again, with the caption 'Slaughtered', 'Murdered' or simply 'Victim' underneath.

Mak adjusted her watch to Tuesday, 5.55 a.m., Sydney time, and rubbed some gritty sleep out of her eyes. *Yuck.* She craned her neck to see the Opera House come into view as the plane dipped its giant wing and banked left. The sky was a brilliant azure, the blue reflected in a vast expanse of Australian waters below. But the dazzling sight only added to her queasiness, thanks to those not-so-fond memories of her last trip.

Surely the worst was over?

Mak strapped herself in and prepared to arrive in Sydney.
*You'll soon find out.*

★ ★ ★

Detective Senior Sergeant Andrew Flynn leaned against the far
wall of Arrivals Gate C at Sydney International Airport, holding
some flowers in his hand and his heart in his throat. His tall,
rough-and-tumble handsomeness drew an admiring glance
from an attractive blonde at the Hertz car rental desk. He failed
to notice her, lost as he was in a battle with his own thoughts.

*Ditch the flowers.*

*No, women like flowers.*

*You look like an idiot. Ditch 'em.*

Barely five minutes after buying them, he chucked the
small bouquet of mixed flowers — he didn't know what they
were — into a nearby bin. He resumed his position, leaning
with his back to the far wall close to the sliding doors of the
main exit, and crossed his arms. Andy felt much better without
the silly bouquet. It had been a stupid impulse, not his style at
all. The truth was, his normally steady nerves were getting a
working over this morning and he worried that he might be
in danger of doing something he would regret later. A fax had
come in overnight that threatened in not-so-subtle terms to
jeopardise some of the vital funding of the new New South
Wales Profiling Unit, of which he was set to be a major player
once it was up and running. *Fuck.* But he knew that wasn't
the only thing responsible for his mood. Or even the main
thing responsible for it.

Makedde Vanderwall was arriving from Canada this
morning, any minute now. Andy wasn't quite sure what to

expect from her or their relationship, if that was the right word for what they had. *She is one of those unpredictable types,* he thought. Then again, weren't all women? He hadn't been able to sleep so he figured he might as well come to the airport and try to be useful, but he didn't feel so good as he stood there anticipating her arrival. The midnight Jack Daniels run probably hadn't helped his condition.

*'Are you back on the booze, Andy?'*

*'Oh no, Inspector Kelley, don't worry about that . . .'*

He looked at his watch: *6.20* a.m. It was bloody early, but it could have been midnight or one in the morning to him, he wouldn't be able to tell the difference if it weren't for the light outside. *No sleep.* He looked around for someone brandishing one of those chauffeur's cards with Makedde's name on it, but it seemed there was no one to collect her. He thought someone had organised for Senior Constable Mahoney to pick her up from the airport, but he hadn't seen her or anyone else who was familiar. None of his colleagues were milling around, which was a relief because he would never live down the bouquet thing if they'd seen it.

The sliding glass doors beside him opened with a waft of crisp air and yet another TV crew walked in, surveying the crowd. Now there was a handful of photographers assembled in the arrivals area, and crews from both Channels Nine and Seven. Who were they there to see? Ian Thorpe maybe? He was reportedly coming back from overseas soon. Brett Lee or Shane Warne perhaps? Or one of those Los Angeles–based Aussie actresses he could never remember the names of?

Andy unfolded his arms and put his hands in his pockets. He looked over at the gift shop. Perfumes. Cards. Chocolates.

Flowers. Should he buy her something? Would that be assuming too much? *Yes it would be. Just leave it.*

Some travellers finally began to appear through the arrivals gate. He saw a tired-looking tanned couple with backpacks and an older woman pushing a trolley overflowing with baggage. A young man with a huge Canadian flag sticker plastered to his suitcase followed, rubbing his eyes and looking anxiously at the sea of faces. Mak probably wouldn't be too much longer.

She hadn't returned his last few calls, and he hadn't told her he would be at the airport to greet her. They'd left off their long-distance relationship on a kind of odd note, that much was true. There had been a lot of phone calls since he'd returned to Sydney from his extended work trip to Canada six months earlier. At first everything seemed fine. Then about two months ago she'd said that she thought they should see other people. She'd said that long-distance relationships never really worked and they shouldn't put too much pressure on themselves. Of course he'd agreed. What else was he supposed to say? But then he'd gone ahead and followed through. It had only been a weekend fling, really. A nurse. Carol was her name. A nice girl, but not really his type. Or rather, she wasn't Makedde.

It hadn't taken long for him to realise he had done the wrong thing. And now there was this stand-off. What was he supposed to do? It had been her idea after all. Why would she say something like that if she didn't really mean it?

*Women.* Were they even the same species? Andy thought it ironic that he could map the psychological processes of the worst kinds of serial killers and rapists, but he still couldn't figure out what made the opposite sex tick. They truly were a mystery to him.

A tall, attractive blonde appeared through the arrivals gate in jeans and a zip-up top, her suitcase bearing another of those ubiquitous red and white Canadian flags. Andy stood up straight and looked at her, his heart beating a little faster. But it was not Makedde. He noticed the film crews and photographers edging forward excitedly. And then, without a single flash bulb going off, they shuffled back into place, clearly disappointed.

And that's when it dawned on him.

*Oh shit. They know she's coming back this morning. How the fuck did they find out?*

He panicked.

Andy didn't want Mak to be met with a flurry of invasive questions about the murder trial straight after a twenty-hour trip from Canada. Some welcome that would be. There seemed to be someone tipping off the media lately. Perhaps it was one of the new constables? Never trust an underpaid cop. Andy ran through scenarios in his head, ways he could help her avoid the throng. It would be tough enough for her to face it outside the Supreme Court in a few days, but she didn't need to deal with this now.

He approached airport security.

'Good morning,' Andy said to a sleepy young uniformed guard. He flashed his badge discreetly and asked to be taken into the customs area.

'No problem, detective,' the young man replied, looking somewhat more awake. 'Come with me.'

He hoped he wasn't too late.

Minutes later, when Andy was told that the witness he sought was already being escorted to her hotel, he felt he masked his disappointment fairly well. He didn't punch a wall, or even let out a string of expletives, although those responses crossed his mind. He simply said, 'Good work. Carry on,' and quietly exited the airport where he'd just wasted ninety minutes. He couldn't have been farther out of the loop if he tried.

*Fucking fool.*

By the time he got back to his apartment it was past eight, leaving just enough time for a couple of fried eggs and another wrestle with his desire for a shot of Jack Daniels before he headed to work and forced Makedde Vanderwall safely out of his mind ... for a few hours at least. Then there would be the unavoidable briefing over dinner with Hartwell and the gang.

Andy would have to get his act together and keep it professional in front of his colleagues. They all had a trial to prepare for and it was of great importance that everything ran as smoothly as possible. There was no room for emotional baggage. This was a big one, and the nation was watching.

It was two days till show time.

# CHAPTER 4

'I don't think you realise how beautiful you are,' he whispered. 'There is a flower inside you just waiting to blossom.'

She blushed and tilted her head, leaning against the wall of the corridor with her hands by her sides, as open as a book.

'I mean it. You are beautiful.'

'Shhh. I am not. Cut it out,' she protested, but she was smiling. 'Stevens is coming any minute,' she warned.

Ed Brown leaned a little closer to the bars. 'I can't wait until we're together,' he whispered. 'I think about it every day in here.'

'Oooh,' she cooed and glanced at him lovingly, another warm smile creeping across her face. But then she turned and looked up the prison corridor, and her body language changed completely. She stiffened. 'Stevens. How are you?' she called out in a dull, professional tone.

He could hear footsteps approaching his cell and Ed retreated to the corner of his cot. In seconds Stevens appeared. He was a solid and imposing six foot four, with arms like a gorilla's and a chip on his shoulder. Probably a police academy reject, Ed decided. Stevens worked the day shifts in these protected quarters of Long Bay Correctional Centre, noon till midnight. He was one of the reasons Ed Brown had taken to keeping a nocturnal schedule — anything to spend more time with *her* and avoid the long boring hours with Stevens hovering outside the cell, bereft of any usefulness or even decent conversation. Now Ed slept from five in the afternoon until midnight when the shifts changed, and his woman came back. The lights out didn't bother him. His lawyer had made sure he could have his own reading lamp and TV on any time he wished, as long as he was courteous about the volume. And Ed was always courteous.

'What on earth do you two find to talk about?' Stevens sniffed, running a hand across his shaved head, which was covered in a curious road map of rough scars.

*Oh, but you don't realise we have so very much in common,* Ed thought with a barely detectable grin.

'Gotta do something to pass the time,' the night-shift woman replied.

That was true. Unlike in the movies, most prison guards did not go out of their way to make life miserable for those they supervised. The guard had to be there, the prisoner had to be there — in Ed's case he was still on remand for his upcoming murder trial, now less than forty-eight hours away — so they coexisted as pleasantly as they could manage. No point in making life any more difficult than it already was. There were plenty of conversations had, and friendship, of a sort, was not unusual between guards and some of the more compliant, long-term inmates. So on the surface, Ed's late-night gabbing sessions with the night-shift guard were not odd. It was the subject of their discussions that was unusual, but that remained their little secret.

'See ya tomorrow.'

Relieved from her twelve-hour shift, Ed's budding ally walked away without looking back. Ed could hear her keys jangling as she disappeared, the sound a kind of music in his ears.

It had taken almost thirteen months, but Ed Brown had found his target. She was perfect — a hardened and unattractive woman, no husband, no children and no social life to speak of, a lonely corrections officer who privately longed to be swept off her feet by a romantic suitor. She had been as tough as nails at first, as one would expect, but just as Ed had anticipated, the hard surface had melted with patience and the right touch. Deliberation and equanimity were some of Ed's great strengths. In due course she had cracked like an egg for him, all gooey and messed up in the centre.

Perfect.

'Excuse me, Pete?' Ed politely addressed Stevens. 'Could you please turn that there on for me? The uh ... TV?'

Ed was careful to show servitude and an exaggerated lack of intelligence when he spoke to people like Stevens. It made them assume he was dumb and obedient, his apparent meekness inflating them with false feelings of superiority and security that could be used against them. In many ways Ed could still be mistaken for the pale, bespectacled kid who had been knuckle-bait every lunch hour in school, the wimpy boy with no friends, no pocket money, no clean clothes. But that was a deception. Ed had since found his power, and he was eager to regain the freedom to exercise it.

Stevens flicked the TV on for him. It faced Ed's cell from the safety of the prison corridor.

'Thank you so very much. I do so appreciate it.'

As was his routine, Ed would go to sleep after watching the news and the daytime TV shows, his last bit of homework for the day. 'I don't know how you can watch that shit,' Stevens had once said. Ed had only smiled in response.

*Put your stilettos on, Makedde.*

*I'm coming for you . . .*

# CHAPTER 5

Makedde sat straight up, jolted awake by a nightmare that faded as soon as she opened her eyes. Her heart pounded like a hammer in her chest.

*What . . . ?*

*Oh yes . . . you are safe . . . Sydney hotel room, courtesy of the Crown. You closed your eyes for a moment, that's all,* she recalled. Another nightmare. Should she enter it in her book? For over a year Mak had used a small notebook, a dream diary of sorts, to try to keep track of her strange nightmares and broken sleeping patterns. She had suffered from insomnia after the events of the last Sydney trip, and back in Vancouver, Dr Ann Morgan, now her father's girlfriend, had used Makedde's notes to help her decipher some of those nightmares. One rather telling dream revolved around Mak wearing her father's uniform and watching helplessly as Ed Brown killed her mother in the same fashion he had almost killed Mak herself — with a scalpel.

This time Makedde couldn't remember her dream so she simply entered the date and the word 'Nightmare?' in her notebook. Her jaw ached and she felt an unhappy twinge in her neck. She had probably been grinding her teeth during her doze. After the stress of the past two years it was amazing she had any canines left at all. Mak stretched her sore jaw muscles, opening and closing her mouth in a series of painful yawns. She rolled across the unfamiliar bed in search of a clock, the tangled hotel sheets wrapping her weary limbs like a shroud.

*You've got to get yourself up, girl.*

Mak planned to have a quick stroll around the city to stretch her legs and acclimatise herself before her seven o'clock date with some of the prosecution team. She was dreading it, picturing it in her imagination as some kind of 'Welcome to Sydney where your Worst Nightmares Come True' dinner. *Will Andy be there? Do I care?* She untangled herself from the sheets — her T-shirt seemed to have put itself on backwards — and rolled the rest of the way over to the bedside table. The glowing red digits of the hotel clock were bad news: 6.01 p.m. *You've got to be kidding!* She'd passed out for at least five hours. So much for the stroll. So much for getting a decent sleep tonight. She had just enough time to bathe and change, and try to snap herself out of her malaise before facing the team in charge of Catherine's post-mortem justice.

*That's it, Mak. You have nothing to do now except take the witness stand. There is nothing left to focus on. Just this trial. Just him. Facing HIM in that big bloody courtroom.*

Facing Ed Brown and being forced to recall every last painful detail of the things he had done to her would be hard, she knew, but getting the guilty verdict that would lock him was forever should be a given, shouldn't it? It's not as if there were any question of Ed Brown's guilt. After all, he had been caught red-handed during his attack on her. Both Andy and his police partner, Jimmy Cassimatis, had walked in on the scene. Andy shot Ed right then and there, though not accurately enough for Mak's liking. A criminal could hardly be guiltier than that. How would his defence team even attempt to defend an indefensible position?

Another look at the clock. She needed to catch her father before he went to sleep. *Hmmm … After six in the evening here would be nineteen hours ago in British Columbia, making it just after eleven at night in Victoria.* It was almost too late to call home but she decided to ring anyway, even if it meant waking someone up. She had promised to call and let them know she had arrived safely, and though it was late she knew the chances were good that her worried father was not going to pack it in for the night until he heard from her. She imagined him wide-awake in his office, sorting paperwork he didn't really need to be working on at that hour, or perhaps doing a crossword, surrounded by his dusty police caps and service awards, relics from his days as detective inspector.

The phone rang twice on the other end.

'Hello?' It was Ann.

'Hi, how are you? It's Mak.'

'Makedde, it's great to hear from you. How was your flight? How is Sydney?'

'Sydney is beautiful, of course, though I haven't been out and about yet. Oh, and the flight was fine. Lucky me, a nice boy at the check-in desk in LA decided to upgrade me. We *love* him.'

A laugh.

'Hang on, I'll get your dad on the other line.'

Mak was still adjusting to the happy fact that these days her father was not always alone in the house. She suspected that the relationship between him and Ann was going well.

'Wait ...' Mak said. 'Before you get him, how is he? Is it looking any better?'

'We got the results from the X-rays. Dr Olenski wants to do an endoscopy now. There is a fifty–fifty chance that he will need surgery. The doctor says it is possible that he may improve on the medication if he follows through with the right diet and takes it easy.'

'And is he taking it easy?'

'Well ...'

Mak had taken Dr Olenski aside and asked him if she had given her father an ulcer. He insisted that was impossible, and explained that contrary to popular belief, the vast majority of ulcers were caused by a viral-like infection with a bacterium called *Helicobacter pylori*, not stress. They were only *aggravated* by stress. Same difference, Mak figured. Same damn difference.

'Mak.' It was her father. 'Have you heard anything yet?'

The phone beeped as if another call was coming in. Was that on her end, or theirs?

'Hi Dad,' she said. 'I'm meeting with counsel tomorrow to review my testimony. Tonight I have a little welcome dinner with the local brass in charge of this circus. Should be fun,' she added sarcastically.

'And have you heard anything from *him*?'

'Oh, Andy?' He could mean no one else. She swallowed hard. 'Um, no.'

The line was quiet for a while. She really had expected to hear from Andy at some point. Some part of her had even thought he might come to the airport, but no. There had been no note at the hotel either, and Karen, the policewoman who'd picked her up at the airport, hadn't mentioned him. She supposed it might really be over between them. Perhaps he was seeing more of that nurse he'd dated. He had probably moved on. She really shouldn't have been surprised. It was time for her to move on herself, officially, and accept that they weren't right for each other.

'When are you going in for the endoscopy, Dad?'

'Uh, soon.'

She knew full well that it would be killing him that he wasn't in Sydney with her. There was nothing that she could say that would make him happy about not being there, let alone telling him that it was better for his health. But while Mak appreciated that he wanted to be in Sydney for moral support, she didn't need or want anyone to hold her hand. She was twenty-seven, and more than capable of handling herself, no matter how bizarre things seemed to have become. And besides, her father had a way of getting himself a little too involved in what was going on in her life. It was amazing how far some of his police connections could stretch. She found it embarrassing when he started to meddle.

'I'll let you go,' Mak said. 'There's no news yet, but I'll keep you updated. I was just checking in to let you know I arrived safely. I love you, Dad. Take care, okay?'

'You call us right away if you have any problems at all.'

'Okay. Love you ...'

Hanging up, Mak spotted a red light flashing on the phone.

'You have one new message,' the hotel voicemail declared. 'Miss Vanderwall, it's Gerry Hartwell from the prosecution ...'

*Oh boy. Here we go.* She found herself gripped by an irrational fear that his message would bring some horribly bad news about the case. *What's happened?*

'... just confirming that we will be in the hotel bar downstairs at seven o'clock. Let me know if you need anything, or if you have any problems. My number is ...'

She pulled the sheets up over her head again.

*You're fine, Mak. You're fine.*

*Why do you always expect the worst?*

★   ★   ★

*'I don't think you realise how beautiful you are ... There is a flower inside you just waiting to blossom.'*

Suzie Harpin recalled the words with immense excitement. Her true love had spoken them to her that very morning.

Although there was so much more to do, Suzie couldn't help but take a moment from her grim task to close her eyes and think about the positive turn her life had taken. She let her arms drop to her sides as she thought about love, about the importance of it, and how she had always known that it would find her eventually. She had waited so long and now it was her turn.

*Oh my love.*

A deep breath. A smile.

Suzie had her wedding dress picked out. It was long and beautiful and adorned with tiny silk bows. She had found a picture of it in one of her wedding magazines and cut it out. It was pure white, as white as snow, and she deserved to wear that flawless white as she had not had sexual relations with any man. Not since she was very young, anyway, but that didn't count. That was none of anyone's business. She had since reclaimed her virginity. For over two decades she had saved herself for her beloved husband, and now she had finally found him. Soon they would be together. There were just a few more preparations to make, some of them easy, some more difficult. There were books to study, items to purchase, chores to tackle. She was in the midst of finishing one of those chores now, and with so much more to do she knew she should get on with it.

Suzie pulled another clear sheet of Glad Wrap across the kitchen bench. With her nose wrinkled in distaste, she reached into the bucket and took the left arm. It was heavy and stiff, but at least most of the blood had already drained out into the bathtub. She wrapped it once from fingertip to shoulder joint.

Another sheet.

*Darn it.*

She was running out of Glad Wrap. What if she only got through half? Suzie continued, her eyes averted from what she was doing. She let her fingers do the work, wrapping and tying off. Wrapping and tying. She felt sure she was as efficient as any butcher.

*'I can't wait until we're together . . . I think about it every day in here,'* he'd said.

*And I think about you too, my love,* she thought as she put the arm aside and reached for her brother's head.

★ ★ ★

When Makedde Vanderwall sauntered into the dimly lit hotel bar, Andy Flynn was the first to look up. Her distinctive crown of blonde hair caught his eye as she appeared through the doorway from the main foyer, standing tall in long black pants and a simple toffee-coloured top that matched her fair hair. She had a dark trench coat over one arm and a small handbag slung over her shoulder, and her quick blue-green eyes surveyed the patrons of the bar from one side of the room to the other. Many of them had noted her entrance and surveyed her right back. Andy noticed some poor hubby a couple of tables away get a jab in the ribs for looking at her too long. He hoped Mak hadn't seen that. She would have hated it.

Makedde stood in the entrance until she spotted their familiar faces, by which time Gerry had eyed her and was walking forward to greet her. A barman had also been moving towards her, presumably to ask if she needed any help, but was robbed of the opportunity at the last minute when she strode past him, his assistance unnecessary. Andy felt his throat tighten as she approached. He took a quick swig of his drink to mask his nerves. The ice cubes clinked in the glass as he put it down, and when he looked up she was there, *Makedde*, standing by their table. He rose to greet her.

'Mak-dee Vanderwall,' he heard the young solicitor saying, mispronouncing her name. 'I'm Gerry Hartwell. I hope you've recovered from your flight?'

Mak nodded, politely ignoring his gaffe. She looked unreasonably attractive, that never seemed to change. Andy found it hard to draw his eyes from the lines of her face, her cheekbones, the shape of her lips with that plump pout in the centre.

'Her name is pronounced Ma-Kay-Dee,' Andy interjected, all eyes turning to him.

In her high-heeled boots Mak stood level with his six foot four. She was one tall woman who never seemed ashamed of her stature.

'Andy,' she said in a low voice, acknowledging him.

He reached out and shook her hand in a formal manner that felt aberrant to him, far from the passionate kiss goodbye they had shared in Vancouver a mere six months earlier. She returned his impersonal handshake with a strong grip, her eyes looking into his with a steady, almost challenging glare.

Gerry appeared to be blushing a little. A couple of his pimples had turned a brighter shade of pink. 'Oh, of course. Sorry, yes. *Makedde*. It's an unusual name, isn't it?'

*You know all this, Gerry,* Andy thought with irritation. *Stop falling all over yourself in front of her.*

'Um ... This is Senior Constable Mahoney, Detective Senior Constable Cassimatis and Detective Senior Sergeant Flynn —'

At least he remembers all our names. 'Uh, we've met,' Andy said.

'Yes, we've all met,' Mak confirmed, saying a quick hello all round.

*Obviously we've met. Obviously we've done more than just meet.* Which was why the prosecution was a little unhappy, to put it mildly. There is nothing more likely to cast doubt on a rock-solid criminal case than bringing up the issue of inappropriate relationships during those brutal cross-examinations in the witness box. And it had all been *very* inappropriate between Andy and her — hence his subtle sidelining in the case. Just another of the many reasons he would have to act very cool in Makedde's presence now.

They all sat down, settling into place and trying to look relaxed, leaning on elbows, crossing and uncrossing legs. He noticed Gerry pat his hair a few times in what he guessed was an unsuccessful attempt to smooth its wayward wiriness. He was perhaps five-six, overweight and still plagued by acne in his late twenties. Andy saw his eyes move over Makedde occasionally when she wasn't looking. He guessed that Gerry had never been in the same room as a former *Sports Illustrated* model before, let alone one with an intimidating IQ and a PhD in forensic psychology within her grasp. If the guy started drooling or convulsing he would have to take him outside.

Andy knew what most of them were thinking as they awkwardly sipped their drinks. *How is she holding up? How will she fare in the witness stand? How will Granger present his defence?* He guessed that Gerry might be thinking of something else altogether.

Mak was speaking to Mahoney. 'Thanks so much for coming to get me at the airport.'

'My pleasure, Mak. No probs at all.'

Senior Constable Karen Mahoney, a young detective in training, had been one of the first at the crime scene after Mak had found her friend Catherine sliced up in the grass at La Perouse. She was a good cop with a bright future in the police force, and she and Mak seemed to be getting along very well. Perhaps too well. *What has Mahoney been telling her about me?* Andy wondered.

'I'm glad we won't be seeing ourselves on the news tonight.' Mahoney let out a good-natured laugh and pretended to fluff her red curls. 'I wasn't looking my best.'

Now Jimmy laughed, and Makedde too. Mahoney was a good icebreaker.

'That could have been awkward,' Mak said.

Andy had not told anyone he had been at the airport, and he wasn't planning to spill the beans now.

'*Skata!* Those dickheads shouldn't have known when you were coming in,' Andy's long-time police partner, Jimmy, added with his usual candour. He was built like a teddy bear, fur included, and he had a certain unrefined charm that endeared him to Andy, though not always to everyone else. 'Oh, sorry,' he said, looking at the ladies at the table. 'Pardon my colourful language.'

'*Scheisse, merde, mierda, skata, crap.* It's the same substance, no matter where you come from,' Mak responded, not missing a beat.

Jimmy smiled broadly, clearly impressed that the girl could curse in German, French, Spanish and his native Greek. Gerry, on the other hand, seemed horrified, his fantasy probably shattered. 'Yes, we should try to keep you as inaccessible to the media as possible,' he said, at least seeming in control of his English. 'There is a lot of public interest in the trial.'

When the waiter came over, Mak ordered a bourbon and coke, which made Andy smile and left the rest of the table speechless for a moment. The next twenty minutes consisted of mostly small talk, the alcohol providing the necessary social lubrication. They continued at the hotel restaurant — no one had wanted the responsibility of recommending a place — and surprisingly little was said about the trial. After all, Mak would have a full formal briefing with the prosecutor, William Bartel, QC, the following morning, and there had been no major changes in the way the case would be presented. 'The prosecution has watertight forensic evidence and a cogent argument that Ed Brown is indeed the "Stiletto Murderer" — the man responsible for the death of all nine victims, and the same man who attacked you, Makedde,' Gerry had said with his usual formality. He was a smart kid when all his blood wasn't feeding the wrong part of his anatomy, though he was definitely a little awkward with personal relations. He'd even reeled off the names of the victims in correct chronological order — including Cassandra Flynn.

Luckily, Andy had been dulled enough by the bourbon and cokes that he had been ordering, one after another on par with Makedde, that he didn't even wince when Gerry mentioned his late ex-wife. His partner, Jimmy, had given Andy a sideways glance to see if he was alright, and then wisely changed the subject.

Yes, there were many aspects to this case that Andy would rather just finish with and forget about. Many aspects of his life, actually.

Come to think of it, this case had practically *become* his life.

★ ★ ★

It was past eleven when Andy found himself face to face with Makedde in the hotel lobby, the rest of the group preparing to disperse after dinner.

'I think Gerry's in love with you,' he said, smiling at her and wishing she would smile back.

Makedde didn't laugh. Her arms were folded and her mouth was held tight. It devastated Andy to see just how unresponsive she was. If he didn't know better he would think that he was a complete stranger to her.

'Really,' she finally replied, incredulous and seeming somewhat less tipsy than he was. 'I see AA did you a lot of good.'

Oh, right to the bone every time.

'The odd social drink, nothing more,' he snapped. 'You're no teetotaller yourself.'

'Not exactly. That's true.'

Makedde looked past him to the others leaving the hotel. Jimmy was on his way home to his wife, Angie, and the kids. He waved goodbye, glaring in Andy's direction before walking out the glass door. *Don't you do anything stupid, Andy*, the look said. Gerry was headed for his car in the hotel parking lot, which he would no doubt drive home to a lonely apartment somewhere in the city, or wherever single solicitors went to lay their heads. Karen Mahoney had gone to use the ladies room, or the 'sand box' as she called it, and would probably be back any minute.

'So, are you okay, Andy?' Makedde asked. Her tone was flat and there was still no trace of a smile on her soft lips. 'Is everything going well for you? Life good?'

*My ex-wife was murdered, I almost lost my job over you and now you are finally here and you couldn't be farther from me. What do you think?* 'Been better,' he replied. 'But yeah, I'm fine.'

'Good. Me too,' she said, and looked at the floor. He couldn't read her. Damn, he couldn't read her at all.

Mahoney appeared behind them. 'Hey? How is everyone?' Her red Irish curls quivered like springs. She was well aware of the past relationship between Mak and Andy. She had been there when the two first met at the La Pérouse crime scene, before Andy's whole life was turned upside down, and Makedde's too, he supposed. Mahoney was probably trying her best to keep everything civil in case some emotional battle broke out between them, but Andy wished she'd go away and leave them alone. He wished Mak would invite him for another drink and a chance to talk, maybe invite him to her room the way she would have only a few months ago.

'We're fine, Karen,' Mak said. 'I should be going.'

'Yup, getting late for a Tuesday night. Give me a call if you need anything, okay? Even just to chat or get together for a coffee.'

'Okay, Karen. Thanks.'

Mak said goodnight and strolled off in the direction of the elevators, and Andy watched her walk away, his heart sinking like a stone in his chest. Before he had a chance to chase after her, Mahoney grabbed him by the elbow and pulled him towards the hotel exit, sensing his mood, and perhaps his blood–alcohol level.

'I'm driving you home. Come on,' she said. Andy was too befuddled to protest, and he allowed himself to be dragged away. He found he didn't have much fight in him now that Makedde had looked through him as if he were an apparition.

*Mak . . .*

He had gone and broken the golden rule, he had mixed business with pleasure and he was still paying for it. It had been an accident at first, but quickly became more than that. Much more. In Andy's defence, when they first found themselves in each other's arms he was being dragged through an ugly divorce and Mak was a beautiful unattached young woman peripheral to the Stiletto Murders investigation. But then, of course, she had become much more important to the case — and to him. It had become a Class A fuck-up in every sense. If his superiors had not been so happy that the high-profile case had been resolved, he might have lost his job over the affair. As it was, he'd been kicked off the investigation, temporarily suspended, reinstated and then promoted in a way, thanks to successfully solving the murders and putting Ed Brown into custody.

What if they'd met under different circumstances? Would things have worked out more smoothly? Was Makedde yet another sacrifice for his career? Like Cassandra?

'*You're never home any more, honey. I feel like I'm widowed.*'

He had already sacrificed so much.

Why'd he have to care about Makedde so goddamn much when she clearly had finished with him?

And Ed's defence team would just be getting started.

# CHAPTER 6

Eleven o'clock on Tuesday night, past lights out, and the dark
corridors of Long Bay Correctional Centre were peaceful in
the wing where those in solitary confinement lay their heads.
As peaceful as could be, at least. Robbie Thompson, the
convicted paedophile, flinched in his sleep, and 'Dirty' Victor
Malmstrom mumbled incoherently, conversing in his dreams
with someone safe from his violence — for now at least. Luigi
Valleto, an underworld price on his head, tossed and turned,
racked with insomnia. Half-a-dozen other men dozed quietly
in the darkness of their cells, snuggled into the canvas sheets
that prevented suicide.

But not Ed Brown.

In his small dark cell, the killer who had not seen physical
freedom for eighteen months was wide-awake and deeply
immersed in a fantasy of recollection and sadistic desire. He
recalled the pinnacle of his free life to date, the moment when
he'd had in his possession a young woman he had devoted his
time and energy to ensnaring. A woman he believed, from the
moment he'd first laid eyes on her, must be his.

*Yes. Perfect.*

'Perfect,' he whispered so softly that not even Pete Stevens, who was walking past on his rounds, could hear him.

In his fantasy Ed saw his supplies spread out over the table, as they had been eighteen months before. Supplies he had 'borrowed' from his workplace — the morgue.

Scalpel.

Shiny new enterotome with its bulb-ended blade and fierce inverted point.

Toothed forceps.

Rib-cutters laid out like pruning shears.

All of the autopsy instruments were sharp and clean, glistening in the light like a child's toys at Christmas.

*She will be my finest work, my finest possession.*

Deep within his fantasy, Ed could see her clearly. He could vividly recall the scent of the young woman's fear, the texture of her fair skin, the look of absolute terror in her blue-green eyes when she realised that she could not break her binds, could not escape him.

'Perfect . . . oh yes . . . yes . . .'

*The sweet smell of sweat and fear. The smell of blood. Ready for consumption. Ready for dissection.*

Under the canvas blanket Ed stroked himself, causing the cot to quietly shake. He could feel his pleasure rise, his heart beating faster.

*Mine!*

But just as he moved to finish his final act of possession, the fantasy shattered. There was interference. Things were no longer under his control. His visions of mastery and power faded to nothing, and all that he could see was that cop's face.

*Andrew bloody Flynn.*

Ed gasped, overwhelmed by his frustration. A warm tear strayed from the corner of his eye. Even now he could almost feel the searing pain in his shoulder where the bullet had entered his body, signalling his defeat.

The end of his perfect moment.

The end of his freedom.

*Nooooo! Mother!*

It was predestined, he believed, and no passing of time could change destiny. The defeat had to be temporary. It had to be. And now Ed had a plan that would give him the second chance he needed to fulfil his destiny. That thought was the only thing that kept him going in this foul, stinking place.

*She will be mine. My perfect number ten. It's destiny.*

Ed pulled a small, ragged newspaper photo of Makedde Vanderwall out from behind the unframed black-and-white snap showing his mother in her younger days. He kept Mak's picture taped flat against the back. The corrections officers wouldn't let him have a photo frame in his cell: too many sharp points. And his original photo of Makedde and her model friend Catherine — *Me and Mak making it big in Munich!* scrawled on the back — was forever taken from him as police evidence. They wouldn't let him have it back, which secretly made him furious. But he had this news clipping. He had cut her face out and it was good. Anyone could see the resemblance was remarkable, particularly in grainy black-and-white newsprint.

*Mother. Makedde. Mother. Makedde. Mother.*

He enjoyed the sight of her for a few minutes, and then carefully taped the clipping back into place. In less than an hour the night-shift woman would begin her rounds, and Ed would give her the final instructions that would see him free in mere days. Everything was progressing better than he could have hoped. Yes, it was destiny. It had to be.

*I'm coming for you, Makedde.*

# CHAPTER 7

At nine on Wednesday morning, Makedde Vanderwall took a seat in the chambers of William Bartel, Queen's Counsel, and did her best to appear confident and emotionally prepared for what she would have to endure in the Supreme Court in the following days. She was adept at the art of conveying composure in testing circumstances — delivering a lecture at university, grinning and bearing it in a designer swimsuit on a freezing winter coastline, being briefed on what to expect of the multiple-murder trial that had already changed her life forever. Whatever ludicrous extremes life demanded, she could handle them ... she hoped. Her life had been laced with plenty of surprises so far, and she saw no sign that the trend was set to end.

Sitting in a creaky antique chair in front of Bartel's massive wooden table, Makedde willed herself not to fidget. She cast her eyes over the modest prints on the QC's walls and the impressive view of Sydney from his eleventh-storey windows. Mak had not enjoyed her first night in the beautiful city. Her body clock was still set to Vancouver time and her nap the previous afternoon had sentenced her to a long restless night in her hotel room, wracked with relentless worry.

'I trust you arrived safely,' Bartel said.

'Oh, yes. Thank you.'

The prosecutor was a tall, thin man with a light moustache and beard peppered with silver. He wore an old-fashioned red tie and a navy pinstripe suit that seemed to exaggerate his vertical stretch. The suit seemed as old as the dusty books on his shelves. After referring to some papers, he peered at her with a pleasant smile and intelligent eyes that she imagined would not miss a thing.

'I understand you are studying forensic psychology?'

'Yes. If I can ever finish my thesis, I might actually be able to use what I've learned.'

He laughed. 'Oh, I think everyone feels like that at some point. I almost quit law school on a couple of occasions. If it were easy everyone would be doing it.'

'You're probably right.' Once all this was over, Mak planned to concentrate on her PhD, and if all went well she would be practising as a clinical forensic psychologist in British Columbia in a couple more years. There certainly had been a lot of distractions lately, but she had come too far to give up, and she was set on reaching her goal.

'What is the subject of your thesis?'

'Variables affecting the reliability of eyewitness testimony.'

He nodded. 'Our eyes can deceive us, can't they?'

'And our memories.'

It was remarkable just how much eyewitness accounts could differ, Mak mused. Human nature leads us to colour facts with our own notions, prejudices and perspectives. And human memory, that fragile and ever-changing instrument, could not be fully trusted, as Mak was discovering. She panicked for a moment trying to clearly recall her mother's face. It was somehow blurry and intangible. Only two years after Jane's death from multiple myeloma, all Mak could see of her mother's face was what she knew from photographs.

Her eyes ... were they green or blue?

There was a knock on the door and the solicitor Gerry Hartwell arrived bearing steaming styrofoam cups from the coffee shop downstairs. He took a seat near Makedde, handing over her skim milk latte with an eager smile. He was wearing the suit from the night before, but with a pink tie that brought out the ruddiness of his pimply complexion. Though an accomplished, well-regarded solicitor, he brought to mind an obedient lapdog in the eminent barrister's presence, all 'yes sir', 'thank you sir', and bowed head.

Sipping his cappuccino, Bartel refocused their attention on the trial. 'Makedde, I will be calling you as the first witness tomorrow.'

'Oh ... yes,' Mak responded, somewhat awkwardly.

'Does that bother you?'

'Not at all. I was told that was what to expect. I didn't mean to sound surprised.'

Bartel continued. 'I have been considering the issue of live-feed video testimony. My instructor,' he motioned to Hartwell, 'mentioned that you had concerns about the presence of the accused in the courtroom.'

'Well, I ... yes.' *Ed Brown. In the very same room. Tomorrow.* 'Yes, that's right,' she managed.

'That is not an unusual issue in cases in which the crime is of an intimate nature.'

*Tied naked to a bed and sprayed down with some kind of weird disinfectant is pretty bloody intimate*, Mak thought.

'It can be an intimidating experience for many. However, Makedde, my feeling is that the trial would be better served by your physical presence in the courtroom in front of the jurors.'

She had considered this. 'I thought you might say that.'

'So unless you feel very strongly about it and you wish to press for that request, I would prefer that we have you in the witness box throughout your testimony.'

'Okay,' Mak agreed, without giving it any more thought. 'I'll do whatever it takes to nail him.'

'I appreciate your attitude. Frankly, I feel the same way. This individual is an aggressive fetishist and a sexual sadist. Very dangerous indeed. Fortunately, we don't come across guys like this all that often. Not of his calibre.'

*How fortunate.*

Makedde reflected on just how colossally bad her luck seemed to have been in recent years. Then again, she was still alive. She had all her limbs and digits — barely. Things could have been much worse for her.

As if on cue, the big toe of her right foot began to tingle, exactly where the micro-surgeon had sewn it back on eighteen months earlier. At first, after the surgery, it had been numb and there was some doubt as to whether she would ever regain feeling in it. But now there was a worse problem, this irritating itch that drove her to distraction. It only ever seemed to itch when she thought about how the wound had been inflicted. Ed Brown had severed her toe with a scalpel during his bizarre ritualistic assault. He had no doubt planned to keep her toes — together with those of his other victims — in the formaldehyde jar that had been found in his bedroom. She wondered how Ed's defence would try to talk their way around that piece of evidence.

'You might not have been aware in Canada that there is considerable interest in the trial both here and in the UK,' Bartel continued.

'The UK?'

'Because of Rebecca Ross, one of the last victims. She was in a soap opera. *Neighbours*, I believe. It's quite popular over there.'

*Great.*

The responsibility of justice in this case was not just for Catherine, or for what Mak had endured herself, but for eight other women who had lost their lives to Ed's sadistic obsession. That responsibility weighed heavily on Mak.

'We will do our best to protect you as you come in and out of the courts. Remember you are not required to speak to the media. In fact I would prefer it if you did not, at least until the trial is over.'

'I understand.' She wanted to get back to the issue of the trial itself. 'Can I ask, did the defence push to have the cases tried separately?'

'Yes they did. But they didn't succeed.'

*Good,* Makedde thought. A defence team sometimes tries to obtain separate trials for each individual crime, making it harder for the prosecution to prove its case. The accused might win a couple of the trials because of lack of evidence or due to an unshakeable alibi, and in subsequent trials the defence team can then say, 'But your Honour, the same man must have committed all these crimes and our defendant has already proved that he did not commit a number of them, so he could not possibly have committed this one.' It had been done before. It was highly unlikely that any defence team could pull off a stunt like that with the wealth of evidence stacked up against Ed Brown, but still, they would try anything. With the cases tried together, a great deal of damning evidence would be seen by the one jury, and if the prosecution could not prove beyond reasonable doubt that Ed had murdered one or more of the victims, that should not affect the case in respect of the others. That, at least, was positive news.

'And the insanity plea? Do you think they will try that?' Mak pried. It was a strong rumour.

'It is possible. The law stipulates, of course, that we must make full disclosure of our case — and how we will be presenting it — to the defence before the trial begins. But Mr Brown's team does not need to disclose anything to us in advance. They only need to give us notice if they plan to call new expert witnesses in order that we may have our own experts on hand to refute the defence evidence. Other than that, they could have almost anything up their sleeves. And Mr Granger, well, he usually has a few good tricks at his disposal.'

Mak knew there would be a forensic psychologist on hand for the prosecution to state the Crown's case that Ed was a psychopath, *not* insane, and thereby shouldn't be able to plead not guilty on the grounds of insanity. He had known what he was doing to his victims — and knew it was wrong. He was warped and evil, but *not* legally mad.

Her toe began to itch harder and she bent down to pull off her shoe and scratch it.

'Are you unwell?' Bartel asked.

Mak felt herself blush. She didn't want to flash her scarred bare foot but it was impossible to ignore the itch. 'You can call it psychosomatic, but my toe itches when I, um … when I think about all this.'

'Good. We'll use that,' he said, to her surprise. 'Does the toe operate fully now? Is your walking or exercise ever impaired?' He was taking notes.

'Not any more.'

He seemed almost disappointed. Perhaps he'd pictured her hobbling up to the witness box, a twenty-seven-year-old woman using a cane. Effective.

'Can I ask another question?' Mak said.

'Of course.'

'How is it that someone like Ed Brown can inspire an advocate like Phillip Granger to put his hand up for the case? Who is this guy? Have you met him before?' There was a distinctly cutting tone in her voice that took Makedde herself by surprise. She hadn't intended to sound so bitter.

'Oh, yes, I know Mr Granger very well,' Bartel replied. 'He is a first-class advocate, one of the most respected in Australia. He's been practising since the sixties and is adept at handling high-profile cases like this one.' He shuffled a few papers around on his desk, his face grim. 'What you have to remember, Makedde, is that a man is on trial for extremely serious crimes here. For justice to be served, he must receive the best possible representation. That is the way the system works. It's not personal, it's legal. Mr Granger will try to find an alternate explanation for the killings, and he will present it. In the end, once the rival theories are presented to the judge and jury, justice prevails. It's not the defender's job to judge his client, only to represent him as best as he is able. And it's not my job to judge either. It may not be a perfect system, but it is the one we have, and I have dedicated my life to being part of it.'

Mak nodded, feeling embarrassed to have inspired such a defence of the legal system. She knew he was right, but it was hard not to feel angry that Ed Brown, sadistic and heartless killer of her friend Catherine and so many others, would get his day in court represented by the best. The killer's defence would try to make the jury believe that Ed was insane, or that the forensic evidence against him was inconclusive, that Makedde was a poor witness, that Detective Jimmy Cassimatis was a bad cop, that Detective Andrew Flynn had acted unprofessionally and had a personal prejudice in the case that made him unreliable. It was not only Ed Brown on trial, but all those who had brought him to justice. *That's* how the system worked, Mak reflected ruefully. A detective inspector's daughter could not be naïve about these things. She knew too much.

It was the trial she had dreaded for a year and a half.

And it would all begin tomorrow.

# CHAPTER 8

Suzie Harpin sat at her kitchen table in fuzzy slippers and a pair of fleecy spotted pyjamas with a soft lace collar. She had the remains of a TV dinner growing cold on one side of the table and the *Yellow Pages* open in front of her to page 499, 'Carpet — Carpet &/or Furniture Cleaning and Protection'. *A steam cleaner should do the trick*, she thought. There had to be someone who would hire one out, without demanding his or her own people do the work. She couldn't have anyone coming to the house and poking around, that was for sure.

*A good clean and it will be presentable.* Suzie frowned momentarily, thinking of the stains Ben had made on the hall carpet. *Just a good clean*, she tried to reassure herself. She did not have much experience with such things.

It was two in the afternoon, and Suzie was home from another long but enjoyable shift. She had needed a couple of pots of drip coffee to keep herself going at work, and now she was looking forward to the welcoming comfort of her fold-out bed. She hadn't got any proper sleep since Monday, what with so many important errands to attend to, and she had spent a lot of her time off fixing up her new house. Now she would sleep like a baby.

The curtains in her Malabar apartment were pulled closed, as always. If she opened them she would only have a stark view of the tall barbed wire fences of Long Bay Correctional Centre, right outside the door of her apartment complex. The closed curtains were how she managed to trick her body into sleeping during the day.

Suzie surveyed her humble abode unenthusiastically. Her pet bird was silent in the centre of the room, a dark cloth thrown over the cage for much the same purpose as her own closed curtains. Some daisies spread limply from the top of a glass vase on the kitchen table, needing to be thrown out. Her discarded prison guard uniform lay untidily over one of the chairs. She had never been the homemaker type before, never houseproud at all, but now the shabby apartment seemed beneath her. The dim single room, with its fold-out bed and kitchen nook, seemed bleak and claustrophobic. She never had much enjoyed coming home to it. It was just a room to sleep and eat in. But soon she would have somewhere else, somewhere so much better. The thought lifted her heart.

Despite a small space heater that blew warm air against her ankles, the sparsely furnished apartment was cold and Suzie had fastened the buttons of her pyjamas high on her strong neck. She managed a small smile. Her thoughts would keep her warm.

*Ed.*

Suzie had over a decade of experience in corrections, and had slowly edged her way up the food chain. Women had to work twice as hard in jobs like hers. And they had to be twice as tough. And now Suzie, with her strength and her determination and her constant battling through life, had finally found a ray of happiness.

Edward A Brown.

Their conversations excited her, especially their conversations on her recent shifts. *Wow!* She was enthusiastic about what they had planned together. Ed was an amazing man. He somehow remained so sane and focused and giving, even in the face of this horrible trial. *Amazing.* And sweet. Just when she thought he couldn't be any more romantic, he would say something right out of *The Bold And The Beautiful*, just like Ridge. It was breathtaking how deep their bond had become. She had not experienced anything like it before. Not since she was a teenager anyhow, but that was completely different. That was not a time in her life that she wanted to think about.

Suzie turned her thoughts to the hardening blister on her forearm, wanting so badly to run her nails over the itch through the thick fabric of her sleeve. But she refrained. She had been sprayed with some body fluid during the clean-up — she had never done that sort of thing before and it took a few tries to figure out how to bag the body and fit it in the freezer, the best spot she could think of for now. During the ordeal she had got some mess on her arm, just above the protection of the rubber dishwashing gloves. Despite her immediate and thorough rinsing under the tap, it had stung and become a disgusting blister. It horrified her that her brother's blood had touched her bare skin, and worse, had disfigured it, even if temporarily. At first she wondered if the remaining poison in Ben's blood would take her with him, but now she was not so worried. It was only a superficial blister and it was starting to heal. The real worry was if it got inside her body somehow.

There was a story she had heard about cantharidin, or Spanish fly, in which a fisherman had put it on his bait in the belief that it would make the bait more attractive to fish. Getting it on his fingers was fine until he stuck a hook in his hand and 'dropped dead' from absorbing the poison. After her little experiment on her brother, Suzie doubted that 'dropped dead' was the right description. But if she accidentally broke the skin on her forearm, the poison might absorb into her blood-stream like it did with the fisherman. She certainly wasn't going to go to hospital for treatment, but she had to be careful not to touch the blister in her sleep. *I'll bandage it up some more before I go to bed*, she decided. The bandage had come off a couple of times already, so she would double it up.

Suzie focused her thoughts back on the object of her affection, blocking out the unpleasant memories: *the body . . . the cleaning . . . the blood . . . the stench . . .*

Ed Brown was one of the more high-profile inmates she had worked with, a tabloid celebrity of sorts and someone with whom the virulent jail grapevine of gossip was frequently obsessed. As in the childhood game of Chinese Whispers, the stories morphed and twisted themselves and came back to her as full-blown fantasies. Sometimes it made her laugh.

'*He killed dozens that no one wants to talk about. Their bodies are buried under the church . . . no one ever wrote about that. He'd been working with the clergy. The church covered it up . . .*'

'*Apparently he's the one who killed Fredrick. He just spoke to him through the bars, like Hannibal Lecter, and Fredrick rammed his head into the cell walls until he died . . .*'

There was not much else to do in Long Bay except gossip, Suzie supposed. The strength of the grapevine was unmatched on the outside. No Catholic girls school or small town rumour mill came close.

Then there was the tabloid press.

*The Stiletto Killer.*

*Sydney's Ripper.*

*The Stiletto Murderer Strikes Again.*

Suzie had read the headlines and press coverage with some interest at the time, and then when they had brought in this sweet man, this mere mortal named Ed Brown, she couldn't believe it. He wasn't anything like the monster they'd portrayed. Of course Suzie put absolutely no faith in the reliability of the media and she certainly had no time for gossip, innuendo and the sensationalising of crime and its perpetrators. But still, *this man* was the monster the public wanted to lynch in Martin Place? *This man* was the Nosferatu the nation feared? *This man?*

Ed Brown was innocent until proven guilty, that was the way the system worked. Except the jail gossip and the cruel press didn't play by the system. That's why he was in the special wing of Long Bay. Ed was isolated for his own protection. Someone as gentle and sensitive and famous as he was would not survive with the rest of them. It was fate, really, that he should come under her care.

*Ed.*

*My love.*

*I've made the perfect love nest for us.*

*We'll be so happy together. You just wait and see . . .*

# CHAPTER 9

Makedde stood in her hotel room, absentmindedly patting the creases in her suit pants as she folded them over a padded hanger. She hung the suit carefully, regarding it as the armour she would wear into battle the following morning.

'I hope you have a suit that's appropriate. Nothing sexy,' Bartel had said, in a statement that was probably unintentionally condescending, as if she were a silly schoolgirl or perhaps Britney Spears. As if a miniskirt and long flowing hair would scream, 'Look at me! I wanted to be abducted! I deserved it!' He needn't have worried. Her ongoing employment as a fashion model hardly made Makedde prone to sheer micro-minis or gold Lycra disco jumpsuits, and her choice of courtroom pantsuit was suitably conservative.

Mak frowned as she contemplated the hours stretching ahead of her before her appearance in court the next morning. She was basically on her own in the southern hemisphere. She had all but given up on the idea of spending any time with Andy Flynn. Even if she did want to see him, just to talk things through and resolve what had gone on between them, she sure wasn't going to be the one to make the first move. Particularly now that it appeared he was seeing someone else.

Were Andy and Carol getting serious? Mak wondered. What was she like? Did Carol make Andy laugh? Did she understand his work better than his late ex-wife, Cassandra, had? Did she understand him even better than Makedde, with her father's police experience and her forensic psych studies? Nurses and cops were an obvious match. They dealt with violence and misfortune all day. Were Carol and Andy a good match?

*Does he love her?*

Mak wanted to call him, but she knew she shouldn't. Andy knew where she was. He knew how to dial a phone. If he wanted to see her, he would simply pick up a phone and call.

*Get him out of your head, Mak.*

She had to. That was the rational and smart thing to do. And she had to try and get the trial out of her head for a while, as well. She had run over her testimony with Hartwell and Bartel; there was nothing left to prepare. All she could do was roll with the punches once she was on the stand.

★  ★  ★

Mak plonked herself down in a seat against the floor-to-ceiling window of the café.

She was at Starbucks to meet up with her make-up artist friend, Loulou, whom she'd called after trawling through her address book in desperate need of someone to talk to. Now that she was seated Mak had the uncomfortable feeling that she was in a fishbowl. The café was one big glass box. At least she had her back to a solid piece of wall, having chosen the closest thing to a 'Clint chair' she could find in the room. Mak could rarely relax in public until she found the seat that Eastwood's Dirty Harry would have wanted, the spot where the main door and cash register were both visible and her back was covered. She had spent so much time with police officers over the years that she could no longer sit with her back to the middle of a room. If she did, the feeling of vulnerability was smothering.

The glass walls still made her feel nervous and exposed.

She tried to calm herself. For the next few minutes she watched the busy street: a lot of businesspeople rushing this way and that, a few tourists wandering around in comfortable sneakers with backpacks and fake Akubra hats. The sky was blue, reflecting in the multitude of sunglasses that passed by on strangers' faces. Those who didn't have the foresight to wear shades squinted at the world around them, shielding their eyes from the glare as they stepped over a curb or looked for a taxi. Makedde wore huge Jackie O style glasses, which she had not taken off inside the café. She was dressed in long black pants and trench coat, a far cry from the colourful attire of her friend, whom she could now see bounding across the street.

Loulou was impossible to miss. Eccentric to an extreme, she wore a denim dress with frayed edges, purple nylons with fishnets layered over the top, and her usual black military-style boots — a kind of Kelly Osbourne meets 1980s queen Cyndi Lauper look. Mak felt comparatively drab in her dark ensemble. Understated could be boring sometimes. It was good just to see Loulou. She had been by her side when things had gone bad in Sydney last time. She was an ally, albeit an odd one.

'Mak! Darling!' Loulou declared as she burst through the glass doors. Everyone in the café looked up, as did several people on the street. 'Oh my gawd! I read that you were going to be back here soon!'

'Would that be the "Serial Killer Slayer" headline or "Model Witness"?' Mak wondered, rolling her eyes and accepting Loulou's generous hug.

'"Supermodel Stiletto Survivor",' Loulou replied with apparent seriousness.

'Yeah, great, I get abducted and finally I get to be a supermodel. Why the hell didn't I think of that before?' quipped Mak.

'. . . But I like the "Serial Killer Slayer" thing,' Loulou went on. 'That's cool. Very catchy. I read that you would be back for the Sydney trial any day now. Doesn't the trial start like . . . tomorrow?'

'Afraid so.'

'Sorry about the Starbucks thing.' It had been Loulou's choice of meeting place. 'I am like, a totally pathetic addict. There must be nicotine in this stuff, or something. Or there ought to be for the price.'

Mak laughed.

They settled into their plush leather chairs, nursing frothy oversized coffees and smiling excitedly. Loulou crossed and uncrossed her legs like a nylon cricket. She had changed her hairstyle completely, probably several hundred times since Mak had seen her last. At the moment it was styled into a kind of trendy mullet, blonde and orange through the front, and black down the back. It was hard to resist staring at it.

'It's so great to see you, Mak! It's been like . . .'

'A year and a half,' Mak said.

'A year and a half!' Loulou exclaimed. 'Well, I'm so glad you called.' She examined Mak's face. 'You look good. The layered hair works.'

When Loulou had seen her last, Mak was still recovering from the injuries inflicted by Ed Brown, including broken ribs and jaw and the now infamous severed toe. She had also suffered a subdural haematoma, or brain haemorrhage, courtesy of the large workman's hammer, wielded by Brown, that forensics discovered with her blood and hair on it. A small part of her scalp had been shaved for the surgery that drained the internal bleeding. Loulou would know perfectly well that Mak's hairstyle was a stylish improvisation to cover the uneven growth, not a fashion choice. The evidence of the wound was now invisible under masses of thick mane. Much like the rest of her wounds — invisible unless you knew where to look.

'How's the toe?'

Mak frowned. 'The toe irritates the crap out of me. Sometimes I wish they'd left it at the scene.'

'Ewww! Don't say that!' Loulou covered her ears.

'Well I guess if they'd left it, it would make a few things more difficult ... minor issues like mobility, balance ...'

'Shoe shopping.'

'Oh yes, that too.' Mak laughed and stirred some more sugar into her latte. 'Hmm, do they make prosthetic toes? I bet they do. That would be something wouldn't it? I could paint it differently for each photo shoot ... red polish or natural? French manicure? Fake tan or no fake tan?'

'Mak, you are gross!'

Makedde was smiling from ear to ear. Loulou was one of the few 'Darling!' people she liked, and her high spirits were contagious. The unsinkable, unstoppable make-up artist was a rare gem, brimming with genuine enthusiasm and possessing an undeniably good heart.

'Have you lost weight?'

'Spoken like a true make-up artist, Loulou. Yes, it's called the "Stress Diet". I *don't* recommend it.' She rubbed her temples. 'And truth is, I look rather gaunt. But I love you for being polite. How's work at the moment? Busy?'

'Well, as you know, Paris sucked for me, unlike *some people* ... so I've been keeping it pretty local, but I've had some good money work with DJs and some celeb pieces for *Who* magazine. Dannii Minogue. Sophie Monk. Sarah O'Hare.'

'Good for you. That's great.'

'And by the way, you don't look as bad as you think you do. You never manage to look bad. A little sleep is probably all you need.' She took a sip of her cappuccino, leaving a large purple lip print on the cup.

Mak let her eyes follow some of the passers-by on the street, wondering what they wanted to be. Superstars? Olympians? Billionaire businessmen? Surely none of them aspired to be an occasionally successful model with a stalled thesis and a serious psycho-magnet affliction.

'Still modelling?'

'I'm afraid so. At eighteen it was amusing. At twenty-seven it's more like the joke is on me. I can't resist the pay. Every time I try to get out of the game, it sucks me back in. I guess that's a blessing considering my thesis is all but dead in the water. Gotta make a living somehow, and I won't be starting a practice for a couple of years at least.' She wondered how much longer her modelling clients would be interested. She had already outlived the average model lifespan by a few years. 'I've been offered the Ely Garner show next week in Hong Kong, which is exciting, but I don't think I'll do it. I'm not sure I'll be feeling up to it after all this, and besides, the defence team might still have me on the witness stand … asking me what kind of underwear I had on and if I asked for it.'

'Ely Garner? That would be huge.' Loulou uncharacteristically paused for a moment. 'Am I allowed to ask what happened with the other thing?'

Was she talking about the relationship with Andy? 'Um … I think you know most of it, don't you?' Mak replied cautiously.

*Should I call Andy today? It might be good to just talk a bit. Would that be the right thing to do?*

'At UBC, I mean,' Loulou said.

*Ah, the University of British Columbia … that little debacle.* Loulou had alluded to something in their email correspondence, and Mak wondered how much she knew of it. 'Nope. That's a no-fly zone. Please don't be offended.' Mak had firmly put her latest dramas out of her head. There was no need to revisit those experiences now, when she had such pressing matters to deal with. It would be all too easy to let her horrors intermingle, distorting and growing on one another. That could be dangerous. But still, when lightning strikes the same spot often enough, it is natural to wonder why.

'I thought so,' Loulou said, successfully pulling Makedde back from the slippery slope of her own thoughts. The colourful young woman brought a painted fingertip to her lip, thoughtful. 'It's only okay if I get to call you Buffy. Deal?'

'Buffy? The vampire slayer?'

'Buffy the serial killer slayer.'

'Sure,' Mak agreed, dully.

'How's the love life? Are you still seeing that hot detective?'

'Any other subject will do, I think.' Mak chuckled awkwardly to loosen the lump in her throat. So many no-fly zones for one human being. 'The short answer is no. It's complicated.'

'Tell me about it! It's always bloody complicated. I was seeing this guy for like, three days last week, I thought I was on to something, and he stays over on Friday night and *snap*.' She clicked her fingers together. 'No sooner are we alone together than he's asking if he can wear my undies. I mean, why do I attract these freaks?'

Mak smiled. 'I've got a psychological test for you. Wanna hear it?'

'Yeah, okay.'

'This is a *real* psychological test,' Mak continued. 'I want you to listen carefully. While at the funeral of her mother, a girl met a guy she didn't know. She thought he was really amazing, her dream man. She felt that she was falling in love with him from that very moment. But unfortunately she didn't ask for his number and she could not find him.'

'Oh no. I hate when that happens.'

'Pay attention, Loulou. This is where it gets interesting. A few days later, the girl killed her own sister.'

'What?'

'So the question is, what was her motive? Think about this carefully before answering.'

'Do I get to phone a friend?'

Mak smiled. 'This isn't *Who Wants to Be a Millionaire*.'

'Okay, um ...' Loulou looked down at the cooling remains of her cappuccino. 'I don't know. She found out her sister was

'... actually responsible for their mother's death, and a fight ensued and she killed her?'

'Is that your final answer?' Makedde prodded.

'I guess so. How am I supposed to know her motive for killing her own sister?'

Mak leaned forward with a Cheshire cat grin, and her friend fell silent. 'Bzzzt, wrong answer. Her motive was this: she was hoping the guy would appear again at the funeral.' She paused for effect. 'If you answer that correctly, you think like a psychopath. Many arrested serial killers took that test and answered correctly, so I'm pleased you got it wrong.'

'Did *you* get it wrong?'

Makedde did her Cheshire cat impression again.

Loulou stared.

'No, I am *not* a psychopath, but thanks for wondering. Geez, I've missed you, Loulou.' Her eyes were drawn to movement outside the window and she froze. 'Oh, fuck.'

'What is it?'

It was Andy. She could see his face as he leaned out of the window of his car and adjusted the side mirror. He was stopped at the intersection just outside. 'That's Andy in the red car waiting for the turn signal.'

It was he who had told her about the psychopath test. He was still in her thoughts, and now in her view as well.

Loulou stared, mouth open. 'Oh my gawd, how freaky. He must be coming or going from work. Police headquarters is on the other side of the park on College Street, I think. Are you guys talking, or what? Last time you emailed me everything seemed to be going okay. You totally had the hots for him.'

Mak was too shaken by the vision of him to answer her friend. As she watched, the light turned green and her former lover drove away, disappearing into a sea of rush hour traffic heading towards Kings Cross. He was still driving the shiny red Honda. It had been his late ex-wife's car. Mak remembered they had still been fighting over it when Cassandra was murdered. Now that Mak was in Sydney, there seemed to be no avoiding Andy. It was uncanny. They had skipped the 'It's not you, it's me' conversation and jumped straight to being complete strangers, despite passing each other constantly. That optimistic kiss goodbye at the airport in Canada had led to this. Mak could hardly believe it.

'Are you okay?' Loulou asked.

'I don't know, Loulou,' Mak said, fighting a sour lump in her throat. She felt unbalanced by the sight of Andy, the knowledge of all they had shared and endured. She had so few people she could speak frankly with. 'Um, Loulou, I was um ... wondering —'

'You *are* going to have me glued to your side through this trial,' Loulou cut in. 'It would be my pleasure to be there for you. I would consider it an honour.' Her bright lips curved into a giant smile. 'I know you too well, Mak. That whole "I can do this on my own" thing doesn't work with me.'

'Oh no, I don't need anyone to hold my hand —'

'Of course you don't. But you don't have a choice. You are my friend and I am going to be there for you all the way. That's what friends do.'

Mak hung her head and laughed.

'When are you on trial ... I mean, *at* the trial,' Loulou corrected herself, though she was probably right the first time. 'When's our first appearance?'

Makedde chuckled again. 'Our appearance? If only it were a sitcom. Let's see ... I take the stand in ...' she checked her watch, '... seventeen hours.'

'That's it. I'm taking you out and getting you completely pissed.'

'My, what a healthy alternative to sitting in my hotel room with my head in my hands. Loulou, I don't think that's a good idea.'

'Come on ... just one then.'

# CHAPTER 10

At one in the morning the night before his trial for the crimes of murder, assault and abduction, Ed Brown sat curled against the bars of his cell with a lover's smile across his face. His hair was combed and scented, his prison-issue clothes straightened as respectably as he could manage. His woman had to walk her rounds, but when she came back they would discuss the plans some more. The seed he had planted so many weeks before was beginning to blossom into a beautiful flower. Plans were devised. Progress had been made.

Whispers now.

She was back, smiling, running a cool hand against his as he gripped the cell bars. He noticed a strange bulge under her shirtsleeve that wasn't there before.

'What's that?' he asked her, mostly out of mock concern and politeness.

'Oh nothing. It's a bandage. Just a scrape.'

'I will kiss it better.'

She blushed and wrinkled her nose affectionately. 'Oh Ed . . .'

Ed Brown gazed into the face of the night-shift guard, seeing only the glorious freedom the plain woman would soon bring him, and the access that freedom would give. Access to Makedde Vanderwall, whom he would see again in only eight hours, and counting. He would look into her face from across the courtroom, and she would know she was destined to be his. And then, finally, he would have her to himself, the way he had always been meant to.

*Makedde.*

*I'm coming.*

*It is our destiny.*

# CHAPTER 11

Detective Andy Flynn sat facing the window, blinking at the world outside.

The city buzzed with energy below, lights still glowing in windows and people moving through the streets despite the late hour. His apartment provided a good view of Darlinghurst. Cassandra had left him most of her assets. She had been divorcing him at the time of her murder but hadn't got around to updating her will. It seemed a cruel irony that he would find himself sitting alone in an apartment bought, in part, with her money. In the end she'd hated him so much it would have pained her to think that she would end up leaving him everything.

*'I feel like a police widow already, and you aren't even dead.'*

The modern apartment, though a sensible investment, had thus far given him little happiness.

The rough handshake of Jack Daniels greeted him again, the liquid growing smooth and mellow on his tongue, slipping down his throat and warming his hollow belly. Andy placed the bottle carelessly against the cushion of the sofa, his fingers sticky. He rubbed his eyes. He wouldn't cry, didn't want to. Men don't cry. Men pick up a bottle and move on.

Seeing Makedde had shattered him.

He had never imagined it would be like this. Here she was, back in Sydney. Finally the waters and continents of the world no longer divided them. But he had stuffed up. He had stuffed up with Cassandra. And then he had met Mak, and she was lost to him too. He'd had his brief moment, and wasted it.

What had she said? *'I see AA did you a lot of good.'*

*Yeah, sure.* He wrapped his fingers around the sticky rim and brought the lip of the bottle to his mouth again. There it was, satisfying, dulling. It took the edge off, that was all. Not an addiction — a friend.

There was a time when Makedde had gazed at him with passion and admiration. There was a time when he had even looked at himself with some pride. And now, in this apartment, with his friend the bottle in his hand, he found himself rejected by the only woman he'd probably ever truly loved, and holding the only thing he'd flatly promised himself that he would reject.

*She'll be sleeping now, Andy, not wasting a single thought on you.*

He looked to the bottle by his side.

*You know you won't be able to stop drinking if you don't throw it out now.*

In a push of self-preservation Andy snatched up the bottle, still half full, and walked it to the garbage bin in the kitchen. He opened the lid and slammed the bottle home amongst the messy remains of his Chinese takeaway dinner and a few cracked eggshells.

*There. You did it.*

It was too late to call his partner, Jimmy. He was at home with his wife and kids. Angie wouldn't appreciate a call at this hour. Andy had not returned Carol's calls, so he was home alone. His infatuation with Makedde left him uninterested in any other woman's company. In fact, some part of him knew that he was sitting alone by the phone hoping against hope that she would call.

*Makedde.*

It was too late to go anywhere, the night before the trial. It was too late to distract himself. It was just too late. Through eyes blurred with alcohol and some kind of irritating water he would not accept as tears, Andy refocused his attention on the garbage bin.

Within twenty minutes, the bottle of Jack Daniels was back in his hand. He didn't even bother to rinse the eggshells and slime off the sides before eagerly tasting it again.

It was not an addiction, it was a friend.

★  ★  ★

'Want my pants?'

'Excuse me?' Mak tried to shoo the man away with her hand, knocked over an empty shot glass instead, and watched as it rolled as if in slow motion off the table to land at the edge of the dance floor. Miraculously, it did not break.

'Want to dance?' the stranger repeated. This time Makedde heard him correctly. The music was loud, and so was the buzzing in her head. To say she felt vague would be an understatement.

'No thanks,' she managed to say.

The young man courteously bent down, picked up her glass and put it back on the table.

'Can I get you a drink?'

'No, no. No more. Please . . .'

'Come on, dance with me,' the man smiled.

Her bold suitor was young and attractive — dark hair, dark skin, almond eyes and well-formed arms in rolled-up shirtsleeves. But Makedde was not interested in engaging with him, just as she had not been interested in anyone all evening. She was busy trying to numb the dread in her heart and she had no time to open it up for anyone else, not even for a simple spin on the dance floor. Loulou had already called her a party-pooper three times during the evening, and she was probably right. Getting plastered had not helped at all.

Loulou appeared unexpectedly from behind her and grabbed the young man's wrist. 'I'll dance with you,' she exclaimed. 'Come with me.'

The young man's face registered shock as bright-haired Loulou dragged him back into the throbbing mass of dancers. Wednesday was salsa night at the Arthouse Bar. Who knew? Certainly not Mak, who couldn't salsa to save her life. Learning some Latin dance was on the end of a long 'must do before I die' list, along with learning to fly a helicopter, scuba dive and speak Cantonese. Her coordination in her current state would not be the most graceful, so this was hardly the time to start lessons.

Loulou and her handsome prey disappeared amongst the twirling bodies, her colourful mullet occasionally visible through a parting of dancers. Mak was alone with her empty glass.

The Arthouse Bar had some of the best mojitos Mak had ever tasted. And the most lethal. Two of those and a few shots of the pornographically named Cock Sucking Cowboys, which Loulou insisted she have, and Mak was pretty well blotto. Unfortunately, the alcohol had started to magnify her mood, rather than numb it, and her worries and loneliness seemed more intense than before.

Mak shook her head in an attempt to clear it.

Her thoughts swung randomly from memory to memory, evoking flashes of things she did not want to recall, stirred up and brought to the surface like crud from the bottom of an old jar. She saw Catherine streaked with blood in the tall grasses, she imagined putting her broken body back together again. 'It's okay, it's okay, you'll be fine Cat, just fine ...' She saw Andy beneath her, slick with sweat, exciting and warm, and she saw him walking away to his departure gate, turning to wave, smiling.

*Gotta pee.*

Makedde forced herself up and half shuffled, half staggered away from the dance floor into the nearby corridor. She searched for a sign to lead her to the toilets. Instead, she found herself facing a public telephone.

*Don't ...*

Within seconds she had somehow managed to slide some coins in and dial Andy's mobile number. She heard it ring once, twice. She leaned hard against the wall to support herself, phone receiver jammed up against her ear.

'Hey, I wondered where you'd got to!'

Mak jumped. The receiver swung away. It was Loulou.

Loulou hung up the phone. She must have read Mak's pathetic expression. 'No, sweetheart. Never drink and dial.'

'Busted.' Mak lowered her head and crossed her arms, utterly embarrassed. She felt deflated and empty, her thoughts dark and confused. Her eyes could no longer focus.

'Call him tomorrow, but not now, sweetie. Just trust me on this one.'

'I know, but tomorrow I'll be on trial.' It came out in an awful slur. 'I'll be on trial, Loulou . . .'

'No, honey, you are not going to be on trial. Ed Brown will be on trial, and you will nail his arse. Come on, girlfriend, I'm takin' you home.'

'He . . . he saved my life . . .'

'Come on.'

Loulou put Mak's limp arm around her neck and led her out.

'Hey!' came a voice behind them. It was the boy Loulou had been dancing with. He was covered in sweat and he followed them out like a puppy dog.

'Call me,' Loulou said, and pressed a business card into his hand. 'But not tonight.'

He nodded, mouth open.

Loulou took Mak in a taxi back to her hotel, let her heave her unfortunate guts out in the toilet and then put her to bed. And like the kind of sister Mak wished she had, Loulou stayed the few remaining hours of the night in the double bed with her so that Mak wouldn't be alone. At seven in the morning Loulou woke her up before going home to quickly change. Gerry Hartwell would be picking them up just after eight.

It was already the day of the trial.

# CHAPTER 12

The Supreme Court in Taylor Square, Darlinghurst, has the unmistakable aura of neglect. Rusty gates open to a once-grand circular drive, flanked by parking signs peeling paint. The increasingly dilapidated sandstone structure is no longer proud, ignored as it is by the sex shops and trendy cafés that have sprouted all around it. Junkies shoot up around the corner, and rent boys sell their human wares down the block at night, along 'the Wall'. Despite the wealth of popular nightclubs that have set up shop nearby, the pain and desperation of the streets has not really faded since the time of the convicts and the gallows. It is simply a different kind of pain now, and this new world does not spare much thought for Justice with her blindfold. She has become all but invisible.

*Justice is not only blind*, Andy Flynn thought, looking at the courthouse long overdue for a refurbish. *She's tired and she wants to go home.*

Across the road on the steps of the Sacred Heart church, a homeless man with a matted beard watched the flow of traffic from behind his shopping trolley. No doubt he wondered what all the fuss was about. Outside broadcast vans and news crews filled the courthouse parking lot, and journalists jostled for position to be the first with a scoop on day one of the Stiletto Murders trial.

Andy crossed the street towards the court, his partner, Jimmy, close behind him.

'Look at the trash this trial brings. They should put Ed up for public hanging after this. I could make millions selling tickets.'

Andy didn't respond to Jimmy's comment, but he couldn't help but wonder what it had been like in the days of public hangings in Darlinghurst. Would the satisfaction of seeing Ed Brown die with a noose around his neck be enough to help Andy forget that he had aimed to kill him and had missed?

Security officers passed them through the X-ray machines, nodding their hellos.

'Andy . . .'

'Hey Jimmy . . .'

The boys were getting a workout today. The normally sedate courtroom five, which dealt day in, day out with a depressing roster of domestic violence, assault, bar brawls turned lethal and the like, had come alive with the rare buzz of public interest and was already packed out. Today, the dry, slow-moving wheels of justice promised so much more than usual: it was day one of the most anticipated murder trial Andy had seen, and the show was about to begin.

Law students, reporters and morbid tourists of all kinds had come to watch as it unfolded in all its grim detail. Today would feature the opening remarks of the prosecution and defence. It was the day the Crown would outline its case against the man accused of murdering nine young women, and try to ensure the jury's favour from the start by putting their star witness on the stand — Ed Brown's only surviving victim, Makedde Vanderwall. But Andy would not be able to watch her testimony. As a witness himself, he would not be admitted to the courtroom until he took the stand. Even though he was the senior detective who made the arrest, the 'informant' in legal parlance, he would not be the first called to give evidence, and he could not watch the testimony of others in case he was swayed in his recollections by what the other witnesses said.

Andy was shut out, a familiar feeling in recent years. He waited tensely for the brief moment he would be able to give Makedde a nod of support before she walked into the courtroom. And that was all he could do. Just nod. The feeling of impotence did not sit well with him.

'Fifty bucks says they question her today about whether or not you porked her.'

'Jimmy!' Andy rubbed his temples. 'My head hurts.'

'Come on. Betcha fifty!'

Andy covered his ears.

'Wow you went hard last night,' Jimmy finally said, realising how fragile his partner was.

'Yeah.'

Andy's brain ached from his late-night session with his mate Jack Daniels. He had managed to cut it short by tossing the bottle in the garbage again, but only after downing a full three-quarters of it. And that had been a chaser for a couple of seemingly benign beers from his fridge. So far, that was one battle he didn't seem to be winning. He would have to do better the night before he was called to the stand, or his binges could spell serious trouble for him once again. He probably would not be called to give evidence for another few days, after Makedde took the stand and endured the intense examination and cross-examination process. The prosecution was bringing out the big guns first for emotional impact: the only first-hand account of Ed's demented violence in this horrifying case. Mak's testimony would be pivotal in hitting home the human cost of what the man had done to his victims.

*'Don't call me a victim, Andy. I'm a survivor, not a victim . . . please don't ever call me that . . .'*

Andy's heart twisted in his chest at the thought of her, and how intimate they had been when she had spoken those words. Things were different now.

'Did you see Ed's ma?'

Ed Brown's mother. Yes, Andy had spotted her too. 'The lovely Mrs Brown,' he replied.

Her date with the court had prompted Mrs Brown to dress somewhat more conservatively than usual. The white rolls of flesh that had been proudly on display in the past were now covered in a drab navy suit that fitted her like a potato sack. The wardrobe was different, but the scowl she wore was apparently a permanent one, and had not faded in intensity since last they'd seen her. She was by all accounts a bitter, difficult woman, a disposition earned from years spent working the streets before a house fire sentenced her to a wheelchair-bound existence. What did she think of her son? Andy wondered. And would she see him differently by the time this trial was through? Would it finally bring home to her what he had done?

'Hello, Detective Flynn.'

Andy looked up with a start.

*Damn.*

It was the ubiquitous Pat Goodacre, arguably the most tenacious reporter in Sydney. He'd expected she would show. Her presence was both good and bad. She would report the facts more accurately than most, but she would get *all* the facts, and that could be worrying.

'Pat, how are you?' Andy said cautiously.

'Yeah, you chased any pretty ambulances lately?' Jimmy added, ever the diplomat. He sat with his arms crossed, practically sneering in the journalist's face.

'You should get a muzzle for your dog,' Pat replied, not even sparing a glance at him. Her pleasant features seemed to sharpen, her eyes narrowed. 'The staff at the hotel say you don't tip so well, Andy. I was wondering if you have any comment on their service.'

Pat was clearly having a bit of a fish around.

'You don't have anything, Pat.'

'The Westin has always been good to me,' she said.

'You've got nothing.'

'The Hyatt?'

Andy remained silent.

'Where is Miss Vanderwall staying?' she finally asked outright. 'Come on Andy, we're friends. There's a lot of international media on this one. Someone's going to get the scoop. You know I'll do the right thing by you.'

Andy looked at his watch in an intentionally exaggerated motion. It was almost ten-thirty.

'You wouldn't want to lose your seat, Pat.'

She left them. The real show would be starting any minute. She would deal with him later, he felt sure.

Ed Brown would be on his way from the cells by now, about to take his place in the dock. The courtroom spectators would finally get a real live glimpse of the man who was allegedly Sydney's Stiletto Killer. Would he measure up to their expectations? Would he appear monstrous, or merely human, just a man like any other?

If convicted on all charges, Ed Brown would sit in history's books as one of the most prolific serial killers in Australia.

★ ★ ★

'Miss Vanderwall?'

Makedde's heart flew up into her throat at the sound of her name. She had been waiting for it, but it still gave her a fright. The opening remarks seemed to take forever, and now, after an hour or more of quiet fidgeting, she had been called.

Mak took a deep breath. 'Uh, yes.' She stood up, and put the wrinkled copy of the *Australian Women's Weekly* she had been pretending to read back on the chair. She had been too nervous to concentrate.

The tipstaff who had come to collect her was clothed in a dapper grey uniform, gold crowns polished proudly on his lapels. He looked a gentlemanly type in his fifties, his mouth firm, but his eyes friendly.

'You'll be fine,' he said quietly.

With a pleasant but formal demeanour, like some kind of butler for the great courts, he led Mak from the room where she had been waiting and out into a hallway. The tall door of the courtroom was opened for her.

'Mak . . .'

Her breath caught in her throat. It was Andy. He sat with Jimmy on a bench outside the court. His eyes looked bloodshot.

'Good luck,' Andy called softly to her. Detective Cassimatis nodded in silent support. She nodded back, barely able to think. The tipstaff urged her on, and without further delay she stepped inside.

*Oh God.*

The courtroom was much smaller than she had anticipated, but much more crowded too. Her entrance was met with collective silence. All eyes were on her, and most of those who stared made no attempt to pretend they were doing otherwise. Spectators, journalists and jurors looked her up and down. She'd worn a black pantsuit, her long hair pulled back behind her shoulders, and she could feel the instant judgement of her appearance, her apparel, her hairstyle. The room momentarily exploded in excited murmurs. An artist began sketching her likeness. Court reporters scribbled in shorthand.

Makedde remained stony-faced as she walked down an aisle past the seated crowd to the witness box at the front of the court. She coughed quietly. Her hands felt clammy. She hoped she was ready.

'Please state your full name,' the tipstaff said.

'Makedde Vanderwall.'

'And your occupation?'

'Psychology student and fashion model.'

'Raise the Bible in your right hand and repeat after me,' he continued. She raised the Bible. 'I swear by almighty God that the evidence I give in this case shall be the truth, the whole truth and nothing but the truth.' She repeated the words.

'You may be seated.'

*Don't look at him. Don't do it.*

Mak knew everyone was watching her, including the sober-looking judge and her associate, but only one set of eyes disturbed her. She could feel *his* eyes burrowing into her, she could feel Ed's stare as his gaze moved over her face, her neck, her bare hands. The sensation made her want to scream. She concentrated on taking in her surroundings instead. There was the stenographer waiting to record her every word, the tipstaff taking his seat, the twelve-person jury, all watching her, binders and pencils poised, each with a thick book of evidentiary material in front of them — photos of crime scenes, images of mutilation and murder. Pictures of Makedde's injuries would be among them. And of poor Catherine left lifeless in the tall grass.

The thin, distinguished-looking figure of William Bartel, QC, approached her. He looked different with his wig and gown. His expression was one of grave sincerity, but Mak detected a barely perceptible wink of encouragement as he ran through the formalities and moved into the examination-in-chief.

'Miss Vanderwall, did you know a young woman by the name of Catherine Gerber?'

'Cat? Yes, she was my best friend. She was from my home town and I helped her get into the modelling business.'

'And did you travel to Australia to see her?'

'Yes. About eighteen months ago I flew to Sydney to stay with her and do some modelling work.'

'And what happened?'

Mak measured her words carefully. She didn't want to cry in front of all these strangers. There was no way she was going to let herself cry. She feared that once she began, she would be unable to stop.

'I arrived in Sydney and Catherine wasn't at the airport to meet me, which surprised me. It wasn't like her at all. I went to the address she had given me and no one answered there. Eventually I got a key from the model agent who'd organised the apartment and let myself in.'

'I see. And what happened next? Did you see your friend Catherine Gerber?'

'Well it was clear that she was staying in the apartment, her stuff was there, and there were phone messages for her. She hadn't left a note or anything for me to explain where she was, and I became concerned that something might have happened to her. Then I had a photo shoot the next day at the beach at La Perouse ... and that's when I found her body in the grass.'

There was another collective intake of breath in the courtroom.

*Oh, Cat.*

Ed was still watching her. She could feel it. She was sure of it now. She wasn't going to look at him. He could stare all he wanted but she was not going to acknowledge his presence.

'Were you asked to make a formal identification of the body?' Bartel asked.

'Yes. The next day Detective Flynn asked me to meet with him at the Glebe morgue to identify her body. I was the only one available who really knew her.'

'And was it your friend?'

'Yes. It was Catherine. And at the morgue, that was where I first saw Ed Brown. He was the morgue attendant.'

Bartel leaned forward across the bar table. He didn't look at Makedde in the witness box, but aimed his question towards the judge and jury, as if trying to impress something upon them. 'Did the defendant, Mr Brown, say anything to you at that first meeting?'

'Yes. Something about how I could touch her if I wanted to, and that he had saved some of her hair if I wanted it.'

There were mutterings of disgust from the public gallery.

'I suppose I was pretty emotional and I didn't think much of it at the time,' Mak went on. 'Sometimes families ask for things. I was the closest she probably had to family. But later it did strike me as odd.'

*He got off on that*, she wanted to say. *Ed got off on my seeing her dead body, his handiwork, while he stood there and offered a lock of her hair . . .*

★   ★   ★

It was well into the afternoon before Bartel began questioning Makedde about her abduction at the hands of Ed Brown. And it was this questioning in front of the crowd of strangers and reporters, *in front of Ed*, that she knew she would find extremely challenging. She didn't even dare think ahead to her cross-examination by the formidable Phillip Granger, that would commence all too soon, perhaps tomorrow. Recalling the facts required a difficult journey into places in her memory that she did not want to travel to. Ed had planned to kill her — *to do even worse than simply kill her* — and he would have done just what he pleased if Andy had not intervened and saved her from becoming Ed's tenth unfortunate victim. In the end, injured and bound as she was, she had been unable to successfully fend for herself. That was the truth. For someone as fiercely independent as Mak, the reality of that vulnerable state was very hard to accept.

'Can you tell us what happened next?' Bartel asked her patiently.

She saw the stenographer typing away, recording every word. The defence counsel and his instructing solicitor wrote notes, and whispered back and forth to each other and their juniors. An artist turned her sketchpad to a new sheet of paper. One of the jurors, an elderly woman wearing round spectacles, looked at a crime-scene photo in her booklet of images. Mak thought she must be looking at an image of Ed's van, the one he had kidnapped her in, or perhaps the autopsy instruments he had stolen to use on her, and the thought of it made her feel like vomiting.

'Miss Vanderwall . . . ?' Bartel prompted.

She had to answer him.

'I . . .' she began. Her voice shook. 'I don't remember every detail. There were curtains across the front of the cab . . . so I couldn't see anything, couldn't see where he was driving me to. I tried everything I could to get free. I started talking to him, trying to convince him to free me. I told him he could let me go and I wouldn't do anything. I told him he could just let me out on the side of the road and I wouldn't tell anybody. I told him he could take my money. But he just became more and more agitated. He kept telling me to shut up. I think he must have looked away from the road while he was speeding, because the van went out of control and plunged into a river. There was a huge crash. He had me in these handcuffs on a chain. When the van went over it threw me into the air and I hit the inside wall hard. Later, I found out my ribs had been broken. I think the chain broke with the impact because I could finally free myself. There was water pouring into the van. I managed to climb out through the front window and wade through the water. I was freezing cold and disoriented, but then I remember finding the shore and out of nowhere something hit me on the head. The next thing I knew he was standing over me.'

At this point, her tears, which up until then had stubbornly clung to her lashes, finally let go in streams down her cheeks. 'I realised that I was tied down,' Makedde recalled, beginning to sob despite her best efforts not to. 'I realised that some time must have passed since I was in the water. I must have blacked out for a while. I was in a lot of pain. My head really hurt. I couldn't move. I was cold and I was naked. And I saw instruments.' She took a deep breath and tried to control her voice. 'He said he was going to perform an autopsy on me. He said ... he said something like, "I will save the fatal incisions for last".'

Makedde stopped short and covered her mouth.

'Do you wish to take a break, Miss Vanderwall?' Justice Knowles asked.

Makedde couldn't help it. She looked in the direction of the dock and her eyes locked with Ed's.

*Don't look at him! Don't look!*

His pale blue eyes were totally unfeeling. She registered not one single emotion in them. Not one tiny trace of remorse.

And then she saw his lips move.

'I'm guilty,' came a soft voice.

Half of the courtroom had heard it, and they turned to stare at him. Mak could scarcely breathe.

'I'm guilty,' came the voice again. Ed stood up. Mak could not believe she was hearing him say it. 'I'm guilty,' he repeated, louder this time.

Ed's defence, Phillip Granger, jumped up so abruptly that his wig shifted on his head.

'I killed them and I killed others too,' Ed declared to the stunned court. 'I want to plead guilty to all of the murders I have committed.'

*Oh my God! What on earth is happening?*

'Your Honour, clearly I need to obtain some instructions. May I request that the jury be excused?' Granger spoke hurriedly, but decisively.

'Jury, you are excused until further notice.'

The jury was led out.

'Your Honour, may I have permission to approach the dock?' Granger asked.

'Permission granted.'

The usually calm Queen's Counsel hurried over to confer with his client. At first Makedde could not make out exactly what was being said, but there were urgent words exchanged, then Ed could be clearly overheard saying, 'No, I want to plead guilty.' No one in the courtroom could have missed it.

*Yes. Admit it, you bastard. Admit what you've done.*

The courtroom was reduced to chaos. Whispering turned to outright cries of shock.

'Order in my court,' the judge called and slammed her gavel down. On her word the room fell silent, as if everyone had momentarily forgotten where they were and only needed that reminder to compose themselves.

Mr Granger addressed the judge. 'Your Honour, I would like to request an adjournment while I confer with my client.'

*He's guilty. He is guilty and everyone knows it.*

'I am guilty of murder, and I want to confess,' Ed stated calmly from the dock.

'We have heard you, Mr Brown,' the judge told him. 'Mr Granger, I will grant your adjournment. The court will reconvene at four o'clock. Miss Vanderwall, you may step down.'

'Oh my God,' Makedde could not help but mutter.

'All rise.'

With that, the judge left the courtroom. Ed was handcuffed and led away. Mak stepped down from the witness stand, shaken. She was confused about where to go, what to do. William Bartel and Gerry Hartwell retrieved her and led her towards the exit doors, protecting her as best they could from the onslaught of questions being thrown her way.

*'Miss Vanderwall, what do you think about his confession?'*

*'How do you think the victim's families feel?'*

*'You seemed very upset giving your evidence; how are you coping now . . . ?'*

From the corner of her eye, Mak caught a glimpse of Andy struggling to get to her through the surging mob of reporters. She opened her mouth to call to him, but found herself half jostled, half shepherded into a small waiting room by the prosecution team. The clamour outside faded, and Mak, drained and bewildered, sank gratefully to a chair, her tears still falling, but hope daring to flicker in her heart.

# CHAPTER 13

*Pop!*

At midnight, another champagne cork flew loudly from a bottle of Moët & Chandon, bouncing off the ceiling of Bondi Icebergs restaurant to a chorus of tipsy laughter and applause.

'We did it!'

'Ha ha. *He* did it,' Jimmy added. His wife, Angie, gave him a jab in the ribs as instant karma for his tasteless pun, but since they'd polished off the previous bottle of champagne the joke seemed amusing to most at the table. Everyone except Gerry Hartwell let out a chuckle. He had just one thing on his mind. Champagne was poured and glasses raised.

'To justice served!' Mahoney said.

'To justice served!' the group toasted.

'To never seeing that ugly bastard again!' Jimmy added.

'I'll toast to that, too.'

When court had reconvened that afternoon, Ed Brown was pronounced guilty on all charges, with the sentencing hearing set for three weeks' time. Mak would not need to be present then. Her previous testimony and evidence would be enough. She was finally free. Andy understood how much that would mean to her.

Andy and Jimmy, Angie, Karen Mahoney, Gerry Hartwell, Loulou and Mak had enjoyed a celebratory dinner at Bondi Icebergs in honour of the long-awaited guilty verdict. For the past hour they had been sitting in the restaurant's groovy bar area, drinking like fish. Icebergs was a new, trendy establishment, patronised almost exclusively by the young, beautiful and tanned, all wearing expensive clothing with logos that Andy could not decipher. *Why does that skinny girl have 'Buddhist Punk' written across her arse?* But the food was a noticeable improvement on the pub menus of Andy's local haunts. The view, however, both inside and out, was what took the cake. The bar had an almost *Barbarella*-esque decor, with white plastic egg chairs hanging from the ceilings and convincing stage candles lined up in stylish arcs above the patrons' heads, their faux wicks seeming to flicker in a non-existent breeze. The crescent shore of Bondi Beach and the raging ocean beyond could be seen through huge panes of glass facing north and north-west. Directly below their table shimmered the illuminated turquoise lap pool of the Icebergs swimming club, bright spotlights picking out waves as they broke into white foam across the concrete structure. Even with the balcony doors closed, Andy could hear the ocean. The corner bar where they sat, and in fact the entire complex of the restaurant, the Returned Services club below and the swimming club below that, seemed to dangle precariously on the edge of the cliff.

'Wow, great champagne! I can't believe the Crown is splurging on us like this!' Loulou gushed.

*Neither can I,* Andy thought.

'Oh yeah,' Gerry said and flashed a gold card proudly. 'This one is on us.' With that he gave Makedde an awkward smile and squared his shoulders.

Andy knew all too well that this was beyond the Crown's budget. He guessed that the solicitor was trying to impress Mak and her friend. For her part, Mak wasn't taking any notice. If Gerry wanted to show off at his own expense, let him.

*Fool.*

It had been a big night of celebration. Jimmy and Angie Cassimatis had enjoyed their now rare experience of dining out. Andy knew they didn't get out much at all, let alone together, and he doubted they had ever dined in an expensive restaurant like this. Watching the budget had been one constant in their many tumultuous years of marriage. Now that they were thinking of trying for another child, Angie would probably start pulling the leash tighter.

Gerry, too, was the most relaxed Andy had seen him. The young solicitor had loosened his tie and was sipping gingerly at his champagne, grinning from time to time, mostly at Makedde. *It was probably way past his bedtime,* Andy thought — or hoped. He shook his head.

Karen Mahoney, Makedde and her odd-looking friend, Loulou, sat close together across a long leather lounge against one wall, laughing and carrying on like sisters in crime. Andy could not help but smile at the sight of the trio elbowing each other and exchanging jokes, some of which were spoken in low voices that Andy couldn't make out. Some complex form of female bonding was going on. The sense of relief at the table was palpable, and for most of them this celebration had been a long time coming.

'I've got another one . . .' Mahoney said, loudly enough for anyone to hear. She seemed barely able to stop laughing long enough to share one more of her strange Celtic sayings. 'Okay . . . *Go n-ithe an cat thu, is go n-ithe an diabhal an cat!*'

'What the?'

'May the cat eat you, and may the devil eat the cat!'

*Aren't women supposed to chat about shoes and stuff?*

Makedde laughed, shaking her head. 'I'm kicking myself for not knowing any good Dutch curses. Um . . . *rukker*! That's one! It means wanker, I think.'

Loulou let out another squeal of laughter.

To Andy's relief, Mak seemed happy, unburdened by what she had just been through. Her cheeks were flushed from the champagne, giving her a delectable glow, and her grin was so big that at times he could practically see every one of her perfect white teeth. Andy had not seen her smile like that since she had arrived in Australia, or perhaps ever. He had only ever known her through her struggles, and she through his. Andy revelled in being able to watch her from across the table. Her happiness was beautiful to observe, and it reminded him of why he had fallen for her in the first place. Although part of him worried that the night would end in headache and heartache, for the moment he did not care.

'Tell us another one of your stories, Andy,' Mak said, grinning. She turned to Loulou. 'He always has the best stories.'

Andy needed little encouragement. He leaned forward, shifting into full storytelling gear for the amusement of his small audience. 'This one should qualify for the Darwin Awards,' he said. 'One night, years ago, Jimmy and I end up in this stupid foot chase with a car-jacker, a teenager, who'd taken off like a shot through all these damned backyards. We're jumping over fences, there are dogs barking at us, this goon is sprinting like a rabbit, the whole catastrophe. And it goes on forever. God this kid can run. I start getting winded, and I don't know if you noticed, but Jimmy's no Cathy Freeman. I'm thinking this moron is going to give him a heart attack,' Andy added, poking his laughing partner hard in his ample gut. 'He's wheezing and lagging behind like an old man —'

'*Skata!* I was the one waiting for you!'

'Eventually we hop this fence and come onto a residential street and he's gone. We've lost the guy, we're thinking, and man, Jimmy is pissed. Fuckin' this, fuckin' that, and breathing so hard I think he's gonna drop dead right there. And then, as Jimmy and I stand panting on the road trying to catch our breath, a gunshot goes off out of nowhere and the guy falls out of a tree right in front of us like manna from heaven. The idiot had climbed the tree and shot himself in the groin by accident!'

Angie Cassimatis dragged her husband away soon afterwards. Jimmy looked a little disappointed, and drunk, but at least he'd had a few hours of fun. Their departure left Andy and Gerry to share the company of the three boisterous women who seemed content to swear at each other in exotic languages when they weren't rapt, listening to Andy's cop stories. As a senior constable in training to become a detective, Mahoney didn't have nearly as many juicy tales to tell. And Gerry's dry legal anecdotes certainly didn't have the same cachet, which was just fine by Andy. He was rather relishing the female attention.

Makedde had begun looking at him from time to time with a warm, open smile. Andy savoured her affectionate look and wondered how long he could make it last.

It was after one in the morning when the five of them stood by the doorway of the restaurant, blinking in the light of the lamppost beaming down on them from across the road. The air was crisp and salty, the roar of the ocean so much louder outside.

Now that the trial was over and they no longer needed her testimony in court, Andy knew that Makedde could fly back to Canada at any time. Soon she would be gone, but he couldn't let her leave without at least trying.

Desperation made him bold.

'Would you like a lift?' he asked.

Andy clutched his keys in his hand, directing his words to Makedde alone, and purposely avoiding the gaze of anyone else who might have taken up his offer, particularly Gerry. If she accepted, he could talk with her at last. It might be his only chance.

Andy's throat tightened, waiting for a response. He felt Mahoney's eyes on him. Even twelve hours ago she would have dragged him away from Makedde, but now that the case was closed, the guilty verdict locked in, she seemed less determined to babysit. She simply waited for Makedde's response.

'Um, that would be nice, Andy,' she replied, much to his relief. She nodded. 'Thanks for that.'

'I would be happy to drive you back to the hotel, Make-eddie,' Gerry Hartwell said, pronouncing her name incorrectly again. He was a real irritation, Andy thought, standing close to Mak and trying to look casual. Andy didn't know how much longer his patience would last.

*That's it. I'm blowing this guy off.*

'Gerry, let me help you get you a cab.' The words practically exploded out of him. Andy jabbed an arm in the air and tried to wave down a taxi that was cruising past. Unfortunately the vacancy light was not on and it did not stop.

*Damn.*

'My car is right there.' Gerry pointed to his sedan, irritatingly thick about being in the way. Or perhaps he knew but didn't care. 'I'm safe to drive. Would you like me to give you a lift, Mak-a-dee?' He looked at Makedde expectantly.

*Oh, Christ . . .*

'That's okay.' Mak took one encouraging step towards Andy and then stood awkwardly between them while neither man budged. 'I'll be fine.'

Mahoney offered Loulou a ride, and she accepted. 'Come on, Gerry,' she said, trying to get him to budge as well, but he had not yet taken the hint to make himself disappear.

'Are you sure you are safe to drive, Mr Flynn?' Gerry challenged.

*Mr Flynn? Oh man . . .*

'At least as safe as you are,' Andy snapped.

*The prick.*

'Um, we're going now . . .' Mahoney said, grinning knowingly. She could see exactly what was going on. 'See ya.' The girls left, but Gerry was still hanging on.

Andy was ready to take the solicitor aside when Makedde made a move. She turned and gave Gerry a firm handshake. 'Good night. Thanks for everything,' she said in a devastatingly formal tone. It seemed to cut off any possibility of his sticking around. And then, best of all, she grabbed Andy's arm and pulled him with her up the street. 'Let's go,' she said in his ear.

Mak led him along the road away from Gerry. It was in the opposite direction from his car, but he didn't stop her. When they reached the end of the street, they stopped and looked towards the dark waves below. Andy knew Gerry would be watching.

'That was a little weird,' Mak whispered, observing Gerry over her shoulder.

As they waited, he finally marched to his car and drove off.

'I think he might be jealous,' Andy said, by way of explanation for the stand-off. 'Of our ... past ... um, relationship,' he added, not wanting to sound presumptuous.

*You sound like an arse, Andy.*

'Yeah, well . . .' she began, but didn't finish her sentence.

*Yeah, well what? Yeah, well he has no reason to be jealous because I hate you, Andy? Yeah, well our relationship can never be saved?*

'That dinner was all about Gerry Hartwell, not the Crown, wasn't it?' she asked.

He nodded.

They stared at the lights on the shore for a while, watching the distant traffic on Campbell Parade that curved along the boardwalk and the near-empty beach of pale sand that was now dark and quiet. 'It's beautiful, isn't it?' Makedde said. 'I never got to really enjoy it, I guess.'

She had lived at Bondi for only a week or two, her stay marred from the second day by the discovery of Catherine's mutilated body. Her every moment in Australia had been tainted by her friend's tragic murder and the events that followed. That was no holiday.

'That trip didn't bring you what you expected,' Andy replied, stupidly, he thought. *Of course she didn't expect to find her friend murdered, you idiot.* He was unable to find anything profound or even sensible to say.

'Are you in a rush to get home, Andy?'

'No.' *Home to what?*

'Do you want to walk with me for a bit? Now that all this is over, I'd like to … I don't know, breathe the air or something.' She chuckled. 'Or maybe I'm just afraid you're drunk too and shouldn't be driving yet.'

He laughed. 'No, I'm fine. But I'd be happy to walk with you.'

They made their way down a set of concrete stairs that led to a roughly paved path. The path would take them along the edge of the coast all the way to Bronte Beach, several coves away. Joggers, tourists and dog-walkers frequented the track, especially on sunny weekends, but at this hour they were alone. Although he could hear sand crunch faintly under their feet, Andy could barely even see his own shoes. There were no lampposts to illuminate their way. The only glow of light was in the distance behind them.

'You know, I saw you driving yesterday. You were stopped at an intersection on Elizabeth Street,' Mak said. 'I was with Loulou at a café on the corner. It was funny to just look up and see you there.' She sighed quietly. 'I can't believe that was only yesterday. So much has happened since then.'

Andy was unsure of what to say. There were many things he wanted to tell her, but none of it seemed important now. All that time spent missing her and thinking about her, and now he found himself tongue-tied.

They continued for a time in silence, Andy's thoughts growing calm as they walked. As his eyes slowly adjusted to the dark, he could make out the white caps of the distant waves, the shapes of rocks and tree branches at the side of the path, some writing on the concrete under their feet. The music and laughter of the restaurant had faded behind them, the noise replaced by the ocean's timeless crashing rhythm. They strolled in the faint moonlight side by side, a strangely comforting experience. They did not touch, or speak. Andy kept his hands in his pockets, his eyes focused variously on the uneven path or on the dark horizon across the water. He did not want to look at Mak. He thought it might make him crazy if he did. He didn't want to ruin the moment with talk of what had gone wrong, whose fault it was, what they had lost. There was no need to add the pressure of his longing for her.

'Keep walking?' Makedde asked.

They had reached the base of a steep set of stairs that would take them further along the path to McKenzie's Beach and Tamarama. Andy knew of a great lookout about five minutes' walk past the top of the stairs where they would be able to admire the winding coastline in both directions. Mak was eager to continue, and they forged on in silence. He noticed that she had no trouble bounding up the steep steps, even when his own breathing had started to come hard, a faint ache growing in his thigh muscles.

Mak's voice floated down from above him. 'Oh, how exhilarating!' she exclaimed. 'It's even better than I remember!'

He smiled at her enthusiasm and climbed the last few steps, feeling like an old man. He briefly caught sight of her several metres away, then she disappeared behind some shrubs as the path turned.

Mak was waiting for him at the base of another set of stairs. Her cheeks looked rosy, her breath visible in the cold night air. She smiled broadly as she took in the view, hands on hips and standing tall. Andy resisted the urge to bundle her into his arms and lift her off the ground. She used to love that. She had said that he made her feel as light as a feather.

*Oh fuck it. I want to kiss her.*

But he didn't. He didn't pick her up, either. Andy kept his hands firmly in his jeans' pockets and stared in the direction of the ocean. The view from where they stood was breathtaking, but he could hardly focus on it. He had begun to feel regret that they were not truly sharing the moment — the unexpected confession and swift court victory, the end of the Ed Brown saga — the way they once would have, the way he had imagined they would when Ed was finally locked away for life. The whole experience had brought them together, but eventually pulled them apart. They should have been kissing, laughing, enjoying the victory together. *We should be making love*, he thought. He could barely think or breathe for all the restraint it took to stop himself embracing her. It didn't feel right to be so impersonal with her like this.

Andy felt a fingertip on his wrist, and jumped. It was Makedde's hand searching for his. She had moved closer. He pulled his hand out of his pocket and squeezed hers, unsure whether it was safe to be even that intimate. Her hand felt smooth and cool in his. For a while they stayed that way, holding hands and looking out to sea.

'My God, Andy. What happened with us?' she said with a tremor in her voice. 'Was it a mistake from the start? All of it?'

Andy didn't reply. He pulled her in front of him and gazed into her face in the low light. It was lovely to see her up close. The wind blew her hair back, and the distant lights of Bondi glowed like a halo around her head. Her eyes looked into his, speaking silent emotions that he could not read. He wanted to tell her all the things he had felt in the past few months, but could not find the words. It didn't matter. In the dark, Makedde leaned into him until her lips met his. Her kiss was a shock of cold from the wind, then warm and welcoming inside her mouth. The surprise of it jolted him into arousal. There she was, her fingers touching his arms, her tongue running slowly across his lips. He parted his lips further and kissed her deeper. Harder. He felt her exhale and melt into him. Her fingers slid across the back of his neck, gently pulling him into her. Andy bent to meet her, allowing himself the pleasure of her kiss, unsure how long it might last. Now she was pressed firmly against him, her body like a puzzle piece filling every gap between them seamlessly, knee to knee, groin to groin, the swell of her breasts crushed against him. His blood surged at the feel of her, and some part of himself let go. He cradled her in his arms as he had always loved to. It felt so damn good. It felt right. He wanted to swallow her up with his rage and pleasure and anger and love. He loved her so damn much and nothing ever seemed to work between them.

Was it worth it to allow themselves this? Was it worth the gamble?

*Yes.*

Andy had no choice. He picked Mak up and carried her. She clung to him, kissing, squeezing, encouraging. He didn't put her back down until they were near the edge of the tall cliffs, metres away, by the entrance to a rocky nook. Nothing but raging seas and whipping wind surrounded them. There was no one to see. With unspoken understanding, they crawled into the small shelter together, not even registering the cold, uncomfortable rock beneath them. Guarded from the elements, they kneeled torso to torso and began a slow ritual of sensual reacquaintance, hands reaching eagerly for every part of one another. He slid his grateful hands under Makedde's coat and the soft fabric of her knitted top. Her skin felt warm and silky to his touch, his fingers seeming far too rough to be permitted such a pleasure. Makedde's mouth felt hot and willing on his, her writhing form pushing him to a point of carnal urgency. He was painfully hard, his body eager. She squeezed his buttocks and ground his stiffness into her. Her fingers found him, caressing the shape of him through the restraints of his clothing.

'Fuck me, Andy,' she whispered. 'Please.'

Andy pushed her down without hesitation. She gave welcomingly under his weight, wrapping her long legs tightly around his hips. Eagerly, she pulled at his belt buckle, tugging until he was free and pressed rigid against her thighs.

In the dark they came together, trembling and holding tight, bodies arching and sighing as they pleased one another, blissfully unconcerned about their numbing knees and elbows, and the biting cold of the whistling autumn wind. It was over an hour before they ventured from their rocky bed to find another, more private place to continue their renewed passions unhindered.

# CHAPTER 14

*Feeling rough.*

At nine forty-five on Friday morning, Andy Flynn reported to Detective Inspector Roderick Kelley's office, as requested. He felt like a train wreck. He gingerly carried a styrofoam cup of watery drip coffee, and dragged himself through Central Homicide. His head was agony, though his heart was a great improvement from the day before. When he stopped at Kelley's door, he straightened his collar with one gravel-rash afflicted hand.

*Ouch.*

Andy had woken to find his palms and knees roughed up from the sharp bed of rocks that he and Makedde had enlisted as a makeshift mattress on the Bondi cliffs. Not that he had felt any discomfort at the time. He had been far too busy focusing on more pleasant sensations.

He found Inspector Kelley staring pensively out of the large window of his office with his hands clasped neatly behind his back. Andy did not want to disturb him — in fact he wanted nothing more than to crawl back into Makedde's warm and inviting hotel bed whence he had come. But that was not an option just yet. Andy rapped on the open door. 'Sir,' he said simply.

'Flynn. Take a seat.' The words were spoken without Kelley even turning his head. Andy took his cue, settling into the chair with a rigid attentiveness that he hoped would compensate for his bleary-eyed morning face.

Andy waited for Kelley to continue.

And waited.

The minutes ticked by painfully as Kelley pondered something at the window. He always did this when he had an important matter to discuss. It perturbed Andy somewhat, though he could not think of anything that he had to fear on this occasion. The outcome of the trial had been surprisingly good, but being called to Kelley's office was still a nerve-racking experience. Andy had been in the hot seat more than a few times in this office — what was it now?

Andy found his mind ticking nervously over the possibilities of what might have occurred to necessitate one of these meetings.

*Jimmy in trouble? Problems with the media?*

After what seemed an eternity, Kelley left his spot at the window to take a seat. The leather chair creaked under his weight. He leaned forward across his broad desk, resting on his elbows and clasping his hands together thoughtfully. Andy noticed that the cuticles of his fingers were raw.

'You must be happy today,' Kelley finally began, observing Andy with sharp, slate-grey eyes that took in every detail. The crow's-feet in the corners of his eyes turned up and he pressed his mouth tight in a stern, but not unfriendly expression.

*Does he know about Makedde, or is he talking about the Ed Brown verdict?*

'Very happy to have Ed Brown behind bars permanently, sir. Very happy,' Andy replied. That was, of course, quite an understatement.

'Yes. That guilty confession ... Quite a courtroom drama, I hear.'

'Yes sir, a guilty confession and a courtroom full of witnesses to hear it. You can't argue with that.' He found himself tapping one foot against the leg of Kelley's desk. He stopped.

Kelley seemed in no hurry to move things along. He was evidently contemplating something, and Andy knew that his silences were not an invitation to fill the air with talk.

*Tick.*

*Tock.*

Kelley flexed his jaw and flipped through a couple of papers on his desk. Andy watched him silently. He was still lean and fit well into his fifties, a man with a lot of arrests under his belt and a lot of his life spent on the beat before he worked his way up to the rank of detective inspector. Kelley was no paper-pushing political mouthpiece, like some of the others. He knew about the work. He'd been there. Like many of the detectives, Andy respected Kelley enormously, and despite being somewhat in favour thanks to the ultimate success of the high-profile Stiletto Murders case, he still feared him a little too. He supposed all mentors were like that — feared by those who revered them.

'The profiling unit, Andy. How is that coming along?' Kelley asked.

'Well, as you know, a green light on the unit doesn't mean a thing if there's a red light on some of the funding,' Andy said with some regret. It was an area of great frustration among many in the police force. 'It's stop, go, stop ...'

'Politicians.'

'Yup.'

Andy gritted his teeth. The Commissioner, Rex Gibbons, was being attacked from all sides for his strategy on police reform and his allocation of taxpayers' funds. The NSW Profiling Unit, which could have been set for full operation later in the year, was meant to be a high-tech national centre for criminal profiling with special focus on instances of serial rape and murder. Instead it was little more than a dream caught in a political and funding limbo. The delay had introduced Andy to a whole new level of frustration.

'Ed's representation, Phillip Granger, is at the bargaining table for his client,' Kelley said out of the blue.

'What?' Andy's heart skipped.

'He is offering two additional confessions, apparently. That would be two of our missing persons cases solved for us, and burial sites for the bodies, too. It would mean a lot to the families to have that kind of closure.'

'Of course it would mean a lot to the families,' Andy responded, trying unsuccessfully to remain calm. 'But what does *he* want, sir?'

'A reduced sentence, of course.'

*No fucking way.*

Andy stood up and practically screamed the words in the office. 'That's not even a consideration, is it? Tell me that's not a consideration.'

Kelley was grim-faced. 'Sit.'

Andy did.

'I know what you're feeling here. But he'll still be behind bars for a long time. The public outcry would be deafening if they let him out in even twenty or thirty years. They know that.'

'Damn right. There's got to be a better way. What else have we got to bargain with to get those bodies?'

It made Andy's skin crawl to bargain with killers, especially this one, but every experienced cop knew that it was the way of the system. Snitching rapists got special privileges, drug traffickers got early release for helping to nail worse drug traffickers, and killers got reduced sentences by cooperating and providing information about their innocent, decomposing, brutalised victims.

'Granger's pushing for possible parole after some years of rehabilitation.'

'Rehabilitation? You've got to be fucking kidding me!'

'Flynn.' Kelley gave him a hard look, and Andy checked himself.

*Jesus, what the fuck is the world coming to? This can't be happening.*

Andy felt his blood pressure peak violently. He had to try to stay under control, especially in the presence of his superior, but he wanted to hit something so damn badly that he dug his fingertips into his palms with white-knuckle force. His nails bit into the already tender flesh, but he didn't care. He could think of nothing but what he would do to Ed Brown if he got hold of him. A rage of violent thoughts flooded through him until it turned back on itself and he felt a sting of renewed shame at having missed his only chance to put an end to Ed Brown's life. Right then and there as he'd caught Ed red-handed assaulting Makedde, Andy could have ended it. He'd been given the chance, and he didn't do it.

*Fucking Ed Brown. Fucking motherfucking slippery Ed Brown . . .*

'Sir,' he managed, 'we're all aware that those with a homicidal urge like Ed Brown do not become serial killers overnight. This has been an evolution, clearly. He is at an advanced stage of sadistic behaviour — stalking, torture, mutilation. People like that do not change. There is no rehabilitation for people like Ed. How can we even banter the word "rehabilitation" around? That's just bullshit.'

'Try to relax, Andy. This is out of our hands now. It's in the hands of the courts. You know that.'

Andy tried to relax. It was impossible.

'The Crown will only bargain so much with someone like Ed,' Kelley continued, 'and there is good news. He has agreed to lead us to one of the bodies today. He delivers a body, and they go to the negotiation table. That's the deal so far. Nothing else has been guaranteed.'

Andy perked up. The fact that Ed had been talked into giving up one of the bodies before any deal was made was encouraging, and very wise considering how little Ed could be trusted.

'Where do I have to be, and when?' Andy asked.

'You don't have to be anywhere. I'm sending Senior Sergeant Lewis, and Hoosier —'

'What!' Andy tried to hold his tongue, but found his restraint lacking.

'And Cassimatis. Plus a small team from forensics.'

*Jimmy. Thank goodness Jimmy will be there.*

'We have to keep this quiet. The last thing we want is the press getting hold of the fact that our guilty serial murderer is cruising around town pointing out dead bodies. I don't want to see this on the news.'

'I should be there.'

'No, Andy, you shouldn't. He killed your wife and he attacked your girlfriend. You are way too close to this.'

That stung.

*But I'm the one who brought him in,* Andy thought bitterly. *I was under bloody suspicion for my own wife's murder and I brought the killer in. And despite all that I am still being excluded.*

'Sir, may I suggest that it is important that someone be there who has dealt with Ed before —'

'Cassimatis was at the arrest.'

Kelley was right, of course.

'Do I have any say in this?' Andy asked, knowing the answer.

'I'm not letting you near this guy, and you know perfectly well why.'

Andy was defeated. He did not push the issue further. The fact that Kelley was probably making the right decision only made it worse. Andy had been in a fair bit of trouble before. He had a history of anger problems. One incident in particular had nearly cost him his job. He had to admit that he had probably taken his interrogation of one suspected paedophile a little too far. The creep had been hospitalised. Andy knew perfectly well that no one would trust him to be able to restrain himself around Ed. He didn't even know if he could trust himself.

'Cassimatis will go in. That's the best I can do. You sit tight.'

*Sit tight. Yeah, right.*

*   *   ⋆

'Fucking bullshit . . .' Andy was well out of Kelley's earshot when he let fly. 'Fucking sit tight! How can I sit tight?'

'Calm down, Andy,' Jimmy urged. 'It don't matter. It'll be over in a day or two. It's nothing. He's convicted, Andy. It's done. Come on, mate, you can take this off your plate now.'

'No, I can *not.*'

*He killed Cassandra. He brutally attacked Makedde. I can never take that off my damn plate.*

'Kelley, he always prepares us for the worst,' Jimmy continued. 'It's the fucking Crown. They gotta do this shit to get the bodies, man. It ain't like he's gonna walk.'

Andy slammed a fist into Jimmy's desk. It screeched back an inch across the floor. Jimmy had never been good at placating him. 'It ain't like he's gonna walk' was never going to work. Just thinking about it put Andy over the edge. He and Jimmy had seen more than enough bullshit calls to know that almost anything could happen when the bargaining table was open for business.

'He won't have a fucking holiday on my watch, don't you worry about that,' Jimmy insisted. 'No matter what happens, I'm keeping him on a short leash. One wrong look and he's getting a clip in the head.'

Jimmy looked at his watch and tossed his rumpled jacket over one shoulder. Senior Sergeant Lewis would be rounding up the guys soon.

Before he could respond, Andy's mobile phone rang and he reached for it automatically, hoping it was Makedde waking up in her hotel room, missing him. Mak was probably one of the few forces in his world that could lift his mood at that moment. Perhaps he could drop in and see her, now that he had been shut out of the action.

'Hello Andy.' It was a woman's voice, but it was not Makedde.

'Oh, hi,' Andy replied, trying to be as ambiguous as possible in the presence of his partner. 'Hang on a sec.' He turned to Jimmy. 'You got a minute?'

'Just,' Jimmy replied.

Andy put two fingers in the air to denote the seconds it would take him to handle the call. He took it out into the hallway, feeling Jimmy's eyes on his back.

'Carol, how are you?' he said into the phone. He swallowed hard.

'I'm good. But I haven't heard from you in ages! I just wanted to see how you are?'

'Oh, I'm fine.'

'I was thinking it might be nice to catch up soon, Andy. It's been so long ...'

'Catch up? Oh, um ... Carol ...' *Oh shit. I'm gonna have to tell her.* 'Yeah, let's do that. How are you placed in the next few hours? A quick coffee perhaps?'

'Sure! That'd be great.' She sounded unreasonably happy about meeting with him. That was not a good thing.

Jimmy predictably raised his eyebrows as Andy returned from the hallway.

'Mmmm, top-secret rendezvous, huh?' He put one hand to his mouth and stuck his tongue into his cheek, crudely mimicking a blowjob, one of his favourites in his endless repertoire of rude gestures.

'I hate to break it to you, but you ain't gonna get Angie preggers again by getting her to do that to you,' Andy said by way of retort.

'My Angie! Hey, you never mind my Angie.' Jimmy crossed himself. 'She gotta kiss the kids goodnight with that mouth. I'm thinkin' of your Makedde … mmm the one you are banging again. Ain't ya? You lucky dog …'

'I don't know what you're talking about,' Andy countered.

'Oh, come on. This is Jimmy here.' He poked a fat finger into Andy's chest. 'You think I couldn't see the way you two were mooning over each other last night?' He pretended to hump the desk. 'Oohhhhh, Andy! Your jokes are so funny! Tell me another story!' He wrapped his arms around his chubby body and rubbed his hands up and down his back. 'Mmmmm, oh Andy, yes, yes, tell me another one, you big macho detective!'

Andy shook his head. He pressed his lips together to demonstrate that they were sealed.

Jimmy finally cut the crap. 'I guess our mutual serial killer acquaintance has had his day in court, so it don't matter much now. You two can fuck like rabbits till the cows come home.'

'You are a true gentleman, Jimmy. No doubt about it.'

'Anyway, I'm happy now. I just won fifty bucks off Hoosier.'

'Fucking Hoosier,' Andy muttered.

'I gotta go.' Jimmy strolled off towards the door.

'I want updates. I'm serious,' Andy called to him.

'Gotcha.'

Ed Brown. Who would he introduce them to today? The remains of some once beautiful and innocent young girl who'd been on her way home from a bar, the park, from school —

122

and talked to the wrong stranger. How young? And how long would she have been waiting to have a dignified burial?

Andy watched his partner leave without him, and his heart sank. At least Jimmy knew Ed from personal experience, while the rest of the crew really only knew him from his file. Jimmy could keep Andy in the loop. He could be his eyes and ears.

# CHAPTER 15

*Eighteen* . . .

Ed's shoulders shook.

*Nineteen* . . .

Blood rushed to his head. With a steady, slow effort, he pushed up again.

*Twenty* . . .

With a shudder, he performed one last push-up. A line of sweat ran down his temple.

*Twenty-one.*

Having finished his fifth set of twenty-one push-ups, Ed let himself down from his position propped from the edge of his cell cot. He had to remain strong and focused. He would need every ounce of strength and speed that he could muster. Everything was going according to plan. Only a little while longer, and he would be free. Free to have Makedde to himself.

*Makedde.*

*I'm coming for you.*

# CHAPTER 16

There was a knock on the door.

Mak frowned. She thought she had put the *Do Not Disturb* sign on the door knob.

She shuffled across the room, clad only in an all-enveloping bath towel. 'Hello?' she asked through the door.

'It's me, Andy.'

She smiled and started to unlock the chain.

'Hey, check it's me first,' he scolded, his voice muffled by the door. 'Never open up without looking.'

Mak shook her head, but peered through the peephole anyway. 'There. Is that better? I see you. Am I allowed to open the door now? No ... wait ... your nose looks really huge. You can't be Andrew Flynn.'

Through the distorting glass she saw him roll his eyes. Relenting, Mak opened the door and drank in the welcome sight of him. He looked rumpled and unslept, yet obscenely inviting nonetheless. Something about him always seemed to arouse her. She had first noticed his effect on her in the interrogation room during the investigation into Catherine's murder. Perhaps it was his watchful green eyes, or his dark, short-cropped hair that accentuated a masculine, squared jaw. Or maybe it was the indefinable sensuality of his mouth, his slightly crooked nose, the tiny scars on his face that seemed to hint at a fiery soul? Of course, there was the Australian accent and the intoxicating height. Whatever it was, Mak found him irresistible, maddeningly so at times.

He stepped inside and she clung to him, shutting the door with one foot. Her towel dropped to the floor.

'I'm serious. Never open your door without checking first,' Andy said. He sounded grumpy. 'You never know who might have your room number.'

'Yes, sir,' Mak replied with mock seriousness. She kissed his neck. She kissed his rough cheek. 'Sleepyhead here was just about to have a shower, and guess what she noticed, hmmm?' His eyes followed her as she stepped back and displayed an angry rash on her chest and neck. 'It seems that some wild animal with a stubble problem has attacked my tender flesh.'

'Oh Mak, I'm sorry.' He stepped forward and placed a chaste kiss on the slightly raw skin of her collarbone.

Mak looked him over. 'What happened to you? You look a mess. Come on. I'm gonna fix you up.'

She grabbed him by the wrist and tugged him towards the bathroom. Andy offered no resistance, but he seemed surprisingly reserved, a different man from the one she had spent the night with.

'First, we check to see if everything is in working order. Perhaps the same wild animal got to you?' she teased. He stood rigid while she undid the buttons of his shirt, starting at his neck, and eventually crouching in front of him as she reached the bottom. 'Hmmm, no marks yet ...' She pulled the sides of his shirt back to expose his bare stomach, taut and firm, with a thin line of dark hair running down the centre. The sight of it stirred her. 'No, nothing,' she said, and covered the line with kisses. She darted her tongue into his navel. 'Let's see . . .'

She went for his buckle.

'Mak, I should tell you I have a meeting in less than an hour.'

'And . . . ?'

It had been far too long between sensual encounters for Mak. Now that she had thrown off her inhibitions, she could not pull back. She did not *want* to pull back. Her life had turned around — Ed was locked away, she was with Andy again, and it felt good, it felt so damned good to be *alive* again, not some ghost of a woman walking through her days merely *coping* under a shield of protection built by trauma and fear. She was open. Alive. She'd wanted Andy Flynn for so long, whether she had accepted the fact of her longing or not, and now here he was. Her body was greedy for more of him. Andy was the only man she had ever felt that certain incomparable chemistry with, the only man who reduced her to a bundle of wanting hormones. She was greedy for the satisfaction of feeling him inside her, and she wasn't going to wait one moment longer.

Makedde undid Andy's belt and his pants slid to the tile floor, the buckle hitting the ground with a sharp twang. She turned the shower on with one hand, and the next thing she knew, her grateful body was pressed against his tall, muscular form under a stream of hot water. She held a bar of soap in her hand and let it glide luxuriously over the hair on his chest, over his arms, his stomach, between his legs. She savoured the feel of his strong, masculine build, already aroused with sexual readiness for her. Her breasts slid across his chest, gleaming with suds. Her hands squeezed and coaxed him. Andy stood for a time under the showerhead, eyes closed, accepting her attention and holding himself back. A faint moan. A sigh. It was apparent that his restraint could not last. Before long, he guided Mak's legs up around his waist and she felt him press into her. He entered her in gentle thrusts as she clung to the bar of the shower curtain for balance.

'Yes,' she murmured, encouraging him. She wanted to feel him all the way inside, and in moments he was there, filling every last part of her. Everything else fell away, the purpose of their physical design overriding every other thought. Only they existed, one flesh moving together. With frenzied thrusts they joined, lost in kisses and murmurs of 'more'. She gripped him harder with her thighs and felt herself fall as the shower bar gave way from the wall. A split second of panic sent her heart into her throat, but he caught her safely in his arms and the damage was forgotten in building thrusts of passion. He uttered some wordless cry and shuddered as she squeezed him, satisfying herself.

★   ★   ★

Mak slept like a baby for almost an hour after Andy left. The physical, mental and emotional relief that she felt was unmeasured. In the past twenty-four hours every part of her life had come to feel renewed and optimistic. Her sleep was relaxed and content, a truly foreign experience after the events of the previous two years. She finally felt safe. There was light in her world again, and she was so very glad.

When Mak awoke, she rolled lazily over to the phone and called her father.

It was Ann who answered.

'Hi Ann. It's Mak. How are you?'

Ann was clearly taking a lot of time off from her psych practice in Vancouver to look after Les. That was a serious step, and one that gave Mak another reason to smile. Whilst deep down no daughter truly likes to see her mother's role filled by another, even after death, neither can a daughter truly live with seeing her father struggle in loneliness. To Makedde it was a relief to gradually be able to put to bed the image of her father widowed and bereft.

'Mak, it's so lovely to hear from you,' Ann said. 'We got your message. That is great news about the confession.'

'Yes, I think everyone is enormously relieved. All except Ed's defence, I suppose.'

'You must have popped a few champagnes last night.'

Makedde grinned. 'Yes, actually, that's exactly what we did.'

*It is over. It is finally over.*

'Hang on, I'll just get your father. I know he's eager to speak to you —'

'Mak.' It was her father's voice. He had probably picked it up in his office down the hall.

'Hi Dad, how are you feeling?'

'Fine, fine. How are things there?'

'I'll let you guys talk,' Ann said, still on the phone. 'It's great to hear from you, Mak. We'll see you soon, I hope. Travel safe.'

'Thanks, Ann.' The phone made the clicking sound of a hung-up receiver. 'Things are good, Dad. Great actually. I can't express how buoyant I feel with the weight of all of that off me. I think it played on my mind more than I let myself believe.'

'What's this about the possibility of Ed getting a reduced sentence? Have you heard anything about that?' Les said, quite out of the blue.

'What?' Mak sat up.

'There's talk about the Crown doing a deal.'

'Dad, what are you talking about?' She immediately felt edgy. The simple suggestion of a problem with Ed being locked away was enough to throw her fragile happiness into turmoil again.

'There's talk that the Crown is negotiating to reduce Ed's sentence in exchange for some bodies.'

She felt herself get angry with her father. How could he do this? How could he keep her from enjoying the positive turn of events?

'That's ridiculous, Dad. That is absolutely *ridiculous*. I don't know who you've been talking to this time, but Ed Brown is guilty, convicted and incarcerated. We have had success.'

'Has anyone mentioned it to you?'

'No they haven't because there is nothing to mention, Dad. Yesterday I watched Ed Brown confess his murders in court and I watched the judge pronounce him guilty. That's it. That's what's happening over here. Honestly, sometimes I think you just make up excuses to worry.'

Les was always working his police connections, his contacts. The web stretched across the globe. He heard a lot of things, often accurate. But something had surely gone awry in this case. Or, just as likely, her father could not help but imagine worst-case scenarios and try to warn her of them. Either way, she did not appreciate the pessimism.

'Mak, the result is wonderful news, I know, but I think we should be prepared for some pretty serious plea-bargaining,' he said.

'The judge pronounced him guilty of multiple murder, Dad. That's practically a guaranteed life sentence. How can you find a negative in this? Why can't you be happy with such a fortunate result?'

'Makedde, I am only trying to warn you.'

'Well thank you for the warning, based on absolutely nothing. Things are great here, okay? We did it. It's over.'

The world was already weighing on her shoulders again; she was Makedde 'Atlas' Vanderwall once more. She had to control a flash of misdirected anger. Why would he say such a thing just when she was starting to feel happy again?

There was a tense pause.

'Dad, how's your health? How did the endoscopy go?'

'Dr Olenski took a biopsy. We're waiting on the result.' He said the words begrudgingly, as if he hated to admit the possibility of physical frailty. He continued in a gentler tone. 'When are you coming home, Mak?'

Mak had not given a lot of thought to that yet. Her whole world had changed in the past twenty-four hours. All of her plans had been turned happily upside down. If she and Andy started seeing each other again, seriously this time, they would have to address their geographical challenges. They would need some time to discover whether they could make it work or not.

'I don't know, Dad,' she admitted. 'This all happened much quicker than I thought. I might ... stick around for a little while now.'

*I don't want to come home, not yet. Not until I know about Andy.*

'You're spending time with Flynn again, aren't you?'

'Yes, Dad. I am.'

Nothing escaped him. How did he always know so much?

'Be careful, Makedde. Just be careful,' Les pleaded, a father frustrated by the enforced distance between himself and his eldest daughter, in whom he could see both his own stubbornness and the spirit of his late wife.

All of which worried him.

# CHAPTER 17

*Here they come.*

When they arrived to collect Ed Brown from his solitary cell at Long Bay, he was waiting on the edge of his bed, fully dressed, with his hands folded neatly in his lap. It was a quarter to twelve.

'Alright, come on then. You know the drill,' Suzie Harpin growled gruffly through the bars.

Ed was careful not to make eye contact with the Prison Lady. He stared at his feet and tried to appear as mild and obliging as possible, standing slowly as ordered and clasping his hands behind his back in the middle of his cell.

He waited, concentrating on his steady, rhythmic breathing.

*In.*

*Out.*

*In.*

*Out.*

*Calm.*

Ed could not let anything betray the childlike excitement he felt in watching his carefully laid plans finally come into play. It was like Christmas morning and he, for once, would have the most toys.

The cell door clicked behind him, the bolt freed. He stood obediently and waited. Then came the heavy, rubber-soled footsteps of the Prison Lady and two other guards. They took his wrists and handcuffed him sharply in a way that hurt. No doubt this was done intentionally by the Prison Lady, whom he hoped was not overdoing her part. He noticed that today she had not worn her nauseating perfume, the one she had taken to using in recent weeks, apparently for his benefit. That was good. Ed didn't want anyone to notice her attempts at femininity, even subconsciously. There was always a slim chance that someone might see some relevance later on.

They spun him around. The Prison Lady spoke again. 'This is Senior Sergeant Lewis, Senior Constable Cassimatis and Constable Hoosier. They are with the New South Wales Homicide Division and they will be spending time with you today.' *No Andy Flynn*, Ed thought with a rush of relief. *Unless he's joining us outside.*

Brusquely, the Prison Lady turned to the tall, muscular police officer with the military-type haircut. 'Senior Sergeant, he's all yours.'

Ed hoped the Prison Lady wouldn't watch him go. She had been pretty good about acting casual so far. Her shift would soon be over and then she would be gone. Neither of them could afford to slip, even once. There would be too many questions later.

Andrew Flynn's absence pleased Ed no end. He was the police officer who could cause the most trouble. It was much better if he wasn't around, especially while the relationship between Ed and these other officers was so delicate, as it was bound to be today. They would be sizing him up, deciding how much he could be trusted, deciding how to play him. That was a laugh. Them playing *him*? The way each minute of this afternoon's excursion unfolded would lay the groundwork for further cooperation. Ed had it carefully planned. He couldn't have Flynn ruining that.

Ed was led out of the cell without further fanfare, shuffling down the institutional corridors with his shoulders hunched. He kept his eyes to the floor.

*Calm. Obedient.*

The Prison Lady's feet were not much smaller than those of the male guards, he noticed. Those unattractive combat-style boots she always wore actually housed a woman's feet. It was hard to imagine. He sometimes wondered what her feet looked like. Were her toes odd-shaped? Mannish? Square? Tapered? Were they smooth and manicured? He doubted that.

'This way, Ed,' the one introduced as Hoosier said, approaching a reception area. The police signed him out at the desk, like a stray dog or a piece of borrowed equipment. Ed tried not to smile though it amused him.

He knew these officers would do their best to make the morbid parade they were embarking on seem innocuous in public. After all, his was a headline case. He, Ed Brown, had captured the public's imagination. He was famous. He was feared. If anyone were tipped off, the news helicopters would be circling in minutes. The police would have chaos on their hands if Joe Public had any idea that the confessed and convicted Stiletto Serial Killer was out walking around, even with snipers and guards surrounding him.

The corners of Ed's mouth turned up into the beginnings of a sly smile.

They *would* have snipers hidden in the bushes, wouldn't they? How long would it take them to scramble into position once he gave his escort directions on where they were to go? It would be fun to watch it all unfold, he thought. It would be an education. Eighteen months was a long time to wait for a little action.

Now Ed was more than ready.

# CHAPTER 18

'My place is just half a block that way,' Senior Constable Karen Mahoney said.

She pointed out the window of her beat-up Datsun in the direction of a slightly decrepit-looking block of flats. Karen and Makedde had spent the past ten minutes speeding around the back roads of the infamous Kings Cross. Makedde, strapped into the passenger seat, white-knuckling on the fast corners, was convinced that they must surely be turning into the wrong side of the road at every intersection. Kings Cross, once renowned as the domain of red-light entrepreneurialism and questionable 'massage parlours', had over the years attracted a slew of trendy bars and restaurants, not to mention a lot of tourists. It was home turf for Karen, so it featured heavily in her Sydney refresher tour for Mak.

After her unexpectedly unsettling phone call to her father, Mak was happy to get out of the hotel room and blow off some steam. Karen was turning out to be excellent company, even if her driving made Mak's teeth chatter.

'Yesterday must have been a huge relief for you,' the young flame-haired senior constable said, gazing intently at Mak as she spun the steering wheel deftly with one hand.

'Yes . . . a relief.'

Since the conversation with her father, Mak's mind had been ticking over furiously. She had not yet broached the subject with Karen. Nor had she spilled the beans on what had happened between her and Andy, though she figured that, like most women, Karen could probably tell. The effect of good, drought-breaking sex was as obvious as a new haircut.

'I can't believe that he confessed in court,' Mahoney said. 'It sure took me off guard.'

'Yeah. I heard that . . . uh . . . there were some leads to do with the case that are being followed up today. Do you know anything about that?' Mak asked, fishing.

'Come on. You don't really want to talk about that right now, do you?' Karen replied. She smiled. 'But it's true they might be investigating those other admissions. Nothing for you to worry about. If you like I'll see if I can find out something this afternoon when I get to work, but it's still a boys' club sometimes, Mak. I don't think I hear half of what's really going on. Hey, see that place?' She pointed again, this time at a balcony area attached to a hotel. 'Hugo's Lounge. Twenty-dollar martinis. The nightlife is really on fire though. These strips along here and on Oxford Street in Darlinghurst have the most *amazing* bars. Something for everyone.'

Mak smiled to herself. Karen had successfully changed the subject.

'You won't believe this, but I came here with Loulou one night on my last trip to Australia.'

'Oh, now that I *can* believe.'

Mak realised that with her mullet and her fishnets, Loulou looked like a Kings Cross wild child. She seemed to have got on quite well with Karen. Perhaps they had struck up a friendship? 'No, I mean I came to one of these dodgy back-alley places to a photo studio,' she explained.

'You're kidding me. For work?'

'Not exactly,' Mak said. 'Let's just say I was young and stupid and more than a little frustrated with the way Catherine's case was being handled. I thought I knew it all. I figured I'd try and make myself useful by sussing out this sleazy photographer who I thought might have had some contact with her. Loulou was my back-up, waiting outside for me.'

They had rehearsed an emergency scenario in which Loulou would burst in, make a kafuffle pretending to be Mak's jealous lesbian lover and drag her away to safety. As it played out, Mak had got into an altercation with the photographer and escaped on her own, no back-up required.

'Are you for real!' Karen squealed. 'Why you little amateur detective, you! Wait ... I remember this!' Her jaw hung open, recognition spreading across her face. Mak wished she would pay more attention to the road. Karen seemed to be engaging with Mak far more than she was with the traffic. 'That was you?' Karen asked. She threw her hands up. 'Of *course* it was you. Rick Filles, right?' Now she fell over the steering wheel, laughing. 'Oh shit, that is too funny. They sent *me* in there. It was useless. Imagine *me* trying to pass myself off as a model!'

Mak had never put two and two together before. Karen Mahoney was the one they had sent in unsuccessfully to check out Rick Filles before Mak had got the crazy idea to go and do it herself. It was hard to imagine now.

They laughed uncontrollably until Karen had to pull over to the side of the road in tears. After much guffawing, the two finally settled down.

'Karen,' Mak said, coming over serious. 'I'm thinking of postponing my flight.'

'I thought you might be.'

'I'm that transparent, am I?'

Karen just smiled. 'Maybe. So come on, where are we going for lunch?'

'This is your jurisdiction. It's your call.'

'There's a famous place just around the corner, Beef and Bourbon, or Beefsteak something. I can never remember what it's called. It's been refurbished recently. It's better than it sounds. Trust me.'

'Deal,' Mak agreed.

They pulled off down the road again, turning back onto the main strip. Makedde was familiar with the bright neon signage: *GIRLS GIRLS GIRLS! Open 24 Hours!* Some things never changed. Sex shops. Newsagents. Backpacker hostels. Her eyes passed over the window of a modest little café among a cluster of sushi and karaoke bars and she did a double take.

'Hey!' Makedde pointed across the road, beaming. 'That's Andy!'

'Speak of the devil,' Karen said, slowing the car.

'How can this city be so small? This happened before with Loulou at Starbucks. Can we stop for a sec?'

'Sure.' Karen pulled into a parking space. 'Fifteen-minute parking,' she warned. 'Should I find a different spot?'

'No probs. I just want to say a quick . . .'

Makedde's words trailed off.

It was Andy Flynn alright. Unmistakable. He was sitting at a table right in the window of the café. But he wasn't alone. Mak took a few steps across the street towards him, and as she watched, Andy Flynn, the man she had been making love to only hours before, the man she was thinking of postponing her flight home for, the man she had opened her heart to one more time, leaned across the table and embraced an attractive young blonde. Right there. As she watched. It was clear that Andy and the woman were more than friends. Makedde stopped dead in her tracks in the middle of the road. A car barely swerved in time to avoid her. Karen snatched her arm and dragged her to the side of the street.

'What's gotten into you?' Karen began, but then she too saw Andy and the woman. 'Oh, shit,' she said simply. 'Carol.'

'What?'

'It's Carol. The nurse.'

Makedde felt a wave of nausea race up through her body from her toes to her scalp and back down again. A sour lump formed in her throat. She wanted to retch.

*He's still with Carol . . .*

'Oops,' she managed to say with a mouth that felt stiff and awkward. She tried not to betray the true depth of her pain, but she knew Karen would see straight through it. She tried a smile on, but it didn't fit, and she ended up wearing a confused frown as she retreated mechanically towards Karen's car. She had to look at her feet and concentrate on her steps . . . *one step . . . two steps . . .*

'Oh, Mak . . .' she could hear Karen saying. The policewoman was watching her face closely, much the same way she had the first time they met, with Catherine dead and bloody in the grass nearby, and Mak sitting with a styrofoam cup of coffee in a state of numbing shock, surrounded by police cars. Karen was shaking her head now. 'Oh, Mak ...'

If Karen didn't already know what had happened between Mak and Andy after dinner the night before, she could no doubt guess now from the shattered look on Makedde's face. It was obvious that something intimate had gone on between them, something that had led Mak to thoughts of commitment, a relationship. This was not the same Makedde who had been so cool with Andy for the first few days. This Mak had been blatantly love-struck. Until now.

*Do you never learn?*

Karen was speaking, saying kind things, understanding things, but Mak was no longer listening.

# CHAPTER 19

'Come on, let's get this show on the road,' Jimmy Cassimatis grumbled. They were barely out of the gates and he was already impatient.

The unmarked car slowly made its way down the driveway out of Long Bay Gaol to Anzac Parade as per Ed's instructions. Jimmy was in the passenger seat with Ed Brown directly behind him, an arrangement that left Jimmy feeling curiously ill at ease even though the prisoner was safely cuffed at both wrists and ankles. Hoosier was at the steering wheel. Senior Sergeant Lewis was beside Ed in the back, behind the driver. Jimmy couldn't help but admire the Senior Sergeant's dedication to his job. With his rank, he would have normally sat up front. But no. He wanted to take Ed around personally. That was a good call. An unmarked forensic van edged along behind them, ready to dig and examine and bring someone's decomposed remains home. Behind them the audiovisual unit had their own truck, complete with soundman and camera operator to record Ed's directions and the exhumations. Jimmy knew that Lewis had fought for the fourth car, another unmarked vehicle with two more police officers that was cruising behind the audiovisual van. There were always grumbles about using up manpower, but Senior Sergeant Lewis had managed to get it done, thanks mostly to Ed's profile. Vast teams of helicopters, armoured cars, sharpshooting snipers and SWAT squads were only dispatched in big American movies; in real life the average multiple killer usually had only a few officers with him on an excursion like this. Any more than four vehicles and they may as well announce themselves as some kind of cavalcade.

So they had extra manpower, they were taking precautions, they had time and Lewis was obviously taking a special interest. That was good. And while it shitted Jimmy that Andy wasn't there, he understood Kelley's reasons and practically had to agree with him. As professional as his partner was, in the case of Ed Brown things had become very personal indeed. It was probably for the best that he was not sitting in the car with the man. It was only an exhumation, not a day of investigation. Andy's profiling expertise would not come into play.

The only problem as Jimmy saw it was that they were fundamentally handicapped by the conditions of the deal that had been struck with Ed's defence. The prisoner would show them the way *as they went* — and he wasn't going to say a peep otherwise. That was the deal. While it certainly wouldn't be the first time such an arrangement had been made, it pissed Jimmy off no end. Ed's hotshot lawyer could talk all he wanted about doing favours and having rights, but Jimmy thought this show-and-tell shit was sick. Ed would get off on it for years.

*A brunette teenager.*

*A young woman with black hair.*

That was all Ed would offer about the young women he had killed. He didn't know the women's names, their families, their backgrounds. He didn't care. They had never been 'people' to him, only something to be used and tossed away. The vague descriptions of the victims that he had given matched several women listed in the missing persons reports for the area four years prior, which Ed had indicated was the approximate time frame. Now it was a matter of bringing them home and matching up dental records and any DNA they could get their hands on.

They drove slowly along Anzac Parade. 'Where to?' Hoosier asked.

There was a long pause while the prisoner considered his response. 'Could you, ah ... please keep following Anzac Parade this way?' A tilt of his ginger head. 'Yeah ... this way please.'

Ed's voice was distinctive and high-pitched. It never failed to give Jimmy the creeps. He'd heard it in his dreams periodically over the previous eighteen months, Angie having to wake him up to tell him he was having another nightmare, digging an elbow into his ribs: *'Honey, you're talking in your sleep again.'* Perhaps that was why having Ed sit right behind him in the car set him on edge. Jimmy knew he had to play the usual game — *make them relax, make them like you, make them feel comfortable and they'll tell you everything* — but he was not for one minute relaxed himself. He had been with Andy when they arrested Ed Brown during his assault on Makedde Vanderwall and that scene had joined the ranks of those which had burned themselves irreversibly into Jimmy's memory — the infant in the car crash at Wollongong, his first fatal domestic, his first floater. There was a special spot for Ed Brown in Jimmy's nightmares. And now the guy was sitting right behind him.

*Does he even recognise me?*

'Can you do any better than that for us, Ed? Can you give us a location?' Jimmy pried.

'I'll show you. Sorry,' Ed Brown said meekly.

*Sorry my arse,* Jimmy thought. *Sorry my frickin' arse.*

'Please go on, go on driving, ah, and I will show you.'

They had passed the University of New South Wales and the National Institute of Dramatic Art and they were still driving.

'Where next?'

'Please, ah . . . keep on.'

Ed seemed so damned submissive. *Is he on some kind of meds?* The guards had not said anything about that but maybe it was standard procedure over at Long Bay for freaks like him. Was Ed really as meek as he appeared? It was doubtful. Jimmy's father had a saying: 'If there's one thing I know, it's that I don't know a thing.' The Cassimatis men did not have great intellect or status or charm, but they did have street smarts. Jimmy had been blessed with good instincts — maybe not about women, or politics, or what was required at a polite dinner party, but good instincts for the work. That made him a good cop. Although he wouldn't admit it publicly, he knew damn well that he knew nothing about Ed. And in that one way, he was probably the smartest cop in the car.

'Okay, ah, turn right here please. Ah, I think this is the way.'

*That fucking voice.*

'Ah, yes, right turn at the next lights.'

'Mate, would you like something to eat, maybe? A meat pie or anything? Want us to stop and get you something?' Hoosier piped up.

Jimmy wanted to smack him.

Over the years he'd bought plenty of guys beers and meat pies and chips and God knows what else to get them comfortable and compliant. Standard procedure, really. But this was not the guy to play that shit with. Jimmy did not give one ounce of piss about making Ed Brown comfortable. There would be no sucking up to this guy on his watch. He could show them where to dig and then he could go back to his little cell and rot in there forever.

Lewis, who was in charge of the show, said nothing.

'Let's just drive, shall we?' Jimmy suggested. He folded his arms and looked out the window.

Ed led them along some back roads, winding this way and that, pausing once in a while to get his bearings and then speaking up weakly in that creepy girlie voice of his. Jimmy wondered again if he was just yanking their chain. He was tempted to call Andy to tell him that the whole deal was a heap of shit just to make them look like idiots.

And then the words were finally spoken.

'This is the spot,' Ed declared.

They stopped the car. The forensic van stopped. The audiovisual van stopped. The other unmarked car stopped behind them. 'We're here,' Hoosier announced on the two-way.

'Which spot?'

Ed nodded toward a petrol station across the road.

Jimmy blinked. 'That is a *petrol station*,' he said, stating the obvious in case no one else had noticed.

'Ed, are you saying that you buried the girl's body at a petrol station?' Hoosier asked, gentle as ever.

'Ah, this is it. Ah, yeah,' came the high-pitched voice. 'That ahh ... that wasn't there four years ago. Ahh, empty lot. This space was empty. I buried the girl near a tree, right there.' He pointed in the direction of the pumps. 'Yeah, this is the intersection. I know it was here. This is the spot. Yeah, ah ha.'

'*Skata!* You've got to be kidding me.' Jimmy slammed his palms against the dashboard. 'This is a fuckin' joke.'

'Hold on, Cassimatis.' Lewis got out of the car, and stood a few metres away. He looked to Ed waiting in the car, and then looked back at the garage with a frown, probably trying to decide what to do.

'Ed, are you sure this is the spot? You know we can't be of much help if you aren't telling the truth.'

'I am telling the truth. I ... ah ... ah, it was here. Yeah. She is buried here.' Ed gestured near the pumps. His hands were still cuffed, so he could not point. 'There were trees and brush there before. Ahh. Brunette girl. Young. Yeah. I buried her pretty deep.'

'Okay,' Lewis said, tense with restraint, standing alongside the car. 'You are sure it is this exact spot, on this corner?'

Ed nodded.

'Sir, do you want to take him out of the car and see what he can point out?' Hoosier asked.

Going through the rigmarole of leading him around the garage in his cuffs to point vaguely at some areas of concrete was pointless, and would attract precisely the kind of attention that Kelley wanted to avoid.

'Well, we can't go digging up a petrol station now, can we?'

And with that, Lewis got back in and slammed the door. Hoosier drove them back towards Long Bay, the other vehicles trailing behind them. Jimmy could feel Lewis seething. It was one thing to demand that much manpower, it was quite another to go through all that and come back empty-handed. They had to check out Ed's story before they went any further. Lewis would be extremely disappointed.

'Back to the Bay,' Jimmy said into the two-way.

Barely a word was spoken on the drive.

# CHAPTER 20

Detective Andy Flynn sat at his desk at Central Homicide, pushing papers around restlessly. His coat was tossed across the back of his chair. His sleeves were rolled up for no task in particular. Since he'd returned from his short coffee meeting he'd been stuck with distinctly unexciting paperwork. The seconds ticked by like hours. As if to amplify his sense of isolation, the office was almost empty. Most of the guys were still on lunch, and a chosen few of his colleagues were over at Long Bay where Andy wanted to be, tying up the tail end of the Stiletto Murders debacle they would all be happy to have behind them.

Andy had his mobile phone in front of him awaiting an update from Jimmy. So far there had been no word on what was happening. Where would Ed lead them? What would they find? It ate at Andy's nerves to be left out of the loop on anything, worst of all this case. It smacked of history repeating itself. This time Andy wasn't a suspect, as he had been eighteen months earlier, when his ex-wife Cassandra had been murdered. Now he was merely a suspect for unchecked temper. It was an improvement, but still excruciating.

*Come on, Jimmy, call me.*

He thought about calling Makedde just to hear her voice. He planned to take her out to dinner when he was finished at work. Which restaurant should they go to? Nothing he could afford would really measure up to the previous night's meal at Bondi Beach, but no matter. Despite being a model, Makedde was no prima donna.

*Come on, Jimmy, give me some news.*

Andy had one less problem to think about, at least. The meeting with Carol had gone better than he had hoped. He had been as friendly and honest as he could, and there were no tears or long faces from her when he announced that he couldn't see her any more. Carol had offered nothing but uncomplicated friendliness and good cheer. She had never given him reason to expect anything different from her, but still, she was a woman and women were unpredictable. The seemingly sane, level-headed types threw wine over you at dinner without any notice, and the edgy ones who always seemed ready to crack shook hands and were happy to 'just be friends'. Andy had decided long ago that there was no system for figuring out the opposite sex. Forget all that 'women are from Venus, men are from Mars' crap. Andy's theory held that the sexes were probably several galaxies apart.

He felt he had done the right thing by breaking the news to Carol in person. He was giving it another try with Mak and all other bets were off. He couldn't afford any more complications. Considering the rocky path he and Mak had already travelled, there was not a lot of margin for error now. Especially if he wanted to convince her to stay with him in Australia.

Andy was relieved when the phone rang. He jumped on it eagerly, anticipating Jimmy with some news.

'Flynn,' he answered.

'You're an arsehole,' came a voice on the other end.

'What?' It was not Jimmy's voice, but a woman's. Andy was confused.

'I said, YOU ARE AN ARSEHOLE,' the voice repeated as Andy sat stunned.

'Mahoney, is that you?'

What the hell did Mahoney think she was doing talking to him like that? One minute she was a shy rookie straight out of the academy, and now she was mouthing off at him! Who the hell did she think she was — Jimmy?

'You bet it's me, Andy,' Mahoney said. 'Tell me one thing, why didn't you just say that you and Carol were still an item?'

'Whoa, whoa. Hold on ... Excuse me?' He looked around to see if anyone could overhear the conversation. He was still alone. 'We're not.'

'Really? Well take a guess what I've been doing?' she said. 'I've been spending time with your girlfriend, taking her for lunch, showing her the sights. A nice little tour around *Kings Cross*. And who do you think we saw in *Kings Cross*?' She kept emphasising the words, as if they would give him some clue as to what the hell she was on about. They didn't.

'Who might we have seen in Kings Cross, in a café, kissing his pretty nurse friend? Hmmm?'

'Oh, shit!' Andy exclaimed, finally grasping what Mahoney was getting at. He scrambled to recall every move he and Carol might have made and how a bystander might have perceived things.

*We didn't actually kiss, did we? When on earth would we have kissed?*

'Oh shit is right, Andy. Mak seemed a tad put out, shall I say.'

'Oh, Christ —'

'Even he's not going to be able to help you with this one.'

'It wasn't even like that!' he protested.

'Whatever, Mick Jagger. I just thought I'd let you know.'

'That's not how it was.'

'Okay, Robbie Williams, Sam Newman, Casanova —'

'Will you shut up?'

'When we saw you and Carol you were all over each other in the window of that café and you should have seen the look on Makedde's face. You'd think someone had died. Friend to friend here, I've gotta say I never picked you for throwing away the only good chick you had a chance with. Excuse me for saying that you are stupid, Andy, but Andy, you are stupid.'

'Carol and I were not *all over each other*,' he said, genuinely confused. 'We might have hugged goodbye at the most. She probably gave me a peck on the cheek; I can't even remember. I was telling her that I couldn't see her again. I was trying to do the right thing ...' He trailed off, realisation hitting him.

*My God, Makedde must hate me.*

'I can't believe I'm even having this conversation with you,' he said. He had spoken with Karen Mahoney about a lot of things, but never his private life.

'You should have seen her, Andy. It was not good.'

'I've got to talk to her. Where is she?'

'I'm not sure she'd want me to tell you,' she replied.

'Hey, fuck off, Mahoney, this is me. Is she at the hotel?' he demanded.

'Do you promise you'll be good to her?' she asked, now obviously playing it up.

'Come on.'

'Yes. She's at the hotel. I just dropped her off. She should still be there.'

'I'm heading there now. If you happen to speak to her before I do, tell her it wasn't like that, okay? Tell her I'll explain when I get there.'

'No probs. Geez, I sure wish I was a fly on the wall for this,' Mahoney said. 'I'd *really* like to see you talk your way out of this one.'

Andy didn't bother to explain any further. He scooped up his jacket and left as fast as he could.

He ran into Hunt and Deller in the elevator. 'If anyone comes looking for me I'm heading out for about an hour,' he told them.

Constable Hunt looked alarmed. 'You're not thinking about —'

Andy read his mind. 'Don't worry, I'm not going anywhere near our star prisoner. I'll be back in an hour.'

★   ★   ★

Andy parked near Mak's hotel, and wasted no time sprinting up to her room. He knocked lightly on the door three times.

'Makedde, it's me,' he announced, standing in the hall.

He knocked again when she didn't answer. *Please be here. Come on . . .*

'Mak?'

Eventually he heard slow footsteps and saw her peer through the peephole at him.

'It's me, Andy,' he said. 'Please open up.'

'This isn't a good time, Andy,' came her voice through the door. 'Can I call you later?'

*Fuck!*

'No, no, no don't do this,' he pleaded. 'I need to talk to you now.'

There was a pause. She still had not opened the door for him.

'Come on, don't make me do this through the damn door, Mak. Open up.'

Nothing. No response.

It was hardly a surprise that she was upset if she thought he had gone on a hot lunch date with someone else straight after leaving her in bed. With regard to situations like that, men and women were predictably the same. Unfortunately, things between them had been shaky as it was. He had made a lot of mistakes in the past, he knew that. But meeting with Carol should not have been a mistake — that was the most maddening thing. He had been trying to do the right thing. Should he have first told Mak that he was meeting Carol? He wasn't sure.

Andy wasn't going to budge from that door until he had the opportunity to explain what had really happened. Otherwise, Makedde might convince herself never to see him again.

'Mak,' he implored. 'Please open the door. Come on —'

'I'm doing it. Hold on.'

Finally Makedde undid the chain and opened up. The first thing he noticed was her red, but dry, eyes. It was clear she had been crying earlier but was composed now. The impassive expression on her face was as impenetrable as a sealed bank vault, and she had her arms tightly crossed. He knew the look well. This was not the first time he had inspired it.

'Hi,' she said simply, and stepped back so he could come in. She closed the door behind him.

He walked up to her and took her by the elbows. She narrowed her eyes at him but didn't flinch away. 'I want you to know that I am not seeing Carol,' he said.

'That's fine, Andy.'

'I'm serious. I know what you think you saw. Mahoney told me.'

'Yeah, well . . .' Mak said, her words trailing off. She shook her head and stepped away from him.

'I just don't want you thinking that Carol and I are dating any more,' he insisted. 'We're not. We haven't been seeing each other for a while.'

*Yeah, like since this morning,* he could imagine her thinking.

'If that is what you want me to know, I believe you.' She had turned to face the window.

'Come on, Mak.'

'I don't know if I can do this right now.'

Andy went to her and squeezed her hands in his. 'Mak.'

She did not respond to him. Her eyes were on his, perhaps searching for whether or not he was telling the truth.

'Come on, Mak. I don't want you thinking that what you saw was some kind of date, because it wasn't.'

She was exhausted. She was without the playful buoyancy he had seen that morning. Her shoulders were hunched, her head hanging.

'I feel . . . confused,' she said. 'I really don't think this is a good time for us to talk about things. Just give me a little time.'

*Damn!*

'Despite what you might think, I'm not angry with you,' she went on. 'I just want to be alone for a little while. It's been a very eventful couple of days and I really need some time to myself. Things are probably ... moving too fast. I know that is my fault, not yours. I'm not blaming you.'

Andy felt powerless. What could he say?

'Can I call you later, Andy? I'm sorry to do this, but I don't want to say or do anything that I might regret later.'

That sounded ominous.

'When's your flight booked to go home?' he dared to ask.

'My ticket doesn't have me returning for another week,' she said, and his heart lifted. That meant he still had time.

'If you came here wanting me to know that you aren't dating that woman any more, that's fine. I believe you,' she said. 'I have to admit it was a bit of a shock to see you with her, especially so soon after ... but it's none of my business, really. You're entitled to do whatever you want. I don't want you thinking that just because of last night ... and this morning ... that I suddenly think we have some kind of commitment to one another, that I think you owe me some kind of exclusivity. I don't.'

Andy listened and watched, his heart sinking. She had clearly been jealous and upset over Carol in the first place, and now she was closed off, protecting herself. He knew what she was like when she shut down like that. In some ways he wished she would just blow up at him, pound his chest and slap his face, maybe. He knew she wouldn't. Makedde wasn't the type. She would be maddeningly *nice* instead. Logical, nice, *closed* ...

'I see,' he replied, unsettled by her cold words. 'So let me get this right. You're saying that it didn't mean anything to you? One last fuck for good luck, was that it?'

'Andy!' Her head snapped up to look at him with surprise. 'No, I'm not saying that. Don't be like that. That's not fair. I'm just saying, well ...' She paused and took a deep breath. He could see by the moisture in the corners of her eyes that her armour was slowly breaking down. 'I'm saying it was wonderful to be with you again, but really, it was probably a mistake, wasn't it?'

'No, Mak, don't say that. Say what you want, but just don't say it was a mistake. I don't think it was a mistake at all.' Her brow was pinched. 'You don't believe me about Carol,' he said.

'If you're telling me that nothing was going on with her today, then I have to believe you. I trust you. It's just that this is all a bit sudden. You were involved with someone else. I don't want to get in the way.'

'In the way! Carol and I aren't together any more, I'm telling you.'

'And when did you break up? Today?'

She had him there.

'I thought I should tell her in person ...' he faltered.

'Do you see what I mean?' Her eyes were glittery now, her cheeks flushed. 'It seems like every time we get together, something happens. Like today when I saw you with Carol. And like that phone call a couple of months ago when you said you wanted to see other people. I don't think it should be like this.'

'Wait ... did you just say that *I* said we should see other people?' Andy asked, surprised.

'Well, yes.'

*You've got to be kidding me.*

That wasn't how he remembered it. He thought *she* was the one who'd suggested they see other people. Hadn't she said it first? Was it another of their damn misunderstandings? She must have thought he suggested it just so that he could be free to date Carol. No wonder she was hurt when she saw them together.

Andy felt his body tense up with frustration. He was angry, though not really at Makedde. It had not exactly been a smooth road for them, not by anyone's standards. He supposed that was what he was pissed off about the most. They had such bad luck together. It wasn't fair. He paced the hotel room, frowning. What was he supposed to say to her? 'I'm sorry'? For what? He couldn't beg. That wasn't in his repertoire, and besides, he doubted it would have much effect on her. And he hadn't done anything wrong! *She* suggested they see other people, and he had. Or at least that was how he remembered the conversation. And then he was meant to feel guilty about it after she had suggested it herself? And when he tried to do the right thing and break it off with Carol in person, he got to be a bad guy for that too?

*Bloody hell.* He stretched up and pressed his hands against the wall. It was all he could do to stop himself from punching a hole in the plaster. He'd tried to get over Makedde before, but he could never quite get her off his mind. It scared him sometimes. And if she left now he knew he was going to suffer over her worse than ever.

'Can I call you tonight?' he asked.

'How about tomorrow? Is that okay?'

A cooling-off period. Great.

'Sure.' What could he say?

If there was one thing he wanted to change in that moment, it was for him to be able to find the right words for once. He had never been good at stuff like that.

'I can't win a trick,' Andy said, feeling miserable and already visualising a bottle of Jack Daniels with dangerous clarity. 'I can't win one single measly trick.'

Jimmy grinned from one side of his mouth, as if the news were somehow amusing to him. He rubbed his dark stubble, eyes sparkling mischievously. 'So you did *what* with Carol while Mak was watching?'

'Nothing, that's what,' Andy insisted. 'I was just talking to her. She might have kissed me on the cheek or something, I think. Or maybe it was on the lips. I can't remember.'

'Uh huh. In front of Mak?'

'And Mahoney. She said it looked like we were snogging each other.'

'Hmmm. I want your life, I really do. The supermodel, the sexy nurse and the policewoman. I could get used to that.'

Andy wasn't in the mood for Jimmy's quips.

'I reckon you're fucked.'

'Thanks. No really, thank you so much for your encouragement.'

'You're going to chase after her?'

'I'm not chasing anyone,' Andy said. 'I just need to talk to her. What really shits me is that everything was going fine, *more than fine*, until she saw me with Carol. What a fluke. I can't win a trick, honestly. I wasn't even trying to get away with anything.'

'Now, if you were kissing 'em both at the same time you'd be a legend.' Jimmy thought a bit more. 'Or if you got them to kiss each other, like Britney and Madonna. Mmmm, now that's —'

'Get fucked.'

Jimmy was on a roll, inspired by Andy's predicament. 'I'd love to get fucked,' he went on, 'but the old lady's got me rooting her by appointment. It's all, "Don't touch me!" and then, "Do the deed now," and legs in the air for half an hour afterwards. We didn't have to do all this crap for the first three. My momma, bless her,' he crossed himself, 'popped the five of us out like she was shellin' peas. Nothin' to it.'

At least he had changed the subject.

'So tell me about today,' Andy said.

'Yeah, you'll love this. Guess where Ed leads us?'

'I know, a petrol station. I heard,' Andy told him.

'Can you believe that shit?' Jimmy threw his hands in the air.

'It's original, I have to admit, and no, I don't believe it. He says he buried this girl deep? Pretty convenient at a petrol station where we're going to need a ground-penetrating radar system to find anything. And since when does he bury his victims instead of leaving them in a heap under some brush?'

Now Jimmy rubbed his stomach, as if craving some unseen gyros or an ice-cream sundae. 'I dunno, Andy. I dunno. All I know is I can't wait to see the last of this fuckin' *malaka*. He makes my arse itch.'

'What also bothers me,' Andy said, 'is that I can't figure his reasons for confessing in the first place. He doesn't seem the type. Did that seem like classic bragging rights to you? Myself, I'm not so sure.'

Jimmy rooted around in the top drawer of his desk and fished out a chocolate bar. He ripped it open with his teeth and started to gnaw on it. Once he had eaten most of it, he offered Andy the stubby remnant. Andy declined. 'The guy's a freak but you said yourself that he ain't so dumb,' Jimmy observed between mouthfuls. 'He must've known he was fucked. If this was Texas they'd fry him a dozen times just for the hell of it. He's campaigning for a better sentence.'

Andy didn't think that was the answer. He knew the cockiness of the average psychopath was boundless. All the evidence and guilt in the world couldn't get them down because they think they're invincible.

'Any clue about what's next?'

'First we check out the story about the petrol station, then they throw away the key — I hope. We should know in the next few hours.'

'Why confess and then lead you to a body dump if it's a crock? What could he be trying to achieve?' Andy asked, thinking out loud.

'Jerking us around, that's what. He's just taking us for one last ride. Maybe his lawyer talked him into confessing and this is his way of fucking us around for a thrill. His swan song.'

'I'm not convinced. Granger looked pretty shocked. Did you see his face?'

Ed's QC *had* looked shocked, along with everyone else in the courtroom. Andy doubted very much that Granger had known what Ed was about to do. Perhaps even Ed himself hadn't known that he was going to do it? Andy wished he had seen it first hand.

'Well, we ain't gonna know much until we get back the info on that petrol station. If it's been round for much more than four years we can happily hand him back to the judge and they can forget getting any special privileges from anyone, except maybe Big Bert.' Jimmy took the last bite of his chocolate bar. 'Yup, Big Bert's always got somethin' special for lady killers.'

He smiled chocolate.

# CHAPTER 21

Suzie Harpin carefully slid her key into the lock, struggling while balancing her precious cargo. She looked over her left shoulder and noticed with satisfaction that the lines of shrubs down the driveway effectively masked her from the view of the street. She had a story worked out for the neighbours, but still, she preferred privacy. Privacy was always best, especially if she decided to move her brother at some point.

The box she held fluttered and scraped. A chirp. A quiver. The delicate noises lifted Suzie's heart. 'You're almost home, Rose,' she said. 'Almost home.' Without further delay she turned the key and pushed the door open with her foot. She would have to come down again to collect the other things from the car. Once inside the house, Suzie made immediately for the kitchen counter to set her things down. Excited, she shoved the groceries to one side, and with a great rush of maternal emotion opened the shoebox just a touch to peer inside. She couldn't wait any longer.

*Agapornis roseicollis.*

'Hello, Rose. Welcome to your new home,' she said to her newly purchased red and green peachface lovebird. The creature stared at her with shiny, fearful eyes. She shut the box and gently stroked the lid. 'Good girl.'

Suzie scuttled over to a bell-shaped cage, which took pride of place in the centre of her brand-new living room. A black cloth lay over it. She lifted the cloth slowly, and frowned when she saw the dead lovebird on the bottom of the cage inside. It looked impossibly small and frail. The pretty colours had faded, the little eyes sealed shut. This bird had never quite lived up to her promise and beauty, and now she was gone. She had become unresponsive in the days before her death, sitting puffed up and inert, refusing food and water, her feathers turning dull. The move to her new, luxurious home had not helped at all. Suzie knew the breed well, and had seen it before. Thankfully, Irving, Suzie's pet-shop owner, had been able to provide a new one right away. She had hoped for a Danish violet white face, considered one of the most beautiful of the peachface mutations, but this new bird was available and she took it. She wanted everything in the house to be right for her new life there, and that meant little Rose sitting prettily on her perch.

Suzie had a particular affection for lovebirds. For the past two decades she had always kept one as a pet, and they had always been called Rose, the name which Suzie, as a pregnant teenager, had chosen for her unborn daughter. Some of her birds had been male, some female, but the name remained the same. This was her twentieth 'Rose'.

Suzie scooped the dead lovebird out of the cage into a plastic shopping bag. She took it outside, down the staircase and into the carport, and placed it in the garbage bin. Tomorrow would be collection day.

Once back inside, Suzie changed out of her uniform and slipped on her fleecy spotted pyjamas and slippers, which were lying across her new bed. On the bedside table, awaiting her further study, was a copy of *The Anarchist's Cookbook*. She would get back to that later.

With growing excitement, she made her way back to her new pet.

'Rose, darling, welcome.'

The tiny bird was frightened, of course. That was to be expected. When she let it out of the box, it flew frantically around the cage where the other had been, losing small tufts of green feather. Suzie locked the cage carefully and spoke to Rose through the tiny bars. 'Sweetheart, it's okay. This is your new home. *Our* new home. Daddy will be here soon.' She quickly changed the food and water and threw the black blanket back over the cage. Rose would soon go to sleep and then she would be fine, just fine. She would adjust quickly to her new environment. They always did.

With her lovebird installed, Suzie looked around and considered what else needed to be done. This was the first day she would be sleeping at the house. Initially she'd thought she would hold off until she could share her love nest with her other half, as a newly married couple will sometimes wait to sleep in their marital home together as man and wife. But with all the final touches that had to be attended to, it was impractical to return to her Malabar apartment before having to start work again in just nine hours. Suzie would get as much done as possible, and then have a quick sleep in her bed, she had decided. She would still be saving the master bedroom for them to sleep in together once they were married. That was good.

Suzie was excited. When she woke from her nap, she would be so near the end of her loneliness. It would come like a Christmas she had waited her whole life for. Her time would finally have arrived. *Her* time.

*What about Brooke and Ridge?*

Suzie looked over at the VCR. It had finished recording. Perhaps first, before any work, she should watch the latest episode of *The Bold And The Beautiful*? Ben had an impressive, state-of-the-art VCR that she had quickly learned to program. She would never have to miss an episode again. Now she could watch the show first, and then replay it while she unpacked the photo frames and ornaments still in the car downstairs, adding those important personal touches to the house. She had some candles she wanted to set up, and some oil-burners. She wondered what else might please him. What kind of food did he like best? What sort of music?

Yes, she would watch her show and think about Ed while she unpacked. She deserved that special treat after all the hard work she had done.

# CHAPTER 22

'Hey Dad, how are you?'

'Mak, is that you?' He sounded groggy.

'I'm sorry it's so late.' Mak looked at her watch and frowned. It would be past midnight on Vancouver Island.

'You can call any time, you know that.'

Mak gripped the phone and closed her eyes. She sat alone in bed with the sheets pulled up high, feeling the weight of her loneliness. She knew she should be happy about the court confession, that it should be enough to make her feel elated, but an unknown dread had begun to settle in the pit of her stomach.

'Is anything wrong?' Les asked.

'No, everything's fine. I miss you, that's all.'

Something felt wrong. Perhaps it was only her father's suggestion, but Ed's conviction really was beginning to feel too good to be true. What he had said was playing on her mind. She didn't know what to do about Andy, either. If they got involved again, what should she expect? The same roller-coaster of misunderstandings and emotional baggage they had battled on and off since they had met? They lived on opposite sides of the world and they couldn't try to date long-distance. Their last experience had proved that. It would have to be all or nothing.

'When are you coming home?' her father asked.

'I'm not sure yet, Dad. I'll let you know soon.'

The line was quiet for a while.

'Dad, have you heard anything more about that rumour of a deal? Because I haven't heard anything.'

'The word is still strong that the Crown is at the negotiating table with him,' her father said.

Mak's stomach churned. That couldn't be right.

'But what does he have to negotiate with? He's already confessed to murder. He's been convicted.'

'But he hasn't been sentenced yet. He's going to show them the bodies, Mak. I didn't want to tell you over the phone but I just don't want you reading about it in the news. He's supposed to be showing them where he buried his other victims. I'm surprised your friend Andy hasn't told you already.'

# CHAPTER 23

*Here we go again,* Jimmy thought.

On Saturday morning they escorted Ed Brown into the back seat of an unmarked car for the second time, ready to embark on another excursion to recover remains. It seemed possible that Ed had been straight with them about the petrol station the day before. It had been confirmed that it really had been an empty, overgrown lot only two years earlier, so they'd wasted no time in setting up this second expedition. A different location, a different girl. It was improbable that they would be unlucky a second time — or so Jimmy hoped.

'Can we get you anything? Are you thirsty?'

'Ah, no thank you.'

Now that the prisoner had a history of cooperation, neither Lewis nor Jimmy intervened when Hoosier offered him beer, chips, whatever crap most men wanted. It still ate at Jimmy's guts, but he ignored it. Strangely, though, Ed declined everything on offer. He was an odd pup. Jimmy couldn't remember the last con to turn down free booze — or the last mate of his, for that matter. Perhaps having to stay cuffed soured the offer for Ed? Tough luck.

'So you used to spend some time out this way? I spent so many summers down here just soaking up the sun with my brothers …'

It looked like Hoosier was going to chat to Ed while he drove, as if it would make some difference to the amount of information Ed would give in return. Ed didn't have a lot to say so far. He sat still in the back seat, unassuming, placid. He was so quiet that Jimmy could barely even hear him breathe.

'Keep going this way, Ed? Along this road?' Hoosier asked.

'Ahh, yeah. Yeah, uh huh,' came the prisoner's reply.

*That frickin' voice creeps me out.*

'Oh look, a Nando's. Would you like some chicken, Ed?'

*Holy Mother of God!*

Ed shook his head politely.

Jesus Christ, Hoosier was a fucking knob. Playing pals was a good strategy with some cons, and they tended to get a little pampered on excursions like these no matter who they were — paedophiles, axe murderers, rapists. It was not the kind of thing the victims' families needed to know about, but hey, if it got the job done quicker, and more effectively, then chatting and beer was the ticket. But Ed frickin' Brown? Jimmy wouldn't hear of letting him out of his cuffs, as Hoosier had suggested, thinking it might loosen his tongue, and thankfully, neither would Lewis. He didn't care that Ed was outnumbered by more than half-a-dozen armed and trained officers. You had to draw the line in this case. You just had to. And despite Ed's placid demeanour, Jimmy couldn't relax. He could feel Ed's presence behind him like a loaded gun aimed at his back. He kept waiting to hear the barrel click over. He was an Ivan

Milat. A Ted Bundy. A fucking psycho. As far as Jimmy was concerned, he wanted to get this adventure with Ed over as quickly and painlessly as possible, preferably without repeating the previous day's disappointment. And then Ed could rot.

On the prisoner's instruction, Hoosier drove towards Botany Bay National Park, in the opposite direction to the petrol station of the previous day. The forensic van, audiovisual van and unmarked car followed close behind them. With all that manpower on tap for a second consecutive day, the pressure was on Lewis to bag the goods and bring something home.

'Which way now?' Hoosier asked.

'Yeah, ah, into the park. Thank you. Uh huh.'

*This malaka sounds like a frickin' Bee Gee with a speech impediment. A homicidal Bee Gee. Now there's a thought.*

As they passed the sign at the entry to the national park, Jimmy tried to recall what he knew about the area. He wanted to do his best to anticipate their every turn ahead of Ed's instructions. The bushland? The adjacent New South Wales Golf Club? Thankfully, Ed had not pointed them in the direction of the airport, or Port Botany with its hundreds and thousands of freight containers, both in the vicinity. That would have been a logistical nightmare. But if Ed got them to dig in an isolated spot within the national park they wouldn't need to kick up much of a commotion. It wouldn't be the first time they had come across criminal evidence in the area. The park was just out of the way enough to appeal to those with dubious intentions. Just so long as Ed didn't point them to a spot in the middle of one of the busy golf greens, they would be fine. If Ed did something like that, Jimmy would make sure they pulled the plug on this charade without a moment's hesitation. He wouldn't let any one of them waste one more second of their time on Ed Brown.

Or at least that's what he told himself.

In reality, Jimmy didn't have the authority to pull the plug on anything, and he knew it. They would all have to humour this creep for as long as Lewis and Detective Inspector Kelley ordered them to. And Hoosier could offer him all the Nando's in the world. They had strict orders to be polite and helpful — and to bring back the dead without attracting the tiniest bit of attention. That meant no smacking Ed Brown in the mouth. Admittedly, that would have been Andy's job.

'Thatta way, ah . . . yeah, there please,' Ed stuttered, pointing them along the road past the turn-off to the golf clubhouse.

*He ain't asking us to dig up the clubhouse. Praise the Lord.*

Their four-car procession moved slowly along the winding road through the park, flanked by thick coastal scrub on either side. They passed some old military residences that looked to still be inhabited, and they kept going. They came up over a rise, and slowed. The end of the road was in sight.

### DANGER
### PISTOL RANGE
### KEEP OUT

*Oh, here we go. A frickin' pistol range?*

A small parking lot sat to the right of the road and a pistol club complete with an operating pistol range on the left. The parking lot was nearly full. Jimmy could hear the crack of light gunfire. He wondered if this would constitute a security concern, a convicted serial killer near a bunch of live weapons? It couldn't be good. Perhaps he was going to tell them that he buried someone in the middle of the pistol range. Convenient.

But Ed didn't motion towards the pistol range at all. With his chin, he gestured towards the disused remnants of Banks Battery, a cluster of dilapidated concrete structures covered in graffiti which stood near the edge of jagged cliffs, the blue ocean raging below. No people, no boats, no cars. That was looking better.

'Ah, in there,' came the voice from the back seat.

'*In* there?' Senior Sergeant Lewis did a double take.

'Yeah ... ahh ... I put her in there. Yeah,' was Ed's response.

Ed pointed to one of the old underground structures, built in World War I. The entrance burrowed into a grassy hill several metres from the parking lot.

'Okay, let's take a look,' Lewis said.

Thankfully there were no bystanders. Inspector Kelley would be happy about that. The golf course was just beyond view on the other side of the hill, and there didn't appear to be anyone in the pistol range clubhouse. There was no need to camouflage Ed's cuffs, and Jimmy was happy to watch Senior Sergeant Lewis order Ed out of the car exactly like the prisoner he was. Ed blinked in the sunlight and looked around, slack-jawed, like someone who was recalling the fragrance and feeling of the long-denied fresh air.

*Let's hope we don't see a news helicopter whip around the shoreline right about now ...*

Walking slowly in his restraints and monitored carefully by half-a-dozen armed officers, Ed led the way to the bunker, followed closely by the audiovisual crew who recorded his every move and instruction. Forensics walked behind. The closer they got to the entrance, the more Jimmy disliked the look of it. There were two concrete walls spaced about a metre apart leading to the mouth of the underground structure, probably to protect it from seeping sand. Despite this, all manner of rubbish had accumulated in the space. A rusted scrap of unidentifiable machinery lay on the path before them, along with some cracked chunks of concrete, and a small drift of dirt and sand. The entrance was low, less than five feet high, Jimmy figured, and was blocked with a heavy iron gate.

'*Fila mou to kolo*,' Jimmy mumbled to himself. *Kiss my Greek arse.*

'What was that?' Hoosier asked.

'Nothing.'

'So tell us about it, Ed,' Lewis began. 'What are we looking for here?'

'Uh, yeah. I'll show you. She's inside ... wrapped in black plastic bags. I uh ... will show you.'

Jimmy frowned. The heavy gate was obviously an attempt by the Parks and Wildlife Service to block access to the inside, but they had not quite succeeded. One small section of iron had been forced open with something very strong. Jimmy wasn't sure any full-grown adult could fit through the hole that had been made. And even if they could, it sure didn't look very inviting once they got inside. They would need torches. Lots of them.

'When were you here last?' Lewis asked.

'When I ah ... put her in there ... I ahhh, I think two or three years ago? Yeah. Three years?'

'And how did you get in?'

'Through that there ah ... hole. It was like this, yeah.'

'And you put a body in there?'

'Yeah, she's in there. She ah … didn't weigh much. Pretty young one.'

Jimmy's stomach churned.

*He twisted himself into that little fucking hole?* Jimmy thought. *Great. Am I the only one who likes doughnuts here?*

'Okay, Hoosier, you give it a go,' Lewis ordered.

Happy to have his number overlooked as the guinea pig, Jimmy passed Hoosier the small torch off his belt. He turned to one of the officers on the forensic team, a skinny and sunburned young man. *What is his name?* 'How many torches have we got, Simmons?' he asked.

'It's Symond,' he corrected. 'We have half-a-dozen good torches. No worries.' He started back towards the van. 'We've got some bolt-cutters too. I'll see if we can do something about that gate,' he called out.

'Let's not upset Parks and Wildlife,' Lewis said. 'Let's see if we can do this without touching anything.'

*Bolt-cutters wouldn't do a damn thing for a gate like that anyway,* Jimmy thought. Not unless they had a few spare hours and a circus strong man to help it along. Jimmy sized up the hole and looked the team over, one by one. Skinny Symond would find it a cinch to squeeze in there, no doubt. He was built like a praying mantis. Constable Hoosier was a fairly big man, though, pretty much on par with Senior Sergeant Lewis, who was clearly a fan of pumping iron. Hoosier didn't have Jimmy's well-earned gut, but he was taller than both himself and Ed. If someone like Hoosier could get through that damn hole then the rest of the team would probably be fine, he figured. All except himself, of course. He had doubts about his ability to perform that magic trick. He was too old for contortion — and several meals too doughy for such a squeeze.

'Okay, here goes ...'

Jimmy watched with interest as Hoosier attempted the hole. On his first go he hoisted himself up, slid his body in headfirst all the way to his waist, and then tried to pull his lower half through. He wasn't flexible enough and found himself embarrassingly stuck. It was rather gratifying to see him pretzelling against the low ceiling of the concrete hole. On his second attempt, Hoosier tried a different angle and fitted through, but caught his shoe on the bent piece of the gate, falling on his arse in the deep sand that covered the floor. *Bravo.* Jimmy wished badly that Andy could see it.

Symond arrived with the torches and bolt-cutter just in time to see Hoosier brushing the sand off his pants.

'Dead easy. You give it a try,' Hoosier mocked through the bars. He couldn't stand fully upright inside the structure, and he stooped like the Neanderthal that he was. The ceiling was low and the sand had probably built up to a depth of a foot or two as well, making the bunker even more cramped.

Jimmy's stomach churned at the thought of what he was about to do. And beyond the tricky entrance, no one on the team had clear knowledge of what was inside. How deep did it go? Was there anything dangerous to beware of?

'What's in there, Ed?' Lewis asked plainly.

'A girl. Yeah.'

'Can you tell us about the structure itself?'

'Ahh, yeah. A couple of old tunnels. Yeah, and some rooms. Not too big. No one goes in there now, no. Except kids maybe. Yeah. It's mostly sealed up. It's not far to her.'

'Why don't we get him to direct a team of guys, and they

can go in,' Jimmy suggested. 'We'll stay on the surface with him.'

'No.' Ed's response was fast and eager. 'No, no, ahhh, that's not the deal. I get to go in. I get to see her, too. That's the deal. I was promised.'

Jimmy's skin crawled. *Fucking psychos.* He could never get used to them. Ed wanted to see his handiwork, that's why he was there. His type always liked the show and tell. Ed had done the same thing back when he was a member of the free world. He was working at the morgue, in a jurisdiction where he knew that most of his victims would pass his way. *Fucking degenerate psycho freak.* But Ed was right about the deal. He was permitted to show them his victims in person, and there was not a thing Jimmy Cassimatis or any of the rest of them could do about it. He took some small solace in the fact that Ed's thrills would be short-lived, but his sentence would not.

'Sir, why don't we get a couple of guys in there with Hoosier and check things out first?' Jimmy suggested. 'I could get Ed back into the car while we wait.'

'We're here. There'll be no waiting. Let's get this done.'

'Okay,' Jimmy said, 'let's get it done. Anyone know what's in there though? Should we call it in?'

'You got cold feet, Cassimatis?' Lewis scoffed.

Ed spoke up in his eerie voice. 'Ahh, I can show you. It's not far.'

'Okay, let's do this.' Lewis asserted his authority. 'You next.' He motioned to a forensics officer.

Ed chuckled inwardly as, one by one, the team lined up, ready to enter the unknown.

'Ed Brown,' Lewis intoned, as the video camera recorded. 'Do you agree to take part in this re-enactment? You are not obliged to say or do anything, but anything you say or do may be given in evidence. Do you understand ...?'

★ ★ ★

Andy was waiting at his desk with a long face when his mobile phone finally rang. He snatched it up, hoping it was Jimmy able to give him an update, or even better, that it was Makedde calling.

'Andy, how are ya?'

The voice was as familiar as his own. Andy could hear wind whistling in the background, and the sound of distant conversation.

'Jimmy, I've been better,' he admitted, gritting his teeth. 'Go on, what's up?'

'She still givin' ya the cold shoulder?'

*Is it that obvious?* Andy wondered.

'I got a question for ya,' Jimmy said, back on topic.

Andy perked up and leaned forward, as if that would somehow make him hear better. 'Shoot,' he said.

'Ya know anything about Cape Banks? Ya know, at Botany Bay National Park? Banks Battery. Whatever it's called.'

'Botany Bay? Boy, this guy sure likes to keep it local,' Andy remarked. Ed had dumped the mutilated body of Mak's friend Catherine at nearby La Perouse. Andy knew the place. 'Yup, I used to get up to all kinds of shit there as a teenager before they wised up and closed the thing off. I tried to get lucky there once with my childhood flame, but she freaked out and wouldn't go inside.'

'Can't say I blame her, you smooth-talkin' bastard. What's it like inside? It looks like Sydney's arsehole.'

'It's pretty dark and disgusting, from memory.'

Jimmy mumbled some incoherent curse in response.

'There's not much to it, though,' Andy went on. 'There are some rooms with short tunnels connecting them, but the tunnels don't go far and it sure wouldn't be too shit-hot now. All the entrances were blocked last I saw. Is that where you guys are?'

'Yes, but please don't go meeting up with us or they'll have my head. Ed says he dumped a girl in there in black plastic bags.'

'Hmm.'

'Yeah, I was just wantin' your thoughts.'

Andy thought he sounded slightly uneasy.

'He says it will only take about two minutes to get to the spot but I ain't been in there before.'

'How are you guys getting in?' Andy asked.

'There's a hole in the gate. I might have to blame Angie's cookin' for keepin' me out of this one.' He laughed. 'This fuckin' hole is like the size of my damn navel.'

'Can audiovisual squeeze the camera in?'

'Apparently.'

'Is Lewis calling for assistance, maps, anything?'

'Nope,' Jimmy said. 'We're going right on in to find ourselves a body.'

'Mate, keep me updated. Let me know as soon as you find something.'

'You got it, Andy. You shoulda seen Hoosier squeeze his sorry arse in through those bars. I think he just got a sandpaper enema.'

Andy laughed. Now that was something he would've liked to have seen.

# CHAPTER 24

'Sorry man. You alright?'

Ed Brown stood doubled over just inside Banks Battery, coughing up sand. He spluttered and moaned for effect.

'You alright?' Lewis repeated.

Ed had managed to squeeze through the hole in the gate with relative ease, considering they wouldn't take his handcuffs off, but he'd caught his shoe just as Hoosier had before him. Unable to use his arms to brace his fall, Ed had done a face-plant into the sandy floor. Now he was playing it up for all it was worth. The muscly one in charge had picked him up off the ground and was dusting him off.

'Sorry about that, man. We've gotta keep you in the handcuffs,' Lewis said. 'I know it's hard going. We'll take it slow.' They had removed the ankle restraints, thankfully. At least he could walk normally.

'Yeah ... ahhh, that's okay,' Ed replied.

As the shortest in the group, Ed could just about stand upright in the space. The ceiling was even lower than he remembered it. Or perhaps the sand had risen higher? He watched a skinny guy in a crime-scene suit toss a bag of gear and a shovel through the hole in the bars, then squeeze himself through quite easily. The sound guy was crouching so low he looked like he was defecating. The cameraman was recording everything, using a thin but intense beam of light like a powerful flashlight to illuminate the scene. Two more cops stood on the outside, squinting stupidly as they peered into the dark.

Now Ed was inside the Banks Battery system with seven cops. So far so good. He'd gone from nine down to seven in one simple step, and he'd rid himself of the ankle cuffs.

'Down there ... ah ... yeah,' he told them, pointing with his cuffed hands down a steep staircase to the left.

'Edward Brown has directed us to what appears to be a steep staircase with a railing along the left-hand side ...' The video camera light shone down the black passage. So much sand had seeped in over the years that the steps themselves were not even visible. It no longer resembled a staircase at all, but a steep slope of sand that disappeared into pitch black, a concrete garbage chute leading into damp nothingness.

Behind Ed, the fat one was mumbling in some foreign language. He was still brushing himself off following his ungainly entrance through the bars. Ed did not know what his words meant, but he recognised the sentiment. He clearly did not like the situation. 'Why don't we get you in here,' he suggested to one of the cops who had been standing outside the gate. 'You can cover the top of the stairs and your partner can cover the entrance.'

To Ed's disappointment, the one in charge agreed. 'Yup. Let's keep this operation tight.'

One of the two nodded and started the process of squeezing himself through the bars.

'Okay, let's go.'

Now they would begin a slippery descent into the bowels of Cape Banks, where not a single ray of sunshine could reach. The dearth of light was so complete that even with all the torches on and the shaky light of the video camera, it was near impossible to see ahead.

'Step carefully,' Lewis said. Frustratingly, he kept a hand on Ed's arm in a vice-like grip.

'Got it.'

'Ahhh, no worries,' Ed said as a kind of reassurance. 'Ahh, it's not far.'

No one responded. He could sense their nerves.

For every foothold down the stairwell they slipped forward several inches in the loose sand, struggling to maintain balance. Most of the men clung to the rusted railing that extended down the left-hand side of the slope, but Ed, with his hands cuffed behind his back, did not have that luxury. Lewis caught him under the arms twice to stop him slipping and falling over. Torches shone at his feet, and flickered across the low ceiling above him, always moving in someone's shaking hands, the changing light making it harder for Ed to watch his step. The group made painfully slow progress down the steep incline, stepping carefully over scattered garbage, rusted wire and even a damaged fire-extinguisher that looked like it had been tossed there years before.

'What's this?' Hoosier asked.

He shone a light across some heavy wrought-iron hooks that jutted from the wall down the right-hand side of the stairwell, four in a stack and repeated every few feet.

'Would have been for cables I guess.'

*Yes. It was for cables.*

Ed knew they were on their way to the old engine room. He had only been here once before, but he had studied the maps well. Accurate maps of the Banks Battery system had been hard to come by, but the Prison Lady had obtained them from a convict with military connections in return for some banned publications. So far everything looked as he'd anticipated. It was just as she'd said. So far so good.

'Yeah, this way,' he said, but no one answered him.

Now a couple of men had reached the bottom of the steep stairwell. Ed could just make out the flicker of their torches and the sound of their feet in water.

'It's fuckin' wet down here. I should have brought gumboots,' someone said.

Almost there.

The camera and sound men and three other cops were behind him, including the fat, suspicious wog, the idiot who wouldn't stop talking while he drove, and the one in charge, always hanging onto him like a leech. Boss Man seemed to be having a much harder time of it now that they were crouching in a waterlogged tunnel. It was obvious that the surroundings were unnerving all of them. The loud bravado of before had disappeared. The blackness had all but silenced them.

As a group they progressed down the seeping concrete hallway, water up to their ankles, stepping across heavy slabs of broken concrete scattered on the floor. Bits of wood jutted into the air. The wrought-iron hooks lined the wall at waist level, with another line closer to the floor. They were several metres underground now. They should be getting close.

*Where?*

Ed kept searching in the dim light. This should be the spot . . .

*There it is.*

Light swung fleetingly across the wall and Ed spotted the package the Prison Lady had left for him, right at the end of the hallway, exactly where he had instructed.

*Perfect.*

It was an old, rusted letterbox with the top torn off, hung on the last iron hook, right at waist level. Ed paused with his back to it, and leaned against the wall. The recording guys and crime-scene investigators moved with the driver cop slowly into the remains of the engine room to the left, while the wog and the one in charge stayed glued to Ed's side. Boss Man was still irritatingly close, but thankfully he no longer gripped Ed's elbow like a vice. His fingertips were curled loosely against Ed's arm, his mouth gaping open as he looked around him.

'Can you hear us up there?' the fat one called out to the man at the top of the stairs. 'Hey! Up there! Can you hear me?'

*Of course he can't hear you down here, you stupid wog. And your walkie-talkies won't work either. Your communications are out.*

Ed smiled in the dark.

Now a torch flashed in his face. He blinked innocently in the light.

'I-I put her there,' he gasped. 'See the uh, plastic ... there.' He pointed into the engine room.

The men moved forward a step, and someone shone their torch across the black plastic shape and then focused on it. 'I think we found it, sir!'

'Edward Brown has directed us to a form covered in black plastic ...'

Ed's fingertips slipped silently into the top of the metal box, feeling inside for the handcuff key.

There.

The key was glued to the inside of the box with a wad of Blu-Tack. His fingers curled around it. Carefully, he pulled the key off the sticky substance and palmed it. It was a SAF-LOK handcuff key, the standard issue for police and law enforcement agencies in Australia. One key fits all. In seconds he had slipped it into his cuffs and was ready to pull them off, but the one in charge was still close enough to hear. The policeman's fingers were now barely touching Ed's shoulder as he leaned forward, curious to see the black shape on the watery floor. Ed waited for a distracting noise.

'Hey!' the irritating wog called again. 'Hey, can you hear us?'

Ed turned the key and slipped out of the cuffs in one rapid movement. Boss Man didn't notice. Now his hands were free. And he was the only one who knew.

'Let's get this done as fast as we can,' Lewis said.

Flashbulbs illuminated the room like strobes as the crime-scene investigators went to work. The video camera beamed its light from corner to corner and settled on the black plastic.

'Got it.'

'Let's get Ed out of here now. We've got what we came for,' the wog suggested. But Ed didn't want to leave just yet.

Torchlight revealed that the men were standing over the bagged form. 'Let's lift her and get her up to ground,' someone said.

Ed closed his eyes and covered his ears.

'It doesn't smell so bad in here as I thought —' someone began, but their words were cut short when the blinding blast ripped through the room.

There was a bright flash, and a powerful *whooosh*. Ed's chest was hit with a pulse of air.

He opened his eyes to near blackness. The scene around him was one of chaos. One of the torches was still on, thrown to the far corner of the engine room. The camera light was not functioning. There was a loud, incessant ringing in Ed's ears, and beneath it all the sounds of shouting, water splashing, people and objects crashing to the ground.

Ed Brown was moving already. His senses of sight and sound were disabled for the moment, so he concentrated on the feel of the tunnel wall under his hands and clawed his way through the passageway to the right. He groped along the walls in the blackness, and after only a few metres tripped over an object that must have been leaning in the corner. *The damn shovel!* He fell hard onto his elbows and let out a sharp cry, landing painfully on the unforgiving handle.

A strong hand gripped his ankle.

*No!*

Ed rolled over and swung out blindly with the shovel blade, slicing it through the air with as much force as he could muster. It made contact with something and he thought he heard the distinctive sound of exhalation, followed by an agonised moan. It was hard to tell with the ringing in his ears. When the hand let go of his ankle, he knew he had hit his mark. He was free! Ed dropped the shovel and edged away. In seconds he was up and running, slipping and battling his way along the tunnel, stumbling blindly towards the surface, the dark scene of chaos and panic in the engine room fading as he hit fresh air. No more hands like shackles on his arms, no more handcuffs holding him back, just the ringing in his ears and the beautiful, bright vision of the Pacific.

*Yes.*

*Yes.*

*Yes!*

He reached the surface and struggled through the half-blocked exit overlooking the raging ocean. In that moment, the wind in his hair was the most exhilarating sensation he had ever experienced. More exhilarating even than his first kill, which surprised him. More exhilarating than all his planning. The wind was fresh and real and it meant that he had won. After eighteen months he had won. It was not the stale, regurgitated air of his cell, but *real* air and real wide-open space. He could not be contained. He could not be beaten. This was proof.

But Ed had no time to dwell on his euphoria. Almost as soon as he reached the surface he scrambled down the cliff, across the rocks and sand at the water's edge, and ran due east along the shoreline in the direction opposite to the remaining police officers who might by now have sensed that something was wrong, or may even have heard the blast at their posts near the bunker entrance. Ed peeled off his clothes as he went, noticing a spray of blood across the fabric. Not his blood, he smirked. He stripped down to boxer shorts and undershirt, and carelessly tossed the rest in a heap behind some boulders, to be discovered by the police or some unsuspecting tourists in the hours or days to come. Before long Ed had reached the rocky point, his skin flecked with dirt and sweat, and not even slowing to catch his breath he rummaged through thick, prickly bushes that scraped his bare flesh, searching eagerly for the next important item the Prison Lady had left for him.

*There it is!*

The backpack was waiting for him, just as planned, hidden amongst dense shrubbery.

He looked around cautiously, staying low to the ground. He half expected to see police officers running along the sand waving guns, helicopters flying overhead, search boats gathering just offshore. He half expected to hear his name on a megaphone: 'Ed Brown, stop where you are and put your hands in the air!' But he was alone. No other human being was in sight.

Ed opened the bag, unable to contain a broad smile, and pulled on the plaid pants and the white polo top he found inside. He patted his ginger hair down and fitted a cap onto his head. He pocketed the car keys and the note with the street address. He was set.

There was just one last detail to attend to before he could be on his way. He found the golf clubs lying hidden in another flattened section of thick shrubs only a few metres away. He hauled them upright, dusted them off and looked himself over. Everything was in place. He had not forgotten a thing.

Ed started towards the golf course.

His gait was casual, the corners of his mouth turned up in a nonchalant smile. He was still sweating, but no one would notice. He could slow down now. There was no longer any need to rush. In fact, rushing now would draw attention to himself. No, he was just another golfer enjoying a scenic walk, just another golfer taking his time and enjoying a beautiful day by the water. Ed rounded the corner of the point and stepped onto the edge of the golf course. Slowly, he began to saunter towards the parking lot on the other side of the hill. It was at least a five-minute walk across the open fairway and he would take his time. He blended in so beautifully with the handful of golfers already on the greens that no one even looked up. No one seemed to notice that he had appeared out of thin air at the edge of the cliffs. He was back to being the invisible, unremarkable Ed Brown. He was back to living under the radar and making his own rules. He was free. He had won.

Ed did not look back in the direction of the entrance to the tunnel until he was safely on the crest of the hill close to the clubhouse. When he finally turned, he was so far away that the mouth of the entrance, with its iron gate, was a mere speck on the horizon, the figures huddled around it as small and insignificant as ants. It was hard to discern what was going on from such a distance, but it hardly mattered now. They would not think to check the golfers. Not at this point. They would be scanning the tunnels, checking the shoreline for an escape boat. They would be tending to the injured. They would still be panicking, if they even *knew* enough to panic yet. Had the men on the surface even heard the blast? Perhaps they had not. And what kind of carnage had he left behind? It would take some time for them to sort through the mess, and by then he would be miles away.

Less than ten minutes later, as he was driving down Anzac Parade in the Prison Lady's beat-up Volkswagen, Ed heard the sirens. He calmly pulled over and let the speeding ambulance pass. And a few minutes after that, two blue and white police cars zipped by as well, all on the way to Botany Bay National Park.

Ed watched them disappear in the rear-view mirror.

He smiled.

# CHAPTER 25

Andy sped toward the Prince of Wales Hospital, still barely able to register the news. He felt numb, like a distant observer separated from his own body. With a tense grip he drove his car on automatic pilot, fighting to block out the emotion and fear, and the dark conclusions running through his mind. *Ed Brown is out. Jimmy is injured.* The news was inconceivable, the consequences grave. One of Australia's most notorious serial killers was at large, having escaped directly from the custody of the New South Wales police — out of their very own hands, a damning reality. The escape would trigger a public outcry, and quite possibly another Royal Commission. Someone would have to pay, and if they did not act fast to bring him in, more lives would be at risk, Makedde's in particular.

*Lewis had better have some answers*, he thought. *Some bloody good answers.*

The traffic was against him. He was only halfway to the hospital and already he found himself at a standstill. This was not the time for Andy to exercise patience. If Jimmy, his partner and loyal friend of many years, was badly hurt and fucking died on the surgeon's table while Andy was sitting in some mindless traffic jam, that would be the end of it. Andy would never be able to forgive himself.

He flicked on his siren with a loud *whoop*. A man in the car next to him jumped in his seat, startled by the noise. Drivers and passengers gawked, and yet the traffic did not move. He leaned out the window and yelled at the car ahead of him. 'Come on, let's move!' Andy laid in on his horn with all his might, as if that would somehow encourage the cars to move more effectively. It did not work.

Warm tears welled in his eyes, and now they began to spill over. Andy did not acknowledge them, did not wipe them away. He simply rolled down the window of his car and yelled, 'MOVE IT!'

The siren continued to flash and holler. A space opened up on the opposite side of the road and Andy wasted no time in driving straight over the divider into the oncoming lane, scraping his muffler across the top of the concrete. Cars came to a screeching halt. Mouths gaped. He sped through, his heart heavy like a block of ice in his chest. He had to get there fast. He had to know what had happened. He had to know where things stood. He had to see Jimmy.

★ ★ ★

'Are you immediate family?' the nurse asked.

Andy was slick with sweat. He had been stopped just beyond the main reception area of the hospital. His heart pounded in his chest. It was hard to think.

'Excuse me, sir, are you immediate family?' the nurse asked again when he failed to respond.

Speechless with grief and anger, Andy flashed his badge and tried to shove past. She put up a hand to hold him back.

'I am Detective Senior Sergeant Andrew Flynn,' he explained. 'My colleagues are in here. My partner, Jimmy Cassimatis, is here. I need to see him now,' he demanded, somehow managing composed speech.

She pursed her lips. 'Sir, I'm going to have to ask you to take a seat.'

*What?*

Andy shook his head, and ignoring her instruction tried to walk past her again. She put a hand against his shoulder. He wanted to break it off. A young nurse. Bloody hell. What was she doing?

'I'm sorry, sir, I'm going to have to insist you take a seat in the reception area.'

'I'm not taking a damn seat.' In the midst of his anger a moment of inspiration. Carol. 'Is Carol Richardson here?'

'Why, yes she is.' Recognition flashed across the nurse's features. 'Wait here.'

'I need to see Carol Richardson immediately. I'll be the one searching the damn halls.' The inexperienced nurse looked gobsmacked as he pushed past her and strode down the corridor towards the elevator. Where would they be? Emergency? Which direction was it again? He should know. He'd been there so many times. His wits had left him. He was panicking.

Carol was quick to find him. He spotted her jogging down the hall towards him in her whites, her pretty blonde hair pulled into a bun.

'Andy! They told me you were here. It's terrible what's happened. I'm so sorry.'

She ran up to him and hugged him briefly. He was as rigid as a plank. She pulled away.

'Where's Jimmy?' he said bluntly.

Carol took him by the hand and led him around a corner and down a different corridor away from the reception area. 'Andy, I know you must be upset, but I think you should try to calm down.'

'Carol,' he said and stopped in the hall, 'just tell me where the fuck Jimmy is and get the fuck out of the way.'

His words gave her pause. Her eyes widened, the mascara-coated lashes batting once, twice. She was clearly shocked by his manner. Truthfully, he was too.

Andy realised he was being rude and unreasonable, but he was unable to apologise. He needed to find Lewis, or someone who could tell him what had happened. He needed to get the lowdown on Jimmy and on Ed Brown.

'Where's Senior Sergeant Lewis?' he demanded.

'Room 311,' she said softly and pointed towards the elevators.

No sooner had the words left her lips than Andy was jogging down the hallway away from her. Carol let him go, helplessly. She knew him well enough to know she should not get in his way when he was like this.

Room 311. He stopped at the door. There were four beds in the ward. Inspector Kelley was already there. He looked pale. He noticed Andy at the doorway and they exchanged glances. There was a hard look in Kelley's eyes, a battle-weary expression Andy had only seen a handful of times. '*Officers down . . . We have officers down.*' Kelley gave a nod and rose from his seat beside the bed of one of the men. Andy couldn't identify the patient because his head was so heavily bandaged. *Is that Jimmy?*

'Flynn,' Kelley acknowledged him gravely, joining him in the hallway.

'Holy fucking Mother of God,' Andy said softly under his breath. 'Who is that?'

'Symond. Half his face is gone.'

'What happened?'

'Ed had the place booby-trapped, it looks like. Some kind of explosive.' He cast his eyes over the men in the room, and back to Andy. 'There was no body. It was a trick.'

*My God*, Andy thought.

'A booby trap? How?'

'We don't know yet. We're getting statements from the guys who can speak. They were in some kind of underground tunnel system in Cape Banks when it happened. A couple of constables were on the surface and didn't get hit. They say they heard something, but couldn't be sure what it was. One of them went down and saw that it was a mess. And no sign of our prisoner. They quickly raised the alarm.'

*Where would Ed get explosives? How?*

'Lewis is fine, apart from some shock and temporary hearing loss. He was furthest from the blast, they think. He was across the room with Ed.'

Andy frowned. *And the men under his command are dying . . .*

'Hoosier might be blinded. The doctors say it's fifty–fifty he gets his sight back. The crime-scene guys didn't fare so well. Neither did audiovisual. They were right up close to the explosion. Parker lost fingers. Flemming lost an arm. Then there was shrapnel ripping through everything. The doctors think they will recover their hearing. We don't know what kind of explosive it was but we're hoping like hell that Ed was injured by the blast too. That would be the surest bet to catch the bastard. We've got eyes at the hospitals, medical centres, veterinary clinics, anywhere he might go to get fixed up. We don't know how he slipped from Lewis's grip.'

Andy drank up the information, but Kelley had left out one big piece of it.

'How about Jimmy?'

'It's not good, Andy,' Kelley said. Andy waited, but that was it.

'Was he right in the blast? Was it shrapnel?'

'No.'

Clearly Kelley didn't want to say anything more. That was a very bad sign.

'You don't think he's going to make it,' Andy said flatly.

Kelley looked him in the eye, silent. There was a controlled rage in there, and emotion too. Kelley's men had been seriously hurt. In some ways they were like children to him. He would want someone to pay.

'Jimmy is in bad shape. Apparently he was unconscious at the scene. The doctors can't say if or how he will pull through, something to do with his heart,' Kelley said.

Andy stared wide-eyed, disbelieving.

'Let's sit down, Andy.'

'No,' he said. He didn't want to sit. He didn't want to relax. He didn't want to calm down. 'No, no . . .'

'Andy . . .'

Andy noticed Carol behind him. He turned and she took him into the hall while Kelley returned to his men.

'It's terrible. I'm so sorry,' she said, her eyes large with sympathy.

'Tell me. Tell me the truth. What's happened to Jimmy? What are his chances?'

'They don't know, Andy,' she admitted. 'I wish I could give you an answer but I can't. He has AF. He's been on Warfarin.'

'What?'

'AF, atrial fibrillation. The atria in his heart don't pump the blood effectively. Your partner has been a stroke waiting to happen, Andy. He's been on blood-thinning medication to avoid blood clots. Unfortunately, that means his internal bleeding was excessive ...'

'What happened to him?'

'He was struck on the head with a shovel, probably in some kind of struggle.'

*Ed. He was trying to stop Ed.*

'He was unconscious when he was brought in. To staunch the bleeding they had to give him something to reverse the medication. In his case there was a risk of a clot. I'm afraid he suffered a stroke on the operating table. I'm sorry, Andy.' She touched his arm reassuringly. 'He has stabilised a little. There is a good chance he'll pull through.'

Andy felt numb. He took a few moments to respond. 'Is that all you can tell me?'

'I'm afraid so.'

'Thanks, Carol. I'm sorry if I've been ...'

'I understand,' she said, squeezing his hand. 'If I can do anything, let me know.'

She left him, and Andy moved back into the ward to speak to Kelley.

'Has anyone told Angie?'

'We're sending a couple of constables around to inform her. She knows Hunt. He'll be there to let her down.'

*Three kids. Why did Jimmy have to have a wife and three kids to leave behind? He can't die. He just can't.*

'There was no sign of Ed Brown when they got there? Nothing?' Andy pressed.

'His handcuffs were on the ground. He'd already vanished.'

'No one can *vanish*. Have we checked the boats along the coastline? The bushland? The freight port? Someone must have seen something for Christ's sake!' Andy made fists at his sides. 'Has anyone told Makedde that Ed is out?'

'We're sending someone over now.'

'I've got to speak to her first. Give me ten minutes.'

'Flynn . . .'

'Just give me this, sir. Please.'

★   ★   ★

'Makedde . . .'

'Speaking.' Makedde's voice was dull and noncommittal.

'I need to talk to you right now.'

'Well, hello to you too,' she said, recognising his voice.

Andy was so utterly relieved that she sounded okay, he barely registered her coolness.

Kelley had said her phone had been ringing out, but now she was safely inside her hotel room. Safe. *Thank God*. The dread in his heart eased just a fraction. The hotel was the best place for her to be at the moment. It was unlikely that Ed Brown would make a beeline for her there so soon. He would be too busy covering his own arse, wouldn't he? Andy had to keep her inside that room until he explained the situation himself, and it wouldn't take him long to get there. He knew that what he had to tell her would be the worst possible news anyone could give her, and it was only right that she heard it from him directly. Andy couldn't bear the thought of her finding out from some door-knocking flatfoot constable she had never met, or from the officers who were on their way to the hotel now to protect her.

'There's something very important I need to discuss with you,' he urged with as much calm as he could muster. He sprinted across the hospital parking lot with his phone at his ear.

'Are you running?' she asked.

'Um, yeah.'

'I was going to ring you later,' Mak said.

Andy finally reached his car in the hospital parking lot and threw the door open. He slid into the driver's seat and shoved the key in the ignition.

'I can't explain it over the phone,' he managed, now slightly out of breath. 'I need to speak to you in person. I'm on my way.'

'Oh, Andy, I'm meeting up with Loulou in fifteen minutes. I'm just about to leave.'

'Don't go out. Don't go anywhere. I'm coming right over. Just promise me you'll stay put.' His knew his words sounded peremptory, probably even rude. He would have to apologise later. And to Carol too. She had turned out to be a great help at the hospital.

'But . . .'

Andy pinched the phone between his shoulder and his ear, and started his car. It revved up reliably and he was about to step on the gas when he looked up and noticed an old man backing a station wagon out in front of him . . . slowly . . . slowly . . . so goddamn slowly. He pressed the horn in a fit of frustration, knowing full well that it wouldn't encourage the man's driving skills in the least.

'Fuck ...'

'Excuse me?' Mak was still on the line.

'Sorry. That wasn't for you,' he said. *Hurry up, old man! Hurry up!* 'Stay in your hotel room,' he ordered bluntly, his patience waning. 'I'll be there in a few minutes, ten at the most —'

'But ...'

Finally the station wagon was out of the way. Andy laid the pedal down and burned rubber out of the parking lot. The phone was hot against his ear lobe.

'Andy, are you there?'

'Mak,' he shouted. 'I need you to stay right there. Just promise me you'll stay put until I get there.'

'Um, okay.'

'Don't let anyone in the room. I don't care who they say they are. Bolt the door. Use the chain. I'll be ten minutes at the most. *Do not open your door to anyone else, you hear me?* If you know anything about me, you'll know I'm not fucking around. I'll see you in under ten.'

He hung up.

# CHAPTER 26

Ed Brown was apprehensive as he approached the house.

For almost five minutes, he sat in the Prison Lady's car at the end of the street, engine off, still wearing the golfing gear with the cap pulled low over his forehead. He crossed his arms and observed quietly. There was no movement on the street or at the house. To be sure he had the right place, he checked the address on the Prison Lady's note several times.

It wasn't what he had expected.

The Prison Lady had directed him to a large modern-looking family house, two levels, in a quiet suburban neighbourhood. It seemed an unusual home for a single woman. *She must be a widow*, he thought. She hadn't said anything about that. He hoped she didn't have an ex-husband she hadn't told him about who might be lurking somewhere and could cause problems. Perhaps her place was a semi, or she shared it with someone. If that were the case, he wouldn't be able to stick around even long enough to shower and change into some new clothes. He'd have to grab what he could and go.

The lawns on the nature strip were well kept. He saw a

tricycle next to one of the driveways. Ed pictured smiling Brady Bunch families, Tupperware parties and golden-haired children playing under sprinklers in the summertime. It looked like the Australia of 1950s' detergent ads, but it was nothing like the neighbourhood he had grown up in. He had no memories of green lawns and tricycles. He was more familiar with being locked in his room, learning lessons that came by way of a hot iron and a length of rope, and children who liked to break his nose after school and make fun of the way he talked. That was the Australia he knew.

Ed reminded himself that it was Saturday, around midday, so there was an increased chance that some of the families on the street would be at home. Someone might notice him in the Prison Lady's car if he loitered around too much. He needed to make a decision. Should he go in? Ed started the car and drove past the house for another look. He didn't spot any movement there. The curtains were drawn and they didn't twitch as he passed. He circled the block and waited. No one seemed to have followed him from Botany Bay. There wasn't anyone on the street that he could see. It was time to do it, if ever he was going to.

Tense and alert for every movement, Ed parked in the Prison Lady's driveway. He was protected from view by a row of tall shrubs. He turned the engine off, left the driver's door open and the key in the ignition, and stepped out. He hurried to the back door, nervously scanning left and right, still wary of waiting police. Nothing looked suspicious so far. *I will go in*, he decided. He needed somewhere to shower and change. He needed something to eat. He needed cash, or something he could pawn for fast money. Unlike the ex-cons on TV, Ed had not stashed money away in case he ever needed to flee justice. He'd never considered that his freedom might be taken away. He had no fancy contacts to help him with fake passports or illegal guns. He was starting with nothing. He hoped to find everything he needed to begin his new life waiting for him inside this suburban house. Then he could concentrate on his plans.

Ed found the key to the back door under a straw mat, just as the Prison Lady had promised. WELCOME HOME, the mat said.

Ed picked up the key and slid it into the keyhole. It fitted. He turned it and the door unlocked. No alarms. He stepped inside. The Prison Lady had assured him that no one would be around, and so far she seemed to be telling the truth. He closed the door behind him and listened. Nothing. The lights were off. No moving shadows or reflections. He could hardly believe his luck. Could he actually be in the clear?

Surprisingly, the house was *huge*.

Ed spent the next few minutes walking through it, upstairs and down, laughing. It wasn't a semi. He counted four bedrooms, expensively furnished. There were all kinds of things he could sell. VCRs, television sets, golf clubs, appliances. There was a pool table, though he could never get it out of the house to pawn. When he reached the large kitchen he found a note propped against some ham and cheese sandwiches wrapped in Glad Wrap. He hungrily ripped the package open and sank his teeth into one of the sandwiches. Then another. And another. He opened the note.

Dearest Sweetheart,
    Please enjoy this snack. Make yourself at home. I will be home from work by one. I can't wait to be together! I love you.
    With love from your dearest,
    Suzie

A note from the Prison Lady.

Ed had planned to only stay one day, but perhaps he could hang around a bit longer, until he got himself organised. It looked comfortable enough, and it was fairly clean. Ed had debated for the past week about exactly when to kill the woman. She looked like she had money, which was not what he'd expected. Maybe he shouldn't kill her right away? She wasn't his type, so it wasn't like he would enjoy killing her or anything. Perhaps he could get some cash out of her over the next couple of days? Then he could grab some of the valuables from the house, take the car and go. She had been useful so far, much more useful than he had even dared to hope. He would keep her around for a few days and see what else he could get out of her, he decided. If anything went wrong, he could take care of her quickly enough.

Ed had an hour or so before the Prison Lady returned from work. He would shower and change. It would be awkward to see her outside jail. She would be expecting affection, probably. That might pose a problem. But she would be able to tell him all about how his little escapade had gone down at Long Bay. He looked forward to that. They would know by now that there was no body. There never had been one there, or at the petrol station. The police would be humiliated. They'd been had.

Ed grinned.

*I did it*, he thought. *I'm free.*

# CHAPTER 27

Andy arrived at Makedde's hotel room, panting. He knocked on the door impatiently. A fingertip strayed to his gun holster, just in case.

*Please let her be here. Please let her be alone . . .*

He could hear footsteps as someone approached the door. There was a pause as he was investigated through the eyehole, and then with a series of clicks the door was opened.

It was Makedde.

Her hair was tied back in a wet ponytail that left her neck moist. She wore a black T-shirt and leather pants, and a challenging look that seemed to say, 'This better be good.' Her eyebrows were subtly raised and her lips pushed out in a curious pout, wrinkling her chin with tension. The look in her eyes was one of apprehension. Her arms were crossed, as usual. She had bare feet, which made him feel taller.

'I have to say, your phone call really freaked me out,' she began.

'He escaped,' Andy said, point-blank, and closed the door

behind him. He had decided to waste no time in explaining the emergency. No hellos or how are yous.

'Escaped,' she repeated. Her voice was flat.

'Yes.'

'I, um, I don't suppose you would joke about such a thing, or ... or ... I also doubt that you're talking about someone's pet dog, or ...'

Grasping at straws. He shook his head gently.

She breathed deeply and let off a humourless laugh. 'Tell me, Detective, how does one escape when one is a convicted serial killer? I presume that's who you are talking about?'

She uncrossed her arms and then crossed them again. The warm colour had drained from her face, and now her even features were set against a smooth, deathly pallor. There was a slight flicker of nerves around her mouth. She rarely lost her composure, but she looked on the edge of panic now.

'Yes,' she continued, 'A *guilty, convicted serial killer*, who is presumably under *maximum* security? Hmmm. How does one go about escaping then? What, forty-eight hours after his conviction?' Her anger and disbelief were palpable.

'I think we should sit down,' Andy said.

Mak nodded. He knew she would be in a state of shock, the full realisation not yet hitting her. She sat on the edge of the hotel bed. Andy dragged a chair over and sat near her. She watched him silently. He could not read her thoughts, though he knew they would be dark.

'Makedde, I am very sorry to give you this news, but Ed Brown escaped from custody today.' He found himself automatically slipping into the role of a death-knocker, using that gentle, soothing, emotionless tone he had learned with years of practice. *Just the facts. Stick to the clear facts.* 'At this time, we don't know his whereabouts. My partner, Jimmy Cassimatis, is in bad shape.' His voice wavered. 'The other officers who were present are injured, some badly. Ed used some kind of explosive . . . somehow.'

She did not respond, but tears filled the corners of her eyes at the mention of Jimmy. Mak didn't even seem aware of them. A tear ran from an eyelash down to the corner of her mouth. Andy wanted to kiss it away. The frustrating fact that he couldn't, and the truth about Jimmy and his own helplessness with all of it, brought him close to tears again himself. He blinked the feeling away and made himself emotionally distant again.

'Ed was supposed to lead a group of officers to the body of one of his victims this morning,' he went on. 'He's done some kind of deal with his confession. They went to look for a body yesterday as well, without incident.' He paused. This part was hard to say. 'I was not there when it happened. They wouldn't let me near Ed so I was left out. Now Jimmy is in hospital instead of me.'

He shouldn't have said that. That wasn't really true, was it? If Andy had gone, Jimmy would have been there anyway, and he would have still been in danger. But dammit, something could have been done. *I should have been there. How could I have not been there? How could I have allowed that?*

'Oh poor Jimmy. I'm so sorry,' Mak said softly. 'Will he be okay?'

'They don't know.'

Andy didn't know what else to say. He rested his chin on his hands and frowned, lost in his own thoughts.

'So there really was a deal? My dad said something about that, and you know what, I didn't even believe him.' She shook her head. 'How could something like this happen?'

'We don't know,' was all Andy could offer.

'When?'

'About an hour or so ago.'

She shook her head back and forth as she spoke. 'I just don't believe it. I mean, there are precautions, right? Surely there are precautions so things like this can't ever happen? He's a convicted killer. *Convicted*, Andy! How the hell do you guys operate over here?'

Andy didn't know what to say. She was absolutely right. After eighteen months in remand, after eighteen months of investigation and hard work putting their case together, they had finally got him. He confessed. He was convicted in a court of law. Then someone had fucked up. It was unthinkable.

'Was Karen Mahoney there? Is she okay?'

'She wasn't there.'

Mak put her head in her hands, clearly distraught.

'I've gotta go, Andy,' she said.

Her words snapped him out of his thoughts. 'Pardon?'

She stood up. 'I'm not going to stay here like a sitting duck. I'm leaving on the next damn flight out of here.'

Andy stood and grabbed her arm. 'I don't think you can do that.'

'Really?' Her eyes narrowed to slits. 'And why is that? Are you saying that he can roam around freely, and *I* can't? Ha!' She shook his hand off. 'And get your hand off me. You don't have any right.'

'Makedde, I'm sorry. Just calm down. I'll have to check with —'

'No,' she said, her voice steady. 'You tell whoever your boss is these days that I'm getting on a plane out of here. I have a job in Hong Kong and I'm taking it.' She walked over to the chest of drawers and one by one pulled them open, throwing her clothes onto the bed. 'That was my mistake last time. I should have left. I should have just left when I had the chance.'

'What's this about Hong Kong?' he asked, stunned.

'Work, Andy. I have to work for a living like everyone else. I can't just fly around the world spilling my guts at useless multiple-murder trials. And I am not spending the next week here while you guys sit around with your thumbs up your arses hoping for Ed Brown to turn up.'

'Mak, I understand that you are angry,' Andy pleaded, watching her helplessly. 'I understand how you must feel, but we must coordinate things to make sure you are safe. We don't know what he might be up to, or where he is.'

'You *understand how I feel*? Oh, I doubt that very much Andy. I doubt that very much indeed.' She spat the words, and they stung. 'You couldn't coordinate yourselves out of a wet paper bag.'

If Ed was dreaming of any one thing, it would be to abduct Makedde again, as he had shortly before his capture. He was still obsessed with her. Andy knew that. One theory was that Ed saw in Makedde a reincarnation of his mother in her youth. More than any of the innocent young women Ed had murdered, Mak personified for Ed a chance to resolve the abuse he'd received in his traumatic childhood. He was driven to destroy her. She looked passingly like the woman his mother had once been, and that was enough for Ed to target her, just as their choice of high-heeled shoes like his mother's had been enough to make Ed target the others. The police had already turned over Ed's cell and found the newspaper image of Makedde taped to the back of a photo of his mother.

If there had been any belief that his obsession had waned, that find proved otherwise.

It was no surprise that Mak wanted to flee the country.

'Mak, you can't just leave.'

She put her hands on her hips, and gave him what he would describe as a 'fuck-you look'. Her eyes flashed large and then narrowed again. Her sensuous lips were lost in a tight grimace. If she were the violent type, her hands would probably be around his throat. She was right to be disappointed. Perhaps she was even right to want to shoot the messenger.

'Mak, you don't understand —'

'You're right. I don't. And I don't care any more. You can call your superior and tell him, or her, that I have work in Hong Kong, and that's where I will be as of the next flight out of here. And I won't be coming back to Australia except to transfer to that flight home. If they can connect me out of Asia, all the better. You guys had your trial and that's it now. I've done enough. Last time, I stuck around to see that Catherine's killer was caught. Maybe I did the right thing by Catherine, or maybe it was nothing but childish naiveté to think that I could make some difference to the outcome. But this time I have no reason to stick around. None at all.'

He knew what she meant — her words included him.

Angry tears sprang from her eyes. '*We had him*. He was convicted, Andy!' She shoved the chair and it fell on its side. 'Dammit! This can't be real! How could you people let something like this happen?' He put a hand on her shoulder and she relaxed for a brief moment. He moved in to hold her, just wanting to comfort her, but she pulled away.

'I'm really sorry about Jimmy,' she said. 'I know how close you two are.' She pulled her suitcase open, and flung wide the doors of the wardrobe. She grabbed her clothes off the hangers and tossed them into the case.

'Please go,' she said.

He didn't move.

She turned.

'Get out, Andy. *Now*.'

# CHAPTER 28

At one-fifteen there was a light knock on the back door of the house.

The lock turned.

Ed Brown was in the process of raiding the kitchen cupboards, and at the first sound he instinctively ran into the living room and leaped behind a large sofa. His ears were still ringing from the blast. He wondered how much he had not heard.

The door opened and closed.

'Honey? Are you home?'

It was the Prison Lady. Ed debated whether or not to go down and greet her. There was still some slim chance that this was a set-up. He decided to wait for her to climb the stairs and put herself in full view, in case she wasn't alone. He might not be able to hear the footsteps of the police, beneath the constant ringing. When he saw the Prison Lady he would be able to tell by her face if she was fucking him over or not.

'Sweetheart?'

There she was, alone. She appeared at the top of the stairs in her Long Bay uniform. She had a bag of birdseed and a bottle of something wrapped in a brown paper bag.

Ed emerged from behind the sofa.

'Oh, there you are,' she exclaimed excitedly and started towards him.

Ed didn't move. 'Is everything okay? Were you followed?' he asked.

'No, I wasn't followed. I was really careful. But I'll tell you, the police are very upset! There are a lot of guys in hospital. That explosive must have worked a charm.'

It had. The blast was intended as a distraction, as Ed escaped through the back tunnel, but even Ed had been shocked by its intensity. He had been lucky to be clear of the shrapnel.

He could feel himself relax. She was telling the truth. It wasn't a trap. The Prison Lady really liked him. She actually liked helping him.

*In the hospital, huh?* That was perfect.

She put the birdseed and bottle down and rushed towards him.

'Oh, darling!'

Ed had anticipated this would happen. This would be the hardest part. He accepted her embrace, his body squirming at the feel of her against him. He could hardly speak. He hoped she would let go soon.

'I'm so glad we're finally together!' she said, squeezing him excitedly.

'Me too,' was his response. He held his breath again.

'You're speaking in a really loud voice,' she said, and looked at him, puzzled.

It was distressing to see her so close, with no bars to protect him.

He pointed to his ears. 'They're ringing. It's getting better though.'

'Oh, I'm sorry, honey!' Another hug.

'Um, that's Rose,' she said, loosening her grip a little and gesturing to the birdcage that was covered in the centre of the room, her strong arms still, horribly, wrapped around him. 'I hope you like birds.'

*Birds are dirty. Dirty, dirty creatures.*

'That's fine,' he said.

'Oh, sweetheart, we did it!' she cried and hugged him again.

# CHAPTER 29

He tried to put a hand on her shoulder but she pulled away. He wasn't sure what else to do, what to say.

'Angie, you don't have to do all this stuff yourself.'

'No!' she snapped, tears rolling down her face. Angie Cassimatis was at the kitchen counter, sobbing. There was an overcooked moussaka cooling on a tray beside her. 'I can do it,' she said.

Andy felt helpless. He stepped back and watched as she tried to function as if nothing had happened, as if Jimmy was at work late again, and would be home soon.

'Angie, what can I help with?' came a voice from the next room. The TV was on. One of the kids was running around in circles in the living room. He passed the door and did another lap.

'Sorry, sorry,' Angie whispered, scooping up slices of moussaka and trying to arrange them on plates with shaking hands, near hysterical with sobs.

'Don't be sorry, Angie,' Andy offered. 'It's okay. It's alright. You're doing great.'

Angie's mother, Rina, came in and gave her a gentle hug. 'How are we doing here? Angie, sweetheart, you go sit down with your father at the table. I've got it. The salads are ready. Come on.'

'Mum?' came a small impatient voice from the next room. The kids were waiting at the table now for their supper — Jimmy's kids. Andy barely knew them. He'd only met them a few times over the years. He knew Jimmy had not been the best family man. He had left the parenting up to his wife and he'd spent a lot of time at work, much like Andy had when he was married. Cassandra had left Andy, but Angie had stuck by her husband no matter what.

'Where's Pappy?' It was Kris. He had wandered into the kitchen on his own. Although he was the eldest, he still only came up to Andy's hip. He had black curls on his head and long, dark eyelashes. Cleo and Olympia were perhaps too young to even understand why their daddy still wasn't home.

'Kris, come and sit beside your grandpa.' Angie's father came in and carried Kris back into the next room.

Andy had spent much of the day at the hospital, asking questions of the guys who could talk, asking Lewis questions, questions, questions, which had to be written on pieces of paper because he still could barely hear. Jimmy's condition had worsened. It was touch and go, and Andy was getting regular updates. Andy would do whatever he could for Angie, and Jimmy's three young kids.

But first he would find Ed Brown. He would hunt down Ed Brown with a new vengeance and this time when the chance arrived there was no way his bullet would miss its mark.

# CHAPTER 30

Makedde woke on Sunday morning in a small suite in a boutique hotel in the exclusive harbourside suburb of Double Bay. She had moved from the Hyde Park Plaza in the city to the Sir Stamford, courtesy of the Crown, and had been placed under police protection. Since booking in, she had not left her floor of the hotel, or even ventured close enough to the elevator to consider it.

The hotel room was bright from a determined ray of sunshine sneaking through a gap in the heavy curtains. Waking had been inescapable, though she needed more rest. She felt heavy-headed and slightly depressed. Through her grogginess, Mak recalled having tossed and turned for the first half of the night. She had probably slept a solid four hours in the end. She had briefly considered sleeping tablets, and how she might get her hands on some.

*Ah, a new day in Australia with Ed Brown.*

She tried to find the humour in the thought, but failed.

Stiff white sheets were pulled up around her chin, and she pushed them down to look around her. She noticed that the sheets had come free from the corners of the bed, probably from her kicking out in a dream. Her glass of water had fallen on the floor, the carpet already dry around it. The TV table was pulled over to the foot of the bed, where she had left it after anxiously watching in-room movies the night before. There was an empty mini-bar bottle of Baileys on the side table, and beside it a half-eaten packet of salted cashews. Mak's eyes moved to the pen-and-ink sketches in ornate, old-fashioned frames that hung along the bedroom walls. The suite was a painted chalky midnight blue, and furnished with European-style antiques. She had noticed some Norman Lindsay drawings in the lobby. Makedde would have enjoyed a place like this under different circumstances. As it was, it felt like jail.

'Good morning,' she called out, wondering if anyone would reply.

'G'day,' came a deep male voice from the next room.

'Morning. Everything okay?' It was the female officer now, something Sykes was her name. *Alison? Anne?*

'Yup, I'm fine,' Mak called back.

The officers were doing security duty in her suite. They'd been at their post all night, sitting in the living area near the front door, giving the bellboys a fright whenever Mak ordered room service. She didn't envy them, though she supposed there were worse places for guard detail than a Double Bay hotel. At nine o'clock they would finish their shift, and another couple of complete strangers would be hanging around her. Whether Mak liked it or not, for her own safety she would have security covering her every movement until she left the country for Hong Kong. The first available flight out was that evening, and she would be on it.

*Only a few more hours and I am out of here, never, ever to return.*

Mak's father, Les, had been positively incensed when news of Ed's escape had reached him, and was threatening to land in Sydney, advanced gastric ulcer and all, with his own shit-stirring enquiry. Mak thought it would be a pointless exercise now that the horse had bolted. She would wait out the hours cocooned in the hotel until her flight, with nothing but the company of her police escorts. Evidently they had been briefed to stay out of her way, but not to let her go anywhere unless it was absolutely necessary.

'Um, Miss Vanderwall?' It was the woman's voice.

'Yeah?'

'Are you up?'

'I could be.' She rolled out of bed and adjusted her T-shirt and boxer shorts. They'd remained favourites long after their original owner had fallen out of Mak's good books. A hole was widening in one of the boxer's worn seams.

'There is a message here from Detective Flynn. It says he would like you to call him as soon as you are up.'

'Hmmm. Okay.' Her heart tightened in her chest.

'Would you like me to get him on the phone for you?' the woman asked.

'No . . . hang on. Just give me a moment first.'

*Great. Security and social coordinators all in one. Perhaps they'll set us up on a nice date inside some barbed wire fencing.*

Mak brushed her teeth and threw a robe on over her bedclothes. Barefaced and wild of hair, she marched across the bedroom and presented herself in the lounge area where she found her two officers variously sprawled over a chair and a couch near the coffee table, reading the newspaper. Sykes nodded hello. The male officer's eyes widened at the sight of Mak.

'Good morning. Yes, I know ... glamorous, eh?' Mak's words were heavy with sarcasm. She turned her attention to Sykes. 'I guess I'll give Detective Flynn a call now. To his mobile?'

Mak closed the intersecting door and called Andy from the bedroom phone. It felt disturbingly intimate to sit on the bed and talk to him, and it brought to mind their long phone calls of times past. Their attempt at a long-distance relationship had failed miserably. In reality, Mak could not abandon her university studies and her dream of setting up a psych practice in Vancouver, and Andy could not be expected to give up his job and consider a future in law enforcement with the Canadian police. Their situation was confusing, an emotional roller-coaster, unlucky, unworkable ...

Two rings. 'Flynn,' was his none-too-friendly answer.

'Vanderwall,' she said in return.

'Oh, Mak! You called.'

'Hi, how are you?' she asked.

'Ah ... okay.'

Impenetrable.

'How's Jimmy doing?' Mak asked. 'Any news?'

'Well he can't speak and he can't eat and he can't feel one side of his body, but he's alive.'

'How are you coping?'

'Me? Fine.'

That was hardly true, she was sure. 'Would you like to meet up today?' she asked. 'Um ... just, you know, it might be good to see each other before I leave tonight.'

'Yes, I'd like that.'

'Well, I'll be here at the hotel all day, I'm guessing. Not like I have many other options. Everywhere I go I'm a table of three.'

# CHAPTER 31

Ed Brown pulled another drawer open. Scissors, tape, ribbons, business cards, tacks and dust. The desk was filled with junk.

*Come on . . . come on . . .*

He was growing impatient. Ed had already rummaged through most of the house in search of the Prison Lady's bank details and PIN. He couldn't find anything like that. It was almost as if she didn't live there at all. No documents, nothing. He spotted a filing cabinet and pulled the top drawer open. It was empty. Nothing but a paper clip mangled at the bottom.

*Next drawer, nothing.*

The sound of a car in the drive made him jump to his feet. Ed quickly shut the cabinet drawer and sprinted up the stairs as fast as he could. He heard the back door unlock just as he made it down the hall and reached his bedroom.

'Honey, I'm home!' came the voice from downstairs.

Ed didn't respond, but crawled into bed and pulled the sheet up to his chin. He would have to try again later, and if he did not succeed, he would have to get the Prison Lady to an ATM and make her take the money out herself. Once he had her money he could leave. Once he had her money he could get started on his plan. It had been a long wait. He had his freedom. He was already halfway there.

'Sweetheart?'

He could hear her coming down the hall. He lay still with his eyes closed, pretending to be asleep. Heavy sickly odours crowded in on him. It was even worse than it was the day before. Before she left for her midnight shift she had put more of those hideous potpourri bags and ceramic knick-knacks in the shape of puppy dogs and bunnies in his room. He could see them on top of the bureau.

*Just a little longer.*

He heard her footsteps as she came to the door, saw that he was asleep and left. He detected sounds from the kitchen, then, 'Sweetheart . . .'

She sidled through the bedroom door, grinning with her awful, lipless bird-mouth and carrying a breakfast tray with a cup of coffee and some toast and Vegemite. He yawned and stretched and pretended to be tired.

'Hello sleepyhead.' She minced over and kissed him on the forehead. He wanted to recoil, but he couldn't afford to, yet. He needed to get her to an automatic teller first. He just needed a bit more time. He could clean his forehead later, when she wasn't looking. Ed only needed to keep her alive for another day at the most, until he got some money, and got his plan together. He knew this was his best bet for the moment. His mother's place would be crawling with police, making it impossible to go back. That upset him. And worse, his possessions wouldn't be there waiting for him. None of the ones he coveted, anyway. The police had taken them as evidence.

*My girls.*

The police had taken his freedom and his well-earned trophies. But now he would get his own back. They'd see. Andy Flynn would see.

'And how is my little lovebird? Did you sleep well?' the Prison Lady asked.

'I slept very well, sweetheart. You look so beautiful today.' He tried his best to look at her and smile when he said it.

She blushed, her saggy jowls turning rosy. She had gone to great lengths to please him with her appearance, he could tell. She was wearing even more make-up than the day before. He had not noticed any make-up on her when she was at Long Bay, but her thin, downturned lips were painted with coral lipstick now. Her small, black eyes were gaudy with blue eyeshadow. He hoped she hadn't been wearing all that at work. Someone might notice.

'Oh, you are so kind,' she simpered.

He managed a smile. 'Sweetheart, thank you so much for everything you have done. You did so well. And all this,' he pointed to the fussy ornaments and scented gewgaws, 'you've made it very comfortable for me here.'

'You like it? Oh, thank you!'

'Oh yes, but I'm afraid I'm allergic to perfume,' he lied. 'I think I smell some lavender? My nose is starting to ...' he coughed once for effect, 'clog up.'

'Oh no!' she cried, embarrassed. 'I'm so sorry, Ed! I'll get rid of it right away.'

'That's okay, honey,' he reassured her. 'How could you know? I'm afraid I just can't handle perfume.'

She was already running around the room as he spoke, collecting the little ceramic animals and some frilly jars filled with scented candle wax. He watched her with distaste. She wore jeans high on her waist, with a tucked-in flower-print top in pastel colours. She was a stocky, fit woman. Not fat. She would have to be strong for her job, he supposed. Her hair was wiry and brown, with a fringe that hung in her small eyes. He found her face severe and mannish.

Suzie had already bundled up the most offending items when she spotted more potpourri and grabbed that too, then scurried out the door.

*When will I kill her?* he wondered. *And where?* He could worry about that once he had some money from her. She would be easily taken care of after that. She was only a woman, albeit a physically strong one, and she was eating out of the palm of his hand.

She came back into the bedroom, red-faced.

'Thank you so much, darling. I'm sorry about that,' Ed said.

'Oh, no. *I'm* sorry,' she insisted.

'Perhaps now I could have some disinfectant to —' he began.

'Oh, of course!' She ran out of the room, returning quickly with an aerosol can. She sprayed it everywhere, until the room was gloriously foggy.

He felt himself relax. He could clean the germs some more later. But for now, he felt better.

'Do you really like the house?' she asked excitedly, through the tea-tree scented mist, his favourite. They had used tea-tree disinfectant at the morgue where he used to work.

'Yes, I do,' he replied.

*It will do for now.*

'It's the perfect love nest, isn't it?' she said.

'Yes, it is. I'm sorry I've been so tired. I haven't been very good company,' he said.

'Oh sweetheart, you've had a stressful time. You can just relax now. I'll take good care of you. We have all the time in the world.'

'Come over here and sit on the edge of the bed,' he said. He hated having her close, but he would have to deal with it for now. She had made arrangements for them to sleep in separate bedrooms, for which he was privately grateful. But there were things he needed to know. She came over to the bed, beaming. *The disinfectant will make her clean*, he thought.

'Have you heard anything from the police?' Ed asked.

'Oh, no. Don't worry.' She switched out of her ridiculous girlie behaviour and became serious, like she had been at first when they were back at Long Bay. 'Today I was questioned about whether we saw anything out of the ordinary at the correctional facility, but I was prepared. They don't suspect a thing. It was all routine stuff. It will be fine. There is nothing that can link me to what happened.'

He nodded, partially reassured. It probably bought him a couple of days before things got hot, maybe even longer. The police would be combing the airports, the borders, and any place he had frequented in the past.

'Will they come here to question you?' he asked.

'Oh no, I don't even live here. They might question me again at work, maybe. But I have tomorrow off.'

Ed perked up. 'You don't live here?' he asked, puzzled.

'It ... um ...' She seemed a little embarrassed. 'It belonged to a deceased family member,' she explained.

'Oh.' It was her mother's house, he guessed. That made sense, given all the frilly cushions and knick-knacks.

'I come here on my days off and enjoy it, but no one

knows about it. No one comes here. It's a perfect hideaway for us, you see. It's all ours.'

She was keeping something from him.

'Oh, good,' he said, unsure how much he could push her on the subject so soon in the game. Would it even matter? He only needed one more day. 'So you are absolutely sure that no one will be coming here? No friends of yours, or family?' He had asked before, but he needed to be certain.

'I promise, sweetheart. We'll be free here.'

He smiled for her, feigning excitement, but when she came in for a kiss, he recoiled. The Prison Lady put her lips against his and left a big, wet mark. When she left the room to make him scrambled eggs, Ed ran to the bathroom and washed his face with soap and water until it was red from scrubbing. Her lipstick tasted like rancid cooking oil.

# CHAPTER 32

Makedde and Andy met in the small third-floor lobby area of the Sir Stamford late on Sunday afternoon. It had been just over twenty-four hours since Ed Brown's escape.

Mak could see Andy's tall figure as she walked down the hallway from her room. He had not yet spotted her, so she was afforded a moment to observe him and prepare herself to face him. He wore his usual blue jeans and black leather jacket, just as he had on their first dates together. His cheeks appeared more hollow than usual, though, his chin dark with stubble. Just like herself, he clearly had not slept. The effect of his impressive height was diminished by his hunched shoulders, slumped forward as if they carried the weight of the world. *Just like me*, she thought. Though she tried to deny it to herself, Makedde's eyes took in the sight of him hungrily. It was probably the familiar face, or the break from boredom in the hotel, she reasoned. Or the empathy she felt for his anxiety about Jimmy. Nothing more. She couldn't be in love. It wouldn't be good for her if she was. After all, she was preparing herself never to see him again.

'Hi Andy.' His head turned at the sound of her voice. 'Thanks for coming. How are you doing?' she asked.

'Yeah, fine.'

They shared a moment of awkwardness in their greeting. Should they embrace? Shake hands? Kiss on the cheek like Europeans? As it was, they nodded at each other and avoided physical contact.

'There's a nice sitting area over there,' Mak suggested, pointing to a cosy side room. 'They can bring drinks for us and I'm sure we'd be left alone.'

'Sounds good.'

They made their way over, and after another brief moment of uncertainty, found seats opposite one another. In seconds a waiter appeared to take their orders. Mak asked for a latte and Andy copied her request. The occasion seemed to call for something stiffer, but it was barely noon.

'So this is where they have you now,' Andy said, looking around. 'It's sure tucked away. How was your stay last night?'

'Your special guest prisoner was just fine.'

'Special guest prisoner?' he said. 'Yes, I think they have that written on your file.'

'VIP SGP,' she said.

Andy laughed briefly, but silence followed close behind. They couldn't make small talk forever.

'How's Angie?'

Andy shook his head sadly. For the moment he didn't seem able to respond.

'Jimmy is a good guy,' Mak offered. 'Angie seems like a great lady, too. She's strong.'

'Yeah, a good Greek Orthodox family unit. They were going to try for a fourth.' Andy frowned. 'Ed Brown has seriously injured a number of police officers, Mak; that's big. And if someone dies … Not that what he's already done wasn't bad enough, but …'

To an outsider it might have seemed an insensitive statement to make in front of Mak, who had already lost her best friend, Catherine, to the man, as well as being assaulted herself, but Mak knew what Andy meant. By escaping custody and seriously injuring police officers, Ed Brown had taken it one step further. The police protected their own. It was an understood thing. Everyone on the police force would be gunning for him now.

'I don't think the boss knows quite what to do with me,' Andy admitted. 'Now that Ed is out, the feeling is that they need me. I caught him last time. But now with Jimmy as he is, they can't even *let* me work until I go through the whole procedure of critical incident counselling and an evaluation to make sure I'm "stable", as they put it. I'm getting evaluated tomorrow. Can you believe it? I should be combing the streets for him right now and they won't let me work. That was the problem in the first place. If they'd only bloody let me do my job this might never have happened.'

'I understand how you must be feeling. But there's a reason for those protocols. You're not immune to grief, Andy, no one is. I'm sure they have everyone available on the case. You can take one day away from it. Ed is not solely your responsibility.' Mak worried that Jimmy's state would put Andy straight on the bottle again. That was probably what his superiors were worried about too.

'Well, don't you just sound like the shrink now?' he quipped.

That stung. She supposed he was joking, but the words hurt. She was only trying to be a friend.

'Can we talk about something else?' he said.

That was fine by Mak. 'I actually realised this morning that we haven't talked about much of anything at all, in fact. We've barely spoken since I've been here.' The incident on the rocks at Bondi Beach, though intimate, didn't involve much chitchat. Nor did their water conservation in the shower. 'I'm sure what you *really* want to do right now is talk about us. 'Now *there's* a light bit of conversation.' She laughed.

'I feel bad about what happened the other day.'

'With Carol?' Mak asked.

'It wasn't what it looked like, you know.'

'It's okay, you don't have to explain.'

'I *do* have to explain if you don't believe me, Mak.'

'I believe you, Andy. That's not an issue.'

'It's not?'

'I've always believed you.' The thing with Carol didn't matter. What mattered was that theirs was an untenable liaison. It could never last. What could she say to him? That she thought they ought to jump in the sack together, only to be separated by the continents again in a few more hours? 'It doesn't matter. We've made too much of a big deal about it already.'

The waiter came with their lattes, served in tall glasses with long spoons. Mak emptied a packet of sugar into hers, and spooned it up like a dessert.

'So what do you think of my posse?' she asked.

The officers of the day were sitting in the breakfast area near the elevators across the lobby. Although they were in plain clothes, they were conspicuous by their 'alert-idleness' — reading the paper with their eyes elsewhere, backs too straight, looking a little too awake. Mak had noticed that they were watching her and Andy with interest. Perhaps they knew something about the past they had shared. She supposed everyone knew.

'Yeah, I spotted them.'

'Recognise them?'

'No,' he said. 'They're not detectives. They've been alright with you, I hope?'

'I couldn't say yet. I've only had those two since nine this morning.' She leaned towards him and lowered her voice. 'So do you really think Ed would bother coming after me? It would be a bit risky for him, wouldn't it?'

Andy didn't say anything at first and Mak waited for an answer. She went to take a sip of her latte, but her stomach had begun freezing up at the thought of Ed.

*Will he really come after me?*

'Mak, I don't think we should take any chances,' Andy told her. 'I'm glad we have protection for you while you're here. Risk and rationale have little to do with how someone like Ed Brown operates. The whole time he was in remand they kept his cell pretty spartan, but when they turned it over the other day they found a newspaper photo of you taped to the back of a picture of his mother. That's not good. He would have had to go to some lengths to hide it, too.'

The base of Makedde's skull began to ache. *He had a photo of me.* Her toe began to tingle. It soon became a full-blown itch.

'Right,' she said in a dull voice.

'I wasn't sure if I should tell you that, but I think it's best that you know everything. Unfortunately, he doesn't seem to have forgotten about you. I thought you should know.'

*Jesus. He is going to try to come after me. He really is.*

'Mak, I . . .' He trailed off. 'I'll be sad to see you go tonight.'

'I know, Andy, but I think we both agree that it's best.'

He took her statement in, and said nothing. She wanted him to say something, anything. She realised that some part of her wanted him to protest. But he remained silent.

'I had a good time, Andy,' she said, holding back her emotions.

'Me too,' he said.

It really was over. That was it.

# CHAPTER 33

Lisa Milgate was in a foul mood.

In her own mind, she had long since reverted to her maiden name. Inconveniently, however, she was still technically Lisa Harpin, though not for much longer. Her soon-to-be ex-husband had not returned any of her recent phone calls, and now she had to resort to knocking on his door. His lack of respect for her time infuriated her. Did Ben think she had nothing better to do than chase him around?

*This is probably some lame attempt to rekindle our relationship,* Lisa thought as she parked her new baby-blue Jaguar in the street — a gift from Heinrich, complete with custom paint job. She stepped out of the car and squinted narrowly at the house that was once their marital home. The yard looked unkempt. Ben had obviously not cut the lawn recently. *The neighbours would be unhappy with him,* she thought. There were certain standards that must be kept.

*He knows I'll come knocking. He'll be loving this. The arsehole.*

Lisa wanted her divorce. Now. And she wasn't going to take any more of Ben's procrastination. It had been just over a year since she had moved out and moved on, and now she wanted to make it legal. She stormed up the driveway to the front door with her fists clenched. The familiar doorbell chimed through the house. Lisa waited impatiently for the sound of Ben's footsteps. She thought she heard something stir upstairs.

*Come on, hurry up.*

She pressed the bell again and anticipated his presence at the door, probably wearing a filthy T-shirt and jogging pants, looking as if he hadn't left the house in days. She stood ready with her hands on her hips, chest out. Her new car was parked directly across the lawn so he couldn't possibly miss it. He would take one look and know how beyond him she was. Success is the best revenge. He couldn't argue with that.

Lisa was distinctly uninterested in having any discussions with Ben about saving their marriage, or about the prospect of marriage counselling, which is what he kept asking for. He'd fucked around on her and the time for negotiation was over. She was with Heinrich now, and that was that. Heinrich, who among other positive characteristics had a job, for starters.

She leaned on the doorbell.

No answer.

*This is bullshit. He's in there. I heard him. He's in there sitting on his damn couch in front of the damn television drinking a damn beer and ignoring me.*

Lisa tossed back her hair, set her mouth with grim determination and laid into the door with the palms of both hands.

'Open up!'

★  ★  ★

'Who is that woman? What does she want?' Ed Brown demanded, holding the Prison Lady tight by the arm and squeezing fiercely. He had her on her knees, frozen with fear. The two were in the living room near the closed curtains, being as quiet and still as possible until the intruder went away. Ed pulled the curtains aside a fraction and peered out at the stranger, not letting go of Suzie's arm. The woman was not budging.

'Who is this person?' he whispered again, angrily.

With the Prison Lady kneeling on the carpet in pathetic, numb silence, the strange woman continued to drum on the front door and yell. Was she a neighbour? A friend of the Prison Lady? Would she bring the police? Was *she* a plainclothes police officer herself?

'Ben, open up!' the woman shouted, and rang the doorbell several times in quick succession.

*Ben? Who is Ben?*

'Ed, sweetheart, just calm down,' the Prison Lady began in a whisper.

Ed looked down at her impassively. Pleading on her knees as she was, she looked like she was praying to Jesus, as if he, Ed Brown, were the Saviour himself. It was almost enough to make him laugh out loud.

'I can explain ...'

'Dammit, I know you're in there!' came the screeching voice outside the front door.

'Who is she?' Ed demanded with another hot flash of rage. With one mighty shove he pushed the Prison Lady to the ground until her face was squished into the carpet.

'It's okay, honey ... just relax. I'll explain everything, I promise,' she managed to say in a voice muffled by the carpet. 'Don't look out the window again or she might see you.'

Ed let go of her and stood rigid next to the closed curtains. He wanted to peek out again and see if the police were surrounding the house. But maybe she was right. Someone might see the curtains move. He turned towards the entrance to the kitchen and spotted the knife rack. He could take one of those and put it to the Prison Lady's throat. He could use her as a hostage if the police stormed in.

'It's okay . . . It's okay . . .' the Prison Lady mumbled, still on her knees.

He ignored her and listened for movement outside. After a few tense minutes, the knocking finally stopped.

Ed heard heels click on the driveway. He peered through a crack in the curtains and saw the woman get into the shiny blue sports car, slam the door and drive away. Relief. Things were quiet again. The emergency had passed. For the moment, at least.

Ed paced in circles in the living room, trying to calm himself and decide what to do. Ed did not like surprises. He did not deal well with surprises. When he did anything, he planned it carefully. Everything had to be perfect. Organised. The last time he had been surprised it was by Andy Flynn and his detective partner when he had been alone with Makedde, and that surprise had led to his arrest. The deep, jagged scar on his shoulder was testament to the bullet that had brought him down, but not killed him. No, he did not like surprises at all.

Ed had never before been at the mercy of someone else in a situation like this, except for his mother. His head was full of murder now. He imagined grabbing the Prison Lady and gutting her with one of the kitchen knives. He'd spotted a hefty butcher's blade that would be suitable for that purpose. He could gut her, grab whatever valuables he could carry and speed off in the car. Then there would be no more surprises or unanswered questions. No more of this ugly woman with her awful kisses and dirty mouth. It would all be up to him again. He could be out of the city in an hour with a carload of things to pawn. The main problem was that if he killed her now, the hope of getting a decent amount was gone. The money he got for what he sold would quickly dry up, he knew, and getting a job at the moment was not an option. That simple reality stopped him. He'd waited this long. Killing her now was not in his plan. He had to calm himself and think.

*Be nice to her. You still need her money. Don't kill her yet. Just find out who that was and how much time you have to get out.*

'Sweetheart, don't worry. That was nothing ...' the Prison Lady was saying, still trying to placate him. Noticing that he was calming down, she rose slowly from her knees, apologetic. 'Darling, I'm so sorry. I understand you must be scared. Just trust me. There is nothing to worry about. I can explain,' she said.

Now Ed was calm enough to talk and to hear her explanation. He tried his best to be civil for the sake of the money. 'Oh, darling,' he said, '*I'm* sorry for getting angry. I guess I'm just so worried about the police. I'm sorry if I hurt you.'

'It's okay, honey. I understand!' She rushed to him and squeezed his hand. She seemed surprisingly eager to forgive his temper, and grateful that he was being kind to her again. Ed had not seen this sort of behaviour before. Not towards him, anyway.

'Let's sit down and you can tell me why someone was at the door,' he said gently.

They walked to the couch holding hands. Her skin felt greasy and he looked forward to washing as soon as he decently could. Ed was still on edge, but his panic was gradually fading. The sweat had dried on his brow. His head was quiet again and he could think rationally. He sat beside the Prison Lady and let her speak.

'Well, I . . . I wanted this lovely home for us. A perfect love nest,' she began.

'Yes, darling. But we can't have people knocking on the door.'

'I know, I know . . . but, what I am trying to tell you is that this house was my brother's before you came, you see.'

'Your brother's?'

'Yes, Ben. Ben is my brother. The deceased family member I was talking about. That was his wife, Lisa, at the door. But this isn't her house. She left him. It's Ben's . . . This is where I must make a confession. I should have told you before, I guess, but I didn't want to burden you. I hope you're not angry with me.'

'Just tell me what it is. How could I be angry with you?' He stroked her ugly face with the same hand she had already dirtied with her sweaty palm. 'You, the woman who believed in me? The woman who saved me?'

She smiled with thin lips. Now she seemed ready to tell him.

'I had to get rid of my brother so we could stay here,' the Prison Lady said.

*What was she saying: 'get rid of'?*

'Sweetheart,' he said. 'I understand. You just did what you had to do, right?'

'Yes.'

'That's okay, darling. I'm proud of you.'

'Really?'

'Yes. Where is your brother now?' he asked her gently.

'He's in the freezer downstairs.'

★   ★   ★

Suzie Harpin took Ed Brown by the hand. He was her first boyfriend in two decades and she already knew that he was the love of her life. Ed was the man she had waited for and was destined to be with. He was the man she would marry. And that was why she knew he would understand what she had done.

They descended into the basement of the house Suzie had made theirs. She did her best to explain it all to him, and he had seemed very understanding so far. Now all that was left was to show him. He had insisted that he wanted to see.

*I had to do it for us, you see. So we could be together . . .*

Suzie really hoped he wouldn't be mad with her. They just had to get through these first few days, and then everything would be wonderful for them. She just had to explain everything and he would appreciate how much she had sacrificed for him. Then they could live together like Brooke and Ridge without anyone getting in the way. Not Ben and his bitch of an estranged wife. Not the police. Not anyone.

'Sweetheart,' Ed said as they walked down the stairs, 'you know we have to share everything now.' He squeezed her hand gently.

She nodded. He was right. She was so glad that he understood.

Ed, her boyfriend, had lost his temper. She had to accept that. It had been scary and Suzie had not liked it at all. It wasn't right for him to push her down like that and she had thought momentarily of retaliating. Suzie had imagined hitting Ed with something hard until she could overpower him, and then locking him in the bedroom until he apologised. But she was glad she hadn't done any of those things. After some calm consideration she had realised that those kinds of little hiccups were to be expected. Even the world's greatest romances sometimes got off to a rocky start. Ed had spent over a year and a half in a cell on his own at Long Bay. That was a lot of time, and Suzie knew first-hand that it could be a harsh and loveless place. It would take some time for him to feel safe again and to trust another person after all he had been through. That was okay. Suzie would show him how safe and loved he was. She would show him, and then things like what happened when Lisa was banging on the door would never happen again. She had to allow for a period of adjustment. That was only fair.

But first she had to show him what she had done.

'Sweetheart, please don't be upset with me,' she repeated as they reached the bottom of the stairs.

'How could I be upset with you? You saved me, darling. You are the love of my life.'

Suzie smiled. Ed was just like Ridge Forrester sometimes. So romantic. So forgiving and understanding. She had to be understanding, too, she reminded herself. She had to overlook any little temper flares he might have in the beginning. That was a natural, normal part of any relationship. Just look at Ridge and the time he and Bridget had kissed. Ridge and Brooke were able to get past that little indiscretion, and have a happy, romance-filled marriage. It was not Ed's fault that he got nervous or scared or paranoid or angry. It was not his fault if he was sometimes taken off guard. He was only human.

They reached the internal garage door. Suzie opened it and switched the light on. The fluorescent tubes flickered on with a hum, the air chilly and a bit dusty. Suzie was wearing little lacy socks that she had bought especially to look pretty around the house, and the cold of the concrete seeped through the thin fabric to the soles of her feet. She shivered.

'That's the freezer there,' she said, pointing. 'I'm sorry about the mess. I had to make room to fit him in.' There were still a couple of wet spots on the floor.

Ed looked at the floor and frowned. Now Suzie felt bad that she hadn't mopped it up. She was new at all this domesticity and it didn't come naturally. She just never imagined that she would take him down there. Not so soon, anyway. She would have cleaned it up perfectly and mopped up every last drop of water if she had known. He was so tidy himself.

Ed started towards the freezer, walking around the water on the concrete floor, as one walks around cockroaches or dead rats.

'So, ahh, your brother is in here?' he said, gesturing to the freezer.

She nodded.

The freezer was about a metre and a half long, and deep enough that it came up to Suzie's waist. Suzie stepped up to it, curled her fingers under the top and lifted. The suction let go with a tiny *fwaap*.

'Just understand that I did this for us,' she said. 'I had to.'

'I know, honey. You did what you had to do. I'm proud of you,' he said.

*He loves me. He really loves me.*

Now Suzie and Ed peered inside the freezer together, looking down at a variety of frozen foods and ice.

'He's well hidden, you see,' she explained. 'I was careful.' Someone could come in with their groceries and not have any idea that her brother was in there. He was near the bottom and there was a fair lot of food on top, even after the things she had taken out. She began to pull the food out and Ed helped. Eye fillet. Roast. An ice cream container filled with leftovers. Frozen meat pies. White bread. A bag of frozen peas bearing the image of the smiling Jolly Green Giant.

And there, under the Jolly Green Giant, was Ben's head, looking like a fleshy pink-coloured shrink-wrapped bowling ball, and almost as heavy. If you didn't know what you were looking at it might take some time to figure out the contours. Suzie pulled it out and Ed took it out of her hands without saying a word. He turned it this way and that and examined it through the layers of Glad Wrap. He started to unwrap it.

*Please don't let him be mad at me. Please.*

It had been a messy job. Unpleasant to be sure. The bathtub had been a swamp of flesh and blood by the time she was done. But it was nothing that hours of scrubbing had not eventually fixed. In the end, she had managed to fit Ben inside the freezer in only eight pieces — head, torso, upper legs, lower legs and arms.

Ed had unwrapped part of the head, leaving only a layer or two of Glad Wrap around it, making the features of the face — eyelashes, swollen lips and tongue — visible beneath the clear plastic. He was now inspecting the other seven parcels with interest.

To Suzie's delight, he did not seem upset at all.

*He understands.*

*He loves me.*

*I'm so lucky to have found him. He is my perfect lovebird.*

# CHAPTER 34

'I guess this is goodbye,' Makedde said.

Andy nodded.

The porter had taken her bags, and now they stood ill-at-ease in the foyer of her hotel suite. Andy had his hands in his pockets.

*Don't go.*

Mak was wearing a woolly pullover that fell off one smooth, tanned shoulder, and a pair of designer jeans with stylish but unnecessary pockets all over them. They fitted her beautifully, as everything seemed to. She had flat shoes on for once, so she didn't seem as tall as she usually did. Her hands were in her pockets as well, and her head down. Her carry-on bag, an oversized black leather purse, was on the floor by her feet. The door was closed behind them and Andy was painfully aware that this might be their last moment of privacy, perhaps ever. Her flight was at 21.35, less than two and a half hours away. She had to go. If he was going to do something, he had to do it now.

'It's probably for the best,' Mak went on. 'And if it's not for the best, well ...' She offered a close-lipped smile and a tiny, restrained laugh. 'Well, then we will probably end up running into each other again anyway.'

That had seemed the way for them so far, brought together and pulled apart like a couple of rubber bands. Only now he had no conferences to fly to Vancouver for, and she had no more trials in Australia. What possible excuse would he have to see her again?

'Are you sure you don't want me to come with you to the airport?' Andy asked. He wanted very much to be there to see her off. It only seemed right after all they'd been through.

'No Andy, please,' she said. Her voice cracked. 'I think this is best. They've got it all sorted. Karen will be here to pick me up any minute.'

'Mahoney. Okay. Okay, I'll leave it at that.' He didn't push it. He could see she was on the edge as it was.

*But I don't want to leave it at that, Makedde. I really don't.*

'Thank you,' she said.

*Stay with me.*

'Will you let me walk you down to the car?' he asked.

'Of course.' With that, she lifted her bag to her shoulder and moved towards the door. The moment was lost. That was it. She was leaving. He had not kissed her and told her to stay. He had not said the words he had rehearsed in his head. He had done nothing at all.

'Mak,' he said, his voice tight.

'Yes?'

She turned to face him. Her eyes were bright and glittery, on the verge of tears. This was hard for her too, he could see that. She was covering it as best she could but he knew her too well to miss the pain running strong beneath her brave smile.

'Um, I'll get the door for you,' he said weakly, having lost his nerve.

He held the door open for her and she started down the hall.

The two plainclothes police were waiting in the hallway. They did not look at Andy or acknowledge him, but walked one ahead and one behind Mak, leaving him tagging somewhere behind. The procession moved towards the elevator. Mak smiled and nodded to the woman behind the desk in the lobby. 'Thanks for everything,' she said. 'Have a good day.'

Someone pressed the button to call the lift.

*Do something. Anything. Tell her the truth. Tell her you don't want her to go. Tell her you don't think Thursday night was a mistake.*

The elevator arrived and the four stepped into it in silence. Any feeling of intimacy was well and truly gone now. Packed in like sardines, Andy felt like he could not breathe, let alone speak. Mak was leaving. This was it. Should he do something when they got downstairs? Pull her aside? Was there something he could say? But what? Andy knew there was probably nothing he could say to make her stay. Not now. Ed Brown's escape had sealed the fate of their relationship even more effectively than their misunderstandings. Mak was so guarded now that she wouldn't consider giving it another try. As possible as it had seemed that night at Bondi Beach, he now knew that the chances of a happy reunion, with Ed convicted and safely behind bars and both of them able to free themselves from the saga that had come so near to ruining their lives, were all but gone. For those few hours it had seemed within his reach. An illusion.

The elevator stopped on the ground floor. The doors opened. They stepped out on clean white tile. Sliding glass doors opened to the outside world. Andy ran his eyes over the patrons of the Cosmopolitan Café next door, people walking across the dark street, faces inside passing cars. He noticed a man standing in the shadows across the street, leaning against a wall on his own. He seemed to be looking their way.

*Ed*.

Then a woman in a long coat approached the man, and he lifted her off the ground and embraced her. Holding hands affectionately, they set off up the street, passing under a lamppost. He saw the man's face. It was not Ed Brown. But that did not mean that he wasn't out there watching, somewhere. He was dangerously cunning, always finding ways to get what he wanted — information, access. Andy automatically did another scan of the street. It looked clear.

Mak and her entourage had reached the unmarked car. Senior Constable Mahoney was behind the wheel. She nodded when she saw him. 'Hey, Andy.' She stepped out and leaned against the door. The porter had Mak's bags ready and loaded them into the car. He opened the passenger-side door for her and waited for her to get in.

Mak stepped up to Andy. His heart flew into his throat.

'Goodbye, Andy. Thanks for everything,' she said. The statement could only be a courtesy, nothing more. What could she possibly have to thank him for? 'I hope Jimmy will be okay.' She squeezed his hands affectionately as they hung tensely at his sides.

'Take care of yourself, alright?' she said. 'I'm really glad we had that time together.'

Mak moved forward and hugged him before he could react. His throat felt like it had closed up. Her arms were around him, squeezing him tight, and then she was gone. She slipped into the car and the porter closed the door. Andy backed away in a daze. He had not said anything. Why hadn't he said anything? Karen Mahoney caught his eye. She brought her hand up to her face in the sign of a phone, and mouthed, 'Call you later.' He nodded.

The car pulled away.

Andy didn't wave. He didn't move.

He felt as empty as a drum.

Andy Flynn watched the car disappear down Knox Street, and when it was gone he went in search of some Jack Daniels. He had noticed a bottle shop on the adjoining road. It was still open. He had a long restless night ahead and he could use the company.

# CHAPTER 35

The Prison Lady's hand was still touching his arm. Ed Brown wished she would remove it. He *needed* her to remove it — immediately.

The Prison Lady was growing impatient, that was obvious. Now that there were no bars between them she clearly expected him to propose. She clearly expected affection.

'But sweetheart,' she cooed, 'when do you think we should get married?' She stroked his face, and let her fingers run down his chest.

Those fingers . . . *touching* him.

The Prison Lady wanted sex.

SEX.

She wanted to have sex with him. He knew it. She'd said she was a virgin, but look at her. She was just like the others. All women wanted one thing. They wanted *sex*. Ed was utterly repulsed by the thought of having sex . . . real live messy sex with flowing body fluids and sweat and unclean smells and germs and —

The Prison Lady put her hand on his shoulder again and

Ed pulled away violently, ending up with his back against the wall, panting with real fear.

*No!*

The Prison Lady looked stunned and hurt by his response. Her painted face was screwed up with disappointment, her horrible mouth hanging open limply. 'Darling, don't you want to marry me any more?' she whined, on the verge of tears. 'Did I do badly to get this house for us?' Her eyes were wide, pleading. She was desperate for his reassurance. Ed did not know what to make of the body in the freezer. Had she done that herself? For him? Had she done it on her own?

Ed knew that he could not afford to offend her. He still had to use her to get some money, otherwise this day of waiting would have been for nothing. It was Sunday night and her bank would be open on Monday. If he played his cards right, in less than twelve hours he could have, say, $20 000 in cash. Maybe even more. So far she had followed his every instruction, so why wouldn't she withdraw her savings if he asked? He had made it this far and he only needed to last until the next morning. Killing her now would be wasteful. Simply wasteful. Once he had enough money to live he could discard her and he could find Makedde, wherever she was. He could follow Makedde across the world, to Canada, to Europe, whatever it took. But without the Prison Lady's money he would have to learn to steal, and that would put him at risk of being caught. Ed was not a common thief. He despised thieves.

'Did I do the wrong thing . . . ?'

'No, honey. You did good,' Ed managed to say. When it came right down to it, he couldn't care less about the stiff in the freezer or how it got there. All he cared about was getting out, and getting fast money to live on and to find Makedde.

'Just . . . I want to wait for the perfect moment for us before I propose,' he explained. 'You'll see.'

He only needed to hold her off for a while longer without losing her trust and adoration. That would be hard. He had no experience in these matters. And little patience. Each time she got too close his violent thoughts were deafening. It was difficult to think.

*Think about the money.*

'Darling, I love you.' The Prison Lady stepped close to him. She put her hand on his arm again. Her mouth came dangerously close to his, that greasy lipstick threatening to touch his lips. 'I've been waiting for you for so long. Let's not wait too much longer.'

Ed did not reply. He was occupied in a struggle to quiet his violent thoughts.

*Just kill her now. Just slice her up and leave her here. Take the stereo and go.*

'Don't you love me, darling?'

*Kill her. Slice her throat.*

'Honey . . . ?'

*Think about the money.*

'Sweetheart, yes, of course I love you,' he said, holding back with every ounce of strength he had. 'You are a beautiful woman.' He managed to smile at her, and touch her limp hair with his right hand, which he would need to wash very soon. He had complimented her so much in the prison. What had he said? What were the right words? The words from the television show she liked so much?

The Prison Lady still did not look happy. She sat down on the edge of the bed and pouted with her thin bird-lips. Ed had to think of something. If she kept touching him he would have to kill her, and that would be wasteful.

'You are the only woman for me,' Ed said. 'I want you to be my wife.'

'Oh, Ed!'

'I will propose to you properly when the time is right. Just be patient.'

They'd talked about it in Long Bay. There was a stack of wedding magazines in the living room, crowned with a heart-shaped candleholder. He couldn't have missed them. He only needed to string her along a little bit longer.

'Please be patient. I love you,' he said. 'You are the only one for me.'

The words were coming to him now. He realised that he had successfully averted a terrible problem. His reassurances would keep her off him until he had her money.

Then she could die.

# CHAPTER 36

Andy held the bottle in both hands. Tears streamed freely down his face. A drop landed on the back of one hand and he quickly wiped it away as if it were acid, then stared blankly at the place where the moisture had been. He was shocked by his crying, not quite able to come to terms with it. Andy was not a man who cried. That was one of his late wife's many criticisms of him. Cassandra had more than once accused him of having no emotions.

*And look at me now.*

It wasn't that he didn't have emotions. It's just that emotions didn't help anything. Emotions had no value. How could emotions help when a child lay murdered on the road and there was a crime to solve? How did emotions help when a good detective was in hospital and a sadistic psychopath was walking free?

The sight of the Cassimatis family at the hospital that morning had brought Andy to breaking point. Angie and the kids had a look in their eyes that he had seen before — the lost look of those uncertain about the future, uncertain about their faith and their place in the world. The sight of Jimmy's desk further brought the reality home. All day it had been empty, his mess of papers right where he'd put them before he had left for Long Bay to get Ed Brown. It just seemed wrong. *Unnatural.* What if Jimmy was never coming back? In his own perverse way, Ed had got the better of Andy once more. He had targeted Cassandra Flynn and murdered her and now he had got to Jimmy, too, slowly pulling away the vital parts of Andy's life until the profiler who had hunted him and brought him in was as alone and isolated as the killer himself.

And Ed had come so close to taking Makedde. As long as he was out, she was better off far from Australia. It was only Andy's selfishness that made him wish she had stayed. He should have been able to accept Makedde's departure, but it seemed to compound his loss. When for months he had known she was coming to Sydney for the trial, it had been bearable to wait, to ignore the rift between them. He had let it slide, thinking that there would still be time to make things right. But now she was gone and she had no reason to come back. His chances were spent.

The words he had wanted to say to her, but had not, scrolled through his mind over and over again.

*I love you, Mak. Stay with me.*

'Goddamm it, you didn't say anything!' he cried to the unresponsive ceiling. 'Fool ...'

He had not even waved goodbye.

The truth was, Andy thought Mak would have said no. Why would she stay to be with him? He had nothing to offer her.

*You weren't there for Cassandra. You weren't there for Jimmy. You are a failure, a drunk ...*

His destructive thoughts were deafening, and the apartment he sat in, the swish new bachelor pad bought with his dead wife's earnings, felt more than ever like an empty box. The walls were closing in around him. Caught in the throes of a desperate loneliness and grief that he could not, *would not*, accept for what it was, Andy's every habit made him reach for his phone to talk with his injured and speechless partner, his late wife, his lover, *someone* to take his mind off its destructive course.

There was no one to call. There was no relief.

The only relief he knew was at his fingertips, the bottle waiting quietly to bless him with its mellow numbness — although the comfort would not be without consequence.

*You are being evaluated tomorrow, Andy. If you do this, it's over,* he reminded himself.

He stared at the bottle in his hands. It was the poison and the cure in one. If he gave in, and lost control, his career could be jeopardised for good.

*Perhaps one sip won't hurt?*

# CHAPTER 37

'Do you understand now, darling? Do you see why it's too
dangerous to stay here?'

It was Monday morning, and Ed Brown was buckled into
the passenger seat of the Prison Lady's car, trying his best to
explain the reasons to her. He had strained every last ounce of
his patience to make it through the night and now here they
were on the way to the bank to withdraw the money. It was
the first time he had risked leaving the house since he had
arrived there on Saturday just after his escape. He was going
to get her to withdraw all her money now, and he was
driving with her to the bank to see that she did it. Now that
he had got this far with her, he didn't plan on going back to
that house for any longer than it took to eliminate the
woman and clear out all the valuables. The only way he could
get her to empty her bank account was to say that they were
going to go travelling together. He had hoped she would be
excited by the idea, but she didn't seem happy at all. He
couldn't figure her out. Weren't females supposed to find
travel romantic?

He was frustrated, his patience nearly spent. He wanted to get rid of this woman as soon as possible.

*Think of the money.*

'Darling, don't be upset,' he said. Exercising great control, he managed to put a hand on her knee and squeeze it gently, as he had seen couples do on TV.

*Don't put your hand to your mouth. You must clean it first.*

They waited at a set of traffic lights. The Prison Lady was at the wheel, gripping it tensely, her thin, mean mouth turned down. She was not looking at him. He could tell she was upset.

'We'll just take a little trip until things settle down,' he said, doing his best to cheer her up.

*Kiss her if you must. Do what you have to.*

Ed leaned across the seat and kissed her on the cheek. Her skin was rough, and covered in foul-tasting yellowy make-up. Ed wanted so badly to wipe his mouth that it started to twitch. There were disinfectant wipes in the car within his reach. He wanted to grab one. The sight of the package on the dashboard was very distracting. Ed knew he had to wait till she got out of the car. He couldn't let her see him do it. That would make her even more unhappy.

*Calmly now. Do whatever you have to.*

Finally the light turned green and the Prison Lady drove them through the intersection. Ed was happy that there was little traffic. The fewer people, the fewer witnesses. He spotted the blue signage of an ANZ bank branch clustered among a handful of shops in an outdoor mall. 'Is that it?'

She nodded.

'Pull in here,' he said, pointing to an available spot in the parking area of a convenience store two shops down from the bank. The Prison Lady did as he said. She turned off the engine.

'But why must we go, darling?' she whined. Her face was petulant with disappointment. She wrung her hands in her lap. 'Why can't we stay at the house a bit longer? We could have at least a month there before anyone misses Ben. He never does anything! No one would miss him. And if they did they'd just think he went away for a holiday or something.'

*Oh, just shut up and get the money!*

Ed had never dealt with a woman like this before. He had never had to. Most of his previous interaction with the opposite sex had been limited to his mother, and the girls he had taken off the streets. One female had worked the night shift at the morgue from time to time, but he had managed to stay clear of her. Now Ed had to concentrate hard to think of how to best handle the situation. He thought of the episodes of *The Bold And The Beautiful* that he had studied. For the moment the lines escaped him.

'Ahh, think of that woman who came to the house yesterday,' Ed said in a calm, even tone. 'We can't have that happening again, can we? She could get the neighbours suspicious. She's bound to come back, darling. I'm sure you realise that.'

'Damn Lisa! Damn her! That stupid cunt has ruined everything!' She slammed her fists against the steering wheel, tears springing from her eyes.

Ed had not seen her angry before. It spooked him even more than her confession about what was in the freezer. He couldn't have her make a scene like this. Someone might notice. He didn't know what to do. Why, oh why couldn't he have found her PIN? Ed thought about giving up, taking her home, slicing her up in the garage and giving a search of the house another try. But even if he found her PIN, he might only be able to take out $500 at a time. Or even less. He had to get the Prison Lady into that bank.

Ed put his hand on her knee again, still trying to placate her. He had come with her specifically to make sure she took out all she had. But she didn't seem convinced yet.

*Two minutes. If she doesn't do it in two minutes she's dead.*

'I'm sorry. I'm sorry for my bad language.' She hung her head, appearing to calm herself. 'Oh, sweetheart ... it's just that I wanted so badly for that to be our love nest and now it's all ruined. I dreamed about it for so long. You don't understand. Now you're saying that we can't even stay there!'

'It's okay, honey. We're going to be fine. All I need is *you*,' he said. 'And we can come back to the house when things have quietened down. Just take out as much cash as you can right now so we can travel for a little while. Think of it as our honeymoon. We can't use credit cards because they'll be traced, so we need cash. Just cash. Once things settle down we will come back and I will repay you. We'll be a team, like Bonnie and Clyde.'

*Ninety seconds and she is dead.*

What he said seemed to please her. A broad smile grew across her sagging face. 'Bonnie and Clyde ...' she murmured. She squeezed Ed's hand affectionately, undid her seatbelt and stepped out of the car. He watched her walk into the bank.

Now Ed smiled as well. And it was a genuine smile.

*Come on, do it. Take it all out. Quickly.*

Ed stayed low in the passenger seat. He wore one of the dead guy's baseball caps that he had found in the poolroom downstairs. It was red and white with 'Sydney Swans' written across it, and the brim was long enough that it hid his face fairly well. There were a lot of security cameras near banks and convenience stores. When the police found the Prison Lady dead, they would track her banking transactions and they would eventually look at this footage. But they would not have a clear view of Ed Brown. He would be nothing but a quiet blur of baseball cap. And that would piss off Detective Flynn no end. He would be long gone and Andy Flynn would have failed once more.

# CHAPTER 38

'So, are you on, like, step thirteen?'

'Excuse me?'

Andy Flynn was walking down Victoria Street, Kings Cross with Senior Constable Karen Mahoney. She had insisted on taking him out for breakfast, knowing that he had been placed on forced leave until his evaluation later in the day.

'Your AA thing? Is this the thirteenth step?' Mahoney said. 'The step where you go back on the booze and forget the first twelve?'

'Hey,' he said. *Cocky thing she's become.* 'I'll have you know that I have not fallen off the wagon. I didn't go drinking last night at all.'

'Really?'

'Really.'

But he had been close. Too damn close. After one more horrible, beautiful sip of Jack Daniels the truth had hit home. If he went on a drinking binge, his career was over. Ed Brown was out and Andy needed to catch him. He needed to do it for Jimmy, and for Cassandra and for Mak. He needed to do it for himself. If he went for the comfort of the bottle once more, he would be a write-off, his pride gone forever, and Ed Brown would have won. Andy took the full bottle of whiskey and walked it to the garbage chute near the back stairs of his apartment building, listening with a mix of pain and relief as it plummeted down the metal shaft and shattered into hundreds of pieces in the basement skip. There would be no going back for it now. Or ever.

'Just a word of advice, keep away from your friend the bottle, or you won't be passing muster on anything, much less proving yourself to be emotionally stable and mentally sound. The powers that be are watching you pretty carefully.'

'Thanks for the heads up.' Andy was determined not to fall into his old patterns. It scared him that he had been so close to sabotaging his career, his future, his chances of catching Ed. 'I told Kelley that there is no way he can keep me away from this case, especially now that half our good men are in the hospital. I think he saw the wisdom in my view.' *I hope he did.* 'I don't think he'll be able to afford to say no.'

'I don't think he'll have any reason to, just so long as you don't take off on one of your binges. At this point I think he's just following protocol ...' Her words trailed off.

Andy stopped. 'What?'

'Oh shit. Look.' Karen pointed at the window of the newsagent across the road. Her mouth gaped.

'Bloody hell,' he said, forgetting their conversation.

'Shit, shit, shit ...'

They examined with jaded disappointment — but not disbelief — the headline news of the Monday morning paper displayed in the shop window.

MODEL WITNESS FLEES TO HONG KONG.

'Ah, you've got to be kidding me,' Andy mumbled, and ran a nervous hand across his mouth.

'Well, she looks great anyway,' Mahoney commented, only half seriously. 'Though she does look a bit like she's just seen one of those *Nightmare on Elm Street* movies,' she added. 'Or been in one.'

Makedde was caught in a blurry photograph prior to boarding her flight for Hong Kong. Karen had warned Andy that the press had managed to track them down at the airport, and there had been a bit of a scuffle. Now, looking at the result, Andy's heart bled. She had the appearance of a scared animal caught in the headlights: hair wild, eyes wide with panic, her lips held in a surprised 'oh'. In real life she had never looked so vulnerable, not even when she was laid up in hospital. In that captured frame were all the elements of a glamorous victim.

'Look at me, though. I'm a shocker,' Karen said, tilting her head to one side and frowning.

Half of the young senior constable's face had made it into the shot. She appeared to be yelling obscenities, and her hand was reaching out towards the camera. *It was a shame her hand hadn't made it all the way to the lens*, Andy thought. It was a bloody shame.

Andy reassessed his disappointment in not going to the airport to see Mak onto her plane. If he had been there, his presence would not have gone unnoticed by the press. The headline would have been all about the 'widowed-detective-hero and the model-victim-ex-lover reunited!', or some such garbage. And some photographer's lens, and face, would have probably got itself accidentally broken. Andy didn't need assault charges on top of everything else. Kelley would have been really unhappy then.

Karen made a move towards the door of the newsagency and Andy followed. Inside, he perused the morning's offerings with a dull feeling of grief, as if they documented a significant loss in his life, which in a way they did. It looked as if every newspaper had some mention of Makedde on the front page, be it large or stamp-sized small, and he noticed that the same photo appeared several times. One of the tabloids had blown up the blurry image to cover the entire front page, along with a small mug shot of Ed grinning eerily in black and white. The accompanying article was penned by none other than Patricia Goodacre.

Andy could imagine the water-cooler talk in offices everywhere: 'Oh the poor thing! I can't imagine how she can carry on!' Mak's plight, the police force's apparent ineptitude and the name Ed Brown would be fuelling talkback radio, café gossip and dinner conversation. It was something he knew Mak would hate. In that way, he was glad she was not in Australia to face it.

Karen and Andy each bought a copy of every newspaper, five in total, some from interstate, and headed back onto the street carrying their grim booty.

# CHAPTER 39

Ed's hand reached automatically for the packet of Clean Wipes, snatching it up eagerly for the second time as he waited for the Prison Lady to come out of the bank. He smeared the wet, stinging tissues across his mouth again and again, feeling the relief of cleanliness. Back and forth. *Better. Better now. No germs.* He wiped his hands and discarded the tissue by his feet.

*The small television set,* he thought. *The VCR. The stereo. The cappuccino machine. The two sets of golf clubs. Jewellery? Where does she keep her jewellery?*

Ed wondered about that. Did she have any valuables that he had not found? Maybe she kept them at her own place, wherever that was. Perhaps he should get her to take him there? Or would that be risky? And he also still wondered about something else — the corpse. The Prison Lady's story was hard to believe. Had she been thinking that it would impress him? Ed was not interested in male bodies. Never was. Not when he worked as an attendant at the morgue and not now. Did she think he was gay or something? No, he was fairly sure that this woman couldn't have done that herself, and now it hardly mattered as she would soon be joining the dead guy in the garage anyway.

*Leave her in pieces by the freezer with her freeze-wrapped brother. Flynn will love that. Perhaps I'll leave a note for him? Dear Detective Flynn, I hope you like my surprise . . .*

Something in Ed's peripheral vision caught his attention, something that made his heart leap . . .

It was an image of Makedde's face.

MODEL WITNESS FLEES TO HONG KONG.

Ed did a double take, and leaned forward to take another look. Yes. It was her. At the entrance to the convenience store just ahead of him, just past where the Prison Lady was now walking back towards the car, a series of little metal racks displayed the morning headlines. And there she was, unmistakable on the front page.

*Makedde.*

*Mother.*

*Makedde. Mother. Makedde. Makedde. Makedde.*

She was right there, just outside the shop.

Looking at him.

# CHAPTER 40

Makedde Vanderwall gazed with quiet excitement out of the window at a new and foreign world.

*Hong Kong.*

The nine-hour flight from Sydney had been the red-eye dash, and Mak felt gritty and unrested. But it was a shiny new world outside, and she had already begun taking it in while she stretched her legs and circled her wrists to rid herself of what she called the 'economy cramps'. The remarkably clean and efficient airport express shuttled her towards central Hong Kong at breakneck pace, travelling through a stunning, yet somehow eerie dawn landscape. The city was awash with light morning mist, painting everything in pale watercolour tones. It clung to the expanse of water off the shoreline, and the inland was pierced by grey apartment buildings stretching as far as she could see, like Lego blocks stacked one upon another, and side by side by side by side, each with hundreds of identical square windows and identical square air-conditioning units. Every window held the outlook of another life, yet the only hint of individuality was in the various plants hanging off the tiny sills and in the infinite variety of trousers, shirts and stockings that hung limply from makeshift clotheslines.

Mak began to get a sense of the lives of the seven million residents of the city of Hong Kong. They clearly did not live with the same sense of space that she knew. Everything was big in North America, she reflected: big cars, big houses, big people — but not here. She looked seawards again, and the mist began to clear. The water was speckled with hundreds of fishing trawlers, cargo ships and the occasional traditional Chinese junk, dwarfed by the modern freighters anchored nearby. An even denser city area was visible in the ghostly distance.

Makedde planned to stay in Hong Kong one week, hopefully a prosperous week, before catching a flight home. If everything went well, she might get more work after the Ely Garner show. She would be rooming in the area called Mid Levels in a models' apartment organised by her agency. She would pay her modest rent after Tuesday's catwalk show. That suited her fine. She only hoped there weren't too many other models there. Models' apartments were usually cramped, and sometimes uncomfortable, depending on the personalities present.

Makedde had not travelled to Asia before, because for many years there were limited modelling possibilities for very tall models like herself, and now the prospect of exploring its famed gateway was a welcome escape. It distanced her from all that she wished to forget, took her away from all the death that seemed to stalk her. To every face, she would be a stranger, inconsequential and without scandal. Her eyes would rest on each sight anew, and nothing would remind her of horrors past.

And after a week of being a no-name foreigner Mak would be ready to return to Canada and face the fall-out of what had happened in Sydney. Her father would no doubt still be steaming. She would try to play it down for the sake of his health, but she doubted she could keep anything from him considering his contacts.

*Oh Dad, please try and take it easy . . .*

# CHAPTER 41

'Just promise me you'll try to take it easy.'

Andy stood up immediately, glad to be out of the hot seat.

'Detective Flynn ...' Dr Fox gave him a raised eyebrow when he didn't respond.

'I will. I will take it easy,' he said.

If he had given in the night before, the outcome of the evaluation would have been less than favourable, he knew. After his pre-trial jitters, there was nothing left to drink in the house, not even mouthwash. And he had successfully tossed away the Jack Daniels he'd bought in Double Bay. That had not been easy, nor had resisting the urge to jump in his car and find the nearest bottle shop. But he'd done it. That was something. That was a step. And here he was, clean for his evaluation, and Dr Fox had no reason to believe the alcohol was a problem any more.

'And lay off the booze,' she said. 'You won't have any liver in a few years if you don't cut back.'

He nodded sheepishly.

Dr Louise Fox wasn't bad, for a shrink. She would do the right thing by Andy, he was sure. Now Kelley would have to let him take on the case.

'Promise me you'll keep tabs on yourself. We can't have you disappearing on a drinking binge like you did when your wife —'

'Thank you. I got it.'

'Don't underestimate —'

'I got it, I got it,' he said. 'Thank you, Louise. I appreciate it.'

'No problem,' she said, and shook her head. She waved a hand in his direction. 'Go on, get out of here.'

Andy was relieved. Evaluations and counselling were standard procedure after a critical incident or death, but they were always nerve-racking nonetheless. And if the guys found out somehow that you had to go back for another session you never heard the end of it. Jimmy, for one, had never failed to pester the crap out of anyone seeing the police psychologist, making loony faces and constantly quoting lines from *One Flew Over the Cuckoo's Nest* ... 'If that's what being crazy is, then I'm senseless, out of it, gone-down-the-road, wacko.'

Jimmy.

*Dammit Jimmy.*

The best thing Andy could do was throw himself into his job, and for the moment try to forget about Jimmy and Mak. Having work to focus on was a godsend. After all, what else did he have now apart from work? If he stayed clear-headed and used all he'd trained for, Andy could crack the case, and that's exactly what he intended to do. He was going to hunt Ed down and bring him in. That was it.

★　★　★

Andy hunkered down at his desk and read for the second time the stack of transcripts of Ed Brown's mother being interviewed after her son's escape. Employing what he had learned about statement analysis from his time at the FBI academy at Quantico, Virginia, he went over every word for inconsistencies or unusual phrasing that might reveal that she had been deceptive or was withholding information. So far, he was uninspired. The main things that jumped out from the interview were that Mrs Brown was a woman who hated the police and hated authority, and, most alarmingly, that she was probably more upset that her son was acting without her involvement than she was about the heinous nature of his crimes. But Andy already knew what she was like from the first time he had met her. What he wanted to know now was whether she knew something important that she wasn't telling them. He could not yet be certain.

Assuming that Ed needed an accomplice to plant the homemade bomb that aided in his escape, the conundrum for Andy Flynn was who it could possibly have been. Ed was a distinctly unpopular guy, not a charmer like Bundy or a first-class manipulator like Manson. Ed was smart enough, but socially challenged, and his speech problems and diminutive frame wouldn't have helped in his dealings with others. Andy was sure that Ed Brown had few, if any, old friends to speak of, and he wasn't the type who would be able to make new friends easily. Who would possibly stick their neck out for him? What kind of person could he threaten, pay off or entice to come to his aid? And if his escape was not organised before he went into remand, how were the arrangements made from within the confines of the high-security prison?

So Ed's peculiar relationship with his mother was the focus of Andy's enquiries. Despite evidence of severe neglect in Ed's childhood during Mrs Brown's years as a single mother and drug-affected prostitute, and despite the fact that young Ed may have lit the fire that led to his mother losing her legs, Mrs Brown was probably the closest person to him in the world. The two were strangely co-dependent. She was Andy's prime suspect for helping Ed escape. Though her disability meant that she could not possibly have planted the bomb herself, she might very well have had a hand in its making, and found someone to hide it in Banks Battery. If anyone knew something of Ed's whereabouts, it would have to be her.

Ed Brown and his mother made up one hell of a family unit. Ed had been living at home when he was arrested, and his mum hadn't moved house since, despite the violent Polaroids, fetish magazines, severed toes and scraps of human flesh that had been found in her son's bedroom. Any normal parent would not be able to live in a home where her son had kept victims' body parts and souvenirs of murder and mutilation, let alone sleep at night in close proximity. But Mrs Brown was evidently a unique woman. She seemed unfazed by the nature of her son's crimes and the evidence against him. That would set off alarm bells for any detective. Her apartment was under surveillance twenty-four hours a day now.

Unfortunately, Ed had not yet gone home to his mother.

Andy turned to say something to his partner. 'What was that ...?' He stopped. His throat tightened. It was so damned automatic to expect Jimmy to be there. It was like trying to reach for something and remembering that you didn't have any arms. He leaned back in his chair and closed his eyes.

'Hey, Andy.'

Startled, Andy opened his eyes and found Karen Mahoney standing over him.

'You okay?'

He nodded.

'How was the shrink?' she asked.

'Dr Fox gave me the all clear.'

'I figured as much.'

'And how was Long Bay?' he asked.

'Yeah, good,' she said. 'We reinterviewed all the staff who had contact with Ed. They are adamant that he didn't have any connections with any of the other prisoners. He had been isolated for his own protection from the start. As we thought.'

'Yeah.' Linking Ed to a cellmate who had recently been released was the kind of brilliant lead they had hoped for, but they had already known that the possibility was beyond remote. 'And visits?'

'Records say his mum visited once a fortnight religiously.'

'What about the nose man, uh ... George Fowler, the building superintendent?'

Andy had sensed from the first time he met George Fowler that he was not simply the superintendent of the apartment block where the Browns lived; he was intimately involved with Ed's mother and was very protective of her. Their body language spoke of an illicit affair, despite Fowler's ongoing marriage. That made him a suspect in aiding Ed's escape. How much would he do for Mrs Brown and her son? Fowler had been endowed with an unusually large nose, which had reddened and swelled with drink and age. It now resembled a rotting tomato. Hence his nickname within the task force: Nose Man.

'He usually came with her. Other than them, it was strictly lawyers and shrinks.'

'Popular guy.'

'Tell me about it. We've scrutinised all the prison officers, the records, visits, times, dates … His mum still seems the best suspect. And this Fowler guy.' Mahoney put her hands on her hips and flicked her head to the side to get a red curl out of her eyes. 'Anything juicy in the transcripts?'

'So far, nothing I didn't pick up originally,' Andy said, disappointed.

'What are you looking for again? How does that work?'

'Statement analysis is fairly simple. You're already familiar with body language and interviewing techniques, Mahoney. Statement analysis with transcripts like these allows you to remove the words themselves from all of the other influences in the interview to see if they reveal more than the interviewee intended. In this case, we already know that Mrs Brown is hostile and uncooperative from her previous actions.'

'Yeah, she's a *bee-atch*,' Mahoney said.

He laughed.

'Looking at this statement, I have no doubt that she would not be bothered by guilt if she helped Ed escape custody. She would happily lie if she felt like it. What I'm trying to discover through statement analysis is whether or not that is the case, or if she knows more about his escape than she has told us.'

Mahoney pulled up a chair. 'I know you've told me this stuff before but can you give me an example? What's the pronoun thing again?'

Andy flipped through the statement on his desk. 'So far I have less than I was hoping for. But here's an interesting answer.' He pointed to one of the early pages of the transcript.

'She is asked here whether she would phone the police if her son contacted her, and she says, "We'd do the right thing."'

Mahoney nodded vaguely, unsure of the significance.

Andy explained. 'There are two main things going on here. The first is the use of the pronoun "we". She is not personalising her answer. She says "we" and yet the question was asked of her, and she was not accompanied by anyone else during the interview. She should have said "I". People use "we" when they are trying to distance themselves from what they are saying. The other time people use "we" is when they are feeling kinship with someone, consciously or subconsciously. In cases of false rape allegations, for instance, investigators may become suspicious if the alleged victim refers to herself and the alleged rapist as "we". An actual victim would not refer to her attacker using such an intimate pronoun.'

Mahoney nodded, impressed.

'In this case,' he pointed to the page, 'it indicates that Mrs Brown probably thinks of George Fowler as a partner of sorts, and she is trying to fob her answer off on him by saying "we" even when he isn't there. The other important thing here is that she did not in fact answer the question. She says, "We'd do the right thing," but what is the right thing in her mind? For us to be confident that she would call us if her son contacted her, she would have to have answered either with a simple "yes", or said something like, "I will tell you if I hear anything from him."'

Karen ventured an opinion. 'Her saying "we" could mean that she and Nose Man have somehow collaborated with respect to Ed already? That when it comes to her son, she and Nose Man stand together?'

'You're on the right track, Mahoney. I can give you another classic example that you've probably heard before.

When pressed in an interview, someone might say, "I am trying to be as honest as possible." That sounds like they are cooperating, doesn't it?' Andy waited for Karen to jump in with reasons of why it didn't. 'What do you think?' he asked.

'What do I think about that statement? Well, um . . .'

'Well, for starters,' Andy explained, 'the person who says that is not saying that they are being honest. They are saying that they are "trying" to be honest. The "trying" implies failure. The "as possible" implies a limitation to the amount of honesty they are willing to give.'

Karen nodded.

'And that, Mahoney, is the end of today's lesson. Now tell me something. There's got to be some new lead that you picked up at Long Bay while I was busy having my head shrunk. Come on, what were your impressions?' he pressed.

She bit her lip and rolled her eyes skywards as she tried to recall the details. 'No one had anything much new to say. They all seem pretty relieved that the responsibility of the escape doesn't lie on their own shoulders, frankly. I can't say as I blame them.'

'What about the ones who had the most contact with him? They had to have opinions. Did they see anything coming? Were they suspicious that his mother was up to something? Was he up at odd hours planning?'

They'd found very little in his cell, which was a disappointment. No bomb-making plans, no nothing. Ed had been careful. Too damned careful.

Mahoney did some mugging again. She chewed the inside of her lip. 'Well, actually, something that one of the guards said sort of surprised me,' she finally offered.

Andy's ears pricked up. 'That's what I want to hear. What was it?'

'One of the guards said that Ed slept really weird hours, like five to midnight or something. So yeah, he actually was up at odd times during the night.' She flipped open her notepad and flicked through the pages.

'Five in the afternoon till midnight?'

Ed had worked the night shift at the Glebe morgue before he was fired for stealing autopsy tools. Perhaps he was accustomed to being a night dweller? Nevertheless, they were odd hours to keep. Andy couldn't rule out that it could be significant.

'That's what this guy said,' Karen explained. 'Pete Stevens works the shift from noon to midnight. Ed would go off to sleep right after his meal. Stevens didn't mind; it made his job easier,' he said.

Andy could imagine.

'He said Suzie Harpin was around for most of Ed's waking hours. He said they seemed to get on.'

'Get on?' Andy asked. 'They're the words he used, "seemed to get on"?'

'Uh, I think so.' She checked her notes. 'Yeah.'

Andy sifted through his file of interview transcripts. 'What was the name? Harpin?'

'Ms Suzie Harpin.'

'Here she is.' Andy pulled her information and statement from his file. 'Thirty-nine years old, single, never married, no children. Been working in corrections for most of her adult life . . .'

He silently skimmed through her statement.

'What about his old work? Did he have friends at Glebe morgue?' Mahoney asked.

'Wait a sec,' Andy said, raising a hand. He ignored her question and reread a section of the interview:

DET. HUNT: Did you notice anything suspicious?
HARPIN: Not really, no.
DET. HUNT: Not really?
HARPIN: I mean no.
DET. HUNT: I understand you had some conversations with Ed Brown during some of your shifts?
HARPIN: Oh. We kept odd hours.
DET. HUNT: How do you mean?
HARPIN: I mean to say, I worked the night shift. Everyone else was asleep.

Andy stood up and pushed the transcript away. 'Come on, we're going back to Long Bay.'

Mahoney looked surprised. 'What is it?'

'We've got a "we".'

He had a familiar feeling of excitement, like he did when he was on to something. When he got that feeling, he was like a dog on a scent. He didn't know what the scent was exactly, but he wasn't going to let it go. What if Ed's odd hours had something to do with this woman? This woman who used 'we' when referring to a dangerous inmate? Not 'I spoke to the prisoner a few times,' or 'I spoke to him,' but '*We* kept odd hours.'

At this point, a simple pronoun was the most promising thing he had to go on.

# CHAPTER 42

Irving Milgrom closed his shop at 5.34 in the evening. He flipped the sign over on the door and walked back towards his cash register to balance the till. It had been a slow day, mostly bird feed, a few goldfish and a cat scratching post. The music was still playing in the shop, and as he walked past the portable CD player he turned the volume a touch higher. It was a bit of Vivaldi that he liked, and he hummed along to the music. Congo Congo, his best talking parrot, hummed back at him.

'Shhh, Congo! You're ruining it! This is the best part.'

'Congo, Congo!' it squawked back.

Congo Congo, Irving's Congo African Grey, had a habit of repeating himself. He was a prized bird with a good vocabulary, and yet no one wanted to buy him. It seemed that customers couldn't look past the $1950 price tag. They didn't know value when they saw it. Exotic birds were Irving's specialty and he was practically an expert, but everyone these days wanted a 'cute bird', something low maintenance and predictable that their kids could point at over Christmas and then shove in a cage somewhere.

A knock came on the door.

*What, a customer now?*

Irving went to shoo them away, but recognised the visitor as one of his regular clients. He walked to the door, unlocked it and opened it a fraction.

'Suzie, how are you?'

'Oh, are you closed?' she said.

*Obviously I'm closed.*

Suzie Harpin was a good client, but she had always made Irving uneasy. It was the eyes, perhaps. They were round and impossibly dark, and she seemed to hold them open a touch too wide so you could see the whites all the way around. Crazy-person eyes, some would say. He'd heard that she worked in some kind of institution. Perhaps it was a mental ward and some of it had rubbed off.

She had the shoebox with her that she had left the shop with a few days earlier. *Don't tell me she's done something to it?*

'What's this? Is there a problem with the peachface?'

'No, well ... yes. I am not satisfied,' she said.

He opened the door reluctantly, wanting nothing more than to tell her to come back the next day. But he couldn't do that. She bought her lovebirds from him year after year, sometimes as often as a few months apart. And the ones she liked were not inexpensive. He needed her business.

'Please come in. You'll excuse the music.'

Suzie and her shoebox came in, and Irving closed the door behind her.

'What seems to be the problem?'

'I'm just not satisfied,' she said again.

That was a first. Suzie had purchased the red and green peachface lovebird just a few days before. It had been in perfectly good health when she had bought it.

'Does it not get on with the others?' he asked.

'What?' She seemed confused. 'What others?'

'With your other lovebirds?' She must have a fair few by now.

'Oh, no. Well, yes. That's the problem. She doesn't fit in.'

Irving frowned. She was a strange woman.

'So you would like to exchange it for another? I have a lovely Dutch Blue coming in that I think you might like.'

'No, I just want to return it.' She handed him the receipt and the box. He felt movement inside. There was a flutter as it changed hands.

'I see,' he said.

*I should have just closed the shop.*

Irving opened the till and returned her money to her.

'Thanks,' she said distractedly as she left.

The door rattled as it shut. He locked it behind her and watched through the glass as the strange woman went to her car.

*There goes the day's profits*, he thought bitterly.

'*Squawk!* What? What others? *Squawk!*'

'Oh, shut up, Congo.'

'Shut up Congo, shut up,' the bird replied.

# CHAPTER 43

The model agency, Wang Models Hong Kong, had placed Makedde in a sparsely furnished three-bedroom apartment in a towering high rise that looked out over the city through huge panes of glass. It was built in the sixties, Mak guessed. Some of the fixtures were worse for wear, and the once-groovy elevator was tiny. A frail Cantonese-speaking concierge who sat behind a metal desk at the entrance had given her the keys and pointed the way up.

Two other girls from the same agency were already sharing the same place: a sweet-looking American girl named Jen and an English model named Gabrielle whom Mak had not yet met. Mak had not had the chance to speak with the American model for more than a few minutes, but she seemed nice, and very young with incredibly pale porcelain skin, as if she never left the house without a parasol to shield her face from the sun. Jen had directed Mak to put her things in the far bedroom, and when Mak dragged her suitcases inside she found a small space with a low window that came right to the head of a short, unmade bed. On the floor and inside the closet were dozens of mangled wire hangers, but there were no bed sheets. The lights worked, however. And the room was spotlessly clean. A relief. On her first trip to New York she had arrived alone off her flight at midnight to a room with no sheets, no light bulbs and a box of maggot-infested Chinese food under the bed. By comparison, this was luxury.

Mak wandered around the apartment in her stockinged feet, taking in her new surroundings. One near-empty fridge housing some organic low-fat yoghurt, a carton of low-fat soymilk, a peach, two oranges and two bottles of champagne. Clean cupboards with a few mismatched dishes. A Post-it Note on the countertop saying that the cleaners would be coming the next day. There was a faint smell of cigarette smoke, not quite disguised by spearmint freshener. A small bathroom crowded with cosmetics. Hmmm, three women in one bathroom — never really a good thing. A Pokémon shower curtain. Loofah sponges. Nail polish remover. Fake tan. Clearly Jen wasn't the one using it. The living room looked comfortable, with a couple of sprawling couches with embroidered silk scatter cushions and a big coffee table covered in fashion magazines. By the door there was row upon row of shoes, most of which looked to be designer labels. A logo-covered Gucci hat sat on the arm of a chair. A logo-printed Bottega Veneta bag. Someone here was making good money.

The place was neat and clean, the view spectacular, and she didn't have a couple of police officers hanging around in the background every time she moved. This would be Makedde's life for the next several days, and that was just fine by her.

She got dressed and went in search of some full-fat groceries.

Andy arrived with Senior Constable Karen Mahoney at Long Bay only hours after Karen had left there with the other officers. Despite the added disruption, the warden made an effort to accommodate their needs. Andy was keen to interview Pete Stevens as soon as possible. Waiting until he was free from his shift at midnight was not an option. Ed could be anywhere, doing anything. If there was even a remote possibility that Stevens knew something valuable it might be a turning point for the investigation. At this rate, it might be the only fresh information they had.

Suzie Harpin could not be reached since she had finished her shift on Sunday. Monday was her day off. She was not answering her phone, and when Andy sent Hunt around to her apartment she was not home.

The warden explained the layout to Andy while they waited. It was nothing he hadn't heard and seen before. This and the high-tech Supermax facility at Goulburn were where the most serious, violent offenders came to stay. There were more than a few men at Long Bay who would not soon forget the detective who had put them there.

Stevens didn't keep them waiting long.

One look at him, and it was clear why he was a prison guard. For someone like Pete Stevens, life as a guard, soldier, firefighter or bouncer was perhaps inevitable. He was almost two metres tall, and at least fifty kilos heavier than Andy, with thick, hairy arms and a shaved head. He wouldn't have to do much to scare the crap out of someone, no doubt a useful attribute in his chosen occupation.

'Thanks for speaking with us again today,' Andy began. 'Now, you told my colleagues that the prisoner Ed Brown slept odd hours. What were odd hours?'

'Like, five in the afternoon or so until midnight.'

'Can you tell us anything else about that? Any impressions?' Mahoney said, mimicking Andy's own style of questioning, and trying not to lead him too much about the night-shift guard, Harpin. 'Why do you think he did that?'

'I don't know. I barely spoke to him at all myself, but he was definitely odd, even compared with the others. And not just the sleeping.'

'How do you mean?'

'Well, he talks funny, I guess you already know that,' Stevens said.

Andy nodded. 'What about his habits? Anything else that stands out?'

Stevens scratched the stubble on his head with one mighty hand. Andy noticed scars on his knuckles. 'Well, he is a clean freak. Really afraid of germs. He was always very, very clean, *obsessively* clean, which you don't see a whole lot of in here. There're always guys defecating on the floors and spitting, smearing stuff on the walls. But Ed kept his cell real nice. Oh, and he, ah ...' Stevens laughed. 'He watches soap operas.'

Andy was stunned.

'*Soap operas?*'

'Yeah, *The Bold And The Beautiful*. He watched it religiously, the last six months or so.'

'It can be addictive,' Mahoney murmured.

'Brown was always courteous, and never caused me any trouble. Maybe it made my job easier that he was asleep. Ms Harpin seemed to know him better.'

'What do you mean by "She seemed to know him better"?' Andy pressed.

'I don't mean anything by it, it's just that I know she spoke to him on occasion and I certainly didn't.' Stevens seemed on guard suddenly. 'I don't mean to say there is anything to it. I'm not going to rubbish Suzie.'

'We understand.' Andy shifted in his chair. He was definitely on to something. He'd hit a nerve.

'Look, Ms Harpin has been here for as long as I can remember,' Stevens went on, visibly uncomfortable. 'She is a solid worker, tough and professional. Practically part of the walls.'

He seemed reluctant to suggest anything negative about his colleague. Andy respected that, but dirt was what they wanted, not teamwork. If there was something suspicious about Harpin, he would have sensed it.

'But you were concerned . . .' Andy coaxed.

'I had never seen her chat with one of the prisoners like that before. It struck me as odd, that's the only reason I mentioned it,' he said. 'But he slept all day, and there was no one much up at night so they might have been talkative because of that.'

'So, most of his waking time would have been on Ms Harpin's shift,' Mahoney jumped in.

He nodded.

'And how long have you known Ms Harpin?'

# CHAPTER 44

'What on earth are you eating?'

Mak sat cross-legged on a sofa cushion on the living-room floor in the early evening, watching the bright lights of Hong Kong through the tall windows. She had her dinner in a bowl in one hand and a copy of Sandra Lee's *Beyond Bad* in her lap. She looked up to see a tall, dramatically thin brunette with arched eyebrows standing in the doorway. She spoke in a Cockney accent.

'I'm eating soup. I think,' Mak replied.

Finding a good grocery store within walking distance had proved a challenge, but Mak had stumbled across a tiny, hole-in-the-wall kiosk and bought some packages of noodles with Chinese writing all over them from the fantastically wrinkled old lady who smiled kindly at her from behind the counter. Mak had just cooked up a bowl of the stuff and it actually tasted pretty good, though salty, a bit like ichiban.

'Yuck, carbs,' the woman said.

'You are Gabrielle, I presume?'

'Gabby, yeah. Who are you?'

'Makedde Vanderwall. It's nice to meet you.' She stood up.

'Don't go in the first bedroom. That's mine,' Gabby said flatly.

'Yes, I know.'

'And don't touch my towels. They're the white ones hanging over the towel rack.'

'Okay.'

'I'm off. Meeting some friends at the Felix.'

'Ah, I love Philippe Starck's designs. I've heard it's fabulous,' Mak said, still trying to be friendly.

'What?'

Mak had seen magazine stories on the Felix bar and restaurant. It was a marvel of design with sloping walls and a circular bar with illuminated floors. Apparently, there were faces of some of the designer's friends sculpted into the walls.

Gabby looked blank.

Mak forced a smile. 'Um . . . well, have fun,' she said.

Gabby was already jogging to forbidden bedroom number one as Mak resumed her solitary position by the window.

The shower went on in the bathroom, and then off again. Mak heard bare feet and then the click of shoes, the sound of closets opening and closing. In less than fifteen minutes Gabby was gone.

Her first night in Hong Kong, and Mak had plenty of time to ruminate on the events of the previous week. What was happening in Sydney? Were they any closer to catching Ed? *God, I hope he hasn't hurt anyone else.* It was tough to fathom his escape.

The thought of him walking free disturbed her right to the core of her being.

# CHAPTER 45

The immigration officer looked them over. He was a short Chinese man in quasi-military dress, and he held their two passports in white-gloved hands. Shrewd black eyes looked carefully at the passport photos and back to them, back to the passport photos, back to them. Looking, looking.

Suzie Harpin.

Ben Harpin.

They didn't look much like brother and sister. They did, however, look like they could be husband and wife. Ed Brown wore a gold band on his ring finger. It had belonged to Ben Harpin, the Prison Lady's dismembered brother, and she had happily thawed the frozen hand that was wearing it and removed it for Ed's purpose before they left. It was a plain wedding ring, much like the one Ed had worn in the past to help lull his 'girls' into a false sense of security. The band was a bit big for Ed's thin fingers, but he was careful to keep it in place. The Prison Lady wore a cheap costume jewellery ring on her left hand. The glass stone could have been a diamond, if you didn't look very hard. But it was enough. It was enough to make them look like Mr and Mrs Harpin, coming to visit lovely Hong Kong on holidays.

Ed noticed with a touch of uneasiness that there were a number of heavily armed guards at Hong Kong airport, dressed in pressed and polished military uniform. The Red Army, he supposed, although they weren't dressed in red. The security at Sydney airport hadn't been toting submachine guns like these men. None of the guards were looking at him, he didn't think. Not yet. Their weapons hung from their necks on long straps, their fingers held close to the trigger. Ed had never been to an airport before boarding this flight to Hong Kong. He had never flown before. The thought of being in the air made him nervous, but the security and immigration officers gave him much more concern. And the guns. He didn't like the guns he saw now, especially after experiencing the destructive impact of a bullet from Detective Flynn's Glock pistol.

'Well, I just can't wait to see Hong Kong,' the Prison Lady gushed. 'We've always wanted to come.'

The immigration officer did not respond.

*Shut up, woman.*

The black eyes narrowed, looked them over again, looked at the photo of Ben Harpin ...

Ed had dyed his hair dark brown to match it, with a messy dye that had stained the porcelain sink in the big suburban house, but he was much thinner in the face than Ben appeared to have been. He was also shorter, and his nose was different too. The tenuous resemblance was probably enough for a glance. Enough for a glance, but for this? He had wanted to discard the Prison Lady, especially after she had proved that she was not useful as a source of money, having only withdrawn a measly $200 from her account. She'd said that was all she could access; most of her money was tied up, apparently. But the game had changed once he he found out where Makedde had gone. Ed knew well that the authorities would be looking for him at every port. A man travelling alone would stand out as suspicious, but a man and his wife? The relief at slipping through Sydney airport had been enormous. He was good at keeping his cool, but he knew perfectly well that he never would have made it through without his 'wife' and his changed appearance. He was not home free, though. Not yet.

Black eyes examining, squinting . . .

*Come on, wave us through.*

The officer was stalling. Other people were being waved through, but not them. Ed could feel himself begin to sweat. Did he look nervous? Did those black eyes sense that something was wrong?

He waited to hear, 'Would you come this way, please?' or more likely a fast string of Chinese words that would bring the armed guards down upon them to haul them away to prison. At Sydney airport, he had been nervous when he'd had to take off his shoes and belt going through a big metal detector, but the security man on the other side had smiled and sent him and the Prison Lady on their way to the gate without incident. As it turned out, no one was interested in an innocuous looking brown-haired man and his plain wife. That's exactly what Ed had counted on. But what if the police had caught up with them? Perhaps they had cottoned on to the Prison Lady's involvement.

'Thank you,' the man said, unsmiling, and waved them over to another officer.

Ed's stomach dropped.

The other officer looked the same to Ed — same uniform, same black eyes taking in their every move. He led them over to a large machine that Ed did not recognise, and made motions to see their passports. They handed them over, Ed's heart pounding.

'Australian?' they were asked in a heavy accent.

They nodded.

The officer examined their passports.

Behind the strange machine a woman with a surgical mask pointed some kind of sensor at them and peered intently at a computer screen. Ed could not see the screen display. He felt a bead of sweat roll down his temple.

'Thank you, yes,' the officer said, and handed their passports back with some documentation.

Relief.

It was a brochure on SARS. The nurse behind the computer had been checking their body temperature for flu symptoms. They were free to go.

Ed smiled.

He and the Prison Lady collected their luggage, walked past more armed guards and finally emerged through sliding doors into the sweltering cacophony of a Hong Kong morning.

They'd made it through.

Ed Brown was in Hong Kong.

And there was no Andy Flynn this time.

# CHAPTER 46

By eight-thirty in the morning on Tuesday Makedde was already wandering through the Central District of Hong Kong, feeling remarkably positive and relaxed. She gawked at the sights around her.

The giant Bank of Hong Kong building loomed above her, extending higher than the rest of the impressive concrete towers that crowded the sky in all directions. Puffs of cloud reflected in thousands of office windows spread over blocks and blocks of dense urban jungle. So many millions of people on one island. Mak had the peculiar sensation of wading through a solid, chest-high sea of strangers as she moved along the bustling streets. But of course she was the stranger. Her towering height and Western features stuck out like sore thumbs, but she was politely ignored for the most part.

Sparkling designer shops with impressive window displays beckoned from all directions: Louis Vuitton, Gucci, Givenchy, Dolce & Gabbana, Christian Dior. Like most models, Mak wore their clothes in photo studios and on catwalks but couldn't afford to buy them. It was fun to window shop, though, and dream.

Spotting the ubiquitous green signage of a Starbucks across the road, Mak had to laugh. Starbucks had popped up everywhere in the world, as McDonald's had done decades before. She shook her head and thought of her meeting with Loulou in Sydney. And of Andy.

She hadn't called him.

*And what will you say when you do?*

She was tempted to get in touch, though they seemed destined to be apart. The thought of letting him go made her sadder than she was willing to accept.

'Copy watch! Copy watch!' someone cried out. She spun around, startled. It was a tall Indian man with a stack of photocopied brochures. He tried to press one into her hand. 'Rolex?'

'No thank you,' she replied, and moved away from him, crossing the street with the flow of pedestrian traffic. A young girl in pigtails and neon space boots pointed at Mak and said something excitedly to her friend. Who knew what they thought of the gargantuan lumbering white woman with the big blonde head? If she were them, she would laugh too.

'Faith Hill! Faith Hill! Photo! Photo!'

*What?*

The girl with the pigtails ran up to her. She and her friend had the Tokyo punk look, and Mak wondered if they were visitors as well.

'Faith Hill!' the girl said again, clearly excited.

'Oh, um . . . sorry, I'm not Faith Hill,' Mak replied.

Her statement didn't register. The glowing smiles and excited giggles did not wane. Mak thought momentarily of telling them her real name to prove that she was not the tall blonde country singer they sought, but thought better of it. If they didn't speak English, the words 'Makedde Vanderwall' wouldn't help.

'Photo!' The girl with the pigtails nodded eagerly. 'Photo!'

Now a shiny compact digital camera had been produced, no larger than a cigarette lighter, and the girls looked around for someone to take their photo. *Fine.* Mak posed beside the giggling duo, who she guessed were no older than thirteen, while a grim-faced businessman stopped to take the photo for them and exchange some quick words in Cantonese. Once the girls had their picture, they took off, still excited.

'You're not Faith Hill,' the man said in flawless English.

'I know,' Mak replied, and stood on the street alone.

# CHAPTER 47

Lisa Milgate-Harpin knocked on the front door of Ben's house with one hand, and held her mobile phone to her ear with the other. Her face was set in a frown, eyes narrowed.

There was still no answer at either the door or the phone.

This, she had decided, would be the last time she would attempt civility with him. Ben was being rude and unreasonable, not even returning her calls or bothering to make any attempt to cooperate. He was obviously trying to avoid a divorce by simply not responding to her. It was an irritatingly immature attitude, another item to add to her list of things she could not forgive Ben for.

*That's it. I'm coming in.*

Lisa stuck her key into the door. It still fitted. After everything, he had not changed the locks. She was hardly surprised. Changing the locks would take effort, something Ben was not adept at. Lisa turned the key and the door opened with a creak. There was no sound inside the house. Lisa gave a quick glance over her shoulder, as if expecting to see her soon-to-be ex-husband approaching behind her, but there was no one on the drive, no curious neighbour watching from the safety of their manicured lawn. Lisa quickly shut the door behind her.

'Hello?' she called. 'Helloooooooooooooo?'

With an unexpected rush of triumph, she climbed the stairs. She had not entirely anticipated that she would come inside, or that her key would still work, but now that she was in the house it felt good. There had been no car in the drive this time, and she had noticed a couple of days' mail in the letterbox by the door. So he had finally taken a holiday, had he? Ben Harpin had been the disappointing kind of husband who thought that an episode of *The Simpsons* was as good as a night out at an expensive restaurant, and a spot of smelly fishing with his mates was more fun than a luxury cruise. Come to think of it, he was probably fishing now. The bastard might have said something to her if he was planning a trip. Maybe she should call his mate Brad and see if he was with him. It would have been nice if Ben had left a message for her somewhere so she didn't have to waste all this time.

Nevertheless, Ben's absence was a blessing. If he wasn't going to return her calls, then she owed him nothing. While she was at the house, she would pick up the cappuccino machine. He couldn't stop her, and really, it was hers. So what if Heinrich had a perfectly good Krups? It had been Lisa's decision to put the Gaggia cappuccino maker on the wedding gift registry, therefore it was hers. Ben had not done any of the research. He probably didn't even know how to use it.

Lisa was almost at the top of the stairs when she sensed that something was amiss. Perfume? The house smelled strangely of lavender.

'Hello? Is anyone there?'

The house responded with eerie silence. Lisa walked into the living room and her jaw fell open.

*What is this?*

The biggest shock for Ben's wife was that the house was spotlessly neat. Ben was not a tidy man, left to his own devices. And there was an empty birdcage in the centre of the room. Since when did Ben have the faintest interest in birds, or pets of any kind? But that wasn't all. The place had been more or less redecorated. There were knick-knacks and photo frames everywhere. Lisa walked across the living room to take a closer look at a woman's photo on the mantelpiece. *No way*, she thought with disbelief. Does Ben have a *girlfriend*? Wait ... she recognised the face. It was photo of Ben's sister, Suzie, but she looked different, somehow. She was wearing make-up and smiling for a change. Lisa inspected another photo, puzzled, then put it down and backed away. Who was that — the soapie actor Ronn Moss? Then there was a cut-out of some television wedding in a heart-shaped pewter frame. A stack of wedding magazines. What was all this stuff? There was heart-shaped crap everywhere, and that horrible lavender smell.

Is he *living* with someone? Is he *engaged* to someone?

Lisa headed for the bedroom. She stopped at an awful streak on the carpet in the hallway, like red paint. *So he'd managed to ruin the damn carpet?* She shook her head with disgust. It would have to be recarpeted before it was sold. How much would that cost?

*I'll be damned if I'm going to pay for that. He can forget it.*

The master bedroom was completely different to how she'd left it. And the bed was neatly made. Very unlike Ben. There were more of the frilly knick-knacks everywhere, and there was make-up on the dresser, alongside more photos of

Ben's damn sister. Lisa went for the closet and was shocked to find that it was nearly cleared out, with only some women's clothes on hangers and a handful of Ben's old clothes shoved to one side. She fingered an ugly flower-print blouse, confused at its presence in what used to be her closet space. Lisa walked to the guest bedroom and checked that out too. The bed had been slept in, but it too was neatly made. There was a stack of newspapers in one corner with a pair of scissors and some blank paper. More wedding magazines. It looked like someone had been making cuttings.

Lisa walked back into the hall in a daze, stepping over the stain.

*How completely weird . . .*

Had Suzie moved in with Ben? If so, things in the family had certainly changed. Last she knew those two barely got along. The Harpins had not been the closest family even at the best of times. His sister had not come to their wedding, saying that she had to work that day, which had seemed a poor excuse. Ben and Suzie only saw each other a few times a year — Christmas and birthdays. And didn't she have her own place near the prison where she worked? Was she trying to move in on Ben's money now that Lisa had left? There was always something odd about that Suzie. It wouldn't surprise Lisa at all if she was getting greedy about the house.

Lisa stood in the living room feeling increasingly uneasy.

*Why would he let her move in?*

Come to think of it, it was more like Ben didn't even live there any more. Where was all his stuff?

# CHAPTER 48

Tuesday afternoon, and Ed had been loose for a full three days.

It had been seventy-two terrifying hours of waiting for a fresh body to turn up with Ed's signature all over it. So far they had not found any unfortunate young woman who had been in the wrong place at the wrong time. So far . . .

'He still hasn't shown,' Detective Flynn confirmed.

Senior Constable Karen Mahoney grimaced. The detective-in-training was buzzing around Andy's desk, unable to take her mind off the case.

Disappointingly, Ed Brown had not yet made contact with his mother, at least that they knew of. The telephone intercepts had not yet been fruitful. If she was the one who had helped her son escape, they were being very cautious about contact now. The warrant to search Mrs Brown's apartment was taking more time — a common source of frustration. They needed to search the apartment for letters, notes or other information that might help to solve the puzzle and reveal any escape plans, or even better, suspicious traces of fertilizer, nitrates or even something more exotic that might have used to make the bomb. An exciting phone call picked up through the telephone intercepts would have helped their cause considerably, but in Andy's eyes they still had enough for reasonable suspicion. As usual, the wheels of justice seemed to move far too slowly. The warrant would be issued imminently, Andy hoped.

And then there was the other lead Andy had. They would need some more evidence to move forward on that one . . .

'When's the briefing?'

'In ten. You'd better get your arse over there.'

Andy was about to brief the task force on the Ed Brown escape. He was not heading the case as he had when they were first trying to track the killer down, but at least he was a part of the team to bring him back in. He knew all too well that if he had lost it and gone off the rails, he wouldn't be part of anything. He was grateful for the opportunity. If he had been put on forced leave, he would never have forgiven himself.

'Andy, she's still not answering any calls.'

'The guard, you mean?'

'Yeah.'

He already knew that. Tracking Suzie Harpin down was proving hard, suspiciously so. Was she staying with friends? Family? A boyfriend no one knows about? Everyone seemed certain that she was single. She had a small apartment near the prison and by all accounts seemed to live for her work. She had not taken sick leave or holidays in years. Why now? There was something there that wasn't right. Something . . .

'You know those weird hours that Ed was keeping?' Mahoney said.

He nodded.

'Last night I got to thinking that maybe it was on purpose, that he was actually wanting to be awake for those hours because of this guard. Like they had some kind of friendship going.'

'We'll talk after the briefing,' Andy said.

'But what if she knows something? Apart from Ed's mother, the pickings are pretty slim for someone who he would talk to. We need to find her. Maybe there's some clue at her apartment. We don't have enough for a warrant, do we?'

'There is a small thing called "reasonable suspicion" that they may have told you about at the academy, Mahoney.'

As with the warrant for Mrs Brown's apartment, they would need to be able to convince a magistrate via an affidavit sworn on oath that they had reasonable suspicion or grounds to believe there was evidence in Suzie's apartment to connect her to the escape. Without that, they could not search her premises for the 'fruits of the crime', detonators, chemicals, wiring, nitrate and so on.

'We'll talk about it after the briefing,' he repeated.

'I just feel that we need to find this woman.'

'I agree with you, Mahoney,' Andy finally told her, and Mahoney's expression changed. 'Suzie Harpin may very well be important. Let's hope she turns up soon. Just don't get so fixated on this woman we want to question that you can't see any other leads. You could get "linkage blindness" and not be able to see other suspects or patterns here. Now get your arse over there for the briefing.'

Mahoney left and Andy prepared the last of his notes. He had presented his notes on Ed Brown once before, when they were hunting down the killer the first time. Back then, they didn't have his name, only the remains of his victims and crime scenes as clues. Now they knew almost everything about him, except the most vital thing . . . where he was.

Detective Flynn stood at the front of the room, feeling more alive than he had for days. In a way, he was in his element.

'Thank you for your dedication to this case,' he began, looking over the faces of the task force. 'In your notes,' he said, referring to the pages of references they had each been given, 'you have a full description of the subject's profile and particulars, and the details of his previous nine known murders, and his recent escape from custody.'

He swallowed hard. He couldn't believe that Jimmy wasn't there. Andy realised he had never done one of these briefings without him in the room.

'We have a serious time crisis here. It won't take Ed Brown very long to work up the confidence to begin killing again. Let's remember that the moment his murders started getting written up in the papers, he began picking off victims with a higher profile. He will want to rub in his escape, and I am hoping that this may be part of his downfall. Let's not allow him to take any more lives before we catch him.'

Mahoney, who sat closest to the front, appeared deep in thought. He knew she was fixated on the guard.

'This killer will do what he can to embarrass the police, and any individuals who attempt to get in his way,' Andy continued. 'As many of you are aware, I was singled out personally when I was in charge of the case. He attempted to discredit me and throw the investigation itself into turmoil by framing me for the murder of my ex-wife, Cassandra Flynn.'

Some shifted uncomfortably in their seats. It was a hard topic to bring up, but it was true and it was relevant. Andy knew that his police work was the direct impetus for

Cassandra's brutal murder. She had been nothing more than a tool for Ed to get at Andy. His ex-wife would never have been targeted had he not been on the case. This case had cost him so much, he could not bear to add up the loss.

'Ed Brown does his research,' Andy said, bringing the danger home. 'He knows who we are. He knows who our loved ones are. We have to consider that he may have ways of finding out how much we know. He is a psychopath with a high IQ, cunning, and adept at manipulating any situation to his benefit. His escape shows a great ability to con his way out of tough situations. Let's not underestimate him.

'As you all know, we are watching Mrs Brown very carefully. The phone intercept has not yet picked up any calls from Ed, but we are hopeful. I'm also hopeful our search warrant will come in the next few hours. But there is also a new person of interest that I want to introduce you to.'

Andy took a stack of files off the top of the desk at the front, and asked that a copy be handed to each officer. Mahoney's eyes widened as she received her file with a photo of the guard stapled to the front.

'This, ladies and gentlemen, is Suzie Harpin. She is the night-shift guard for Ed's protected quarters at Long Bay. Thirty-nine years of age. Single. No children. Parents are deceased. She has one brother, who we have thus far had no success in contacting. By all reports she is a loner, and she grew quite close to Ed during his time there. She requested leave around the time of Ed's escape, and has not been seen since.

'This woman is wanted for immediate questioning.'

# CHAPTER 49

'Hello?'

Lisa Milgate-Harpin looked up in the direction of the noise and frowned. She moved along the hallway.

'Is someone there?' she called.

She had been sure the house was empty, but there had been a noise in the kitchen. There it was again. A loud bang.

'Hello?' she repeated with apprehension. She reached into her purse and took out her keys, gripping them like a weapon.

*Bang.*

She stepped into the kitchen, her arm extended, and saw with relief that the window was wide open. The venetian blinds were catching the wind and banging against the window frame.

She exhaled and lowered her arm.

Now she was here she would get the Gaggia, and a few odds and ends like the Alessi corkscrew. Ben was out fishing with his mates, and she was tiptoeing around the house, freaking out at every little noise. Christ, he was a bastard. She would take what she wanted and he could get stuffed if he didn't like it!

Then Lisa saw something that made her freeze.

She paused mid-step, her eyes riveted to the bloody mess in the kitchen sink, just below the open window.

*Oh my God, Oh my God, Oh my God!*

She screamed.

It was a severed arm. A man's arm, cut off at the shoulder.

# CHAPTER 50

The stairs creaked under her feet. Loud disco music drifted up from the bar downstairs. A couple could be heard grunting next door, a bed squeaking. Suzie Harpin climbed the stairs of a run-down apartment complex in the Wan Chai district with a plastic bag of Chinese takeaway in her hand. She was prepared for a confrontation, if it came to that. Her face was set in a frown. She positively hated the apartment that her boyfriend, Ed, had rented for them with her money. She hated this place called Wan Chai. In less than a day she already hated Hong Kong. Why did they have to come here? *Why?* Suzie could never be happy here, she knew that already.

Wan Chai seemed to be a red-light district. Strip clubs and girlie bars lined the main streets, and there were tourists everywhere, mostly men. Suzie guessed it was the type of place people who lived a safe distance away visited to do lewd and unsavoury things in anonymity. Ed had explained that it was the best cheap and fully furnished apartment he could find on such short notice, in an area where people were conveniently slack about formalities like identification, home addresses, credit cards. But surely anything had to be better than this? Suzie couldn't believe they had left the comforts of the love nest she had made for them in Sydney to come to this irretrievably hideous hellhole. They would have been so much happier if they had stayed; it had been a terrible choice for them to leave her beautiful, cosy house. Suzie felt she was taking a huge step backwards after working so hard to finally get somewhere. She had worked so *hard*.

She put her key in the door and turned the handle. It creaked. The plastic bag she was carrying caught on one of the rusty, loose screws that kept the door handle in place. She untangled it with a grimace. She entered the apartment and found Ed sitting at the kitchen table, just as she imagined he would be. He looked sombre. He didn't jump up to greet her. There was no 'Welcome home sweetheart, I've missed you!', no 'Honey, you're home!'.

'Hello darling,' Suzie said, closing the door behind her and locking the bolt.

There was that smell again. Stale cigarette smoke. Despite the noise from outside Suzie had kept the windows open all day, but it did little to help the odour. Now it was simply loud *and* smoky.

'Sweetheart, where have you been all day?' she asked.

'I came home and you weren't here,' he replied in an unfriendly tone. He didn't even look up at her.

Suzie walked into the kitchen area and spread the takeaway out on the counter — sweet and sour pork, noodles, some kind of soup. As she watched, his eyes went to the food and then back up to her face.

'I just went out to get some food,' she lied, quietly seething. 'I didn't know when you were going to come back. I got enough food for both of us, just in case. Would you like some, darling?'

In fact, Suzie had followed Ed's every move from the moment he had left the apartment that afternoon. Ed had camped out near a model agency called Wang Models Hong Kong for more than three hours until they closed up and everyone went home. He had then followed a couple of the young women from the agency to a restaurant in Lan Kwai Fong, a place swarming with expats from around the world, particularly Englishmen, Americans and Australians, as far as Suzie could tell. There he had drunk beer and watched the girls from across a steep, cobblestoned alley. The whole time Suzie had thought about confronting him. But she was interested to see what her boyfriend would do next. Eventually he had headed back to Wan Chai, not having even spoken to the girls from the model agency. He didn't notice Suzie tailing him, barely a block behind. Suzie had bought the takeaway just before following him back inside the apartment. She wanted an excuse to have gone out.

'Oh,' Ed replied, uninterested. He didn't bother to explain where he had been. Did he really believe she had spent all afternoon and evening pining for him in that sleazy little apartment? He actually believed she would sit around and wait for him while he went looking for that girl?

That girl. *Makedde Vanderwall.*

Suzie had seen the headline too. She knew what was going on.

MODEL WITNESS FLEES TO HONG KONG.

'In Asia we could afford to live like kings on the money we have,' Ed had said only a few days before. 'We can get married there, no questions asked.' But she knew the reason he wanted to be in Hong Kong. He wanted to be there because of that girl.

*I'm no fool, mister.*

Suzie knew she needed to be patient. If the only way for them to move forward was to get this girl, so be it. She was willing to be patient, even help out if she could. She wanted Makedde Vanderwall off the face of the earth as much as he did. But what about his lying? Ed's lack of honesty caused her pain. And his behaviour was changing. She was beginning to see that this might not turn into the romance that she had imagined. She'd had such high hopes. Every once in a while she would get a glimpse of her dream man — he would become sweet and affectionate, but then he would switch. He ran hot and cold, worse than the taps in this awful, run-down, stinking apartment.

*He hasn't proposed yet. When will he propose?*

She hoped he wasn't another of her disappointing loves. There was Michael when she was just fourteen, he was experienced and exciting, but it turned out he already had a fiancée. And the next year brought sweaty evenings spent in the back of Colin Garrison's creaking car, and news that she had become pregnant. Suzie was sure it would be a beautiful baby girl, that her daughter Rose was in her belly waiting to be born. But *he* didn't want her. Colin made Suzie kill her, and as soon as the abortion was done, he too was gone. She'd since focused her attentions away from wicked men. She got her first bird when her parents were still alive and she was living at home, and she called him Rose after her daughter. He didn't sing like he was supposed to, and after six weeks Suzie stopped feeding him. The next one was a female. She lasted a little longer.

When Suzie met Ed, he was in a cage of sorts, and now that he was out he was not living up to his promise. Like the new little peachface Rose she had bought the day before Ed came. It sang beautifully in the store, but when she got it home it wasn't the same. She was glad she had returned it and got her money back, though in truth she hadn't known what else to do with it once Ed had convinced her she had to go away. But it wasn't good enough anyway. When their feathers grew dull and the singing stopped, she knew they would soon be gone. Would it be the same with Ed? Was he growing dull?

'Darling, would you like something to eat?' Suzie persisted.

He didn't respond. She served him some soup anyway, and sat across from him at the table. She noticed that he had some tourist maps in front of him. There were areas circled in red felt pen. Ed picked up his spoon and ate his soup quietly. Not even a thank you! Not even a sorry for being gone all day!

*Be reasonable, Suzie. Be patient.*

Although Suzie knew that she had to make allowances for Ed, disappointment was seeping into her bones like acid. Her head was filling slowly with dark thoughts until she felt she could barely breathe. Ed was *not* giving her the love and attention she deserved. Suzie had freed him. She had taken leave from work, just as he'd suggested. She had taken almost all of her money out of her savings, just like he asked, and then charged two flights to her credit card that she couldn't afford. And what about the house she had made for them, and what she had done to get it? She deserved something in return, dammit! She deserved his devotion.

*I won't let him leave me for this stupid girl*, she thought. *I've done all the work. She's not going to have him.*

'Sweetheart, let's do some sightseeing tomorrow,' Suzie said. 'Please?' She reached across the table and squeezed his hand. 'There is so much I want to do with you.'

*And if I have to get rid of her myself, so be it.*

# CHAPTER 51

The vast warehouse smelled of smoke and expensive perfume.

*Damn this corset is tight . . .*

Hong Kong socialites, film stars and fashionistas were crammed in side by side, their perfumes, personas and personal assistants fighting for dominance. The din of excited gossip was rivalled by a loud smoke machine to the side of the stage that sent pale clouds tumbling across the T-shaped runway, spilling into rows of media and VIPs waiting to view Ely Garner's latest collection, EG.

It was Ely's first major show since she'd severed the partnership of Nobelius Garner, and the PR machine had been in overdrive to secure her status as the winner in the fashion fight. The front row was armed with the necessary arsenal for media success — Leonardo DiCaprio sat next to Chloë Sevigny, with Lucy Liu nearby, a wisp of couture falling open to reveal an expanse of toned thigh. There was a slew of local starlets Mak did not recognise, but it was clearly a paparazzo's wet dream. Flash bulbs and bleached teeth got a workout. The international names were no doubt wooed by personal friendship, if not the promise of clothing and front-row status. The locals were just lucky to be there.

Anyone not deemed important enough for the front row was bitching about who had been chosen over them. There was the usual sneering, leering and whispering. The models backstage jostled for a quick peek of anyone famous, their heavily made-up faces peering out from behind the curtains — all except Makedde's. She'd already glanced at the celebrity royalty and was now busy begging one of the backstage hands to loosen the corset on her dress.

'Pssst.'

*This thing is killing me . . .*

'Psssssst!'

'What is it?' The woman finally turned around. She wore head-to-toe black, and a heavy belt weighed down with a crackling walkie-talkie. A neon-pink streak of hair fell over harsh, squinting eyes.

'You speak English?' Mak said, surprised.

'What was your first clue?' Attitude. Fair enough.

'Could you do me a favour please and just loosen this corset a fraction?' She spun around to reveal the tight lacing up the back of her leather dress. 'It's absolutely killing me. I feel faint.'

The woman looked at the dress. 'Oh, I don't think I should do that.'

'Come on. I don't want to pass out.'

'Ely doesn't let us touch anything. I really should call her over.' She raised her hand and was about to shout.

'No, don't!' Mak pulled the woman's hand down, horrified. The last thing she wanted was to offend the designer who had seen fit to fly her all the way over. She probably wouldn't have too many more of these jobs as it was. 'Never mind,' she said. 'Everyone's busy, so don't bother. I guess it's only for a few more minutes.'

But Makedde had already been waiting too many minutes. Her ribs had begun to ache, and she felt dangerously dizzy. *This can't be healthy.* Sitting was always banned once models were dressed, and there were never any chairs backstage at fashion shows. Anyway, sitting down would probably make the boning in the corset buckle and pierce a rib, or at the very least cause some further repositioning of vital organs. Mak was stuck standing and panting.

'If I pass out and die, can you make sure my body is sent back to Canada?'

'What?' The model behind her gave her a frown. Or perhaps the frown was permanent.

'Never mind.'

*Why is it against the rules to ever start a fashion show on time? Why?*

The show was already thirty minutes late, now forty minutes, forty-five, fifty … Mak could feel the restlessness of the crowd on the other side of the curtain. She scanned the waiting line of models for the girls who were staying at the apartment with her. She didn't see either of them, or maybe she didn't recognise them under the make-up and hairpieces. Mak was up front, standing a not-so-close second in line behind the magnificent Brazilian supermodel Gisele — the star of the show and probably the main reason Leo DiCaprio was in the crowd. Her appearance would be costing Ely at least a cool $20 000 over Makedde's humble fee. In modelling terms, Mak was eating Gisele's dust.

'I'm dying for a fag,' someone said.

A petite man wearing artfully ripped jeans and a black T-shirt brushed past Mak to reach Gisele. He sprayed oil on her bare, bronzed flesh without saying a word. For her part she turned when he had finished her stomach and chest, so he could spray down her back and buttocks. Then he disappeared. Not a word was exchanged. Mak stayed well out of the way of the nozzle.

Finally, after what had seemed an eternity of shallow breathing, the grumpy woman with the walkie-talkie made her signal. Gisele, newly oiled, slinked gracefully into position, as 'Get Me Off' pumped through the powerful speaker system, drowning the din of the smoke machine, the chatter, the clicking of Manolo Blahniks on impatient feet. The lights came up on the stage, sending shafts of red through the smoke, and revealing Gisele positioned with her hands on her hips, clothed in a black leather bikini and impossibly high stilettos with straps that snaked all the way up to her knees. She waited for her cue, her lithe body firm and voluptuous, and when the first raw beats had come and gone and the chorus began, she strutted down the runway to the raunchy rhythm, every ounce of her considerable sex appeal aimed at the audience and cameras.

It was almost Makedde's cue.

'Go!'

Mak was shoved forward, barely recovering herself, striking a practised pose just before the spotlights found her. As a second act to Gisele, Mak felt that she would hardly be noticed, but the audience dutifully turned to watch her. Cameras flashed. She set her features in the mandatory mask of mild disdain, and made her way down the catwalk. On automatic pilot after years of shows, she placed her feet perfectly, jutting her hips forward, head held high. The corset was still too tight, but under the glare of the spotlight she didn't feel a thing.

Then, at the end of the runway, a pale, ginger-haired man with a camera around his neck lunged forward, catching her eye, and Makedde's organs fairly seized up.

*Oh my God . . . Ed Brown!*

The tiny hairs on the back of her neck stood on end. Her legs went rubbery with terror, she felt like she couldn't take another step . . .

On second glance it wasn't Ed Brown at all. The man was merely a member of the overseas media contingent sent to cover the fashion show. He barely bore any resemblance to Ed, in fact. But it was too late, Ed had invaded her thoughts and she was rapidly spinning towards panic.

*This is Hong Kong. Ed is not here. You are safe. Ed is not here,* Mak repeated like a mantra in an effort to calm herself.

Ed Brown was still able to poison her thoughts, even now, so many miles away in a new and exotic country. Even on the job, he was there in her mind. It was as if she had never really escaped his clutches at all.

Makedde's stilettoed feet continued to do their job with precision despite the inner demons that tormented her, threatening to overwhelm her. She glided back along the catwalk under an impenetrable veneer of poise, and the hundreds of eyes and camera lenses that studied and captured her every move were ignorant of the fear pulsing fiercely within.

# CHAPTER 52

*Thirteen . . .*

As many in Wan Chai slept, and others partied with strangers and friends in discos and bars, Ed Brown was wide-awake and focused on his future in his solitary bedroom.

Neon signage glowed through the open window from the strip outside, filling the space with a feverish pink hue. The door was pulled shut, the Prison Lady asleep in the next bedroom. Ed was confident that she would not be able to hear his movements above the incessant street noise. He was confident that she would not attempt to bother him tonight. He had time to think, to plan.

Ed had his nose to the wooden floor. His feet were propped up on the bed, elevated half a metre above his head. His whole body strained with the effort of keeping braced and steady. His obliques twitched. His shoulders ached with lactic burn. Blood began to rush to his head. With a steady, slow effort, he pushed up with his arms and back down again.

*Fourteen . . .*

With a slightly strained exhalation, he executed another push-up. Up and down.

*Fifteen . . .*

It was good to have space to think. The Prison Lady agreed that it wasn't proper for them to sleep in the same bed until they were married, but he knew she was growing impatient. She would expect a proper proposal soon. It mattered little. Soon he would have no further need of her.

Tomorrow Ed would stake out the model agency for Makedde again. He hoped for more success this time, but even if his prize did not appear, he probably had a few more days to find her before there was a risk that she would leave the country. And if she went to Canada he could follow her there too, with the help of the Prison Lady again under the guise of a happily married couple. He would follow her wherever she went until he had her. But he hoped it wouldn't come to that. He did not want to risk travelling through customs and immigration again, and he did not want the Prison Lady around for much longer, if he could avoid it. But most of all, Ed had waited so long — a whole year and a half since his moment with Makedde had been so rudely disrupted by Andy Flynn — and he didn't want to wait any longer.

If by tomorrow afternoon he had still not found her, he would have to take further measures.

*Eighteen . . .*

Ed's triceps began to shake, his shoulders tiring. A line of sweat ran from his forehead to his eyebrow.

*Nineteen . . .*

Once he knew his time frame for having Makedde, he would be much happier. The time frame dictated the amount of risk that would be involved in kidnapping her, and how long he had to suss out some good, quiet areas for his purpose in Hong Kong.

*Twenty . . .*

Much was still up in the air, but it had been an important day for Ed. He had successfully entered Hong Kong without interference or detection. He was out of the clutches of the idiot Australian police force. He had located Makedde's model agency — it hadn't been hard, he'd just phoned her Sydney agent, and familiarised himself with some of the areas she might frequent. Things were going well. If only he could think of some way to find out where she was staying. Who would be willing to tell him? What story would convince them?

*Twenty-one . . .*

Having finished his fifth set of twenty-one push-ups, Ed let himself down and turned over onto his back. Some things still bothered him, things he was still mulling over, searching for satisfactory conclusions. He knew it would be risky for him to return to Australia. That was unfortunate. In choosing a reunion with Makedde above all else, he had forsaken his homeland. And it would be close to impossible to get Makedde to travel back with him, no matter what means he used. He'd dreamed for so long of spending time with her there, in those familiar surroundings he had grown up with. He'd envisaged tying her up in his garage and keeping her for weeks. There he could do what he wanted — indulge in simple pleasures like walking around the block while she waited for him, bound and gagged; speaking to her, telling her his every secret and wish; closing the door and leaving her in the dark if he so pleased; feeding her by hand; touching her. And when the time was right, he would perform the final act of possession, and take from her the souvenirs he'd been robbed of before. Destiny demanded it. He had a set-up for her room planned out in his head, and in Sydney he knew where to get the things he needed — binds, metal trays, tools, equipment, sterile gauze, anaesthetic, formaldehyde. But those dreams could not come true now, not exactly the way he had imagined them. He was busy forming other ideas. He would adapt, now that everything had changed. He *would* spend time with her, just as he wanted, taking as long as he wished until he was satisfied. That part was certain. If that had to be in Hong Kong, then so be it. He would find a way.

And there was the issue of how it would be afterwards. It was hard to see beyond such a goal. Would he stay in Asia indefinitely? Take on a new life? He might never see his mother, or Australia, again. He had mixed feelings about that. And without Mother, what would he do for money?

Troubled, Ed scrambled to his feet, slipped his shoes on and collected his jacket. He cleaned his hands with some Clean Wipe tissues and pocketed a small packet of them for later. He slid twenty Hong Kong dollars into his pocket. The Prison Lady's cash was fast running out.

It was time to trawl the bars on the strip, he decided. Perhaps he would find a way to get some money, or even better, perhaps tonight was the night he would find Makedde.

He opened his bedroom door cautiously, and finding the living room empty, ventured to the bathroom to splash water on his face and wash his hands — twice, three times — before going out.

*Can you feel me, Mak? Can you feel me coming?*

*Put your stilettos on for me.*

*It is our destiny.*

# CHAPTER 53

'Hey, what's your name? Ummm, Macayly right?'

Makedde looked up from her menu at Gabby, the abrasive English model from her apartment. Sitting hunched in her chair in a silk singlet with her bony shoulders jutting out and dark make-up smudged around her feline eyes, she looked even more rail thin than she had the night before. When Gabby stood she looked as if her body had been stretched.

'It's pronounced *Mak-kay-dee*, actually,' Mak told her. 'But you can call me Mak.'

After the Ely Garner show, the American girl, Jen, had invited Mak to join her and some other models for a late dinner at a restaurant called Che's. There were eight models in all, dressed in the usual uniform of fashionably sloppy jeans and skimpy tops.

'*Mak*. Right,' Gabby huffed in response, as if she didn't care what the name was and would no doubt mispronounce it again.

Jen, seated to the left of Gabby, beamed at Mak. She and Gabby were chalk and cheese. Jen was fresh-faced with a cheerful Midwest accent, as wholesome as freshly cut hay and apple pie. She hadn't been around the apartment much since Mak arrived, but Mak already liked her. Gabby, on the other hand, was a pouting drama queen for whom a smouldering cigarette and unwelcoming attitude seemed permanent attachments.

'Red or white,' Gabby asked — or snarled. It was hard to tell.

'Red thanks.'

'Everyone else? Red, yes?' She called the waiter over. 'We'd like two bottles of your Canonbah Bridge shiraz.'

The waiter nodded and scurried away.

'So is this a regular hang-out for you guys?' Mak asked Jen. She felt it was better to address the friendlier of the two models she knew. She'd hardly caught the names of the others. 'I have to admit that I thought immediately of Cuban food when you said "Che's".'

Jen looked blank.

'Because of Che Guevara,' Mak explained.

'No, this is a Chinese restaurant,' Jen replied, still not registering. 'It's owned by one of the local movie stars! We hope he'll come in later,' she gushed excitedly.

The fact that the restaurant was traditional Cantonese had not escaped Mak's attention. It was hard to miss the tanks of fish and the opulent gilded décor. There were even jars of mysterious dried substances in cases along one wall.

'That would be so great if he shows up!' Jen blurted, evidently still thinking of her movie star.

Gabby nodded vaguely, not interested enough to speak on the matter of Hong Kong movie stars or the Cuban revolution. Mak wondered just how old — or young — Jen was. She went back to studying her menu. She quickly realised that deciphering the items on offer would be a challenge. This was not exactly Ming's on Quadra Street.

'Um, can anyone tell me what Double-boiled Sweet Superior Bird's Nest is?' she asked. There was laughter from those on her side of the table.

'It's bird spit,' the model beside her said in a disturbingly familiar Australian accent. He leaned forward and grinned at her mischievously. He was a deeply tanned bloke with unkempt hair, a ripped $300 T-shirt and Tsubi jeans — the advertising industry's version of a Bondi surfer. His name was Shawn.

'Bird spit,' Mak replied flatly. She raised an eyebrow and waited for the joke.

'I'm not shitting you. It's bird spit. A delicacy.'

Mak regretted that she had unwittingly sat next to the only Australian at the table. *What if he recognises me from the press about the trial?* Instinctively, she buried her face in the menu.

Hmmm. Ducks' Jaws in Maggi Sauce. Snake Fillet with Chinese Herbal Medicine. Pig's Colon in Soya. Elephant Trunk Shellfish. The menu read like *Ripley's Believe it or Not*. Sea Whelk. Twenty-five-headed Abalone. And there was a whole section devoted to something called 'Conpoys'. There were probably things here that weren't even legal in her native Canada.

Leaning across the table, Mak whispered to Jen. 'Help, what the heck is a conpoy?'

Jen pointed at the jars of strange-looking shriveled lumps stacked along one wall. 'Sun-dried scallops. They're big on conpoys here.'

*Right. Perhaps I'll just stick to steamed vegetables*, Mak thought. Her usual philosophy when travelling was to throw herself into local culture and customs, but tonight the thought of exotic food was repellent. She had a headache and felt vaguely queasy. Was it just jetlag — or was something more sinister doing her head in?

She spoke sternly to herself. *Get a rip, Mak. You're in Hong Kong. You are safe. Ed is not here. You are safe* . . .

# CHAPTER 54

'Hello, you looking for company?'

The accent was exotic, from somewhere Ed didn't recognise. He stared impassively at the girl who had approached him — at her dark brown eyes and golden skin, and her large puffy lips, and though he said nothing she did not move away. She batted her eyelashes and smiled. She had tiny pimples all over her forehead, and she smelled faintly of yeast.

'What do you want?' he said.

'You want company? You very *handsome.*'

The petite Filipina girl was not at all attractive to Ed. She wore chunky sandals with a miniskirt and her toes were awful and squarish. She had not even painted them. Her feet revolted him.

'No, I do not want company.'

'You have wife?' she asked.

'Yes. I have a wife.'

He still had the frozen guy's gold wedding band on his finger. There had been a time when Ed used to wear one like it at least once a week, on his nights off when he was cruising for girls. He used to enjoy polishing it up. Over the years he had learned that it put girls at ease to think he was on his way home to a wife. It made him seem harmless. The wedding band sealed the deal, when the offer of a lift home in the rain from a kindly bespectacled good Samaritan was tempting, but not quite tempting enough to make a girl let her guard down and get into his van. *'I have to be home for dinner any minute, but I saw you walking by yourself and I thought you looked lost. You looked like you might need help. It's not safe around here you know ...'* For the others, the hookers and the strippers, money was usually enough to get them into the van. If they refused, he would simply offer more money, and more, until they gave in.

Ed had bought his ring at a garage sale — a funny thing to sell, he'd thought — and now it was sitting somewhere in police custody in a small cardboard box of measly possessions labelled *Edward Brown*. Ed could replace the ring, but he couldn't replace the other things the police had stolen from him. He desperately missed his souvenirs. He had been so proud of them. Over the years he had painstakingly collected several of his girls' toes, only the best ones severed neatly from the foot, in a shoebox in his bedroom. It had taken patience and practice to make the incisions neatly and perfect the method by which to store them. He had even kept one whole foot in formaldehyde in a jar and it had been a beautiful artefact, one he had enjoyed looking at often. She'd had perfect, symmetrical toes, the nails manicured and painted red. Just perfect. The curve of her arch had been exquisitely formed. Now he would never see that arch again.

'Want to drink with me?' It was the young dark girl again. She was still hanging about, smiling at him and twirling her black hair between the fingers of one hand. She rested the other hand on his arm, the long, chipped, artificial pink nails touching his bare wrist.

'Go away!' Ed snapped and pulled away. If she was even half worth the effort he would cut her open right there on the tiled floor of the disco. That would shut her up. That would stop her touching him.

The girl recoiled at his response, and finally left him alone. He saw her retreat to her girlfriends, with whom she exchanged some words. They looked at him with scowls and then looked away. One of them pointed out a tall fat man in a suit standing alone at the bar, and the girl approached him next.

Ed surveyed the room. No Makedde Vanderwall. There were lots of American and Australian men, and a lot of Asian girls. Was this where he would find Makedde?

He finished his cheap drink and slumped on his stool. How long would it take to find her? And once he had her, where could he keep her, and for how long? The beats of the disco music rang in his head, the flashing dance floor blurring in his vision. He felt tiredness set in. The jet lag and the time difference had begun to catch up. He would walk back to the apartment, perhaps after one more lap around the strip.

*I will find you soon, Makedde.*

*You can't hide from me.*

# CHAPTER 55

By 1 a.m. the models had left Che's and were standing on Lockhart Road, discussing whether or not to go for one last drink. Mak was weary, and she wanted nothing more than to head back to the apartment and rest her aching head. Most of the group, however, seemed determined to have one more for the road. They didn't have jet lag and her draining anxiety to contend with.

Lockhart Road was rife with girlie bars: a handful of modern, trendy establishments incongruously nestled between the strip clubs. Amongst abundant and equally bright Chinese symbols, neon signage for *Pussy Cat, Cavalier, San Francisco Club, Dreams Café, Club Carpenter* and the subtly named *Cockeye Model Dancers Club* adorned the street, beckoning foreigners in English. Westerners, the majority of them men, hung about the entrances with lazy smiles and flushed cheeks, keeping an eye out for a good time.

'Pluto's?' Shawn suggested. He threw an arm around Gabby, which she shrugged off.

'Hell no,' Gabby said. 'Not Pluto's.'

'Well, let's go somewhere else then,' Jen suggested peaceably. 'The Felix?'

'It's a bit late for the Felix, hon,' Shawn said. 'Especially by the time we get there. Come on, let's show our newcomer the *real* Wan Chai.'

Mak raised an eyebrow. 'I might be a bit exhausted for the "real" anything right now, but thanks.' With the two-hour time difference from Sydney, for her it was about 3 a.m. already. She wasn't much of a party girl, she reflected.

'Come on, just one drink,' Shawn coaxed.

Mak looked to Jen and Gabby for support, hoping to hitch a ride back to the apartment in Mid Levels with them. Somehow she didn't want to walk into the empty apartment alone.

'Pluto's is rank,' the elfin-faced model called Amber complained, wrinkling her nose.

'One drink. Come on. It's part of the initiation.'

*Initiation?*

'Okay, enough already,' Gabby said. 'One drink. Let's go.'

Mak's heart sank.

With a flurry of tired air kisses, Amber and her friend Raquel parted ways from the rest of the pack and jumped into a taxi to head home. *Ah well, the 'real Wan Chai' sounded vaguely interesting*, Mak thought. It might be worth ten minutes of her time.

★　★　★

Pluto's was a basic bar with a dance floor. At first glance at least, anyway. They took a side table and ordered drinks. Makedde sipped her free gin and tonic sceptically.

'So, what kind of an initiation is this, exactly?'

'It's just a glimpse of the Hong Kong underbelly, that's all,' Shawn answered.

'What makes this the Hong Kong underbelly?' Mak wondered aloud. 'There are no locals here.'

'Well spotted.'

To Mak, it was obvious. Although the bar was crowded with revellers, not one of them was Chinese. There were Caucasian businessmen, some Indians and Africans too, but the girls were all South-East Asians, mainly Thai or Filipina, Mak guessed. With Raquel and Amber gone, Jen, Gabby and Mak were the only three Caucasian women in the place. No one would let any of their group pay for drinks, which Mak found odd, and a bit suspicious. She tried several times to push Hong Kong dollars into the waitress's hand but the woman refused.

'So these are foreign sex workers, I'm guessing?'

'The women are 90 per cent workers, yeah,' Shawn said. 'They come here on short-stay visas and make all the money they can. Most of the money goes home to their families. Back in their villages, they would be heroines for paying the bills. Anything that puts bread on the table.' Shawn seemed to be experiencing a sudden streak of sensitivity.

Mak nodded thoughtfully. What a life they must have. And she thought *she* had problems.

Not surprisingly, Shawn's maturity was short-lived. He pointed towards the bar with glee. 'Oh, she's hooked one! Yep, hook, line and sinker.' He began to laugh. Gabby rolled her eyes.

A pretty girl in a tiny skirt and a lycra top was smiling alluringly at two American men in jeans and pressed dress shirts, batting her eyelashes and flicking her hair. She was no more than five feet tall, and the men towered over her. They were clean-cut and a little overweight, probably not used to getting such eager female attention back home. They looked like college boys to Mak. They looked like someone's brothers. What did they think they were doing accepting forced affection from an impoverished sex worker? In moments the girl had giggled and cooed her way into being offered a drink. She leaned against the shoulder of the taller one, smiling flirtatiously. She put a manicured hand on his waist. He looked delighted. Negotiations would be next.

'Mak,' Shawn said in a lowered voice, 'I wanted to ask you something.'

He had her immediate attention. She braced herself for the worst.

'Are you the same Mak from Canada who was just in Sydney for that trial?'

Mak cut him short. 'No,' she blurted.

'Let's get out of here,' Jen broke in, seemingly oblivious to the conversation. Mak saw her tug at Gabby's sleeve. 'I've got a photo shoot tomorrow.'

'Oh, live a little. You'll be fine,' Shawn complained, sipping his free cocktail. At least she had distracted him.

'It's a test for my book. I need some sleep,' Jen insisted.

'I'll go back with you,' Mak offered, jumping at the chance.

Jen's face lit up. 'Great!'

'Thanks for the tour of the underbelly, Shawn,' Mak said. 'Don't forget to tip well. Bye Gabby.'

With that, she and Jen climbed the stairs to the street.

'I hate that place,' Jen complained, once they were outside. 'It's so creepy. I don't understand why people like it.'

'Well, I don't reckon we are quite the demographic, somehow. I think Shawn rather likes the free drinks. Come on, let's flag a cab.'

The red taxis of Hong Kong Island zipped past on both sides of the road, all occupied. Mak began to feel uneasy. Goosebumps stood up on her forearms. Were they being watched? Yes. She could feel it. Was it just the bouncers at the entrance to the club, or was someone else watching them?

*Why do I keep worrying about Ed here, when I am so far away?*

★ ★ ★

Suzie Harpin blinked once, twice. Yes, it had to be her. A tall young woman with a mane of blonde hair had emerged from a doorway not half a block from her.

*Makedde Vanderwall.*

Suzie stood on a corner directly across from the seedy-looking bar Ed had disappeared into. She'd heard the front door close when he had left the apartment, and quickly followed. Her boyfriend was after this girl Makedde, and here she was, right in Suzie's sights. It was her. And Suzie had found her.

With violence bubbling over in her heart, Suzie walked briskly towards the woman who was the cause of all the uncertainty in her relationship. Makedde was the reason she did not have Ed's true devotion. Makedde was his distraction. Makedde was the one thing that could bring them down. Makedde stood in their way. Makedde was the enemy. *Makedde Vanderwall.*

Only a few feet away now.

Suddenly she turned and looked right at Suzie. She had bright blue-green eyes that took in Suzie's face with surprise and some alarm. Did she recognise her?

'Oh, here!' A taxi pulled up in front of them and the back door opened automatically with a strange little hydraulic lever. Makedde and the other girl quickly climbed in. Suzie lunged towards the cab but missed the door as it swung shut again.

*Dammit!*

★  ★  ★

'Did you see that woman?'

'Who?' Jen asked.

'That woman with the crazy eyes. She was staring at me.' Mak was shaken.

Jen turned around and looked out at the street. 'She wanted this cab pretty bad. Look, she's trying to hail one now.'

Mak turned too. The woman was trying desperately to hail a cab but none were stopping for her.

Makedde's heart pounded from the unsettling encounter. 'Mid Levels,' she told the driver and settled back into the seat. 'I'm glad we found a cab. I think that area creeped me out a bit.'

# CHAPTER 56

'Wake up, Andy. We got something.'

Through his congested thoughts he managed to croak, 'I'm awake, I'm awake,' though truly he wasn't. With one eye open, he saw the bedside clock indicating ten minutes to six. He rolled straight out from between the sheets clutching his mobile phone to his ear.

'Don't tell me you fell asleep at your desk again and didn't get home until late?'

'Just tell me what it is, Mahoney. Is it good?' He grabbed a shirt off the floor and started to put it on.

'There's a homicide in Seven Hills. Probably related. Want me to pick you up?'

*Oh damn. A body.*

Andy had been wondering how long it would take. Who was she? Whose life had Ed cut short this time?

'Only if I get to drive,' he said.

'No way. I mean, yes, sir. Whatever you say, my superior. Local police got a call last night from the wife of the brother of our Long Bay guard, Suzie Harpin,' Mahoney explained.

'She said that someone had moved into her husband's house. That he was missing. And there was a human arm in the kitchen sink.'

'An arm?'

'I'll explain the rest on the way.'

# CHAPTER 57

'Are you okay?'

The words came through the bathroom door in a whisper. Mak looked up with a start. It was barely four-thirty in the morning. She opened her mouth to answer, but felt another wave of nausea take over.

'Blaaaah,' was the noise she made instead of speech.

'Makedde?' Another whisper, and a thump, as if someone were now pushing against the door.

*Go away, please* . . .

'Just a . . . uh, minute,' Mak groaned. She wiped her mouth and rose from the toilet bowl. 'Yes?' she said through the locked door.

'Are you okay?'

'Yeah sure,' she replied. *Yeah right.* 'I'll be out in a sec.'

Mak found her toiletries bag shoved into the back of the bathroom cupboard, behind someone's cosmetics and bottles of Dior fake tan. She brushed her teeth and spat into the sink. She splashed water on her face.

Apart from her episode the night before the trial, Mak couldn't remember the last time she had been sick. She hoped this wasn't going to become a regular occurrence. Puke for worry. Puke for excess alcohol consumption. Puke because you love Hong Kong. All this vomiting was a sure sign that her life was going down the toilet.

Feeling slightly less nauseous, she opened the bathroom door and found Jen sitting on the arm of the couch, gazing at her with worry. She wore boyish pyjamas, her face clean and shiny, hair pulled back in a ponytail. Without make-up, she looked about twelve.

'It's all yours,' Mak managed to say.

'You aren't fat, you know. You're just tall,' Jen replied.

'Excuse me?'

'I'm just saying . . . you know . . .' Jen looked sheepish. She was sitting on her hands, Mak noticed. 'I'm just saying that you aren't fat.'

Mak was confused. *Why is she saying this to me now?*

'I know I'm not fat,' she replied.

Then Jen looked towards the bathroom and back to her, and Mak got her meaning.

'Oh, no, no. I'm not bulimic!' Mak exclaimed. 'No. Thanks for your concern, but no.' The chucking up was probably something Jen had seen before. 'I'm just, well . . . *sick*. It might be something I ate last night, those conpoys I ended up trying, or that abalone thing.'

Jen nodded, partially reassured.

'You ought to go back to bed,' Mak said. 'I'm sorry if I woke you. It's so early. And you have that test today.'

For Mak it was 6.30 a.m. Sydney time, so she doubted she would be able to get any more sleep. This would be the start of her day, and what a start it had been.

Jen's sheepish look had appeared again. 'I don't have any test,' she admitted. 'I just ... wanted Shawn off my back. He's a bit of a party animal.'

Makedde laughed. 'I see. Do you usually get free drinks?'

Jen nodded. 'At some places they offer free drinks if we bring our composite cards.'

In any fashion capital there are plenty of places willing to offer free drinks to models who frequent their establishment. When Mak was starting out in Milan, some of Italy's richest playboys were known to pay top dollar to club owners to lure young models. Some clubs even had agreements with model agencies to encourage the new girls in town to party with them. Most of the new models were unsuspecting of the set-up, and their being underage and impressionable was not considered a problem to certain powerful men. Mak had only managed to escape one slimebucket's attentions by being, as the man described, *'intimidazione'* — an almost six-foot-tall fifteen year old who commanded an impressive right hook.

'Um, please don't think I'm rude, Jen, but can I ask ... how old are you?'

*Please don't let her be fifteen.*

'Seventeen.'

Mak was relieved. 'I'll be twenty-eight this year,' she said, by way of sharing. In Europe at fifteen, she'd been invited to all kinds of wild parties. Hamburg, Munich, Milan, London, Paris, Barcelona, Madrid. Wherever there was work, there were parties. She very quickly decided not to go to any of them. The early nights had probably added eight years to her model resume.

'You have beautiful skin, you know,' she told Jen. 'Don't ever bake it in the sun.'

*My God Mak, you are beginning to sound like someone's mother.*

With that thought, she rushed back into the bathroom to be sick once more.

# CHAPTER 58

*A dismembered arm . . . ?*

'We've an absolute goldmine here, Detective Flynn.'

Andy Flynn and Karen Mahoney were met by a young constable who explained as much as he could as they got out of the car and walked towards the pleasant suburban house.

It looked to Andy to be a family-oriented neighbourhood. Nice green lawns. A tricycle on a driveway. Sprinklers. A basketball hoop in the garden next door. Some chalk lines drawn on the bitumen for hopscotch, or something similar. The house that had been blocked off as a crime scene was one of the larger, newer ones on the block. It looked well kept, although the garden was a bit of a jungle. If this was one of Ed's victims then why was the lawn so overgrown? Ed had only been out a few days.

Some of the neighbours were standing around, gawking. One woman was actually in a robe and hair curlers, like an extra in an old Doris Day film. An elderly man watched from his yard several houses down through a pair of binoculars. No kids about, thankfully. No one screaming and carrying on. Yet.

They stepped over the blue-chequered crime-scene tape and followed the constable towards the front door of the house.

'Detective Flynn!' came a loud voice from the street.

They turned in unison.

'Pat Goodacre. Oh shit. Media's here guys,' he said under his breath.

Andy walked calmly back across the lawn. 'Fancy meeting you here,' he greeted her.

'So what have we got?'

He kept his smile. She was annoyingly good.

'We don't have anything of interest for you at this time, Pat. Sorry I can't help you out.'

'Oh, I think you can.' Pat smiled back unflinchingly through her pearly whites, her keen eyes searching his face. 'What has been found in this house, Detective? And how is it related to the Stiletto Murders?' She brandished her tape-recorder like a weapon. Mightier than the sword, indeed.

'We don't have any reason to believe that anything here is related to the Stiletto Murders. Sorry, Pat. There's no story here. Our media liaison will be able to let you know if there are any developments.'

The journalist smiled. 'But Andy, you and I both know that the story is wherever you are, and you are wherever the story is.'

'Flattery won't get you anywhere, Pat,' Andy said, walking away. Pat stayed put at the edge of the barrier. She wasn't budging. She knew a story when she saw one. Andy Flynn wouldn't be house-hunting in Seven Hills right after Ed's escape unless there was a bloody good reason, and they both knew it. The only saving grace with someone like Pat was that she was so good at getting her scoop that it was possible that not even her boss knew where she was or what she was chasing. If anyone else caught wind of it, the news helicopters would be tipped off in no time and then they would find themselves on the morning news.

Following Mahoney and the constable into the house, Andy was relieved to leave the crowd outside and close the door.

'Hey, Flynn.' It was Sampson, a junior task force detective. He was at the top of the stairs next to an officer dusting for fingerprints. The white railing was sooty with carbon powder. The black rim of a frame was cloudy with Lanconide.

'It looks like our man has been spending a lot of time here,' he said. 'There are some *bee-yoo-tiful* prints all over this place. We ran them and the initial analysis says we probably got a pretty damn good match. Bloody brilliant.'

*Bingo. A lead. Finally.*

And this Suzie Harpin was related. As hostage, or accomplice?

'We got prints in the kitchen, the bathrooms, bedrooms everywhere. Our man hung around here for a while. Got real comfy. He even cut out some press clippings about himself,' the officer said between dusting spots.

'Tell me about our John Doe,' Andy said. 'Or John Arm. Who does it belong to?'

'Oh, we found the rest. The woman who called us, a Lisa Harpin, is going to try to ID the head. It was well preserved. Probably her husband.'

'Yeah, wrapped like a frozen turkey,' the young constable commented, and picked his teeth with a hangnail.

'Thank you!' Mahoney said and shook her head, curls bouncing in every direction.

'So the victim is . . . male?' Andy said.

A nod. 'You're going to want to take a look at the basement first up, then I'll take you through the rest.'

*What are you up to, Ed? Coming here and killing a man? You wouldn't bother killing a man unless he got in your way . . . like Jimmy. And since when have you wrapped and frozen your victims? That's not your style at all . . . Who is helping you — and why?*

# CHAPTER 59

Wednesday morning, still bright and early, and Mak was seated on the deck of one of the famous Star Ferries, leaning her elbow on the rail and admiring the impressive view as the ferry bobbed along through the darkly polluted water of Victoria Harbour. Gleaming skyscrapers of glass and steel rose from Hong Kong Island behind her, offset by blue skies and lush green hills in the distance. She had already snapped half-a-dozen photos with her digital camera, and she raised it now for one more. She was on the way to Kowloon, along with the local rush hour crowd, mostly businessmen and shopkeepers on their way to work. She planned to do some sightseeing on the other side, and perhaps a bit of shopping, though she knew that earrings and handbags would be the only things that would fit her.

*Snap.*

She checked the image on the tiny digital screen. The city looked gorgeous. Small boats bobbed through the water, bathed in morning sunlight. She was having a great run of luck with the weather.

They were halfway across the harbour to Kowloon now. The ferry rolled in the wash of a passing tug. *Lurch.* Thoughts of the weather vanished as Mak felt her stomach churn.

The boat swayed.

Her mouth started watering.

Her tongue squirmed.

Makedde gripped the rail. A cold, clammy sweat broke out over her whole body. *Oh no.* The early morning queasiness had not yet passed. She had been a fool to take a ferry. She felt sick. She felt like she might . . .

With a buzzing in her ears and an uncontrollable urgency in her belly, Makedde began vomiting into Victoria Harbour. She gripped the rail and leaned out over the side, the rocking motion and the direction of the wind leaving a line of brown and yellow sick across the side of the ferry.

*Oh God, how mortifying.*

No one bothered her, or tried to help, for which Makedde was grateful. There was nothing anyone could do anyway until her body decided that it was through.

At last the ferry docked at Kowloon. Pallid and shaken, Makedde followed the other passengers towards the gangplank, wishing the line would move faster so she could escape this crowd of strangers who had witnessed her embarrassing display. As she passed a rubbish bin, she tossed away a still full styrofoam cup of latte. The very thought of drinking it brought the bile to her throat once more. Paper napkin at her mouth and her head down, Mak stepped gingerly onto solid ground.

Her first priority was finding the nearest women's toilet. It was a humble ferry-terminal ladies room, and a not very glamorous one at that, but to Mak it was an oasis. There was running water. She was alone — or so she thought at first. In the corner, a diminutive Chinese woman of perhaps eighty stood watching quietly. The old woman followed her to the sink to hand her a paper towel when Mak went to wash her hands. At the side of one of the sinks sat a dirty upturned cap, half filled with small change. Mak cleaned herself up as best she could with soap, and gargled the tap water, wondering if that was what had done her in. She placed a Hong Kong dollar in the cap before she turned to leave.

'*Dor jeh*,' the old woman said as Mak walked away. Thank you.

Mak paused and smiled at the ancient stranger. She had never seen such incredibly fragile-looking skin, so weathered and thin, like wrinkled crepe paper. There seemed to be dirt in the creases. But the red-rimmed eyes were kind.

Mak paused to search for the words. 'Umm … *m sai haak hei.*' You're welcome.

'*Nay hoy mmm hoy some a*,' the woman said, and put her hands to her stomach.

'I'm sorry, I don't understand,' Mak replied. '*Dor jeh.*'

She walked briskly out of the terminal building and followed a flow of people towards the streets of Kowloon, still trying to swallow back the faint taste of sick. The roads were busy with fast-moving traffic, and she could see that there was no way to safely cross. Subterranean walkways seemed like the only way to get anywhere.

THIS WAY TO THE PENINSULA HOTEL
THIS WAY TO THE NEW WORLD CENTER

Mak walked down a set of steps that took her under the roadway. She followed the larger crowd at every turn, and was soon spat out into the central courtyard of a shopping mall.

Mak found herself facing a four-metre-high beige fake-fur teddy bear. In the middle of the open area was an enormous artificial tree housing hundreds more of the creatures, these ones animatronic and doll-sized, all waving and singing nonsense. The tree was a full three floors high. At the bottom level was a teddy bear themed food court, currently unattended.

WELCOME TO THE TEDDY BEAR KINGDOM

*Right.*

Mak stopped dead in her tracks.

The old woman's hand on her stomach. Her smile and incomprehensible words.

*What if it's not food poisoning, Mak?*

★   ★   ★

Twenty minutes later, Makedde sat on a bench on the lower floor of the New World Centre, waiting nervously for a pharmacy to open. She had her legs crossed tightly, her heart heavy with dread. By contrast, her surroundings were jarringly bright and cheerful. Canto pop music filled the mall, echoing remorselessly off the dazzling white walls and shiny glass shopfronts. There were very few people around, only some sales assistants here and there, busy inside the still closed shops.

Mak shut her eyes and prayed.

*Please let this be a stomach bug or food poisoning. Please let this be anything else.*

She could not be pregnant with Andy Flynn's baby. She just couldn't. That was not in the plan. That would not work at all. They were not together. They were not a couple. They did not even live on the same continent. This was impossible, unthinkable, utterly unplanned. She still hadn't called him. Every time she thought of him her stomach twisted in knots. She hated herself for missing him, for wishing that they were somehow meant to be together, when clearly they weren't.

Mak still felt ill, probably from worry now more than the food poisoning, upset stomach, flu, seasickness, morning sickness ... whatever it was that she had.

*You're working yourself up over nothing. Just think how foolish you are going to feel in a few more minutes when you know for sure.*

★  ★  ★

An agonising twenty-five minutes later, the pharmacy opened. The instant the roller door was pulled up, Mak ducked under it and made for the front counter.

A young girl was at the till.

'Um, do you speak any English?' Mak asked her.

'Thank you. What can I help you?' the girl said.

'I need to purchase a pregnancy test, please.'

'Pregnancy. Test for baby?'

'Yes. Test for baby.' Her stomach churned and pinched.

'One minute, yes. Thank you.'

Mak felt her heart thudding in her chest. It will be food poisoning, she scolded herself. The strange food had put her off. And the food poisoning would naturally have been aggravated by the rocking of the ferry. Nothing to get excited about. Of course it was food poisoning! She'd eaten conpoys and abalone only the night before. And she had also been thinking about the water. Perhaps it was not as safe as everyone kept insisting. She'd brushed her teeth with it.

That could be enough. The food was probably fine and it was the water. She had some kind of common travel bug, that was it.

The girl returned with a small white package, a pregnancy test kit. 'Okay?'

'Okay,' Mak replied.

# CHAPTER 60

'*Nei hou*. Wang Models Hong Kong.'

'Hello, this is Victor Thomas from *Moda* magazine. I would like to book one of your models.'

'Certainly,' the woman said in clear, but heavily accented, English. 'I will put you through.'

'*Nei hou*,' came another voice.

'Do you speak English?' Ed Brown asked.

'Yes, thank you. Please.'

'This is Victor Thomas from *Moda* magazine. I am enquiring about one of your models, Makedde Vanderwall from Book agency in Sydney.'

'Yes. Mak-eddie.'

'I am an acquaintance of hers from Australia. I'd like to contact her.'

'Would you like to leave a message? I could pass it on —'

'It would be easier if I could call her directly,' Ed pressed.

'I'll be able to pass on the message to her, but I can't give out models' phone numbers.'

'That's a shame,' he said. 'What is her availability in the next two weeks?'

'Was it editorial you were looking for?'

'We are shooting in Hong Kong for the next two weeks, and we would like to book Makedde Vanderwall, please. Is she available?' he asked again.

'She is available for the next week. Could you give me your —'

Ed hung up the phone. They wouldn't hand out her details, just as he'd thought.

But now he knew that Makedde was not leaving for one week. That should give him enough time to find her. He would stake out the model agency for her today, and if she didn't show, he would implement another plan . . .

# CHAPTER 61

'Hi Loulou. How are you?'

'Good, girlfriend! How's it going?' It was great to hear Loulou's familiar voice, *any* familiar voice. 'Hey, are you okay?' Loulou asked. 'You sound like you're crying or something.'

Mak was laughing. Uncontrollably.

'Um ... actually I'm laughing.' And crying.

Mak sat on a couch in the models' apartment, alone, holding the test in her right hand and the phone in her left. She looked out at the bustling city below through eyes blurred with tears of relief.

'Laughing?'

'Yeah, you won't believe this. I got sick somehow, must've been something weird that I ate, and stupid me starts thinking I might be pregnant. Isn't that hilarious?'

'You're not, are you?'

'No, no, no. I took a test. Twice. I'm not. Can you believe I even thought that?'

'So you're fine.'

'Yes, paranoid but fine,' Mak assured her.

'You know your departure was, like, front-page news.'

'It was?' Andy had left messages for her, but she hadn't returned them. Maybe that was what they were about.

'Yeah, the papers said you fled to Hong Kong.'

Makedde felt her stomach churn again. 'Oh. I didn't know they would print that. They actually printed that I flew to Hong Kong?'

*Ed reads the paper. Ed knows where I am.*

'The photo looked great,' Loulou said, but Mak barely heard her.

*Ed knows where I am.*

Her toe began to itch furiously.

'Mak?'

*But he can't get to me. He can't leave the country. They would grab him,* she thought.

'Mak?' Loulou repeated, concerned.

'Sorry, Loulou. I'm fine. Hey, I really want to thank you again for being there for me with the trial and everything.'

'Don't mention it. How was the EG show?'

'It was good. Gisele was amazing up close. Skinny as a rail but amazing. Actually, I'm just about to head off to the agency now to see if I have any new bookings. You take care, okay?'

★   ★   ★

Mak walked past the receptionist in the office of Wang Models, and made her way to the booking table, feeling like a pest. Sam, her booker, was busy punching details into his computer. Someone called 'Mink 3' was getting a pretty good paycheque for an editorial shoot. Mak would have liked a job like that herself. It would ease some of her uni bills nicely.

'I'll just be a sec,' Sam said, smiling.

Mak walked over to a wall displaying composite cards and admired the array of fashion models pictured there. *Ying. Alexxus. Phaedra. Ines. Alsou.* Didn't anyone have normal names any more? As if she could talk! There were some stunning Eurasian faces on show, and sweet-faced Chinese models as well, impossibly pale. A few, like Makedde, had European or North American features. All were young, but few were household names. Makedde had watched over the years as the supermodels had slowly been replaced by fresh-faced but forgettable girls who didn't set back fashion designers' bank balances like the big stars of the catwalk once had. The old supermodel guard was largely in retirement now, with a few notable exceptions like the ever-popular Kate Moss, and post anger-management Naomi Campbell, who still made the odd appearance. Mak kind of missed the once-common sight of a full-blooded, healthy-looking supermodel like Claudia Schiffer or Paulina Porizkova leaping athletically across the pages of a fashion mag. Ah, the golden years of supermodeldom. They had made the fashion world look so exciting to the teenage Makedde. These days Gisele was one of the few names recognised outside the business.

*I must be getting old.*

'Mak-eddie.'

Sam had finished with his computer. He swung around on his swivel chair. 'How are you? You're looking well.'

*Am I?*

'Um, thanks.' Standard model agency talk. They practically *had* to say that.

'Some of our clients who saw you at the EG show were pretty impressed. Do you do swimwear?'

'Yeah.' *Still.*

'Fantastic. I'll let them know.'

A new booking would make her trip at least a financial success, if a disaster by every other measure.

'There was another client, *Moda*, who called about you today, but I think they must have been cut off.'

Mak raised an eyebrow.

'Hopefully they'll call again. I think the shoot was in the next couple of weeks. The client knows you from Australia. He asked for your number. A Victor Thomas, I think?'

Mak's chest tightened. *I don't know any Victor.* '*Moda*? The Italian magazine? You didn't give out my number, did you?'

'You don't know this Victor?'

'I don't think so,' she said. *Who would be calling?*

'Well, we never give out personal details.'

Mak was relieved.

She still hoped for another booking before she left, but she didn't want to push her flight home back any further. She wanted to get back to her dad and make sure he was okay. And she wanted to get back to Vancouver Island for her own peace of mind. She'd feel safe there. She needed more distance between herself and Ed Brown. And, maybe, between herself and Andy Flynn.

# CHAPTER 62

Andy sat on the edge of Jimmy's hospital bed, trying to read a scrawled note on a clipboard. He turned it sideways and back again.

'Your writing is crap,' he said.

He detected a smile on the left-hand side of Jimmy's face — the side that still had some expression. The stroke he had suffered on the operating table had paralysed his entire right-hand side. His condition had stabilised somewhat in the past four days, but he wasn't out of the woods yet. He would need to learn to speak again, to walk again, do everything again. In the meantime his main communication was through writing with his left hand. Problem was, he was right-handed.

Jimmy gestured to have the clipboard back. Andy passed it to him and watched while he drew a rudimentary set of testicles.

'Your writing *is* crap. I can't read even half of this!'

Andy was trying to gently squeeze some more information out of his partner about the sequence of events that led up to Ed's escape.

'Flynn?'

Constable Mahoney was at the door.

'Come on in.'

Karen entered the hospital room, her red curls tied back in a springy ponytail.

'Hey,' she said, 'how are you feeling, Detective Cassimatis?'

Jimmy was pale, with dark circles under his eyes. The right side of his face was slack and emotionless, dragging downwards at a strange angle. He curled his lip into a snarl on the opposite side, as if to say, 'How do you think I'm feeling?'

'It's good to see your personality's come back,' Karen said. 'You'll be on your feet in no time. Andy, can I talk to you for a sec?'

Andy got up from the bed and walked with Karen to the door.

'You know about the ID on the arm?' she asked. As a detective in training, Karen was often left out of the details. 'The arm in the sink belongs to the body in the freezer which belongs to ...?'

'Benjamin Harpin,' he replied. 'Married, no children. His wife, Lisa, ID'd him for us.'

'Right.' Karen nodded. She leaned against the doorway and crossed her arms.

'She was in the process of divorcing him.' Andy knew exactly what that was like. 'She claims not to know anything. It's possible that she is telling the truth about that,' he added thoughtfully. She *had* seemed genuinely distressed.

'And what do we think the arm was doing in the kitchen?' Karen asked.

'It was the left arm.'

She clued in immediately. 'Ah, a wedding ring.'

'Precisely. Lisa claims that her husband still wore his gold wedding ring, even though she'd left him. It hasn't been found yet.'

'Ed hawked it for cash?'

'Perhaps. We're checking for credit card transactions, paper trails, anything that can tell us what led up to Ben's last moments. Hopefully his killer will slip up and use his card somewhere. We haven't found his wallet.'

Andy was not convinced that Ed was the killer. Would he really have poisoned a man with Spanish fly and put him in the freezer, gladwrapped? That didn't fit with his usual MO. It didn't make sense. Because of the freezing of the body, forensics were having more difficulty than usual in pinpointing the time of death, but it was possible that Harpin had died before Ed even escaped. Yet Ed was definitely there at some point. He had spent significant time in Ben Harpin's home. The puzzle pieces of this murder had not yet come together.

'Nothing on the sister since the bank withdrawal?'

'Something will turn up soon.'

Andy strongly suspected her involvement, voluntary or not. She was quite possibly a hostage. He'd seen the surveillance tapes from the convenience store next to Suzie's bank, when she made her withdrawal. There was a figure in the passenger seat of her car. They couldn't make out the person's face as they had a baseball cap pulled low over their eyes.

They watched as whoever it was pulled a cloth from a box, which they identified as Clean Wipes disinfectant, and rubbed their face vigorously. Andy was sure it was Ed. Was he armed?

Karen looked to her hands and back up at Andy again. 'Andy, do you think Detective Cassimatis will be okay?' she asked.

Back in the bed, Jimmy held up his clipboard. It said, 'I can hear you.'

'Yeah,' Andy said. 'I think he'll be fine.'

# CHAPTER 63

'Mak?'

Jen was looking at her, head cocked to one side. She sat across from Mak in a tiny Mongkok noodle bar, her slim white fingers wrapped around a warm cup of Chinese tea. She appeared to be worried, as she had that morning when she'd found Mak being sick.

'Sorry Jen, I must've zoned out there for a second,' Mak said. 'I've got a lot on my mind.'

She saw the food coming, a welcome distraction. 'Ahhh, right on time . . .'

A slight Chinese woman arrived with their dishes, two steaming bowls of noodle soup crowned with pork balls, a popular local specialty. There was a small bowl of some type of hot sauce on the table, and Jen piled a spoonful on the top of her soup. Mak followed her lead. She took a ladle-sized spoonful up to her mouth and savoured the broth.

'Ohhh, hot!'

Thankfully, Makedde's stomach had settled. It felt nice to eat something that didn't feel like it would immediately be purged. She realised that between being sick and being upset, she hadn't eaten a proper meal all day. Mak and Jen had chosen this small noodle bar near the Ladies Markets for dinner so that they could go shopping afterwards. Through the steamed-up windows, Mak could see the market stalls extending for blocks in all directions, and though it was already dark, it didn't look anywhere near closing, or even slowing down. Mak couldn't wait to get into it. Thousands of people swarmed the streets in all directions, buying and selling trinkets, toys, clothes, fake watches and copies of designer handbags. It looked like it would be a real adventure.

Meanwhile, the constant traffic of people outside the noodle bar was compelling too. There were funky girls with spiky hair and platform boots. Ancient-looking gentlemen, hunched over with their shopping. Kids on shoulders. Young couples holding hands. Jen and Mak, tall female foreigners, were two amongst thousands. The odd signs for sporting brands like adidas and Nike, crowded amongst Chinese symbols, were the only real hint of Americanisation. The sights and smells were so different from what Mak had seen in her many travels across North America and Europe. She marvelled at the exotic atmosphere, wondering why she had never ventured further east than Istanbul before. Look at all she'd been missing!

Mak felt Jen's eyes on her.

'Mak?'

'Yup?' she said between mouthfuls.

'Last night I heard Shawn ask about that trial. That was you, wasn't it?'

Mak's stomach froze up.

'Um, yeah. It was. How do you like your soup?' she asked, desperately trying to change the subject.

'It's good.' Jen looked away. 'That must've been really scary,' she continued, eyes downcast.

'Yeah. It wasn't much fun. The less I think about it now, the better. Truthfully, I've had a crap couple of years and I'm ready for some good luck now, I think.'

'You seem so positive and smiling all the time. You'd never know.'

*Not all scars are visible*, Mak wanted to say, but thought better of it. She was no victim. She was lucky. She wished they could get off the subject.

'What will you do?' Jen asked.

'What will I do about what?'

'Isn't there a guy in Australia? Mak, are you okay?'

'Yes. Sorry.' She swallowed back a sour lump in her throat, and took a long, slow breath. Her noodles no longer seemed so appealing. Her appetite had almost completely vanished. 'The um ... the guy I was seeing is an Australian detective who I kind of went out with for a while, but we're not seeing each other any more.'

She felt a rush of sadness. There was a bond there, as frustrating and inconvenient as it was. Mak could not deny that she'd been drawn to Andy from the start, and apparently she still couldn't quite keep herself from thinking of him. At the hotel in Double Bay, she had worried for hours knowing she would have to face him, and say a final goodbye. What did that mean? How could he still have such an effect on her?

# CHAPTER 64

*I see you.*

Was Makedde looking at him? Was she waiting for him to come in and get her?

*I see you, Makedde.*

*Can you feel me?*

Ed Brown watched Makedde from across the street. She was eating in a small noodle bar near the night markets. He'd watched her on the crowded subway train and followed her through Mongkok station. With her mane of blonde hair, Makedde stood out like a beacon amongst the Hong Kong locals. In the restaurant she was in clear view, like a window display just for him. She was his.

*You are mine. Can you feel it? You are mine.*

Makedde was eating with a girl Ed had not seen before, a young girl with a ponytail. He wondered how they knew each other. Another model? A friend from back home? Ed had followed Makedde from her model agency all the way here, where she had met with this girl. That was okay. The other girl was easily discarded. The sun was down now and everything was perfect. He had her. His patience had paid off, as he'd known it would. He should never have panicked about not finding her. Of course he found her. It was only a matter of time. Ed knew she would have to come to the agency eventually. He knew that would be the key. No matter where she went he would find her, because that was her destiny. She belonged to him.

The streets were still busy, even though night had fallen. But no matter how many people brushed by him or walked around him, not one person paid Ed Brown any attention. He was 'Mr Cellophane', his unremarkable appearance like a cloak of invisibility that he'd learned to use to his advantage. He could melt into any crowd.

*Makedde, you know you are mine.*

Was she waiting for him? Should he walk straight in and take her?

'Ed, darling.'

Ed turned, startled.

It was the Prison Lady.

*No!*

'I can't believe I found you, sweetheart. How wonderful!' she cooed. She was dressed in runners, jeans and a T-shirt and carried a backpack. She held a plastic bag and a bottle of Evian water. Her upper lip was beading with sweat.

'What are you doing?' he demanded.

*She will ruin everything!*

'I was just shopping. Here, I bought some of these fabulous custard egg tarts. Daan tarts, I think they call them. They are soooo good.' She took one out of the plastic bag and handed it to him. He held it in his hand, shocked.

How could she be there now, when his prize was right across the street? How!

'So what have you been up to, honey? Sightseeing?' She looked down at his hands, puzzled. 'Darling, why are you wearing gloves?'

Ed looked down too. It was odd to wear leather gloves in humid Hong Kong, but he needed them for his task. He had no explanation to offer.

'Oh, I've just been, yeah, sightseeing,' he said awkwardly.

*Get rid of her. Get rid of her now.*

'Mmm, there's lots of great shopping here,' the Prison Lady went on, mumbling through a mouthful of tart. 'Oh, would you like some water?' She held up the bottle.

'No thanks.'

She took a swig of water herself through those awful thin, mean lips and put the bottle into one of the zippered pockets of her backpack. 'I find it so humid here! It's like I'm sweating all day.'

*Do something. Get rid of her fast.*

Ed made a plan. He put the small tart in his mouth in one bite. He grabbed the Prison Lady by the wrist with one gloved hand. 'Honey, I want to show you something,' he said. He pulled her with him. 'I was going to save it for later. But this is the perfect time.'

'Really?' she said, and smiled with crumbs all over her disgusting little bird-mouth.

'Yes,' he said. 'It was going to be a surprise, but darling I just can't wait any longer.'

Ed led her through the crowd, glancing behind him a couple of times to check his orientation, and make sure that Makedde hadn't left the noodle bar. He didn't see her on the street. She'll probably be there for a while longer, he thought. She's barely eaten any food.

*Just get rid of the Prison Lady, get rid of her get rid of her get rid of her . . .*

He headed towards a restaurant only half a block away, its windows displaying racks of barbecued ducks hanging by their feet, eyeballs gone. The restaurant was teeming with people, but when he'd walked past earlier he'd noticed a back alleyway they used for their garbage. It was probably as close to privacy as they needed. They moved into the alleyway, she with that putrid smile still glued on her face, and when they reached a gloomy corner, he stopped her.

'Okay, now this is a surprise,' he said.

She was positively glowing with excitement. She would do anything for him. Anything at all, he thought.

*I want you to die now. That's what I want you to do for me.*

'Close your eyes and hold out your hands.'

She did as he said.

He stole a quick glance left and right. There was activity everywhere, neon signs flashing in the darkness, music, people walking this way and that, but no one was watching. And no one else was in the back alley. The back door to the restaurant was closed.

'Keep them shut . . .' he teased.

'Oh sweetheart —'

He took the rag from his pocket, along with the phial of liquid that had been reserved for his prize. He soaked the rag in one quick action. There was no time to waste.

With force, Ed wrapped one arm around the back of the Prison Lady's head in a lock and held the pungent rag firmly over her gasping mouth — that awful, lipless bird-mouth. She flinched and struggled, spluttering and coughing. He pulled her backwards, leaning in close so anyone watching might think they were lovers enjoying a passionate embrace. She continued to struggle against him, her arms wanting to lash out, but he held them fast, hugging her in a vice-like grip with his strong upper body. She tried to speak, tried to protest, but her incoherent words were mumbled senselessly against the damp rag, shocked eyes open and staring at him. A whimper, a small kick, and then, limp, she fell back into his arms.

The rag was soaked with chloroform. She was unconscious.

He lifted her and walked further into the alley, her feet dragging across the concrete. From a distance they could have been a couple dancing. He pocketed the rag and fished in his pocket for the knife. Still holding her, he rammed the six-inch blade through her T-shirt into her stomach. Her skin gave easily to the sharp steel tip. She twitched. With effort, he dragged it up through her torso, hitting the sternum at the top. His adrenaline soared. Ed had not thought he would enjoy killing her — she was so dull and sexless to him. But ridding himself of her was so very satisfying, and the metallic smell of spilled blood never failed to excite him. He felt alive. He felt like a god.

Ed pushed the Prison Lady away and she fell on top of the swelling plastic bags of rotten garbage, her head hitting the brick wall behind.

She looked almost lovely there. Like a rag doll. He'd never thought of her as lovely before.

Ed leaned over her, barely registering the repulsive reek of the garbage she lay in. He sliced her throat from ear to ear. She bled profusely, her life spilling out from every gaping wound. It gave him a sweet tingle up his spine. It was finally done. The Prison Lady was dead.

Ed paused for a brief moment to admire his handiwork, then quickly covered her in garbage bags, one on top of the other. There was nothing left to see. She was gone.

The job complete, the reality of the alley hit Ed with full strength.

Without looking back, he strode briskly out into the street and around the corner. He took a Clean Wipe from his pocket and cleaned his face. Once. Twice. He wiped the fingertips of his gloves. His jacket had blood on it. He would have to turn it inside out.

He had to wash.

Crazy with adrenaline and the compulsion to cleanse the germs away, Ed rushed through the front door of the restaurant and made a beeline for the toilets at the back. A waiter addressed him but he did not respond. He needed to clean it all off. The germs. There were so many in that alley. He had to get them away . . .

# CHAPTER 65

'We just got notification from Qantas that Suzie Harpin flew out on Monday night on one of their flights. Immigration confirms it. She left the country with her brother, Ben Harpin.'

*Her dead brother. Holy shit.*

'Fuck, that's him. Where did they fly to?'

'You're not going to like this. Hong Kong.'

'That's Ed. That's fucking Ed Brown. Goddammit! How could he get through the airport? Contact Interpol immediately and —'

'It's been done.'

'We need to get to Makedde NOW.'

'It's being done, Andy. Interpol have a team of people in Hong Kong and they promise they are all over this. They are going to track her down.'

*Oh Jesus, Makedde . . .*

# CHAPTER 66

Ladies Market was amazing.

It was absolute sensory overload: the sound of Cantonese and Mandarin, footsteps, laughter, arguments and haggling. Alarm clocks buzzed senselessly in one stall. T-shirts hung over every possible centimetre of selling space in another. There were tables overflowing with sparkling fake jewels, illegal Rolex copies, souvenirs, snow globes, toys, pirated CDs. Music played on cheap plastic ghettoblasters. Woks and frying pans sizzled with the greasy edibles of street vendors. Rich aromas floated out from lively cafés and restaurants, while pungent odours wafted from narrow back alleys.

Wide-eyed, Mak followed Jen through the shoulder-to-shoulder crowd — or in Makedde's case, their shoulders to her waist. 'Copy watch, copy watch,' someone shouted. She threw a look in the direction of the voice but was moved along by the crowd, almost lifted off her feet towards another stall that seemed to carry precisely the same watches. Chinese symbols hung down from awnings in all directions, dilapidated apartment blocks rising like stacks of old shoeboxes above the neon signs and clutter of capitalism. Stains of rust and dirt oozed down the sides of the ramshackle buildings, tiny air-conditioning units teetering on the edges of the windowsills. The living conditions would be anything but first world. No wonder SARS had spread so fast through the plumbing, the ventilation, the sewerage. The city had suffered, but now it was thriving again — cleaner, safer, though still so much more crowded and layered than a Westerner could comprehend without experiencing it first-hand.

Makedde gawked at the stalls, the signs, the buildings — the whole overwhelming streetscape. And all the while, thousands of locals thronged in all directions around her, haggling, buying, eating and moving in a great human sea.

Mak pushed forward and grabbed Jen's arm.

'Oh wow! I don't want to lose you ...'

'Come over here, I've got to show you these bags,' Jen exclaimed. 'They have great copies of the latest Louis Vuitton bag for, like, fifty Hong Kong dollars! That's only ten US dollars a bag.'

'Ten bucks?'

'They're double A fakes. The good ones.'

Mak followed Jen closely through the crowd, arriving at a stall displaying nothing but laminated photographs of what looked like Gucci, Louis Vuitton and Burberry handbags and wallets.

'But where are the bags?' Mak asked.

'Which designer you want?' the vendor said. 'You want Burberry? Gucci?'

'Louis Vuitton,' Jen giggled.

'I bring it. Which one you want?'

'Um ... I want to see that one.' Jen pointed to a laminated

sheet featuring a bag covered with graffiti–like scribbling. 'How much?'

The man brought out a calculator and punched in some numbers. He showed the read-out to Jen.

'One hundred Hong Kong dollars? Too much,' she said.

Mak did a quick calculation. That was about twenty Canadian dollars. A bargain.

'Very good quality. Double A. I show you.' He scurried off behind the stall and down an alley.

'What's happening?' Mak asked Jen. 'Where did he go?'

'They get raided twice a day. It's safer for them to just have the catalogue out. They keep the bags hidden somewhere and bring them out when customers ask to see them. A lot of them work like this.'

The piles of trinkets in the next stall caught Mak's eye. Mao books, Mao toys, Mao pins. The stall next to that had crazy underwear hanging all over it. There was a pair of men's briefs on display with an elephant's head on the front. It was obvious which body part was supposed to go into the long trunk.

'Oh my God. Look at that!' Mak exclaimed.

Just further on was a stall selling Osama bin Laden T-shirts. Mak moved closer. 'I can't believe this ...' she mumbled with disgust. There were T-shirts on the trestles portraying the World Trade Center towers collapsing, with a glowing head of bin Laden in the middle. The illustration looked *pro*-bin Laden. *What the hell?*

Mak turned back to tell Jen, but couldn't see her. She was shoved sideways by a tall teenager in a hurry. Regaining her balance, she looked left and right. No Jen. A Caucasian man caught her eye a few metres away. He was short and slight with dark brown hair and pale eyes. A chill ran up her spine. He was staring at her.

*He looked like . . .*

Mak could feel panic run through her body. The man reminded her of Ed Brown. That was why she had come up in gooseflesh. She was seeing things again, like she had at the fashion show with the red-haired photographer. She had to slow down and think clearly. That could not have been Ed. Ed didn't even have brown hair.

*You are seeing things. Just calm down.*

But she couldn't will herself into calm. The sight of someone who looked so much like him, despite the different hair colour, had spooked her, and now she felt on edge. The crowd began to feel less like an exhilarating sea of people and more like an ocean to drown in. There didn't seem to be enough oxygen. She breathed what she could through short, sharp gasps.

*Get out. Get out of here now.*

Mak ran back towards the stall of fake designer handbags and, not finding Jen, dodged past it, searching frantically for her. She needed to get out of the crowd, find space. She ducked through an unattended stall into a slim corridor that ran for blocks behind the market. There were winding alleys branching off it this way and that — but no Jen. No one familiar. She had to get out. A feeling like claustrophobia threatened to overwhelm her, pulling her away from clarity.

*That could not have been Ed. He is in Australia, not in Hong Kong.*

*Unless . . .*

*There had been that front-page article about Hong Kong.*

*My God, what if it was him?*

She scanned to her left, taking in the crowded street, busy as a mosh pit. There were hundreds, no thousands, of people walking, talking, haggling. Neon signs glowed and flashed and beckoned. $H_2O$. Virginia Hotel. PC Online Gaming. Levis. Fairwood. DVD. Import Fashion. Cantonese writing everywhere, on every surface, and a huge pink banner above it all: WELCOME TO LADIES MARKET.

She scanned to her right. More of the same. The crowds went on as far as she could see. Where was Jen? How could she have lost her? She was sure to stand out. Jen was six inches taller than anyone else. Just as Mak stood out in that jostling swarm, with her height and her fair hair. Perhaps Jen would see her?

*Just calm down, Mak . . .*

★   ★   ★

Ed could see her. She was on her own. Her eyes were wide with panic. Her mouth was open, yelling something no one could hear. She looked confused, distressed.

*Makedde.*

*Mak.*

*Mother.*

She had lost her friend.

It was time.

Ed followed several steps behind her. He matched the height of the crowd, able to watch the top of her blonde head as she turned and looked back and forth, jogging through the stalls. He would have to catch up with her. There was no more Prison Lady to get in the way. She would never bother Ed again. He could have Mak now and they would not be disturbed at the Wan Chai apartment. He would have as many days with her as he liked. There was no one to ask questions. He could take her home unconscious. A cab driver would think she was drunk. He was strong enough to carry her. It would be easy.

Ed reached into his pocket and brought out the rag. He clutched it in his gloved hand, and followed.

★　★　★

Makedde strode back the way she had come, moving briskly and checking each stall for her friend.

*Calm. Calmly now. There is no need to panic. That could not have been him . . .*

Jen had probably gone to look at the bag with the vendor. She would be back at the stall by now. *You have been imagining things. You've had a tough day. You are under strain, that's all.* She reached the handbag stall at last, with the catalogue hung up for show. Or was it? She turned and looked through the crowd. Could she see the strange T-shirt? No. Where was it? It had been right there. Or was she mixed up somehow? Was this a different fake bag outlet? The stalls all looked the same, crowded one into the next, selling the same things, the same watches, the same cheap trinkets. Where was she? Where was Jen in this hellish bustle?

*How did I lose her?*

*Calm down. Stop panicking.*

Makedde felt eyes on her again and turned.

The blood in her veins froze. A deep, gnawing itch began in her toe. Everything seemed to grow quiet except her breathing. The world slowed to a halt . . .

Ed Brown stood no more than four metres away, staring directly at her.

Mak bolted in the opposite direction.

It *was* him.

*How could it be him? How could he be here? Good God, how?*

Makedde could not forget those eyes. The sight of them close to her face had been burned into her memory like the painful brand of a hot poker. *'Are you ready, Mother?'* he'd said. *'You have such beautiful toes. Lovely toes. Would you like to taste them? Suck them for me?'* He looked different, his hair darkened with bad dye, but he was unmistakable this time.

*Scream, Makedde . . .*

*Scream for help!*

Makedde called out. A woman beside her turned as she passed, then looked away and continued up the row of stalls. *'The right foot, because it's right . . .'* Ed had sliced through her big toe with a post-mortem scalpel while she was tied up helplessly, wide-awake in agony and fear. She would never forget that face, those eyes, that voice, the searing pain. And what he had done to Catherine . . . poor Cat, mutilated and abused, discarded in the tall grass like a mangled doll.

*'No, I won't let you go . . . Mother.'*

Makedde raced through the sea of strangers as fast as she could, knocking into people's bags, hitting a young girl in the shoulder. She yelled loudly as she ran — 'Help me! Police! Police! Please someone help!' — trying to raise the alarm, her eyes no longer seeking Jen's ponytail but desperately hoping for the sight of a uniform, police of some kind, someone, anyone, who could help. The swarming crowds went on as if nothing were happening, like the nightmares where she was screaming and no sound came out, no one could hear, no one would help. She could not recall the word for emergency in Cantonese, but it probably wouldn't make any difference anyway. These were people who would mind their own business, especially when it came to a screeching tourist. How could they know that an escaped sadist who had murdered at least nine women was walking amongst them? How could they be warned?

*It is Ed Brown. He is here. He has found me.*

She looked behind her and with a sick despair saw that Ed was still there, matching her pace, moving through the crowd stride for stride. Mak ran straight into the back of a man holding a baby, and the child began to cry. She ran again, slipping past them and watching where she was going, but Ed was still there, so close, only a few paces behind her. She bobbed and weaved, urgently seeking a safe place, a police station, an officer, someone who looked official.

There were only unmoved locals, and the street vendors with their cheap wares, people who were raided twice a day for their fake Rolexes and Louis Vuittons. These people would likely run from the police, not help her find them. There were so many people, and yet she was truly on her own.

# CHAPTER 67

Andy Flynn was coming out of his skin with anxiety. He could feel it in his bones.

*Mak is in dire, immediate trouble.*

His eyes ached from dehydration and lack of sleep. The abrasions on his palms had opened again from gripping his hands too hard. He felt as useless as tits on a bull in Sydney. Makedde was in Hong Kong and Ed was in Hong Kong. That was the worst-case scenario. He prayed they weren't going to be too late. Ed had slipped into Hong Kong as Ben Harpin on Tuesday morning and it was already Wednesday night.

Interpol had alerted the Hong Kong Police. They were determined to capture multiple killer Ed Brown and his companion and had put out a major alert on them, but neither had been tracked down in the short time since the search began, nor did Andy believe that would happen anytime soon. Until they used a credit card or flashed a passport, finding them among the seven million-odd people in Hong Kong would be like finding a needle in a haystack.

Makedde should be easier to find, he hoped.

She, at least, should not be hiding.

# CHAPTER 68

Ed was easily matching Mak's pace through the mass of strangers. They were all moving too slowly, so many people in her way: children, old people, couples, everyone blocking her path as she ran. She had to think of something. She needed to get someone to help her. The last time she faced Ed he had taken her off guard, hitting her over the head with brute force. He might have a weapon now. He would not stop until he had her, that much was certain. He had come a long way for this.

The tables and stalls of cheap goods filled her vision in all directions. She saw no escape, only hundreds of tawdry souvenirs.

*Use them.*

In a flash she snatched a snow globe of Hong Kong off one of the tables.

The vendor screamed something angrily in Cantonese. '*Wai! Gwoh lai a!*'

She finally had someone's attention.

Off the next table Mak snatched up a set of thin chopsticks held together with a pretty red ribbon. They looked like they might be plastic but they had sharp points. She pocketed them as she ran, making a show of her thievery, catching the eye of the incensed seller.

*Yes, come after me. And bring the police.*

With her mane of blonde hair rising above the rest of the pedestrians, Mak had no hope of disappearing into the market crowd. She needed to gain ground and find somewhere to hide, around a corner or through a doorway — to give her just enough time to flee way towards the Mongkok subway station where she'd noticed some uniformed officers earlier. There *had* to be police officers at the station. But which way was it from here?

*There. Behind that last stall. Someone in a uniform.*

'Hey! Help me! Police!' she called out.

Makedde dodged to her right, shielded momentarily from Ed's view by a tall canvas tarp that protected a stall overflowing with toy planes buzzing, toy monkeys clapping symbols, toy ferrets chasing balls.

*Clang, clang, clang . . .*

She squeezed her way into the corridor behind the stalls and found herself at the mouth of a dimly lit alley. Tarpaulins blocked her way, she had to double back — this was a mistake, she realised now. *Oh God, where to?* The alley was filled with rows of garbage bins, each overflowing with rotting food. There was a high chain-link fence at the end. *No officer.* Whoever she'd seen was on the other side of those tarpaulins.

She had a fraction of a second to decide. Go back the way she came? *Or . . .*

*Hide.*

Mak flattened herself against the brick wall and gripped the snow globe tightly in both hands.

*There he is.*

In seconds Ed Brown had appeared at the mouth of the narrow alley, panting. She would not have had enough time to double back even if she'd tried.

Without hesitation Makedde lunged forward to strike him hard over the head with the snow globe. The killer must have sensed movement. He flinched and the globe only glanced against the side of his temple, propelling her forward as she missed her target. She struggled to retain her grip on the globe but it slipped from her hands and crashed on the pavement at their feet, scattering water and fake snow as the cheap glass shattered. Already his hands were on her and they began to struggle like boxers in a hold, he so much shorter but somehow stronger, his power shocking. They wrestled grimly, their bodies straining and twisting. She tried to get free to hit him, to go for his eyes, to reach the sticks in her pocket. Even if they were too flimsy to be effectual, she might scare him, slow him down maybe. She only needed a bit of distance, just a few seconds on her side in order to escape his clutches.

But her strength was no match for his freakish vigour. Ed got hold of her windpipe with both hands and squeezed, the black leather of his gloves creaking as they stretched tight. She batted at his arms in panic, a futile act, and in seconds felt her mind slip dangerously as she began to cloud into unconsciousness. His face was close to hers, those pale eyes burning through her, eyes that were windows to a diseased soul. She had to escape that sickness, that foulness. She would not let it claim her. The instincts of years of self-defence training finally came to her. She braced her palms together as if in prayer and lodged her hands upwards between his, the strength of her shoulders breaking his grip on her throat.

'Mother-fucker!' she gasped, swinging out with one good kick and striking his kneecap hard on the side. He cried out and stumbled backwards, his head briefly silhouetted by a halo of neon. She backed up one step. Two. Shattered glass crunched under her feet. He blocked the entrance to the alley. There was nowhere to go but the chain-link fence and the open ground-floor windows beyond, where she could use a phone, get someone to help. Mak turned and ran towards the fence, leaping at it with force and meeting it a full five feet above the ground, her fingers clawing through the holes in the wire mesh, her feet scrabbling for purchase as she pulled herself up, up, ever closer to the top. She had to get over it, get into the buildings beyond. Someone would have to find them soon, someone who was chasing the thieving Westerner who had run down a back alley. *Where was everyone? Where was the police officer?*

A hand grabbed her ankle and pulled.

Mak struggled to hold tight to the fence. She was almost there, her fingertips only inches from the top, her voice crying out as loud as she could make it, but the hands had her, Ed had her in his grip and he was strong, so strong. She strained with every fibre of her being, tears springing from her eyes. *'I will save the fatal incisions for last'*, *'Have you ever seen an autopsy Makedde?'*, *'You are special . . .'*, *'Such pretty toes . . .'* Her fingers stung as the wire pressed into them, threatening to cut them as his binds had when he had her tied down, immobilised and helpless: her shoulders cried out, he had her by the waist now with both hands, how could it be, he had her, after everything he had her, he was pulling her down with both arms and her desperate determination was no match for his strength. She heard his breath hard in her ear. A sharp smell, like alcohol but stronger, a rag over her mouth, a strange sensation, something lifting, she was being lifted, she felt weightless for a moment — *fight it, fight it Mak* — she struggled and kicked, felt her oxygen fade, her head going, lifting away.

With a final moment of focus she grabbed the chopsticks from her pocket and jabbed them into Ed's neck.

His body jerked from the impact and the sticks snapped in half, the sharp ends left jutting straight up above his collarbone. He clawed at them, trying to get them out, his eyes wild with pain and confusion. He made a terrible noise, and there was a great exhalation of air from his mouth, then blood, blood covering the shoulder of her top and down her front. Mak lunged forward and kicked at his kneecap again, which buckled this time. 'You fucker!' she screamed at him, and was ready to swing again … but he was not fighting back now, he was flat on the ground and she could see him grip his stomach. He had blood all over him. But not just from the broken chopsticks that protruded at a disturbing angle from his neck. There was blood and vomit, he was choking on it, coughing. He held a rag in one leather-gloved hand, clenched tight. *What's happening?* She stumbled backwards and hit the chain-link fence; she turned and climbed. 'Call the police! Someone call the police!' she yelled towards the windows above. She pulled herself up to the top and threw a leg over, panting. Behind her Ed was on the ground surrounded by a growing pool of darkness. She watched him heave, once, twice, and give out a spray of dark vomit. His body convulsed, his head falling back to hit the concrete. He vomited again.

She paused, perched on top of the fence, mesmerised, watching in frozen awe as Ed Brown suffered and writhed in the filthy back alley.

'Why me, Ed? Why, you fucker?' she yelled at him.

He did not respond.

# CHAPTER 69

Makedde sat in her underwear on the edge of an examination table in Kwong Wah Hospital, feeling both exhausted and pumped with uneasy adrenaline. She had been thoroughly checked for injuries. The blood on her clothes had not been hers. She couldn't control her shakes now. Her body tensed and released, tensed again. It wouldn't stop.

'Thank you. You can get dressed now,' Dr Luk said, and pulled the white curtain across for Makedde's privacy. She had a flawless English accent, and was probably one of the few overseas-trained medical doctors to stay in Hong Kong after the handover in 1997.

Mak hopped off the table and reached for a small pile of clean clothing she had been provided with: drawstring pants and a loose top. They reminded her of surgical scrubs. She got dressed and came out from behind the curtain. The doctor was at her desk.

'The shakes are just a bit of shock, all quite normal under the circumstances. They should disappear in the next few hours or so. Try to stay warm and drink plenty of liquid. And rest as much as possible,' she said. 'You don't appear to have any physical injuries apart from those scratches, though you might have a bit of bruising around the neck tomorrow. I have cleaned and bandaged the small abrasions. They should be fine. We would know by now if you had been affected by any of the poison, but just to be sure if you notice any blistering in the next twenty-four hours alert a doctor immediately.'

Mak had been admitted to Emergency covered in blood. Her clothing had been stained heavily with it and would need to be examined. With Ed critically ill, not from the chopstick stab wounds, but from an as yet unidentified poison, they had to be certain that none of it had entered Makedde's system orally, or through any broken skin. As Mak had not fully lost consciousness during the struggle, Dr Luk did not believe that the chloroform Ed had used would have any lasting effects.

Dr Luk got up from her desk and gave Makedde a reassuring look. 'You will be fine. I will let them know we are finished. Good luck.'

'*Dor jeh*,' Mak whispered. 'Thank you.'

Shortly after, there was a knock on the door and a tall Caucasian man stepped inside. 'Miss Vanderwall?' The officer was square-faced and grave. He sat down opposite Makedde and took a deep breath. Mak felt on edge. She wished he would speak.

'Edward Brown passed away a few minutes ago,' he said.

The tiny hairs on the back of Makedde's neck bristled, and somehow her heart *lifted*. He had been such a part of her life for the past eighteen months, subtly invading every thought, tainting everything she did, and now it seemed he was truly, really *gone*.

'Um ... are you sure?' Mak asked, knowing the question was strange, but needing to be certain.

'Yes. He is dead. We thought you would want to know.'

Mak nodded. 'Yes. Thank you. I'm glad you told me.'

That was it. Catherine's killer was dead. Ed Brown was really gone, forever.

'The Australian authorities have requested that you return to Sydney to answer some routine questions.'

'Oh,' she said.

'Will you be okay to leave tomorrow?'

'Yes, that's fine. I was only planning on staying another few days anyway. I can um ... pack up by then.'

She would see Andy again, in that case. And soon. It was probably a good thing that they meet again face-to-face. There was a lot to talk about. She had feelings for him that she needed to resolve. Their bond was not so easily broken, it seemed. Perhaps now, with Ed out of their lives, they would be able to get on with whatever relationship it was that they had — or didn't have.

'Are you feeling alright?'

'Well, yes, actually. Not bad, considering,' Mak responded. Her body was still buzzing, and she was still shaking from time to time, but she was also relieved and it felt good. It felt good to be able to slowly start adjusting to life without Ed Brown. She was finally free of his obsession, and it was wonderful.

'Your friends are here,' the man said. 'Are you okay to see them? They can take you home.'

'Friends?'

Jen had been found through her mobile phone, still in the markets. She had been in the hospital waiting room while Mak was examined. But what was this about friends, plural?

The officer walked Mak back to the waiting room where she found that he was right. She had not one, but two friends waiting for her.

'Oh my God! Macayly!' Gabby cried. Her mascara had run. She looked distressed, her usual look of posed disdain had evidently vanished. 'I couldn't believe what happened when I heard.'

This wasn't something Mak had expected to see.

Gabby engulfed her in a bony hug. 'You poor darling! Are you okay?'

'Um. I think so. I'm fine.'

A sign of humanity from Gabby the model? Life kept getting stranger.

'I had no idea what you had been through! Oh my God!'

'Oh, Makedde!' Jen exclaimed.

'It's over now. It's finally over,' Mak whispered, more to herself than anyone else. 'It's done.'

# EPILOGUE

'Welcome to Sydney. We hope you've enjoyed your flight. Thank you for choosing to fly with us ...'

Mak yawned and stretched.

*I didn't think I would ever see this place again.*

'Please stay seated until the aeroplane has come to a complete stop and the pilot has switched off the fasten seatbelt sign.'

By the time the plane docked in the gate, half of the passengers were up. It felt good to stand in the aisle after so much sitting down. Maddeningly, the first available flight out of Hong Kong had been via Melbourne, so she had needed to wait out a two-hour layover and transfer to Melbourne domestic airport. As if the nine hours from Hong Kong weren't enough. Mak reached for the overhead compartment to get her carry-on. She would be happy to be on solid ground for a few days.

'Miss Vanderwall?'

'Yes?'

It was one of the stewards. 'The police have requested that you stay seated until all of the other passengers have exited.'

Mak sat back down and folded her arms. Perhaps it was standard procedure. She watched impatiently as the plane slowly emptied, passengers pushing past her seat, stretching, chatting. She saw a couple holding hands as they waited. What would she do about Andy? What should she say when she saw him?

Mak wriggled into her trench coat, and something crinkled in the pocket. She fished around and removed a wrinkled and folded envelope. It simply said *Cat*. It was the envelope from the birthday card she had left at Catherine's grave. Tears welled in her eyes and she tried to blink them back.

*Oh, Catherine, he's gone. He's finally gone.*

She found it ironic that just when she had given up on executing justice for Catherine herself, she had been forced to face the killer again. His death did not lie on her shoulders, though. The police had told her that cantharidin poison had killed Ed, though they did not yet know how he had come to consume it. There was a search on for his travelling companion, the prison guard Suzie Harpin. Ed had been found wearing her brother's wedding ring, with the inscription 'with love forever, Lisa'. The mystery remained: was she a hostage or an accomplice? Or, like Patty Hearst, was she a bit of both?

The plane was almost empty now, only a few stragglers left: a mother juggling three children, an elderly man with a cane. They made their way off with painstaking slowness. Mak was soon the only passenger remaining. She wanted to move her legs a bit. She felt cramped.

Finally the steward returned. 'Thank you for waiting. They're ready for you now.'

'Um, thanks.' She followed the woman up the aisle towards the exit. Two tall men in uniform were waiting for her at the door. Police escorts. She had grown accustomed to such company in recent weeks.

'Miss Vanderwall, we are with the New South Wales police. Please come with us.'

'Um, hi,' Mak said. She began to feel nervous. Had something else happened? Had the media been tipped off? Was there some new threat to her life that she hadn't been told about?

'Before we go any further, we need you to put this on,' one of the men said. He presented a piece of black cloth.

'You need me to *what?*' Mak was stunned.

The straight face faltered for a moment, a trace of a smile running across his lips. He took the cloth and put it over her eyes, blindfolding her.

'Um . . .' She laughed nervously.

'Please, ma'am, this is serious,' he said.

'Okay.' She went along with it.

'I'll take care of your bag.' She felt one of them relieve her of her hand luggage.

The officers walked her forward. She could hear the noises of the terminal, people's chatter, departure announcements. The blindfold was slipped off and Makedde found herself standing before a small welcoming committee. Loulou was grinning madly, taking pictures with a tiny silver digital camera. At her side was the young man from the Arthouse dance floor. He was holding her purse for her while she took photos.

*No way . . .*

Between flashes Loulou gave Mak the thumbs up.

A couple of people were holding a cheesy banner that read 'Welcome Back' in primary colours. It was Karen Mahoney and a few of the detectives. No media this time, just friends welcoming her back, or perhaps congratulating her on the new life ahead of her, *without* Ed Brown. It had been quite a journey for all of them, she supposed.

Detective Andy Flynn was loitering behind Loulou. She caught his eye and went straight to him, as if it were inevitable.

She thought of her father again. He was recovering okay. But what about this? *If the ulcer doesn't kill him, getting back with Andy might,* she thought.

They embraced.

There were cheers. A complete stranger took a photo. Loulou's camera flashed.

'Jimmy couldn't make it ... not yet, but he sends his best,' Andy told her. Mak saw that Angie Cassimatis was nearby, smiling bravely. *They will be okay,* she thought. *They're going to be okay.*

Andy revealed a bouquet of flowers from behind his back, and Mak laughed with surprise. Their soft petals were clumsily wrapped in plastic — a gift from the airport florist.

She smiled and hugged him again.

'Flowers, Andy,' she whispered in his ear. 'I'm impressed.'

# ACKNOWLEDGMENTS

In the course of writing this novel I have been fortunate to have the support of some wonderful people. Firstly, I want to thank my 'Super Author Agent' Selwa Anthony, a never-ending source of inspiration. I would also like to thank everyone at HarperCollins for their support and for believing in me from the start. You've made my lifelong dream of being a published writer come true. Thank you.

My research for this novel would not have been possible without the help of forensic polygraph expert Steven Van Aperen of Australian Polygraph Services — you were a hit launching *Split*; the queen of poisons Dr Gail Bell; psychopath expert Dr Robert Hare; medical consultant Dr Kathryn Fox; Sergeant Glenn 'Standing By' Hayward; Donald Deakin-Bell; Barristers at Law Damien Sheales, Jason Pennell and Sarah Fregon, and Philip Dunn QC, for their generosity in letting me into their chambers and cases. I also want to thank crime readers everywhere, and the supportive media for keeping books alive every time they write about local authors.

A big thanks to Bolinda Audio Books, Saxton Speakers Bureau, Chadwick Management, Di Rolle, and the incredible Xen. And thanks to Justin Moran for saving my scoliosis-ridden back. I promise I'll start watching my posture at the computer.

To the Royal Institute for Deaf and Blind Children and the Bone Marrow Donor Institute — you give hope, smiles and tears. Thanks for all you do for so many.

My friends Amelia, Gloria, Linda (forever Miss J), Misty, Nafisa, Xanthe and 'the gang' Irving, Deb and Hugh, and Pete and Anne, each deserve a Nobel Prize for their patience with my hermit-writing-mode, as does my wonderful husband Mark to whom this novel is dedicated. And Bo. Thank you also to the wonderful Pennell, Moss, Bosch, Reimer, T'Hooft and Carlson clans.

To my ice-climbing genius sister Jackie Moss — you are my best friend and so much more cool than Theresa Vanderwall. Lou — thank you for making my Dad so happy. And Dad — despite being a retired appliance salesman you handle the mystique of being mistaken for the formidable ex-detective Inspector Les Vanderwall so very well. Walking around in that FBI shirt doesn't help.

I love you, Mom. I never forget you.

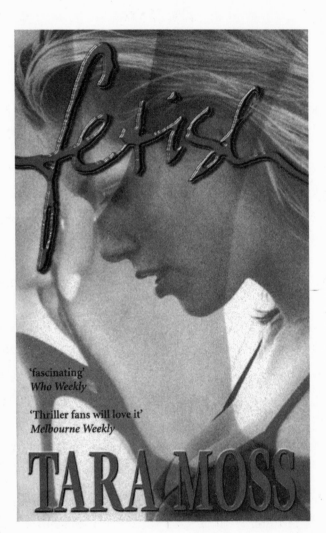

'fascinating'
*Who Weekly*

'Thriller fans will love it'
*Melbourne Weekly*

TARA MOSS

# *Fetish*

MAKEDDE VANDERWALL IS A PSYCHO-MAGNET.

She's a single, Canadian, street-smart daughter of a cop, an alluring Venus who works in the lucrative world of modelling while studying forensic psychology.

When Mak travels to Sydney on assignment and discovers her best friend brutally murdered, she unwittingly opens a Pandora's Box of suspicious photographers, hired thugs and mysterious lovers. She also encounters Andy Flynn, the handsome, cloyed detective investigating the 'Stiletto Murders' — the most violent signature killings Australia has ever known.

In her quest to uncover the truth behind her friend's death, Mak falls headlong into a deadly game of cat and mouse, unaware she has become the obsession of a sadistic psychopath. She is driven into a corner, an evil place where she must suspect everyone and everything.

'. . . full of intrigue and suspense. Thriller fans will love it.'
*Melbourne Weekly*

'Moss's plain and simple depiction of the unglamorous worlds of middle-income modelling and the NSW Police Force is fascinating.' *Who Weekly*

# TARA MOSS

## *Split*

# *Split*

MAKEDDE VANDERWALL IS A WOMAN WITH A PAST.

She is beautiful, street-smart and single, a model paying her way through a degree in forensic psychology. But behind the wit and winning smile is a woman haunted by violent nightmares and plagued by thoughts of Detective Andy Flynn, the ex-lover who saved her from a serial killer in Sydney.

Mak has returned to Vancouver, her hometown in Canada, eager to finish her studies, move on from the ordeal, and find some peace of mind. But instead she walks straight into a city gripped by fear, and a campus where the students are fair game.

As winter closes in and the days grow shorter, Mak is drawn into a shifting world of unstable minds and untrustworthy men, where motives are unclear and desires are unchecked. Her past cannot be so easily forgotten, and she must face her greatest challenge yet ...

'Why is gorgeous international model Tara Moss writing about gruesome, sadistic killers? Because she's good at it.' *Globe and Mail*

'Australia's Glamagatha Christie ...' Jessica Adams